Heritage of the River

~~~~~~

An Historical Novel
of Early Montreal

MURIEL ELWOOD

New York
CHARLES SCRIBNER'S SONS
1945

DEDICATED

to

*My Maternal Grandfather and
Grandmother who were
Canadian pioneers*

CONTENTS

BOOK I

Marguerite

CHAPTER I

PIERRE BOISSART sat on the wooden bench that flanked the doorway of the farmhouse. He was wrapped in a heavy beaver coat tied round the waist with a colored sash. On his head a homemade woolen cap with a perky tassel was perched at a jaunty angle showing the outline of his white hair. Despite his threescore years he was still sturdy and his deeply lined face was the color of well-seasoned leather. He puffed on his pipe and looked towards the river—the River St. Lawrence which in a few hours would throw off its heavy winter covering and herald the start of a new season. The fact that the temperature was only a little above zero did not worry Old Pierre, because over a period of thirty-five years he had become hardened to it. Aye, for thirty-five out of his sixty long years he had watched and waited for the annual "ice shove" and he sighed now as he thought back over those years.

He had come to Montreal as a young man of twenty-five, full of zeal to build a new life, accompanied by a young wife and a son six years old. He had watched the mission town struggling for its life. Even now after half a century it sometimes seemed doubtful whether the town could ever develop beyond a fur trading post of minor importance. When Pierre argued with visitors or new settlers that because of its strategic position Montreal must survive, he always had his tongue in his cheek. If ever they could subdue the fierce onslaughts of the hostile Iroquois perhaps it might have a chance, but up to now all efforts to make peace and keep it had failed. The band of stalwart Catholics who had followed Paul de Chomèdy, Sieur de Maisonneuve, in 1642 for the pious purpose of converting the savages to Christianity had almost all perished after indescribable tortures at the hands of those whose souls

3

they strove to save. And now, forty-six years later, the population of the town was still less than a thousand. The one man who could perhaps have succeeded in bringing about a lasting peace—the Comte de Frontenac—had been recalled to France and the present Governor-General of the colony was afraid of the redskins.

Pierre had been one of the earliest settlers and had come to New France with great hopes but all these had been thwarted when the Indians captured him. Of course, he was fortunate to be alive, for few prisoners escaped to tell the story of their tortures. Had it not been for a loose thong and the fact that the savages had become stupefied with brandy, Old Pierre never would have been able to escape. Tortured for days until his body was a mass of scars, he had been left naked, dangling by his wrists from a tree. He had been able to work one wrist free but the effort had left him exhausted. Finally he had regained sufficient strength to release the other wrist and then had crawled into the woods, too weak to move farther. To reach Montreal had required superhuman effort, for his wounds continually bled and became infected by the swarms of insects. Somehow he had endured the ordeal. His wife had discovered him lying unconscious, a short distance from the house. She had never recovered from the shock of seeing him so hideously multilated and soon after had succumbed.

Poor Marguerite! He thought of her again now. How beautiful and frail she had been. He never should have brought her to a country where the hardships were so great. She had been so brave and never once had he heard her complain, though there was that moment when they had first landed and he had caught the expression of despair on her face before she could hide it from him. Both he and his wife had come from Normandy, lured to the Colonies like many others by the hope of greater freedom and greater opportunity. Ambition was discouraged among the poorer classes in the Old Country and heavy taxation made improvement impossible. In New France, untold opportunities awaited men who were strong if they were good Catholics, for no Protestant was allowed to set foot in the colony. Pierre had heard the reports that were circulated. To those who would emigrate, a gracious King would give as much land as they were able to clear. Pierre had begun to dream and to tell his dreams to his wife and after a time she had caught his enthusiasm. They had sailed away full of hope, much of which was to be crushed before they reached their destination. The vessel was fever-ridden and hundreds died before they reached the new shores. No mention had been made in those dispatches to France of the terrible hardships of the winters or the ravages of hostile savages whose onslaughts prevented the cultivation of the land. These details were carefully withheld, for France badly needed people to inhabit her colonies.

To some extent Old Pierre had been able to realize his ambitions through his son Jacques and his growing family. That family now numbered nine children—an average family for these parts. Even as he sat brooding he could hear them calling to each other inside the house and soon the door burst open as some of them came scurrying out. They were bundled in heavy homespun woolens and paused a moment to adjust brightly colored caps and to tie mufflers, at the same time politely stopping to speak to their grandfather.

"Aren't you coming to watch the ice break, grandfather?" one boy asked. He was a sturdily built lad of fifteen and spoke in the French patois common to Montreal.

Old Pierre shook his head. "No, Charles. I've seen it too many times."

"Do you think it will break this afternoon?" eagerly inquired Etienne.

"Possibly, Etienne, possibly." Old Pierre spoke through clouds of smoke that made the boys wrinkle their noses. It took a long time to get accustomed to the odor of home-grown tobacco.

"Have you been down to look at it?" Etienne asked but his

brother was already on his way and so he only half heard his grandfather's reply. Old Pierre watched them go, a kindly look in his faded blue eyes. How they were growing up! It hardly seemed possible Jacques now had two sons married with families of their own and one daughter married and living at Lachine some nine miles up the river.

From inside the house came the clatter of dishes being washed. They had just finished their midday meal and it had been a good one, for the last harvest had not been interrupted by massacres and this winter the menfolk had been able to keep the larder well stocked with bear and venison. So the Boissarts and their neighbors ate well, devoutly giving thanks for it. Most of them had known years of famine and hardship and they never could tell when they might come again.

Two more children came out of the house. These were the two youngest—Marie, aged twelve, and Philip, aged nine. They were eager to join the others but nevertheless paused long enough to speak to their grandfather, for politeness was an innate part of these people. As their brothers had done, they inquired whether their grandfather was coming down to the river. He repeated what he had said to the other two children and told them to hurry along, for he knew their eagerness to join their playmates. They scurried over the thick snow in the manner of people familiar with it.

Life here in Montreal was lived from ice *break* to ice *freeze,* with every available hand—men, women, children and friendly Indians, working hard for seven months of the year to plant and then to reap sufficient to support them during the five months when all communication from the outside world was completely cut off. Once the St. Lawrence River had frozen over, the Montrealers lived entirely among themselves, knowing nothing of what was happening elsewhere, not even in Quebec one hundred and eighty miles to the northeast. Winter, with its enforced hibernation, was gay enough with hunting, skating parties, sleigh rides and leisure to spend with neighbors, but by the time April came all were tired of idleness and waited impatiently for the ice to melt. As soon as the River was clear all the way to Quebec, ships would begin to arrive bringing news—rumor and fact, gossip, intrigue and scandal—and of more importance to some and less to others, supplies from France and perhaps a new emigrant or two, though these were not as frequent now as in the early days.

Old Pierre became lost in thought. He spent much time this way, for to the old and disabled there was not much else left. He did not at first notice the tall, heavy-set man who came out of the house and stood in the doorway. It was Jacques, his only son, now a man of little past forty. The lines on Jacques' face were serious and the eyes rather stern and dull. He was a man who seldom smiled, even in the midst of gaiety. Yet he was well liked, for he was reliable and honest and ever ready to help a neighbor. Everyone agreed it was hardly to be expected Jacques Boissart would be gay. Since he was twelve years old he had had much responsibility. When he was eighteen he had married and had begun to build up a family of his own. Old Pierre loved his son, but it was love tempered with respect and gratitude rather than deep devotion. A cloud of smoke first called his attention to Jacques as he too puffed upon a homemade pipe. He turned to him and nodded.

"Not going down to the river?" Jacques asked.

The old man smiled slowly. "No, I've seen all the ice shoves I need to, I reckon."

"I reckon so," Jacques replied. "Better not sit out here too long. It's mighty cold still."

Old Pierre nodded and they fell silent. A woman came out of the house and repeated Jacques' admonition.

"I'll be all right," Old Pierre answered and they went on their way. The woman waddled off beside her tall husband and as Pierre looked after them he noticed Marie had grown fatter this winter. Considering the way she worked to clothe and feed her ever-increasing flock, it was surprising she retained so much fat. Although her manner was brusque and entirely devoid of sentiment, Old Pierre was fond of her. She took care of him as though he were one of her own and never once had he heard her grumble about his helplessness, although she was given to nagging and grumbling quite frequently about other things. He had a suspicion that beneath her brusque manner there was hidden a soft heart. This was often shown by the way in which she saw to it that the children did everything they could to make their grandfather's life comfortable.

Of all his son's family, there were two of whom Old Pierre was especially fond—the twins, Paul and Marguerite, now seventeen years old. They hardly seemed to be part of the family for they were so different both in looks and temperament. They had come halfway between the rest of the children and Old Pierre always felt they were a throwback to his wife's family. They had inherited many of their grandmother's characteristics, even to the red-gold of her hair and, like her, were lighthearted and gay. As though they sensed they were different, from earliest days they had centered their interest almost entirely in each other. As Old Pierre thought of them now, he wondered where they were. He had not seen either of them go down to the River. In a few moments his question was answered as Marguerite came to the door and stood looking out for a moment before she spoke to her grandfather. She was an attractive girl in the full bloom of youth. The heavy peasant features of her brothers and sisters were absent, as they were in her twin brother. She had the greenish-blue eyes that complemented the color of her hair, a finely chiselled nose and a sensitive mouth that betrayed the quality of her emotions. As she stood there, the winter sun touched her curly hair and set it aflame with color.

"Isn't it time you came in, grandfather?" she asked.

He turned quickly to look at her and as he smiled, the lines of his weatherbeaten face became deep ravines. "Is it?" he asked. She nodded and returned his smile. "Aren't you going down to the River?" he inquired.

"No, I don't feel like it," she replied.

Old Pierre stood up revealing his great height. "Maybe I should come in," he said and followed her into the house.

CHAPTER II

THE INTERIOR of the Boissart home had little to distinguish it from the homes of the other *habitants*. The original house, built by Old Pierre with the help of his neighbors, had been of wood and had consisted of only one large room. Jacques and his sons had since added two bedrooms, flanking each side of the main room, and a low attic that ran the full length and breadth of the house, providing sleeping accommodations for the overflow of children.

The main room was capacious and served as parlor, dining room and kitchen. It was a pleasant room with low open-beamed ceiling and a huge fireplace at one end. Cooking utensils and a large iron kettle, scoured and glistening, hung before it. The furniture was crude and had all been made by the men of the family from pine and maple trees they had chopped from their own land. Woven underbark formed the seats of the chairs and made them comfortable.

Marie Boissart might be a stolid and unimaginative woman but she kept her house immaculate. The wooden floor was scrubbed every day and gaily colored woolen rugs were scattered over it, giving an atmosphere of comfort. The spinning wheel which stood in one corner was seldom idle, for to Marie fell the task of keeping the family properly clothed throughout the year. Even the shoes on their feet were made at home. Necessity had made these settlers versatile and the men fashioned heavy clogs out of rawhide or moccasins of tanned and oiled skins.

Marguerite helped Old Pierre off with his beaver coat and pulled the woolen mittens from his hands. As he held his hands to the fire, their unsightliness was revealed. The cold air had intensified the scars until they stood in purple ridges.

Both thumbs had been severed below the first joint and all that remained of his fingers was the index finger of the right hand minus the first joint. The others were mere stumps of different lengths and quite useless. But, like most people who have been incapacitated for many years, he was surprisingly adept at managing for himself. He put that solitary finger on his right hand to the utmost use.

He settled himself comfortably in the large wooden chair with the winged sides that Marguerite had drawn up to the fire. She pulled a wooden stool forward and sat with her back against her grandfather's knees. As Old Pierre began to fill his pipe, Marguerite took it gently from him, not because he was incapable of doing it himself but because she loved to do these little things for him. When it was filled, she handed it to him and then took a brand and pushed it into the fire. As she held the lighted brand to him, the firelight shone on her face, revealing the sweet gentleness of her expression. They sat silently for a long time, watching the flames that leaped and curled around the logs, while the room filled with the strong odor of tobacco. What few windows there were, were tightly battened down against the cold winds. Neither of them, however, minded the closeness of the atmosphere for both were accustomed to it.

It was Marguerite who eventually broke the silence. "Grand-father, why am I so restless when the others seem to be quite content?" she asked.

Old Pierre showed no surprise at the question, for he had for some time noticed this restlessness in his favorite grand-daughter. "Maybe you should be thinking about getting a husband," he said quietly.

"Yes, I suppose so," she replied in a flat tone.

"Not interested?" he asked and raised his shaggy eyebrows.

Marguerite thought for a moment or two and then looked up into his face. "Yes, I am interested, grandfather," she said. "In fact, I would like nothing better than to get married, but, well, it's so difficult being different from the rest of the family. I don't seem to think the way they do; things with which they are contented bore me. The monotonous routine of our life is so tiresome. Get up in the morning, listen to father reading prayers, get breakfast, wash dishes, bake, sew, mend, more meals, more dishes, evening prayers, bed. That goes on day after day and nothing ever happens to change it. When I marry, it will be the same thing over and over again, with the addition of a flock of children to take care of." She finished with a sigh.

"I know what you mean, child," Old Pierre said sympathetically. "Your grandmother was the same, and as I have often told you, you are very like her. But"—he paused for a moment, and stroked her hair—"she had the courage to come with me to this savage land and adapted herself to the life. I'm afraid you're going to have to do the same."

"Yes, I know," she said and her tone was despondent. "Am I wrong, grandfather, in wanting to wait until I fall in love with someone? Perhaps I am too romantic . . ."

"Romance is the privilege of youth," Old Pierre said.

"The others seem to have managed without it . . ." Marguerite thought of her older sister, Jeanne, who had been married for two years to dull Louis Benet and, at the age of nineteen, already had a growing family. Old Pierre thought also of the others in the family—all of them unimaginative and unromantic, accepting things as their father and mother had done. Good, stolid Marie's only concern was the care of her large family. She had come to New France as one of the "King's Girls"—those who were selected from good hardy peasant stock to make wives for the settlers. When new shipments of the girls arrived, the men chose the women they thought would best be suited to a hard farm life and could bear plenty of children. It was rather like the way they selected the sheep and cattle for their farms. There was no question of love, though most of the marriages turned out well. Jacques had chosen Marie in this manner twenty-three years ago and when his older sons reached the age of eighteen, they had done the same. It was expected that most of the men would follow suit—all except Paul, for Old Pierre doubted whether he would find a wife that way.

Old Pierre broke into their reveries and picked up the conversation where they had dropped it. "Isn't there any man hereabouts who attracts you?" he asked. "No one with whom you went skating or sleighing this winter?"

Marguerite thought for a moment and then replied. "Only the wrong kind of man and that wasn't anything serious."

Old Pierre looked a little puzzled as he asked: "Meaning whom, my dear?"

"Charles Péchard . . ." Marguerite said and her voice was low.

A frown crossed Pierre's face and he grunted.

"You like him?" he asked anxiously.

"I don't even know that. He's more interesting than most of them. He was on one of the sleigh rides and kissed me. That was all."

They fell silent again for Marguerite's statement had alarmed Old Pierre. The Péchard family and their followers were notorious in the neighborhood because they all preferred fur trading to farming. They went off for months, and sometimes years at a time, into the forests, trading with Indians and living like them. *Coureurs de bois* were looked down upon by the more respectable Montrealers, though many of the so-called respectable families did fur trading on the side, using the *coureurs de bois* as scapegoats.

Marguerite thought about Charles Péchard as she sat before the fire with her grandfather. There had been scarcely anything between them but enough to arouse her emotions and make her restless. There had been sleighing parties as usual that winter among the young people and a lot of innocent fun and frolicking. Charles Péchard had been home because his father was ill. He had unexpectedly joined one of the sleighing parties and no one had objected. In fact, it had made many a girl's heart flutter, for like most of the coureurs de bois he had about him an aura of daring, adventure and fascination. He had chosen Marguerite for his sleighing partner and under cover of the heavy rugs had put his arm around her and kissed her. She had reproved him in the prescribed manner, though at the same time wishing he would ignore the reproof. There had been an exhilaration in that kiss and it had left her excited and hungry for more. No other flirtation had ever stirred her in that manner. She had not seen Charles Péchard since, for her father strictly forbade any of them going near the Péchard seigneury even though it was next door.

"Charles probably isn't as bad as he's represented," Old Pierre said. "But you wouldn't want to get mixed up with a family like that, would you? He's away for years at a time and that would be no life for you."

"No, I wasn't taking it seriously. It's just because I am so restless," she said evasively.

"Now that the ice break is here there'll probably be new people coming and we must see what we can do to help you."

"You're always so understanding," she said and put her lips to the back of his mangled hand. "It helps just to sit and talk to you."

"I'm glad, dear. I'm such a useless old fool . . ."

"No, you're not!" she protested. "And you mustn't say that. If it weren't for you I should be much more unhappy."

"Exaggeration, my dear—but thank you for saying it." He bent and kissed her.

They sat for some time musing, each making pictures in the fire and when a sharp knock came they both started almost guiltily. They looked at each other quickly and Marguerite wrinkled her nose at the interruption of this pleasant hour together. Muttering her annoyance, she got to her feet and went to open the door. Immediately she bobbed a curtsey, for the Sieur de Courville stood outside.

"Welcome, Seigneur," she said. "Won't you please come in?"

"I'm not intruding?" he asked graciously.

"Certainly not, monsieur," she answered politely.

"Thank you," he said with a pleasant smile. Marguerite waited to take the Seigneur's heavy beaver coat but he held it away from her. "That's too heavy for a pretty little thing like you," he said and chucked her under the chin. Marguerite smiled at him and curtseyed again.

"Well, you old rascal," the Seigneur greeted Old Pierre who had come forward to meet him. As they seated themselves by the fire, Marguerite hurried to the other end of the room to find lights. Candles were a luxury they could afford only on special occasions and at the winter's end they had none until new shipments arrived. They managed to get along, however, with iron bowls filled with tallow, from the center of which protruded a wick. Even these were seldom used as they went to bed as soon as darkness came. Marguerite set the bowls on the table, and when she had brought the brandy, left the two men to talk.

Jean-Baptiste, Sieur de Courville, was a handsome man with iron-grey hair and finely chiselled features that showed his aristocratic heritage. He was the owner of the Seigneury and in the early days Old Pierre had been his servant. In those pioneer days Seigneur and servant often worked side by side and when the Sieur's house had been completed, Old Pierre had taken his portion of the land and cleared it. The Sieur was five years older than Old Pierre, though to look at them the position seemed reversed, Old Pierre's hardships had been so much the greater. Over the long period of years they had become very stanch friends and often of an evening they sat around the fire at the Manor House with their pipes and brandy and never tired of reminiscing over the thirty-five years they had known each other. Though one was a *seigneur* and the other a *habitant*, it made little difference, for there were few social barriers in this new colony. Often the seigneurs were as poor as their tenants and, though usually of noble birth, this was not necessarily so. As the years progressed many habitants became seigneurs. All land in New France was held under feudal tenure, the land being granted to the seigneur on condition he had it cleared within a specified time and obtained colonists to farm it.

It was said that Old Pierre was the only one who knew the Seigneur's true story and if this were so, he had kept the confidence well. Unlike many of the seigneurs, the Sieur de Courville had never returned to France. He had made occasional trips to Quebec, though in later years he had omitted even these. It was known he had had a wife in France and that he also had sons, but they had never come to Montreal and he never referred to them. There were sad lines on his face, lines of deep disappointment, and to counteract his personal sorrows he had devoted himself to the lives of those who lived on his seigneury. As a result, no seigneur in Montreal was more beloved than he.

"Pour the brandy, Jean-Baptiste," Old Pierre said. The Sieur filled two glasses, handed one to Old Pierre and they toasted each other. The Sieur smacked his lips in appreciation.

"Good brandy. *Almost* as good as mine," he said and chuckled.

"Almost?" Pierre said and there was a roguish smile on his leathery face.

"Is it some of mine, you old rogue?" the Sieur asked and then threw back his head as his laugh bellowed to the rafters. "Then it must be more than *almost* as good! Think I'll have another glass to see if you're speaking the truth." He filled his glass and sipped it slowly, running the liquid over his tongue. "Yes, it's good."

"How are things down by the River?" Old Pierre asked.

"They're getting excited. It'll break very soon now. Breaking up early this year."

"Aye," Old Pierre agreed.

"What's the latest news?" the Sieur asked.

"Why ask me?" Old Pierre replied in a dry voice.

"No local gossip?"

"If there is, you supply it," Old Pierre bantered.

"Devil take you! I lead a most innocent life!"

"If you do it isn't any credit to you. It's just because you can't find any woman who would want to go to bed with an old fool!"

"Oh, I can't! I'm not so old yet that I can't make a pretty filly just as happy as some of these younger fellows who think they know so much!"

"Huh!" Old Pierre grunted. "What's on your mind?"

"How d'you know there is anything on my mind?"

"I haven't known you all these years without being able to read the signs on your face. Fill up your pipe and let's have it."

The Sieur became more serious as he filled his pipe and he took his time over it. Not until he had it drawing well did he speak again.

"A nephew of mine is coming here," he said abruptly.

"A nephew?" Old Pierre said and looked at the Sieur suspiciously.

Jean-Baptiste hesitated a moment and then said: "Sister's son. I had a special dispatch . . ."

"At this time of the year!" Old Pierre said dubiously.

"Well no—had it some time but haven't said anything."

"Secretive devil."

"Wanted to get it straight in my own mind before I talked about it."

"Why's he coming? Trouble?"

"I gather so. Some indiscretion."

"H'm. When does he get here?"

"He'll arrive on the first ship."

"Going to Quebec to meet him?"

"I suppose so," Jean-Baptiste answered without enthusiasm.

"What are you going to do with him here?"

"Try to make him settle down if I can."

"Won't be easy. These young bloods don't like farm life after Versailles. And he's evidently pretty wild if they had to get him out of the country."

"Probably only an amatory indiscretion and the fellow may have other qualities that are good. After all, who of us hasn't had these entanglements in our youth?"

Old Pierre nodded. "D'you like the idea?" he asked.

There was a heavy look on Jean-Baptiste's face and he puffed on his pipe for a while before answering. He was debating with himself how much of the truth he should tell his friend.

"Oh—it'll make a change," he said finally. "Maybe the fellow will prove better than we expect and perhaps," he sighed, "he might carry on here after I'm gone."

"Maybe," Old Pierre answered. He knew the greatest sadness in the Sieur's life had been that none of his sons had come over to be with their father. After his wife had died, the Sieur had written to his sons in the hope they might be interested, but they had scorned the idea of coming to the colonies.

The two men sat talking for some time, speculating as they all did at this time of the year as to what the new season would bring.

Then heavy rumblings like thunder filled the air and though they had heard it many times, the two men left the comfortable fire and went to the door. There Marguerite joined them and as they went outside they could hear the shouts of the people at the water's edge. At intervals further rumblings rent the air as the ice burst its bonds and crumpled into large jagged blocks, pushing against each other and piling up along the water's edge.

"Well, it's here," the Sieur said. "Now we shall have spring, Marguerite, and new hopes." He put his arm round her and she smiled up at him.

The darkness was falling and they could see the habitants and their families moving across the snow to their homes. Soon the snow would all have melted and the vast lands would change from white to green and yellow. In the background the hills were silhouetted against the sky, with the tall fir and cedar trees holding up their arms waiting to welcome the new life that would soon spring from them.

CHAPTER III

PAUL BOISSART walked away from the Péchard house deep in thought. He had that afternoon come to a momentous decision and now there was much thinking to be done. It was a decision he had been pondering for a long while and, taking advantage of the fact that the family would be down by the shore watching the ice *shove,* he had slipped over to the neighboring seigneury, taking the back way through the uncleared land in the hope that no one would see him. He was anxious his father should not know until he had every detail arranged and an opportune moment could be found for the disclosure. Even then it would probably mean disagreement and perhaps a scene.

Paul was restless and dissatisfied with the monotony of the daily routine of life. It was a law in New France that land should be inherited by all the children of the family in equal portions. Therefore as soon as a son married, a slice of land was divided off with frontage to the River and he would build his own house and begin to rear a family. Already this had been done in the case of the two eldest Boissart boys, Pierre and Raoul. In another year Paul would be expected to take a wife, receive his strip of land and set up his household. But the land, Paul argued, could not continue to provide for all of them and as the families increased there would be far too many mouths to feed. Besides, he wanted to make money so he could perhaps become a seigneur and not have to spend all his days as a habitant like his father. Outside of farming there were only two courses open—soldiering and the fur trade. Soldiering as a profession did not appeal to him. Like all the men of this new colony, he was ready to fight when it was a matter of defending home and rights from the onslaughts of

20

enemies, but that was as far as soldiering interested him. What he was most keenly interested in was the fur trade but his father was rigidly opposed to coureurs de bois. Jacques' objection was engendered largely by their neighbors, the Péchards, and the unruly manner in which they conducted their lives.

Major Péchard had been a member of the famous Carignan-Salières regiment, the first regulars to come to New France in 1665. When a few years later the regiment was ordered home, a number of the officers and men had preferred to remain in New France as settlers. It had been a good as well as a bad arrangement but one which had a strong and lasting influence on the character of the Canadian people. It was good because it not only provided further settlers for a colony that badly needed them, but also provided a permanent military protection. It was bad because soldiers were by the very nature of their calling somewhat wild and restless, and the pious mission town of Montreal could not cope with the increase of taverns and gambling that thrived under their influence, despite all the edicts and decrees that were made in an effort to discontinue them. The younger element in the town secretly applauded these new settlers for they brought a more lively atmosphere to what had hitherto been a pious and dull existence. Some of the soldiers had made good farmers and had cleared and tilled the land allotted to them. Many, however, had neglected their land and instead had taken to the adventurous and more prosperous life offered by fur trading.

Such a family was that of Major Péchard. With him had settled several of the men under his command and they had only cleared enough of the land to build a rough hut in which to live when they returned from the woods. The Major himself had built quite a pretentious house for he was from a good French family and aristocratic blood demanded proper habitation. He and his men used his "castle" for their carousing when they returned each year for a few brief weeks while they sold their beaver skins. Then the entire neighborhood resounded with their drinking bouts and where there was drinking there were women—women the priests had done their best to have deported to France. If there were not enough of these, there were always Indian squaws.

Thus the whole seigneury under Major Péchard had acquired an unsavory reputation, although the old Major himself was liked—even though this might be reluctantly admitted. There was no better man with whom to spend an evening, and as the brandy took effect, he would settle down to telling stories of his escapades in a manner that never became tiresome. His son, Charles, was also liked although there were unsavory stories of his relationship to the Indian women kept by his father, for the Major had no legal wife.

Paul had tried to argue with his father that all coureurs de bois could not be judged by the Péchards and in support of his argument would mention the le Moynes who had originally made their money in the fur trade and were now one of the most respected families in that region. Their seigneury directly across the River was one of the finest and most prosperous in the community. If the le Moynes could do this— the descendants of a humble innkeeper in Dieppe—then why could not he, Paul would argue. The le Moyne family had no better background than the Boissarts and it was upon their success that Paul intended to model his own. But though Jacques approved and admired the le Moynes, he stubbornly refused to listen to any argument in favor of coureurs de bois.

So that afternoon Paul had gone over to see the Péchards. He had known them all his life though he had had little to do with them because of his father's insistence that they should not go near these neighbors. When Charles Péchard had been a little boy, the Boissart children had taken delight in annoying him and occasionally there had been fights. On one occasion Paul and Charles had fought it out bitterly with hard blows. This, however, had made them respect each other and had it not been that their modes of life were so different they might have become friends. But since he was six years old Charles had gone with his father and the men into the woods and was not often home. He was three years older than Paul and at twenty was considered one of the most experienced coureurs de bois in Montreal. Often Paul had watched him set off in his canoe with the Major and had secretly envied him with a constantly deepening envy. His life was interesting and exciting and he did not have to do the dull tasks about the farm that fell to Paul.

During this last winter they had met occasionally, as the illness of Major Péchard had kept Charles at home. But on these occasions there had been no opportunity to talk about fur trading and so Paul boldly took this step this afternoon. When he had knocked on the door, he was not quite sure how he would be received. It was opened by a slovenly Indian squaw who curtly asked:

"Yes, what is it?"

Her manner annoyed Paul and, thrusting her aside, he walked in.

"Where's Monsieur Charles?" he asked.

"Charles is in there," she replied sullenly, omitting any prefix.

Paul turned to the door indicated and then hesitated. He had not meant to be so abrupt in entering this house for the first time. He paused a moment and then rapped. A voice inside called to him to enter and when he stood in the open doorway, surprised faces met his, for no one ever knocked on a door in this house. Their surprise deepened when they saw who it was.

The room was a large one and quite well furnished though it looked dirty and untidy. All the furniture had been imported from France and there were still traces of a former affluence, but that comfortable "homespun" look which was characteristic of homes in the neighborhood was lacking. The Major and Charles sprawled in their chairs before the fire, a bottle of brandy on the table between them.

"Sacré diable! Look who's here!" Charles exclaimed.

"Am I intruding?" Paul asked, nervousness apparent in his manner.

Charles shrugged his shoulders, a sarcastic expression on his face.

"Makes no difference to us," he said rudely. He had consumed a quantity of brandy and was in a mean mood. The enforced idleness of the winter had begun to get on his nerves.

Charles' abruptness was softened by the manner of the Major. "Come on in, boy," he said and motioned him to a chair.

Paul took the nearest chair and refused the proffered brandy. "What can we do for you?" the Major asked. Without further preliminaries Paul began to explain the reason for his call. The Major smiled as he listened. He liked this boy—he was clean cut and healthy, strong too, though he was much shorter than the rest of the Boissart men. This had once been a sore point with Paul, for his brothers, father, and grandfather were all over six feet tall. But he had stopped growing at five feet six and then suddenly realized that his Maker had been kind to him. Had he grown taller he could not have become a coureur de bois, for long legs and too much weight were a handicap in a canoe where every pound counted. In looks he closely resembled Marguerite, with the same wavy, reddish hair and a handsome face roughened by an outdoor life.

"How old are you?" the Major asked when Paul had finished explaining his call.

"Seventeen, monsieur," he replied.

"What makes you want to go into the woods?"

"For one thing, I find farm life monotonous and—frankly I want to make money. There are too many of us to live off the land and also I want to make something of myself when I am older. I want to be more than—just a farmer."

"Ambitious, eh?" the Major said and smiled at him.

"Yes, monsieur," Paul answered and looked the Major frankly in the face.

"Your father won't approve, Paul. Are you prepared to go against his wishes?"

Paul did not answer. There was an anxious look on his face. He had never disobeyed his father, except in trifling childish things. But the more he thought of this the more he felt it was the life he wanted.

"I shall have to, monsieur," he answered quietly. "I've got to get away."

"You mean you are in trouble?" the Major asked and his tone was kindly.

"Oh, no!" Paul said hastily. "I'm just restless."

"You can't become a coureur de bois without a license and that'll cost you a thousand francs," Charles snarled. As Paul talked Charles had been watching him covertly. Although his tone and manner were unfriendly, actually he liked Paul and had more than a passing interest in his twin sister since the night he had kissed her. But because he did not want Paul to know he liked and admired him, Charles assumed an offhand manner.

"I know," Paul said and there was a challenge in his eyes. "And just where I am going to get a thousand francs is the difficulty. But . . ."

"Then you might as well save your breath. Every man who goes with us has to have his own license and provide his own equipment." The expression on Charles' face implied, "and don't think we're going to do it for you," but he did not voice the remark.

Paul met Charles' eyes steadily and because Charles did not like to have people look directly at him, he took the brandy bottle and filled his glass.

"I understand all that, Charles," Paul said. "I came over this afternoon only to find out whether you would be willing to have me join you if I could equip myself."

"I suppose we ought to feel honored that one of the worthy Boissarts wishes to become one of us," Charles said and then added tersely: "But we're not!"

Paul's face flushed and he set his lower jaw firmly. Before he could answer the retort, the Major spoke.

"What makes you want to come with *us*, Paul?" he asked. "There are many other coureurs de bois in Montreal."

This was a difficult question for Paul to answer and he replied rather lamely:

"We're neighbors, monsieur, and er . . . well . . ."

"And you don't think we're such black sheep as your father would make out?" the Major said with a smile.

"Does it really matter what my reasons are, monsieur?" Paul asked.

"No. Only you are building up twice the amount of trouble for yourself. Your father is bitterly against the fur trade and that will be one obstacle for you; he despises me and that will be a second obstacle. Why not find some other trader and have only one bridge to cross?"

Paul considered the Major's words. It was foolish of him to join the Péchards since his father was so against them yet they were the only coureurs de bois he knew.

"He thought we'd be so flattered we would jump at the idea!" Charles said and yawned.

"There's no need for sarcasm, Charles," the Major said reprovingly.

"He's too soft for the woods!" Charles continued, ignoring his father's reproof.

"Come outside and I'll show you whether I'm soft or not," Paul retorted angrily. "I beat you once before and by God I'll do it again!" In his anger he forgot he was swearing.

At the last remark a grin crossed Charles' face but this did not appease Paul. Had it not been that he realized Charles was rather drunk, he would have been tempted to strike him as he sat there. But the Major was talking, pointing out to Paul all the hardships he would have to endure as a coureur de bois, with the intention of trying to dissuade him. Instead it had the opposite effect and made Paul still more anxious to go into the woods.

As the Major talked to Paul he wished these two boys could become friends. He was sixty years old and the hard life he had always led was beginning to take toll. His illness that winter had been severe and his heart was giving him trouble. Soon Charles would have to take over the leadership of the crew and a man like Paul would be an asset. The Major had not yet told his son, but he felt sure he would not be able to make another expedition into the woods. Charles and Paul were opposites and could balance one another. Charles had seen only the crude, rough side of life, yet his experiences would help Paul. Paul, on the other hand, could show Charles some of the more gentle and refined things in life. The Major often worried about his son's irregularities. His own father had been a highly respected man of title in France and his background and early childhood had been one of delicacy and charm. The old man would have been horrified had he known that his grandson was not only illegitimate but could scarcely read or write. The Major had at times thought of sending Charles to France for his education but there was no one living there now to whom he could have entrusted him and if the boy had gone alone the results would probably have been more disastrous than his remaining in New France.

"When do you leave again, monsieur?" Paul asked.

"We usually leave about the end of May," the Major replied with a glance at his son.

"That's quite soon," Paul said anxiously.

"Not too soon for me," Charles said with a yawn.

"I'll probably have to wait until next year." Paul said disconsolately.

When Paul left, nothing had been decided. He walked to the water's edge and looked out over the River that was now stirring restlessly. He felt depressed, for his talk with the Péchards had made his chances appear more hopeless. Yet with it all, he was more determined than ever that somehow he was going to become a fur trader.

CHAPTER IV

In Montreal the excitement pendent upon the ice break was reflected in the attitudes of the people, who stood in groups talking and gesticulating, while the taverns were doing a thriving trade. No town could exhibit such a mixed population as Montreal in this era. Seigneurs in fine clothes; clerks and merchants also affecting fine clothes and imitating their superiors; habitants in their rough homespuns; coureurs de bois in their distinctive garb; soldiers of all ranks; priests in their black robes—all rubbing shoulders with each other and with Indians civilized by the missionaries.

The struggling town lay just above the heel on a boot-shaped island with the toe pointing to the south. Situated at the confluence of two great rivers—the St. Lawrence and the Ottawa, which made it a natural starting point for all expeditions to the west, the town also served as an outpost for warning Quebec and the intermediary town of Three Rivers of the approach of dangerous enemies. Only the previous year, the Governor of Montreal, the popular Chevalier de Callières, had had a stockade erected around the town in an effort to protect the people more adequately from constant raids.

Montreal in the year sixteen eighty-eight was not as fashionable a town as Quebec but it could boast some fine stone houses built by the Government officials and leading merchants. Governor Callières had obtained from the Seminary of St. Sulpice a grant of land on the point where the Sieur de Maisonneuve had originally landed. Here he erected a fine edifice suitable to his position and prestige, and it was later to become known as Pointe de Callières. The le Moynes, although their property was across the river from Montreal, had built a large mansion within the town on the Rue St. Joseph (afterwards St. Sulpice) and their ambitious brother-in-law, Jacques le Ber, one of the most prominent of the Montreal merchants, had flattered his superlative ego by building himself a magnificent establishment.

All these impressive residences were dominated by the Seminary, three churches and the Fort which rose high above the houses. The Seminary of St. Sulpice was a branch of the Seminary of Paris and had purchased the Island of Montreal from its founder, the Sieur de Maisonneuve, some twenty-five years earlier. The Superior, Father Dollier de Casson, was a man for whom everyone in Montreal had the greatest regard and admiration. It was to his farsightedness that Montreal owed its well-planned streets—the first town planning in the colony. Sixteen years before, accompanied by a surveyor, Father Dollier had marked out the streets, many of which were to remain unchanged during the ultimate growth of Montreal into a great city. The Rue Notre Dame was the widest street and was connected by five main arteries to the Rue St. Paul—the business street that ran parallel with the River. On the Rue St. Paul was the Common where the Indians traded their beaver skins and also the public market where the farmers brought their produce every Tuesday and Friday. Here also were the saloons and taverns which continued to thrive in increasing numbers despite the efforts of the clergy to suppress them.

The day following the ice break, the Sieur de Courville drove into town, accompanied by Old Pierre. They were making their way towards Dillon's Tavern, when they saw the Governor's carriage approaching. The Sieur de Courville drew in his horses to let the Governor pass and de Callières stopped to greet them. They had been chatting for a few minutes when they were hailed by a massive figure in black, threading his way with difficulty through the crowd. It was Father Dollier de Casson, and his good-humored face was wreathed in smiles. They returned his greeting warmly, and as he strode on his way, his tall figure towering above all others, the Governor commented:

"He always looks as though he still carried a musket."

"Well, he was a soldier and a good one before he took the cloth," the Sieur de Courville remarked.

"Yes, indeed," the Governor replied. They all watched him striding along to the Seminary and their faces were kindly.

The Chevalier de Ramezay was with the Governor. He and de Callières had come over from France in the suite of the Governor-General, the Marquis de Denonville. Already de Ramezay had distinguished himself as a soldier and in years to come was to be one of the most outstanding men in the colony. Tall, good-looking and as yet unmarried, he was very popular with the ladies.

"Won't you gentlemen join me at my house for some refreshment?" de Callières asked.

"That's the best suggestion I have heard for a long while," Old Pierre said gruffly and smiled.

"We were on our way to Dillon's but I don't see why we shouldn't drink your good brandy instead," the Sieur de Courville remarked. "Thank you, your Excellency."

"Delighted. I shall be expecting you."

The Governor drove on and the Sieur de Courville turned his horses and followed. The Governor's mansion was a model of elegance and good taste. De Callières had been Governor of Montreal for the past three years and his administration had been popular. There were many who wished he had been Governor of the entire colony instead of the rather weak and very pious Marquis de Denonville.

"Well, gentlemen, your very good health," de Callières said when the brandy was served. Each man sipped the golden liquid with the grace of an epicure and admired its excellent quality.

"What's the news going to be?" the Sieur de Courville asked of his host.

De Callières shrugged his shoulders. "I know no more than you do."

"Or if you do, you're not going to tell," de Courville chided.

"No—I know nothing more than anyone here."

"When is the Governor-General arriving?"

"I don't know that either. Probably by an early boat."

"It's probably as useless as ever to look forward to a peaceful spring and summer," Old Pierre remarked.

"We can always hope," the Chevalier de Ramezay said.

They had barely started their discussion of the events of the day, when a servant informed the Governor that General de Vaudreuil was calling.

"Show him in," de Callières said and when the guest appeared he was greeted warmly by all. The Chevalier de Vaudreuil was a newcomer to Montreal, having arrived in Quebec the previous year in command of the forces. He had come to Montreal just before winter had set in and, being a bachelor, had been much courted. Old Pierre had never met him and was now introduced.

"I would like to have you meet one of our most respected citizens," de Callières said. "Pierre Boissart—the Chevalier de Vaudreuil." They bowed to each other and it was inevitable that de Vaudreuil's eyes should rest for a brief moment on Old Pierre's disfigured hands. It was typical of Old Pierre that he was perfectly at home among all these elegantly dressed gentlemen, though he wore the clothes of a farmer. "Pierre Boissart is one of the original settlers here and knows more about our woes than anyone," de Callières graciously told the Chevalier de Vaudreuil.

"I am delighted to meet you, monsieur," the young soldier replied.

"You know, of course, that General de Vaudreuil is in command of our forces," de Callières went on.

"So I heard," Old Pierre replied. "Too bad they didn't send you a larger force to command," he added critically.

The Chevalier de Vaudreuil looked sharply at Old Pierre. He was not quite sure whether the criticism was aimed at him personally or whether he should agree. He decided on the latter.

"We do need a much larger force, monsieur," he said.

"What's the matter with those bone heads in France? How do they expect to keep their colonies if they don't send us proper help?"

The Governor took up the conversation. "That is what we have all been asking. The Marquis de Denonville has written letter after letter."

"Denonville!" Old Pierre exclaimed and his tone was derisive. "What has he ever done for the colony?"

"It is not an easy task that he has, monsieur," the Governor said in defense. "His hands are tied. I have it in mind to suggest letting me go to France to see if I can't represent the case so they will understand and help us."

"Tell them to send back the Comte de Frontenac—he's the only man who knows how to handle this colony. He's not terrified of Indians—like our present Governor-General!"

The Chevalier de Callières smiled patiently. He had heard so many complaints against the Marquis de Denonville but loyalty prevented his giving his own opinion. There was much that was fine in the Governor-General—he was pious and trustworthy but lacked foresight and had made too many serious mistakes.

"I wonder, gentlemen," the General de Vaudreuil began, "whether I might take this opportunity of asking you some questions? I am a comparative newcomer here and during the winter I have heard so much discussion about the honorable Marquis de Denonville. To be frank, could you gentlemen tell me, confidentially, if you wish, just what did happen at the Fort Frontenac when the Indians were made prisoners and sent to France as galley slaves?"

For a moment or two there was an awkward silence. The

Governor took out his snuff box, carefully selected a pinch and placed it delicately to his nostril. He offered the box to Old Pierre, who was sitting beside him, but he declined it. He had no fingers with which to handle it and besides he thought it a stupid habit.

"Well, monsieur," de Callières said, "that has become rather a delicate subject."

"We're all friends here and no one is going to quote you outside," the Sieur de Courville remarked.

De Callières smiled. "I know that, gentlemen. My hesitation is not that I am afraid of being quoted, but that, frankly, my own opinion is divided. I have known the Marquis a good many years and I know how sincerely he tries . . ."

"But can't get over his fear of savages!" Old Pierre retorted.

"There is no denying he dislikes them. Yet I have seen him leading attacks against them and no one could doubt his courage."

"Anyone who comes here has to have that," the Chevalier de Ramezay said.

"Certainly, we all agree he's a courageous man," the Sieur de Courville said. "But he lacks the strength of personality this colony requires in an administrator. With the Indians you have to show them you are stronger than they. He parleys too much with them."

"True, true," de Callières agreed. "It is often difficult to know what is the best thing to do. Personally I think the Marquis has the right idea when he attacks the matter at its source—the English. They insist the Iroquois are subjects of the English crown and there is no doubt they incite the tribes to fight and plunder us."

"No doubt at all," General de Vaudreuil remarked.

"The Iroquois have no more love for the English than they have for us," the Sieur de Courville said. "They are just playing one group of white men against the other. Actually they despise us all—and in many ways we can't blame them. We come into their territory, spoil their hunting grounds and then fight among ourselves as to who is going to get the best land."

"That is correct," de Callières said. "Yet—when fine men have given their lives to come here purely for religious reasons and to try to teach these savages Christianity—you wouldn't have us go away and admit we have failed in our task?"

"I sometimes think it would have been better. Where have we arrived in all these years—a handful of settlers all expecting to be killed any day. Look at this town—what progress has it made?" de Courville said and his tone was heated.

"If we could once make peace with the Iroquois—we could make progress," de Callières said.

"What's the use of peace?" Old Pierre growled. "They keep it as long as it suits them and when it's no longer to their advantage they forget all about the treaty and begin plundering again."

"They have one idea—security of the monopoly of the beaver trade and we interfere with that," de Courville said.

"We should attack the English," the Chevalier de Ramezay said and looked at General de Vaudreuil.

"With the small force we have here? That would be very difficult unless we could take them by surprise."

There was a pause while de Callières passed the brandy decanter and they filled their glasses.

"And we still have not answered the Chevalier de Vaudreuil's question about the galley prisoners," the Sieur de Courville said.

Attention was directed to the Governor and it was obvious the subject was distasteful to him. He cleared his throat and thought for a moment. "That was a mistake in judgment," he began. From the expression on the faces of the others they were all in agreement. "A mistake because he took too literally the orders sent by our illustrious King. The order was to take as many prisoners as possible among the Iroquois and send them to the galleys because they are all robust men. It is obvious, now, the order meant prisoners taken in the wars. Instead, the Marquis deliberately went out to get prisoners by —by—er—a trick." The last word came out quickly as though de Callières hoped they had not heard it. He looked the Chevalier de Vaudreuil directly in the face. "This is what happened, General. The Marquis de Denonville called the Iroquois to a peace parley at the Fort Frontenac. He sent our Intendant, Monsieur de Champigny . . ."

"Another weak, pious fool!" Old Pierre commented and though there was the faintest flicker of a smile about de Callière's mouth he let the remark pass unnoticed.

"Monsieur de Champigny went with a force of men and— well, took the Indians prisoners—after a fight, of course. They had come in peace, not in war paint—that was the error."

"It wasn't so much what was done as the way it was done," the Sieur de Courville remarked. "They torture and murder our people when they take them prisoners and that is much worse than being sent to the galleys."

"Certainly," the Governor agreed.

"And what has happened since?" the Chevalier de Vau-. dreuil asked.

"That is what we are waiting to see. The Governor-General sent an explanation to the Iroquois and has written to France asking that the prisoners be returned . . ."

"And they have not been?" de Vaudreuil said.

"Not as yet—though we expect them as soon as navigation opens."

"And we expect the Iroquois to retaliate before that time arrives . . ." de Courville said.

"We'll hope not," the Governor said.

"Hope? That's what we've lived on for years and it gets less with each new spring."

"Let us drink to the new season anyway—and perhaps to the realization of our hopes this time," the Governor said.

They all drank the toast and shortly afterwards went their

respective ways. As the Sieur and Old Pierre drove home, the carriage slithered and slid over the uneven road with holes already filled with the melted snow. All along the river bank huge blocks of ice had piled, forming mounds of debris before each homestead.

CHAPTER V

Old Pierre stood at the door of the farmhouse, his pipe held between firm jaws, and watched the dawn break over the River. It would be a clear, bright day and the thought satisfied him, for it was to ·be a day of celebration. Throughout the entire colony there would be no work done that morning. Tools and implements would be laid aside and every habitant and his entire family would don their best farm clothes and gather to pay homage to their Seigneur. It was May Day— one of the many feast days that provided a pleasant diversion from the hard work and monotony of farm life. From the western outskirts of Montreal, up to Three Rivers and on to the farthest point of settlement east of Quebec, the same celebration would be taking place.

The hazy light of the morning cleared as the dawn burst its nightly bonds, and as far as Old Pierre could see, the scene was one of peace and beauty. The elms and maples were beginning to show delicate young green leaves and in the sections where the trees were uncleared, wild flowers lifted their heads in colorful greeting. The river, recently a solid mass of white, now moved its deep azure waters swiftly along, impelled by the restless rapids of Lachine. Against the banks, craft and canoes were tied, many in the process of repair and some freshly painted for the busy season. The fields were now plowed and spring sowing had begun.

The children were the first dressed and scampered out of the house to join their grandfather. Old Pierre took his pipe from his mouth and smiled at them.

"Ready?" he asked.

"Yes, grandfather," Philip said eagerly. "May we go over?"

"I don't know why not—unless your mother told you to

38

wait," Old Pierre said and his kindly old face was gentle as he looked at them. Young Philip was so very much like Jacques and Old Pierre thought back to the days when Jacques had been Philip's age.

"Well—mother did say we were to wait for Charles and Etienne."

"Then you had better wait, hadn't you?"

"Yes, only I have a lot of work to do today, grandfather. I'm to climb the Maypole, you know."

Old Pierre's face·beamed. "Why, yes, to be sure, so you are. Quite an honor, Philip."

The look of importance on Philip's face no doubt prompted little Marie to remark:

"I wish they'd let a girl do it one year."

"Girls can't climb Maypoles!" Philip retorted.

"I don't know why not!" Marie protested with all the vehemence of her twelve years. "I climbed higher than you did yesterday!"

"Only because you were there first and took the best position. Girls aren't supposed to do the things boys are."

"Who said they weren't?" Marie argued, and the argument waxed quite heated as she tried valiantly to defend her sex. Having no sisters near her age, little Marie had her difficulties. Philip was her nearest companion and they were always together, wrangling and arguing but nevertheless, before others, always defending each other.

They were still arguing over the relative merits of their respective sexes, when Paul came out and the discussion ceased as they rushed to him.

"Come on, Paul. Let's get over. We shall be late," they cried.

"Such a hurry!" he chided.

"But we've got to strip the tree. Do we have to wait longer?" Philip protested.

Old Pierre smiled at Paul and nodded his head. "All right. We'll go," Paul said and the children raced ahead.

"Looks like a fine day," Paul remarked to his grandfather as they walked towards the Manor House. The sun rose and cast its brightness over the scene, silhouetting the Manor House upon a knoll, overlooking the River. In comparison with the houses that many of the seigneurs had built, the de Courville Manor was not impressive but to those on the seigneury it was a symbol of protection. It was built partly of stone and partly of wood, two stories in height, with gabled upstairs windows.

It was before the Seigneur's house that the ceremony would take place and this was the thirtieth in which Old Pierre had played a leading part. In all those years the formalities had never been varied and though he grumbled about it all being a lot of nonsense, in his heart he was proud of doing the honors. From each farmhouse people were beginning to make their way towards the Manor and while the children scampered about, the older men dragged over a tall fir tree that had been cut the day before.

Paul, hatchet in hand, directed the operations. His brothers Charles and Etienne·had now joined them and, with Philip and other boys from the neighboring farms, were holding the tree while Paul hacked off the branches.

"Hold it firmly now," Paul said and then more sharply: "Philip, hold it still or I'll let someone else do it." Young Philip brought back his wavering attention and gripped the top that he had been told to hold. Marie was busy picking up the lopped branches and putting them in a pile. "All right," Paul said presently, "you can begin stripping the bark. Get it clean but be sure to leave at least three feet at the top."

He wiped his forehead and came over to his grandfather. Jacques had now joined them and watched with the eye of one who had seen it all many times before.

"Warm work," Paul said as he rested from his exertions.

"Looks like a good sturdy tree you have there," Jacques said.

"Aye," Paul replied. "We cut it yesterday. It'll look well when it's ready." The crowd increased as families left their farmhouses to join in the celebration. The babble of voices grew louder and people formed themselves into groups to gossip. This was the first opportunity many of them had had to chat with each other since the ice *shove* some three weeks before, and they took every advantage of it.

Paul took out his pipe and filled it, and when it was going to his satisfaction, he turned to speak to his grandfather. "The same old scene over again, eh, grandfather?" he said.

"The same—yet different. I was just thinking how many changes there have been in these past thirty years—yet not nearly enough changes. The changes have been in the people but not enough progressive change in the land. As I look around here I can't help thinking of these families. These men with deep lines in their faces and anxious looks in their eyes—it seems such a little while ago they were children scampering about like Marie and Philip. And that makes me think too of the many who have gone . . ."

"Many of them before they were old too . . ." Paul remarked.

"Aye. It's not many men who can have the privilege of growing old here as I have. Too many of them have been sacrificed while they still had youth."

"I wonder just how many of us will die natural deaths," Paul mused. "It would be interesting to know the percentage of those who live their normal span—and those who get killed prematurely."

"Eh." Then Old Pierre's expression changed. "But why spend a fine morning like this talking about death?"

Paul grinned. "You're right. I'd better go and see about that Maypole. Come with me."

They strode over together, Old Pierre towering above Paul, yet the resemblance between them apparent.

"How's that, Paul?" Philip asked.

Paul cast a critical eye over the Maypole that was in the making. Its trunk now shone white in the sunlight and at the top was a tuft of green leaves which they called the *bouquet.* "The bouquet is a little too long," Paul told them. "Strip off those lower branches."

The boys grasped the fresh, young branches in their hands and tore them off. "That'll do," Paul said. "Now, where are the pegs?"

"What about the weathercock?" a boy asked.

"That goes on after I have fixed the pegs," Paul told him.

"Here they are," the boy said and grabbed a handful from the protesting Philip.

"You can each hold some," Paul said, endeavoring to avert an argument. "Now, Philip, give me one of yours." Philip handed him a wooden peg which he drove into the trunk of the tree. "Now, Antoine, one of yours," and for a while the boys watched with fascinated eyes as Paul drove pegs at regular intervals into the trunk so that presently Philip could climb to the top. "There, is that all right?" he asked the boys.

"Fine," they all agreed.

"Now we can put the weathercock on. Who has it?"

"I have," Marie called proudly and handed it to her brother, with some reluctance in her gesture for it was pretty to hold.

"Get a firm hold on the tree, you boys," Paul told them and while they were busy scrambling for the best places, he took hold of the top of the tree and firmly fixed the decoration. It was a rod about six feet long which had been painted red, surmounted by a green weathercock adorned with a red ball. This same ornament had been used for years on May Day and each year someone different had had the privilege of affixing it. "There we are." He stood back and surveyed his work. "Now we are about ready. Go and clean up, you boys, or you will be late for the ceremony."

They scampered off and Paul smiled at Old Pierre. "Nice

job," Old Pierre said. "Almost as good as I could have done myself," he added. Paul grinned back at him. Together they walked back to the farmhouse so Paul could wash the dirt from his hands and as they returned Paul thought of the Péchard seigneury—the only one that was quiet on this festive morning. No May Day celebration had ever been held on that seigneury.

Old Pierre followed Paul's eyes and thoughts. "Heard yesterday in town that the Major's quite bad."

"Yes—I saw Charles yesterday. He seemed very anxious."

"I doubt if he'll pull through . . ."

"You mean that, grandfather?" Paul said and his voice was anxious.

"Yes. His heart's giving out."

Paul stopped a moment and looked back. "There's something very sad about that place," he said as they walked on. "The silence around it is ominous this morning. On every seigneury there will be gaiety and that one is so quiet."

"Eh—the Major's been a fool. And if he dies, Charles will probably lose the land unless he develops it."

"He'll not do that. He'll go off to the woods again immediately."

"And come back to find he has no land."

"I doubt whether that would worry him. He's a strange chap . . ."

"Had a strange upbringing . . ."

"Yet, you know, there's something about him I like. I believe if he were given a chance he'd turn out all right."

"Probably—but if the Major dies, I doubt if we shall see much of him."

Paul thought for a moment, weighing in his mind whether he should tell his grandfather of his desire to become a coureur de bois. He decided to let it wait for it needed time for the telling and they were almost at the Manor House.

Inside the de Courville Manor, the Sieur watched the proceedings from his bedroom window. Figuratively speaking the habitants were giving their seigneur a surprise, though no one could really have been surprised with all the hammering and chattering that was going on outside. He had dressed in brocaded coat and breeches, and before going downstairs, knelt at the prie-dieu in his bedroom. This day was a proud one, yet his heart was sad because he had no family to share it with him. In the large dining room below long tables had been set, for custom demanded that the friends outside be honored with a feast.

There was the report from a gun and the Sieur hurried to a large armchair facing the door and seated himself. In a few minutes Old Pierre entered, followed by the heads of the other households on the seigneury. With a courteous bow he addressed the Seigneur.

"Monsieur, we beg permission to plant the Maypole before your threshold as a token of our respect and esteem."

The Sieur returned the bow and in the same formal manner replied: "My friends, I am honored by this gesture and accept it with deepest humility and thanks for your loyalty."

Old Pierre and those with him bowed and withdrew. At the front door they paused and Old Pierre stepped in front of the others.

"Fellow habitants," he said, "our Seigneur has graciously accepted our homage."

A shout greeted the announcement and then all knelt to pray for protection during the day. Inside, the Sieur knelt alone, praying with those outside, and then went to the window to watch the raising of the Maypole. Many helping hands lifted the tall tree now so prettily decorated and eased it into the hole that had been dug. Eager faces were upturned as it was secured in position and the children dashed wildly about in the fullness of their excitement.

Old Pierre was then handed a green goblet about two inches high standing on a plate of faience. Holding it very carefully in his crippled hands he again entered the Manor House, followed by the others of the deputation, one of whom carried a bottle of brandy. He made a low bow to the Sieur de Courville.

"Monsieur, will you be pleased to wet the Maypole before you blacken it?" he asked in formal parlance. He then turned, poured some brandy into the goblet and handed it to the Seigneur.

"We will wet it together, my friends," the Sieur replied and signalled to a servant who brought forward a tray containing further glasses of brandy. Together he and the delegates toasted the day and then one another.

Old Pierre then took the gun held by one of the men and handed it to the Seigneur who immediately went to the open door. The moment he appeared on the threshold, Philip clambered up the Maypole with the agility of a squirrel, and twirled the weathercock three times.

"Long live the King!" Philip shouted, and he was answered by cheers and shouts from the crowd.

"Long live the Sieur de Courville!" he then shouted and this time the cheers were loud and long. The Seigneur bowed his acknowledgments, his handsome, weatherbeaten face showing the emotion he felt. Custom had not staled this ceremony and as year added to year he was proud of the love and loyalty accorded him.

Philip began clambering down the Maypole, hacking off the pegs with a tomahawk as he descended. The Sieur stepped forward, raised the gun to his shoulder and fired a blank charge and the Maypole which had gleamed so white was now marred by a black splurge. Had there been other members of his family present, they would now have taken their turns in the blackening ceremony, but since there was none, the habitants and their families now raised their guns and proceeded to blacken the Maypole, for the more powder that was burned on such occasions, the greater the compliment to the seigneur.

The women as well as the men fired the guns and for half an hour there was a rattling feu-de-joie that made it sound as though the Manor House were being besieged.

When it came to an end, the Seigneur addressed them:

"My friends, this is the thirtieth year you have done me this honor. To some of you it is the first May Day celebration for I see new settlers nestling in their mothers' arms." He could have added that they were screaming protestingly, for the firing had set every baby crying. "There are also among you some who have shared every May Day celebration with me since we came to this new colony to make a new life for ourselves. Our lives have been hard and to a great extent our hopes have not been fulfilled; yet despite all the hardships and setbacks that we have known, I am still confident the day will come when our descendants will praise us for our fortitude and be glad we have endured these pioneer years, confident that our faith is not misplaced." Loud applause greeted his words and it was several moments before he could resume. "Hold fast to that faith, my friends, for some of you who are still young will live to see the day when this beautiful land will be at peace and will prosper. Perhaps this small colony will grow into a great city. Its beginning has been slow, much too slow, but do not lose heart for we have a fine heritage here." Again he was applauded and then he concluded: "Come now, my friends, and partake of the humble feast prepared for you."

There was another rattling discharge of muskets and then all filed into the house, preceded by ravenously hungry children. The food was plentiful but plain and for the men there was a good supply of brandy, with wine for the women. At intervals the guests got up, ran to the door and fired another volley at the Maypole, as a courtesy to their seigneur. When the feasting was finished, the Sieur led them in the rollicking songs of the times and every face was wreathed in smiles.

The afternoon was well along when the feasting was finished and many of the families, after a respectful adieu to their

Seigneur, began to straggle back to their own farms. Old
Pierre lingered to the last, standing outside the Manor House
and chatting with the Seigneur.

"Hear the Major's very ill," Old Pierre remarked.

"That so? Serious?" the Sieur asked.

"Looks like it."

"Why don't we go over and see?" the Sieur suggested.

"That is what I was going to suggest."

"Come along then," the Sieur said and he and Old Pierre
walked to the Péchard seigneury. It looked very dejected in
the closing evening. What land had once been cleared was
now overgrown and even the path to the house was undefined.
A dirty squaw opened the door to their knock—the same one
who had let Paul in some weeks earlier, only her manner was
more respectful as she recognized the Seigneur. The bedroom
into which she ushered them was a miserable sight. The room
was half-darkened so that at first they could scarcely discern
the Major lying on the bed, his lined face purplish against the
pillowcase. He was unshaven and his hair was matted.

Charles was sitting by the bed and stood up abruptly when
he recognized the visitors. He had on an old coat and around
his chin was a growth more than a week old.

"Greetings, messieurs," he said and his tone was embarrassed. "I was not expecting company."

"It's all right, Charles," the Sieur said kindly. "We heard
your father was ailing." Then he turned to the Major. "Well,
Major, you don't look quite yourself today. Anything we can
do for you?"

"Thanks—no . . ." the Major said in a low voice quite
unlike his usual booming one. His words came between gasps
and there was concern on the faces of Old Pierre and the Sieur.
"I'm about—at—the end—of the trail," the Major gasped
and tried to force a smile.

"Nothing of the kind!" Old Pierre grunted. "You're too
tough to let a thing like this get the better of you."

"Hello—Pierre—" the Major said. It was the first time Old Pierre had ever been in the house, though they had met often at the taverns. "It's good—of—you—to come."

"Not good at all," Old Pierre said gruffly. "Heard you were ill." He took the chair Charles set for him and laid his scarred hand on the Major's gnarled one as it lay outside the bed-clothes.

"Seen a doctor?" the Sieur asked.

The Major shook his head. "I've been trying to persuade him to let me get a doctor, but he won't listen," Charles told them.

"Doctor—can't do—any good. Heart . . ." the Major said.

"Been letting too many women get at it, you old rogue," the Sieur said and the Major tried again to smile.

It was obvious his strength could not last long. The silence in the room hung heavy as a velvet curtain and the air was foul. They did not stay long for it was apparent little could be done and that conversation exhausted the sick man. As they left the room, Old Pierre noticed several empty brandy bottles that had been hastily kicked under the bed.

That night, Major Julien François Péchard came to the end of a hard and rugged trail. Old Pierre and the Sieur de Courville had returned with a doctor, but there was nothing he could do. He made his examination and then turned to Father Dollier de Casson who had accompanied them.

"This is your job—not mine," Dr. Peret said and walked away from the bed.

Charles' lips tightened at the words and as he knelt with bowed head listening to Father Dollier's voice his hands were clenched tightly together.

When Father Dollier rose, he turned and said quietly: "It is over, Charles."

Charles remained kneeling, one hand covering his eyes. When he rose his eyes rested for a while upon the set face of his father. Then he turned and walked from the room.

CHAPTER VI

"Is it just because we are twins that we are different?"
Marguerite asked.

Paul shrugged his shoulders as he lay sprawled on his back
with his hands behind his head. "I don't know—maybe . . ."

"Grandfather says we are a throwback to grandmother. She
was redheaded—and an aristocrat . . ."

Paul rolled over on his side so he could see Marguerite as
she sat beside him on the river bank. "And you think you have
inherited her aristocratic blood?" he teased.

Marguerite wrinkled her nose at him defiantly. "No—I'm
not that stupid," she said but did not continue the discussion.

It was Sunday afternoon and every farm was quiet as the
habitants took advantage of this one day to rest from their
labors. Dinner over, the Boissarts were amusing themselves in
their respective ways. Old Pierre, Jacques and Marie would
spend the afternoon sleeping and then go over to Pierre's for
supper. The younger children had all drifted off to play and
Paul and Marguerite had come down to the river bank to
watch the canoes that for two days now had been coming down
the river laden with furs.

Paul broke the silence. "I have about made up my mind to
become a coureur de bois."

"You have!" Marguerite's voice was a mixture of surprise
and interest. "When did this happen?"

"I decided the day of the ice shove . . ."

"You mean—like Charles Péchard?"

"*With* him . . ." Paul rolled over on his face as he made
the remark.

"With him!" Marguerite exclaimed. She leaned on her
elbow studying her brother's broad back. "You've been seeing
him then?" she asked, trying to get him to confide in her.

49

"Several times," his voice came muffled as his face was buried in his arms. Then he rolled over on his side again and looked at her. "Charles isn't bad when you get to know him—in fact, I'm beginning to like him. He likes you too . . ." he added and grinned at her.

"Charles Péchard is hardly the height of my ambition," she said and her mouth was disdainful.

"Oh—I don't know. If Charles were given a chance he would be all right. He has good property . . ."

"And lets it go to waste . . ."

"He's changing that . . ."

"I don't believe it."

"Go and take a look some time . . ."

"And have Father in a rage?"

"Since the Major died, Charles has been different. Father Dollier had a talk with him. I really believe he is going to improve the land—and himself. He's talking of getting a wife."

"He'll have a hard time. His reputation is hardly encouraging for a wife."

"Men do reform."

"Are you suggesting I become interested in Charles Péchard?"

Paul laughed. "No—although he did ask me to speak to you."

"He'll have to do a lot of reforming first . . ." Marguerite said and pretended to be disinterested. "Besides—he's always away in the woods. A fine life that would be for his wife . . . ."

"He says he wants to give up the fur trade—he's made plenty of money out of it already. He's talking of giving it up for a while and devoting his time to his seigneury . . ."

"I can't imagine Charles Péchard ever settling down. He's too restless . . ."

"I agree with you. But at least he's making an effort. He's already cleared all the land around the house. I hope his interest lasts until I can raise the money to become a coureur de bois . . ."

"Won't he lend it to you?"

"No—besides I don't want it that way. If I go I ought to be independent of him. He's a man of moods and if he equipped me for the trip—it might have the wrong reaction in his bad moods. No—I want to equip myself . . ."

"What does it cost?"

"A thousand francs for my license and then money for supplies and equipment . . ."

"Phew!" Marguerite exclaimed. "A thousand francs! Wherever would you get that much?"

"That's the difficulty—I don't know."

"The Sieur de Courville couldn't help you, could he?"

Paul shook his head. "He's not a rich man. You know how little he gets from his tenants each year and he has very little besides that. I couldn't ask him . . ."

"What did you think of his nephew this morning?" Marguerite asked suddenly and she looked out over the river so that Paul should not see how keenly interested she was in his answer.

"Quite a dandy, wasn't he?"

"Yes—but—it's a change to see someone fashionably dressed."

Paul looked at her quickly. "I'm beginning to read between the lines of our talk. You think he'd . . ."

"I'm not thinking about him at all," Marguerite said sharply and by her tone gave the lie to her statement. Paul turned on his back again, a smile on his face and followed his own thoughts.

That morning at Mass there had been quite a stir as the Sieur de Courville had come into the church with his newly arrived nephew, the Chevalier Nicholas de Favien. After the service he had introduced him to the groups that stood about chatting and Marguerite thought now of the remark that the

Chevalier had made as she curtseyed to him. "You didn't tell me there were such beautiful women in Montreal," he had said to his uncle and had given Marguerite a searching look which had made her heart beat faster. They had talked about him at dinner and the comments among the elder folks had not been too complimentary. Dandy—fop—cynic—they had called him all these things. "If he soiled his delicate white hands with a speck he'd be flicking it off with a lace handkerchief," Old Pierre had growled.

In Paul's mind there was also a train of thought about the Chevalier de Favien. It was quite obvious he would not be interested in farming and Paul wondered if there was a possibility of interesting him in the fur trade. "It's probably too ambitious a thought," he told himself, yet he had almost made up his mind to try it. The Sieur had announced that morning that he was giving a ball in honor of his nephew and they all had been invited. Perhaps that would give Paul his opportunity.

A sound came upon their ears and they both sat up abruptly, their faces eager as they strained their eyes towards the direction of Lachine.

"Here come some more!" Paul said and soon the melody of the traders' songs could be heard. Wafted from the distance on the soft wind, the songs presently became louder and then the first canoe rounded the bend, followed immediately by a bevy of others. Marguerite and Paul jumped to their feet and ran to the edge of the water, eagerly waiting to wave a greeting. From out of farm doors people appeared to watch the hundreds of canoes passing on their way to Montreal. Each canoe was laden with stacks of pelts ready for sale at the annual Fair that would begin the next day. The canoes moved in groups of three and four, some manned by robust redskins and others by bronzed and hardened coureurs de bois.

Paul gazed at them, his eyes envious and longing.

"Envying them?" The voice of Old Pierre startled them.

"Why, grandfather, I thought you were sleeping," Paul said.

"I was—but I heard the noise and came down. Fine-looking lot, eh?" Old Pierre remarked.

"Yes," Paul answered.

"Haven't you told grandfather?" Marguerite asked in a whisper. Paul shook his head.

"Whispering? Am I intruding?" Old Pierre asked.

"Of course not, grandfather," Paul said quickly. "Marguerite was just asking me whether I had let you into my secret . . ."

"You don't have to . . ."

"I always do, don't I?"

"We have shared a good many secrets. But—perhaps I can save you the trouble. Would the secret be that you want to become one of those men out there?"

"How did you guess?"

"Well—an old man sometimes has second sight. I've known you were restless and I have noticed the look on your face the last few days . . ."

"And probably the others have too . . ." Paul said.

Old Pierre shook his head. "I don't think so. They are too busy with their own affairs. I've nothing to do but interfere with yours."

"Not at all, grandfather. It's just that you have always been more interested in Paul and me," Marguerite said and linked her hand through his arm. Old Pierre smiled down at her from his height and patted her cheek.

"You're right there. You two are my special interest."

"Am I wrong in wanting to become a coureur de bois, grandfather?" Paul asked.

Old Pierre puffed on his pipe for a minute or two before answering. "It's a rough life, Paul. Weeks of trekking over difficult country, enduring great hardships in all kinds of weather and often running into hostile tribes . . ."

"I know. I wouldn't mind that."

"What has caused most of the objection, Paul, is not the fur trading itself but that after months of such hardships the men return home and plunge into dissipation. They go to extremes—you watch them during the next few days. Montreal will be in a pandemonium—every man will be drunk—and with that, well, there are other things." Old Pierre paused.

"There are many fine men here in Montreal who started as coureurs de bois," Paul said obstinately. "They're not considered bad men."

"No, Paul, they're not all bad men. It's the Church that mainly objects and then, too, the State discourages young men going into the woods because it takes them away from the land and they feel the land must not be neglected."

"There are too many of us to prosper by the land and besides one can't make money that way."

"You're quite right. How about coming into Montreal with me tomorrow and seeing things for yourself?"

"To the Fair?" Paul said eagerly and then his expression changed. "What about father?" Jacques had always forbidden any of them to go near Montreal during the Fair.

Old Pierre's chin went out stubbornly. "I need you to look after me," he said doggedly.

"I hope you can arrange it, grandfather," Paul said.

"Sorry I can't invite you too, my dear," Old Pierre said kindly to Marguerite. "No place for women I'm afraid."

"I understand, grandfather—though I do envy you men!"

"You can be thinking of the Seigneur's ball. You'll need a new dress for that."

"I would like one. I don't know if father will buy me one."

"I'll have to speak to him," Old Pierre said and his arm tightened round her.

The next day when the Council met on the common, Old Pierre and Paul stood among the crowd watching the cere-

mony. Governor Callières sat in an armchair at the head of a
circle, with the Indians ranged around him in the order of
their tribes. Next to the Comte de Frontenac, he was the most
able man in handling them. The Marquis de Denonville was
not present, for he had departed a few days before for Quebec
—some said in order to avoid this annual ceremony.

Paul watched the Chevalier de Callières with admiration.
He talked to the Indians with dignity and his manner made a
good impression on them as they solemnly smoked their pipes
and listened to the harangues made by each tribe. Extrava-
gant compliments passed between the white men and the savages, assurances of friendship were reiterated—and though it
was largely a matter of formality, nevertheless it was impressive and not until it had been done could trading begin.

When the ceremony was finished, Paul walked with his
grandfather through the town. It was hardly recognizable. All
along the palisades merchants had set up their booths—many
of them having come from Quebec a few days before to partici-
pate in the trading. This was an event in which everyone
wished to share, for as soon as the beaver skins were disposed
of, the men hurried to spend their profits, not only in the re-
newal of equipment and supplies, but in trifles and vanities
for themselves, their families or their women. The streets of
Montreal were a strange sight. Some of the redskins were
grotesque, their faces daubed with bright-colored paints and
wearing nothing except the feathers on their heads. Many of
the coureurs de bois had discarded their rough clothing and
bedecked themselves in all kinds of expensive finery. Some
assumed the attitudes of gentlemen and swaggered with swords
at their sides. Others, however, went to the opposite extreme
and having become accustomed to association with the Indians,
now strutted through the streets as naked as the savages. From
tavern to tavern the men roamed, the naked and fashionably
dressed pushing against each other, and often getting into
fights. Gambling and drinking were rife. The priests had from

time to time tried to intervene and curtail the debauchery, but it was useless. If they bore down too hard, there was the danger that the men would break away entirely from the Church.

This was the first time Paul had been in town while the coureurs de bois were there and he was fascinated though a little shocked. He knew now why his father had always forbidden the younger members, particularly the girls, from coming to Montreal during trading time. As Paul had left with Old Pierre, Jacques had a heavy scowl on his face but had made no comment. As they had walked the mile into town, Paul had asked his grandfather whether he had told Jacques where they were going.

"Just told him I wanted to go into town and you were coming along to look after me," the old man replied with a roguish chuckle. Paul had seen his grandfather in these rebellious moods before and it was one of the things that made him admire him so. The old man let his son have his way most of the time, because there was usually no alternative, but when he wanted his own way he got it.

As they jostled through the crowds, Paul watched Old Pierre and his admiration rose. The old man's body had been maimed but his spirit certainly had not. His hands were dug deep into his pockets to keep them out of sight and his pipe was thrust between determined jaws. His tasselled cap sat as always at a jaunty angle over the white hair and because he had defied his son, his blue eyes were dancing merrily. He was a schoolboy playing truant and enjoying every minute of it.

"Never been into Dillon's Tavern, have you?" he asked Paul.

"I've never been into any tavern—yet," Paul answered.

"Time you started then. Can't be a coureur de bois and still have pink ears. Come on."

Paul caught the spirit of his grandfather and had a broad grin on his face as they turned into the tavern. The place was crowded but Old Pierre's powerful build and determined air cleared the way. The atmosphere inside was heavy with the fumes of brandy and tobacco smoke and for a moment or two Paul felt choked. As Old Pierre looked around for a place where they could settle, his name was called and some men beckoned to him from a table against a wall.

"Ah!" he exclaimed in a satisfied voice. "Come on, Paul," he said and they pushed ahead until they reached the table. Paul's face lit up when he saw the men, for among them were the le Moyne brothers, who had always been his heroes.

There were greetings from all and they made room for Paul and Old Pierre to sit down.

"You know my grandson, Paul," Old Pierre said and as Paul bowed politely to the older men they nodded to him in a friendly way.

"Which boy is this, Pierre?" one of the men asked. He was Charles le Moyne, the eldest of the twelve le Moyne brothers. The father of these distinguished men had died three years previously and Charles had inherited the title of Sieur de Longueil. He had married a lady of rank, Mademoiselle D'Adoucourt, lady in waiting to the Duchesse d'Orleans. The previous year a son had been born to them, who would carry the name of Longueil to posterity. The Sieur de Longueil was now thirty-two years old and had distinguished himself not only in the wars of these French colonies but also in France. His ambition was great and on his seigneury of Longueil he was building a magnificent chateau which was to become a landmark.

"The wayward one," Old Pierre replied in answer to de Longueil's question.

"Oh, indeed," de Longueil replied and gave Paul an amused smile.

"One of the redheaded twins," Old Pierre reminded him.

"Ah, yes."

"Wants to become a coureur de bois—so I brought him along to let him see what rogues they are." Old Pierre said.

"Leading the boy astray, eh?" de Longueil said and poked Old Pierre. "What's your father going to say about it? He's against the coureurs, isn't he?"

"Yes, monsieur," Paul said.

"Jacques!" Old Pierre impatiently said. "Sometimes he can't see beyond his nose. A little roughing it in the woods will do the boy good. Louis, bring us some drinks." Old Pierre shouted as he sighted Louis Dillon. Immediately the tavern keeper made his way to their table, greeting them in his congenial way.

"Beer for you, Paul?" Old Pierre said, giving him a lead for which he was grateful. Brandy was a little too strong for him yet.

They had scarcely begun their drinks when two more of the le Moyne brothers came toward their table. Their progress was slow because their entry had created something of a sensation. They were Jacques, Sieur de Sainte-Hélène, and Pierre, Sieur d'Iberville, the two eldest brothers next to the Sieur de Longueil. No two men had gained a higher reputation than these two, for their work was fighting and they had distinguished themselves in the constant wars against the English. They had just returned from a successful expedition to the Hudson Bay region.

Paul was thrilled when he saw them. These older le Moynes were little more than names to him for at seventeen, ten or twelve years difference in age was a wide gap. There was much handshaking as they joined the group around their brother and while people threw questions at them as to their latest prowess, Paul had an opportunity to study them. Sainte-Hélène was tall and powerfully built and had earned a reputation as a considerate leader with a keen understanding of men. He had astonished, and in some instances shocked, the people of Montreal some four years previously by marrying a girl only twelve years of age. He was twenty-five years old at the time and the fact that his bride was an orphan had for some people been sufficient explanation. His young wife had since given him three children.

Pierre, Sieur d'Iberville, was to become the most famous of all the brothers. He was the better looking and was tall and well built. His dark brown eyes were fearless, and though the mouth had humorous lines about it, the general impression was one of ruthlessness. Had anyone accused him of this, he would have laughed and probably replied that they were living in a ruthless age. He would even have been quite frank in admitting that to this he owed much of his success in capturing forts and vessels from the English.

Paul decided he liked Sainte-Hélène and this impression was increased when he turned and included Paul in the conversation. Up to this point Paul had said little, feeling he should be a listener in the presence of older men and particularly such distinguished ones.

"Which one of the Boissarts are you?" Sainte-Hélène asked as he gave Paul a friendly smile.

"The middle one—they usually distinguish us as the twins."

"Oh yes," Sainte-Hélène said as though trying to recollect. "I've been away so much the past few years and you've grown up. Let me see, there's Pierre and Raoul and . . ." He stopped to think again.

"They're my two older brothers," Paul helped him. "Then I have a married sister living in Lachine. My twin sister, Marguerite and I come next."

"Ah yes, the redheaded sister, looks very much like you. She must be grown up now too."

"Yes, we look very much alike."

"You sticking to the land?"

"Er—no, that is, I don't want to. I want to be a coureur de bois, if I can manage to get my license and equipment.

"That's fine. More exciting than farming. But why don't you become a soldier?"

"Doesn't appeal to me very much, begging your pardon."

"Oh, no need to apologize. We can't all like the same thing. But you'll probably have to do soldiering anyway. We're going to have a lot of fighting to do before we get this country settled."

"Yes, I expect so."

"Still, fur trading has its points. It is a good way to make a fortune. My father began that way and my brother Charles does a lot of it still. You'll have to be tough though. They're a hard lot, these coureurs." He looked out over the room and the company bore out his statement. The din was terrific and when some of them would get into a fight, Louis Dillon would give a sign to his helpers and a man would be thrown out of the door. No one took much notice of these things—no one except Paul, who felt like a child at his first circus. Everything fascinated him. There was the long bar just inside the door. This was so crowded now that he could hardly see it, though it was indicated by the rows of glasses and bottles against the wall. Near to where Paul sat was a swinging door that constantly banged to and fro as men went in and out. It led to the gaming room and as Paul watched the men going and coming, he wondered whether he would have to learn to gamble if he became a coureur de bois. It was something he knew nothing about for the Church condemned it. His father would have been aghast had he known his thoughts at that moment.

"Who're you going with?" Sainte-Hélène asked, interrupting Paul's thoughts.

"Charles Péchard, I think. He's the only coureur de bois I know."

Sainte-Hélène did not look shocked or contemptuous at the mention of the Péchard name. "I hear the Major died," he said.

"Yes, about a month ago."

"He was a grand old fellow," Sainte-Hélène remarked.

"I didn't know him very well."

"No, I don't suppose you did," Sainte-Hélène said and smiled. "How's Charles these days?"

Paul did not need to answer for at that moment Charles came out of the gaming room. He was looking rather pleased with himself, presumably because his luck had been good. He was dirty and unshaven and had been drinking. He was about to push his way past when he caught sight of Paul.

"Sacré diable, look who's here!" he exclaimed.

"Hello, Charles," Paul said.

The sensuous mouth curled at one corner and he slapped Paul on the back. "Does your father know you're out, young man?" he asked.

Paul felt himself bristle but Old Pierre said quickly: "Sit down and have a drink with us, Charles."

Evidently Péchard had not noticed Old Pierre before. His manner changed, for he had much respect for him. "Thanks, I will. Brandy," he said.

The difficult moment was bridged and the quick-mooded Charles now turned to Paul and began talking in a friendly way about his plans to go into the woods.

By the time they left the tavern darkness had already fallen. They were all intoxicated and walked along unsteadily, singing loudly. But in Montreal that night, this passed unnoticed because practically everyone was in the same condition. When they reached the Boissart farm it was in darkness and Charles tried to persuade them to come to his house and drink some more. They argued about it and in the stillness of the night their voices carried far.

"All right, if you won't. I'll go and drink by myself," Charles said as his legs carried him uncertainly towards the discomforts of his own house.

Old Pierre and Paul let themselves in like two truants and went to their rooms. Paul's head was throbbing, and without taking off his clothes, he fell on the bed and was immediately asleep. When he wakened the next morning it took him some time to recollect what had happened. He sat on the edge of the bed, holding his head, and resolved never to touch a mug of beer again. When he had sufficiently collected himself, he went outside, and held his aching head under the water pump.

As they all assembled for prayers, he glanced quickly at his grandfather. The old man's eyes were steely and his jaw set. Paul saw he was going to bluff it out defiantly and decided to do the same. Marguerite gave him a friendly smile as her eyes danced and Paul grinned back at her. His father's face was the picture of pious sternness. He picked a text about the waywardness of man and Paul knew this was his way of reproaching both of them. During breakfast he did not say a word nor was there any actual reproach during the day, except that he kept Paul busy every minute, giving him the most unpleasant and toughest tasks about the farm. It was the hardest day's work Paul had ever done and he was glad when nighttime came.

Yet he was happy when he went to bed. He felt a new era had started in his life.

CHAPTER VII

It had been many a long day since Montreal had witnessed anything as magnificent as the ball which the Sieur de Courville gave to introduce his nephew to the colony. Many of the lesser folks had never been to such an affair and for days the excitement was intense. Balls were given in Montreal, especially during the winter months, but these were usually confined to the *noblesse*. The Sieur de Courville, however, followed the tradition of the settlement and invited all the habitants of his seigneury as well as those of the more aristocratic circles.

The days following the invitation up to the very eve of the ball were filled with preparations and for once the bake oven and spinning wheel stood neglected. In the Boissart household there had never been such a period of industry and excitement. There was much running back and forth to Pierre's and Raoul's houses to help with fittings, for though both the wives of these sons were pregnant they would not let that stand in the way of their going to the ball. They would have to sit at the side all the evening and watch the dancing, but that in itself would be entertaining, as they would be able to study all the dresses and the people who were in town from fashionable Quebec.

At times it seemed to Marguerite they would never get their new dresses finished. There was so much detailed work to be done and, too, the clothes of their menfolk had to be put in order. The tailor in town was much too busy to make minor alterations and so Marie had to use all her skill as a needlewoman in letting out seams and renovating garments that had not been worn for years. Paul was the most fortunate of the men, for his father had allowed him to have a new suit made.

He seethed with impatience and fear that it would not be finished in time and only a few hours before the ball was to begin he was sitting in the tailor's shop waiting for his coat.

That night the usually quiet farm was unrecognizable as each one struggled to get into his or her clothes, shouting frequently to one of the others to come and help fasten this or adjust that. The four younger children who were not going, were worn out running errands but nevertheless getting much vicarious enjoyment watching the others dress.

The ball room of the Manor House was magnificent with hundreds of candles reflecting their lights in the shimmering crystal of the chandeliers. Many of the guests were already there when the Boissarts arrived, though their host had not yet appeared as he was entertaining the Governor-General and his suite at dinner. Behind well-arranged shrubbery, the fiddlers were playing, competing with the babble of voices as friend greeted friend.

Paul and Marguerite, as usual, kept close together and exchanged comments and innuendos with each other. Watching them, Old Pierre felt immensely proud, for, in his opinion at least, no one could compare with these two when it came to looks and certainly this evening they did him justice. Marguerite had chosen a soft green brocade for her dress, a color that complimented her beautiful hair. Only the exquisite art of a Frenchwoman could have turned out such a gown in a farmhouse. Paul was feeling very self-conscious in his brocaded coat of deep blue, with breeches and waistcoat of a paler shade. He kept wondering whether he should try "making a leg" and kissing the ladies' hands or whether he should content himself with the stiff bow from the waist which was all he had been taught. Marguerite had confessed to him that she had been practicing a low deep curtsey instead of the usual quick bob curtsey, and they had practiced with each other, having much fun over it. Now that the moment had come, however, she was afraid of getting all the way down and not being able to get up again without falling over.

It was not long before the fiddlers stopped and the lackeys threw open the doors at the end of the room. Their host appeared with Madame la Marquise de Denonville on his arm and behind him the Governor-General escorting a lady of exquisite beauty.

"Who's that?" Paul asked his grandfather but Old Pierre shook his head. All through the room the same question was being asked.

All the other distinguished guests were well known. Immediately behind the Governor-General came the Intendant, Monsieur Jean Bochart de Champigny, and his wife and on the arm of the Chevalier de Vaudreuil was a very plain girl who it was whispered was the Intendant's daughter.

"There are the le Moynes!" Paul whispered eagerly and his eyes were not the only ones full of admiration as Dame Catherine le Moyne came in, followed by five of her distinguished sons. It was seldom they were all in Montreal together and their presence created a stir. Dame Catherine was a native of Montreal and since her husband's death had carried on the administration of the seigneury at Longueil with the aid of her eldest son. Many said it was to her shrewd judgment that the seigneury owed its success. She was beloved by all for her fine character and lovable nature and as she leaned on the arm of the Chevalier de Ramezay, graciously acknowledging the many tributes, her charm was undeniable.

The long line came to an end and greetings became general. It was inevitable that attention should be focused upon the lady escorted by the Governor-General. Madame Hélène de Matier had been the name announced and it was a name that no one in Montreal had heard before. There was no denying the outstanding beauty of the lady and every masculine eye was reluctant to look away. She appeared to be about thirty-five though probably was older. She was tall and dignified,

with manners savoring of the French Court and it was evident
her gown had come from Paris. She had, furthermore, made
herself distinguishable, either by accident or intention, by the
manner in which she wore her hair. The other fashionable
ladies had their hair dressed high upon their heads, but
Madame de Matier wore her jet-black hair in soft ringlets
around her face and cascading down her back in a natural
way. Rumor had it that Madame de Maintenon had cast a
disapproving eye upon so much frivolity in dress and had
ordered the Court ladies to cease overdressing their hair. Was
this simple hair-style of Madame de Matier a forerunner of
fashion, the ladies wondered?

The Sieur de Courville led out the fat Marquise de Denonville and the ball began. Despite his sixty years the Seigneur
still danced gracefully and the eyes of those of his seigneury as
they watched him were admiring. Everyone agreed that he
looked splendid this evening. He was always conservative in
his dress and the royal-blue coat, with embroidered waistcoat
and silver-buckled shoes, was very becoming. This was one
of the rare occasions when he wore a long, white curled perruque.

Many wondered what he thought of his nephew's foppish
attire, for the Chevalier de Favien was dressed in pale pink
brocaded coat, with a waistcoat of silver cloth and the silver
buckles on his shoes were studded with diamonds. The dress
sword which he wore slung across his shoulder with a wide blue
ribbon had a jewelled hilt. All the men in the Governor's suite
wore perruques and that of de Favien was jet black with long
curls draped over each shoulder.

The man for whom the ball was being given had not so far
created a very favorable impression. He made no attempt to
mix with the people of his uncle's seigneury but remained
within the circle of distinguished guests. From the moment he
entered the room, Marguerite had been wondering whether
he would remember her. Then, to her delight, he came towards

her and made the most elaborate leg. As she returned him a deep curtsey, she felt a slight squeeze of her fingers as he bent over to kiss her hand; when she looked up she met his eyes—a pair of steel-blue eyes that were penetrating.

"I have been waiting impatiently for the pleasure of seeing you again, mademoiselle," he said.

"Merci, monsieur," she answered demurely and lowered her eyes.

"May I have the honor of this dance?" he asked and as she accepted she felt every eye in the room upon her—especially of those who lived on the seigneury.

De Favien looked down at her, a smile curling about his lips. "You are very ravishing, mademoiselle," he said.

"Merci, monsieur," she said again and wished she could have thought of some clever repartee. De Favian danced well and as she was also an accomplished dancer there were many comments. It seemed to her the dance came to an end all too soon, but as he returned her to her place, he said in an undertone: "I will get the duty dances over and then we must dance again. I want to know you better. Save me several more dances later."

For answer she just smiled and felt she was being very inadequate. She thought about it for a little while but soon found herself surrounded by officers and gentlemen who wished to dance with her. Never before had she had so many compliments.

During one of the dances she noticed Paul was dancing with Madame de Matier. They were about the same height and at the moment Marguerite noticed them, Hélène de Matier was gazing into Paul's eyes in her most provocative manner. He had had to let several dances go by before he could approach her, and when finally he did, she was surrounded by every susceptible male in the room—or at least it seemed so to Paul. He contented himself with standing on the outside of the circle—a reddish gold and curly head conspicuous among the overburdening perruques. Madame de Matier noticed him and was interested. Skilfully separating herself from her cavaliers, she held out a graceful hand. "Ah, monsieur," she said, giving Paul her most ravishing smile. "How do you do?"

Paul was not adept at repartee, so he merely bowed over her hand and then said quickly: "May I have the honor of a dance, madame?"

"With pleasure. I will have this one with you," she said and, flashing a smile at the other men in the circle, moved off to the center of the room on Paul's arm.

As he danced with her, Paul began to realize how dangerous yet desirable she was. His blood raced and when she fixed his eyes with hers, his hands began to tremble. She noticed it and laughed, a quiet sure laugh that upset his emotions. He had never imagined there were women like this.

"You dance well, monsieur," she said archly.

"With you anyone could dance well, madame," he replied gallantly. "You are *so* beautiful." The words were said in a half whisper and in a tone that was almost reverent.

"You find me so?" she said coquettishly.

"Ravishing," he said breathlessly.

"We must get to know each other better, yes?"

"Yes," he answered, not fully understanding her meaning. He looked into her eyes again and they were dancing mischievously. How beautiful they were! Large, dark and velvety —eyes that could smolder and when angry would certainly dart fire.

"What is your name?" she asked.

"Paul Boissart."

"Paul," she said, drawing the word slowly over her tongue in a way that made him catch his breath. "I like it."

"Thank you. And yours, madame?"

"Hélène."

"I like that too."

"Then we are both happy."

"Very," he said deeply.

The dance came to an end and Paul was wondering where he should escort her. But she kept her hand on his arm, pressing her fingers into it.

"You may have the next dance and then take me to supper," she said. "After—we can talk, yes?"

Paul was elated, particularly as Colonel de Ramezay and several others had requested the honor of taking her to supper but had been refused. Hélène was completely master of the situation. As soon as supper was finished she turned to him:

"I would like to walk a little. It is hot and crowded in here."

"With pleasure, madame," he said.

She led the way out into the grounds. "You are a native of Montreal?" she inquired.

"Yes, madame. My family are pioneers. You can see our land from here," he said and pointed towards the farm. She glanced in the direction he indicated but with little interest.

"You have never been to France?"

"Not yet—but I intend to," he said and there was eagerness in his tone.

"One needs to visit France before one gets too far away from civilization. You are young—you would learn a lot there." She arched her eyebrows and smiled at him.

"I am sure I should. Are you on a visit here or are you going to remain in Montreal?"

"Oh dear no! This place would be too dull for me after Versailles."

"Versailles," Paul thought. Then she must have been to Court. He felt more than ever flattered by her attention.

"You find us—savages?" he asked and smiled.

"Savages?" she said and paused as though weighing the idea. "Er, no—at least not when they are as handsome as you." As she said this she leaned closer to him and again he felt the pressure of her fingers on his arm.

"What brought you to Montreal?" Paul asked naïvely. Her answer was a low laugh which he was to learn was her way of avoiding a direct answer.

"I did not mean to be inquisitive," he said apologetically. "It is only—that you are so different from the people who usually come here."

Hélène de Matier stopped walking and turned so that she faced him. They were at the end of the walk where the shadows were deeper and it would never have occurred to Paul it was by design that she placed herself so the moon cast its full light upon her face revealing all its exotic beauty. It made him draw in his breath sharply and stare at her in silent admiration.

"So—you find me different?" she said and her dark eyes mocked him. He put out a hand to touch her but she stepped back, not in haste, but with a gliding movement so that she was lost in the shadows. Paul misunderstood the movement and took it as a reproof, dropping his hand abruptly. "Come here," her voice said and he also moved into the shadows. "You are a very sweet boy—I am going to like you," she said in a low voice and again his heart began to race. She put her hand up to his cheek and her touch was electric. The cat began to play with the mouse and it was a cat with a great deal of experience.

Unable to contain himself any longer, Paul grasped the hand and moved it over his mouth, smothering it with kisses. The edges of her mouth curled as she withdrew her hand and then swiftly put it round the back of his neck and drew his mouth towards hers. A strange, inarticulate sound came from Paul as he felt her luscious lips against his—lips that were soft and yielding. The fragrance of her exotic perfume tantalized his nostrils, and putting his arm swiftly around her shoulders, he held her there, afraid this ecstatic moment would pass too

quickly. Never before had any woman kissed him this way—
never had he dreamed that a woman's lips could be so intoxi-
cating.

"You are wonderful!" he gasped and looked into dark eyes
that smoldered. He bent to kiss her again but Hélène de
Matier knew how to tantalize and she turned her head away
and slipped from his arms.

"How old are you Paul?" she asked.

"Old enough to know you are more lovely than any woman
I have ever known," he answered.

"Have you known many?" she mocked.

"None like you," he parried, wishing she would not waste
time in questioning him. He moved closer to her and for the
briefest moment she leaned against him—a moment so brief
it was gone before he could fully realize it. "Let me kiss you
again—please," he said and the answer was that low laugh he
adored and hated at the same time.

She began to walk back and he had to follow. At the same
time she said almost indifferently: "Come to see me tomorrow
afternoon."

Paul's heart leaped. "Tomorrow afternoon," he said jerkily
for he was having difficulty with his breathing. "Thank you.
Where shall I come?"

"I am staying at the Chevalier de Callières' house while he
is away," she told him.

The Governor's house! He wondered again who she was
and what she was doing in Montreal, but did not dare ask
questions. Perhaps later he would learn.

"At the Governor's house," he said and tried to make his
voice as nonchalant as hers. "What time shall I come?"

"Oh—about three o'clock."

She seemed to have gone far away from him, as though she
had drawn a steel curtain, and when a few minutes later he
stood in the grounds cooling off from his excitement, he could
not be sure whether he had not imagined that moment in the

arbor. As they had neared the ballroom she had turned to him and had given him one of her flashing smiles.

"Don't come in with me," she had said, and though her tone was sweet, it was a command. She had held out her hand to him and he had kissed it and the feel of it was still upon his lips.

Tomorrow would be Sunday and it would be easy for him to get away. Tomorrow—it was so many hours away and each hour would seem the length of a day.

CHAPTER VIII

THE CHEVALIER NICHOLAS DE FAVIEN was bored—also he was in a bad mood. He had gambled with some of the officers at the ball until dawn, losing heavily and he was not a good loser. Already he had come to dislike Montreal thoroughly and was angry that his uncle had refused to allow him to remain in Quebec. Only necessity had made him leave France at all. He had no love for the colonies nor the people who had settled there. Half savage, uncouth, ignorant—this was his opinion and he could not understand how his uncle could feel so deeply about them. The Sieur had been really proud when he had taken him over the seigneury, insisting that he go into the farmhouses and talk with the farmers. Then had suggested that he, a product of the Court of France, should settle down and take over the seigneury! There was no doubt in his mind that his uncle was becoming senile. It had been convenient for de Favien to have this place in which to take refuge while France remained dangerous for him, but that would pass and then he would be able to return. But to remain for the rest of his life in this far-off, miserable part of the world—never!

He yawned and walked to the window which looked out over the river. The view was pleasing but, to town-bred eyes, monotonous. He thought of Sunday afternoons in Paris, with drives up the Champs Elysées and in the Bois—and sighed deeply. If only things had not become so involved in Paris! His face grew angry at the recollection. "The little fool!" he muttered as he thought of the humiliating situation which had made him an exile. What irritated him was the fact that he had managed it so badly. He had felt sure the girl had understood his meaning when he had told her he would see her again that night. He had slipped into boudoirs and bedrooms

73

many times but this was the first time he had found himself repulsed. For once he had counted too much upon his own charms and had never expected the girl would scream so her father would hear. And the stupidity of it all—to be chased from a girl's bedroom with nothing to cover his nakedness but a quilt he had snatched from the bed! His face flushed as he thought of it, but from anger instead of embarrassment. The aggravating part of it was he had not been in love with the girl; in fact, she had scarcely attracted him. He had only courted her because of her father's influential position at Court. "The old idiot!" he grumbled. "He's probably been in exactly the same position himself many times, only he didn't get caught."

He thought of the ball the previous night and of Marguerite. He wondered how much of his meaning she had understood. Surely, he told himself, her flaming hair was an indication of the quality of her emotions. This deduction had appeared correct when he had kissed her. She was inexperienced, yet when he thought of the warm lusciousness of her mouth, his desire for her grew. But there were so many complications and his more sensible side warned him he had better not get himself involved again. He wanted to laugh when he thought of her naïve suggestion that they should meet at the mill that afternoon. The mill! Of all places for a de Favien to be meeting a woman! Last night the suggestion had cooled his ardor yet he had been so carried away after those brief moments with her that he desired more. It was almost force of habit that had made him ask her if he could come to her the next afternoon, accustomed as he was to women who answered the question by murmuring they would be in their boudoir at a certain hour the next day. And then to get a reply that she would meet him at a mill! He knew her people were farmers and presumed that a dozen or more of them lived in the same house. He could see her point of view, that for him to call would be very awkward, yet he still felt irritable at her idea of a meeting place. Better to leave the whole thing alone. She was hardly likely to come to the house if he did not turn up. No—it would be better to drop the matter and go to see Hélène de Matier. She was always good company for an afternoon.

Yet that thought did not bring him comfort. The difficulty was that at forty he had begun to crave more excitement. Hélène and he had become too used to each other. Though Hélène was undoubtedly the most beautiful woman he had ever known and had all the charm of poise and experience— yet the fire of their passion had burned down. The only way in which he was going to be able to stand these months in this miserable colony was by having someone young and enchanting to amuse him. Excepting Hélène, Marguerite certainly had been the most attractive woman at the ball. He thought again of how she had looked with her head lying against his shoulder, with her pretty face turned up to him. The recollection disturbed him. There was not even the alternative of taking her for a drive somewhere and finding a place where they would be undisturbed. In this uncivilized country one could scarcely move without an armed escort and he had no wish to run the danger of being ambushed by horrible, naked savages.

"Oh, sacré Dieu!" he exclaimed and sat down sulkily. If he did not keep the rendezvous, what was he going to do? Hélène had been rather strange as he took her home and had told him she would be busy the following afternoon. Jealousy swept over him. With whom was she being busy? Had she found someone to interest her at the ball? It certainly might be so for men had swarmed around her from the moment she had appeared. Utterly selfish, he did not want her to get interested in anyone else, even if he were tired of her. Yet, if that were the case, then he, too, had better find someone else to amuse him.

He looked at the time. An hour yet before he should be at

the mill. Irritability swept over him again at the thought of such a place to meet a lovely girl, but he began to dress.

At the farm Paul and Marguerite were having their difficulties. They had been to Mass in the morning and Marguerite had been glad the Chevalier de Favien was not there. Upon their return neither she nor Paul had hastened to change their Sunday clothes. Paul, however, was more fortunate than she. When his father noticed he had not changed, Paul simply said he was going into Montreal after dinner and the only reply was some teasing about his having a rendezvous. Nothing more was said to him but Marguerite was abruptly told to go and put on another dress. "You can't work in your best dress," her mother had said sharply. "Go and change and be quick about it." There was no arguing the point. Marguerite had taken off her dress and laid it carefully on the bed. Perhaps when the family had gone over to Pierre's she could get into it quickly and slip out of the house without anyone seeing her.

But when dinner was over, her hopes sank. The family were all tired from the ball and Jacques and Marie decided not to go to Pierre's as they usually did. Young Etienne was dispatched with a message and the older folks settled back in their chairs to sleep. Marguerite felt angry with Paul, even though it was unreasonable. All he had to do was to walk out of the house and no explanations were asked. Men always had all the luck, she thought. If she walked out of the house with her best dress on, there would be innumerable questions and they would forbid her to go. She took up her embroidery and tried to work on it, all the time keeping her eye on the clock.

What should she do? Was this a hint that she had better keep away from the mill? She knew she was playing a dangerous game in meeting a man like de Favien. All night long she had tossed restlessly, going over and over the incident at the ball. She had gone to look for Paul to tell him her father and mother had said she could stay as long as he did. She had not been able to find him but had run into de Favien. The difficulty was she kept changing her mind as to whether she liked him or not. Against her will she seemed drawn to him and this she knew was mainly because of her restlessness. When she had felt his arms round her and he had begun to kiss her, her emotions had become entangled. Yet he had made her feel stupid and inadequate when he had curled his lips contemptuously at her suggestion that they should meet at the mill. He had seemed so insistent that he wanted to see her again but the idea of his calling at the farm would have been so difficult. She looked round the room at the somnolent figures slumped in armchairs and felt annoyed. Laying down her embroidery, she went into her bedroom and looked at the pretty dress lying on the bed. If only there had been another way out of the house, but the front door was the only exit and then there would be the difficulty of getting back. She would have to give up the idea of changing her clothes and go as she was, if she went at all. It was nearly three o'clock and a decision had to be made. She looked at herself in the mirror and her appearance did not please her. In her short simple linen skirt with a bright colored blouse, she looked very different from the young lady in the pale green silk ball dress.

Going to the window, she looked towards the mill. For a moment she thought she saw him waiting there and it filled her with excitement. She turned away and wandered disconsolately around the room. When she looked out again the figure had disappeared and this added to her indecision. Then almost defiantly she put on her large straw hat and short coat, and crept through the parlor.

There was no one at the mill, though it was after three o'clock. Perhaps he won't come, she thought. She stood on the side facing the river and waited. A few minutes later de Favien came out of the mill and when he saw her in her peasant costume, a cynical expression crossed his face. He stood

watching her for a moment and as he lowered his eyes to her
ankles he smothered an exclamation at the sight of her wooden
shoes. He came up behind her quietly and touched her. She
gave a scream and his annoyance deepened. Were there nothing but screaming women in the world!

"Oh!" Marguerite said. "You took me by surprise."

Was the girl being coquettish and pretending she had not
come to meet him? "Weren't you expecting me, mademoiselle?" he asked and the curl of his lips was not pleasant.

"Why, yes, of course. Only I didn't see you coming. In these
parts we are always afraid of surprises—so many savages lurk-
ing about."

"Well, I'm not a savage!" he said irritably.

"No, of course not. I did not mean that."

As the large greenish-blue eyes looked up at him apologetically he smiled for the first time. There was something so fresh
and lovely about her.

"And now, my fair lady, what are your wishes?" he said
after he had taken her hand and put his lips to it. Her face
flushed for she did not know what to suggest.

"Er—shall we walk along the river?" she asked hesitantly.

"Mon Dieu, no!" he exclaimed. "I never walk." Again that
feeling of annoyance swept over him. Did the girl really think
he would walk up and down the river bank as so many bour-
geois couples were doing on this Sunday afternoon?

"I'm afraid we don't have much to offer in Montreal,"
Marguerite said.

"Indeed you don't! But—we must make the best of it. Come
along."

He took her arm and led her to the door of the mill. It
creaked as he pushed it open and the inside looked dark and
forbidding.

"In here!" she exclaimed.

"My dear mademoiselle, you really don't imagine we're
going to stand outside all the afternoon, do you?" he asked,

his irritation again apparent. "You suggested this strange meeting place."

His remark confused her and she wished she had stayed home. Without further comment she went inside and he closed the door. It was very dark except for narrow shafts of light that came in through the musketry slits around the walls. She could not see him in the darkness and she waited nervously.

"Frightened?" he asked, putting an arm around her.

"A little," she said and her voice betrayed her. He tightened his arm.

"Your eyes will get used to the darkness in a minute. Come over here. There's some straw we can sit on. I took a look around while I was waiting for you."

His voice was kinder now and she began to feel less uncomfortable. She let him guide her to the pile of straw and they sat down.

"I'm sorry I—er—couldn't invite you home," she said apologetically. "I know this must seem very foolish to you."

"Very," he replied "but we must make the best of it."

She noticed he was not wearing a perruque. His hair was smooth and black. She was thinking how much more attractive he looked without the heavy wig, when he asked:

"And what is milady thinking?"

"That I like you better without a wig."

"Thank you." His tone seemed to be mocking. He took her hand and kissed it, turning the palm to his lips. "And I like you better without a hat," he said as he took it off and laid it aside. "Your hair is so beautiful." He ran his hand over the flaming ringlets, pressing her head backwards. She felt his lips on her throat and then on her mouth, persistently and hungrily forcing her to yield. He held her so long that she had to struggle for breath.

"It's very warm in here," she said lamely when she had freed herself.

"Let me help you off with your jacket," he said. He also

removed his own coat and threw himself back on the pile of straw. When he attempted to draw her down beside him, she held back, because she was so disturbed. "Timid little thing, aren't you?" he taunted her. "Evidently no one has ever made love to you before."

The insinuation annoyed her, as he had intended it should.

"I like to take my own time," she said haughtily.

"Oh, pardon me, mademoiselle," he said coldly and, putting his arms behind his head, gazed up at the roof with a bored expression. She looked at him and bit her lips—then, leaning on one elbow, smiled into his face. To her relief he smiled back but those steel-blue eyes were hard and he made no move. She had said she liked to take her time and he was waiting to see what she would do next. Because she was feeling very inexperienced and uncomfortable she did what she knew she should not have done—dropped her head on to his chest and buried her face in the soft ruffles of his shirt. Then she felt his lips against the back of her ear and her Norman blood began to tingle.

It all happened so quickly—afterwards she was never able to piece it together. She struggled desperately with emotions that swept her beyond control and the eyes that looked into his were scared—scared of her own weakness that was carrying her away. For a moment or two she endeavored to keep a grip on herself, but as he became increasingly ardent, she slipped away completely into a world where she seemed to be floating. It seemed as though there was nothing beneath her and it was hopeless to try to keep a hold on her thoughts of right or wrong. Her mind was numb and she knew only that the floodgates of her emotions were open and she had entered an ecstatic world.

Then the gates slammed with a crash as de Favien suddenly pushed her away with the exclamation: "Mon Dieu, what is this!"

"What is the matter?" she asked, scarcely able to bring her-

self back from the world into which he had transported
her.

"Do you always wear those?" he asked with distaste. Then
she saw he was referring to her long drawers.

"Mind your own business!" she said and pulled her skirt
down.

"Oh, excuse me," he said and withdrew his arm. To her
annoyance she began to cry. She had been feeling so happy
and now they were involved in another awkward situation. She
lay there wondering whether she should get up and go home.
She knew she should and that she was behaving in a way which
would have shocked those who had brought her up so strictly.
With the intention of being strong and leaving him, she sat
up and straightened her dress, but he pulled her to him.

"You sweet little innocent—you're irresistible. You're a
devil in long drawers!"

She smiled at him rather lamely and let him kiss her again.
Once more he transported her into that ethereal world and it
was bliss. She was so dazed she did not resist as he undid the
front of her blouse and then with a swift gesture buried his
face between her breasts. Time flew by on that peaceful Sunday afternoon.

Paul walked into Montreal, feeling very pleased with himself. He passed many people he knew and waved gaily to
them. His self-assurance was not quite as great as he reached
the Governor's house and he walked past it several times before he could make up his mind to enter. He looked around
cautiously before going up to the door. He told the guard that
Madame de Matier was expecting him and felt reassured when
he was allowed to pass without further question. Almost immediately the door was opened and when he gave his name, a
lackey ushered him in. They walked along a wide corridor
past several closed doors, until they came to tall, double doors
at the end. The lackey threw these open and waited for

Paul to pass. Trying not to make it obvious, he glanced quickly around and concluded this must be a separate suite of rooms. The lackey went to the other end of the room and tapped discreetly upon a door. Paul heard Hélène de Matier's voice reply and his heart leaped.

"This way, monsieur," the servant said and, bowing, left Paul to enter alone. He hesitated a moment with his hand on the door, bracing himself to make a dignified entrance. Though it was the middle of the afternoon, the room was in semi-darkness and it took Paul a few moments to get used to the dim light. At first he thought the room empty, until a low laugh drew his attention to the chaise longue where Hélène was reclining.

"Come in, my friend," she said. It was such a different reception from what he had imagined that all his self-assurance left him. He began to walk towards her but she stopped him. "Close the door, first," she said and he retraced his steps.

Looking down at her, he was again perturbed by her exotic beauty. She was wearing a deep-rose gown of some soft material, her hair loose and lying in soft ringlets over each shoulder. In the dim light she looked young and very desirable.

"I'm glad you came," she said and looked up at him. She was completely poised and master of the situation. Paul was so overcome he could not speak. He managed to take the hand she extended and to kiss it conventionally. When he raised his eyes to hers, he saw they were dancing mischievously.

"Sit down," she said and gave him a half-amused smile that he did not understand. She moved her lithe body to one side and tapped a place beside her. "Sit here," she said and he obeyed her. She was a woman who liked to have men in her power and enjoyed the feeling of having this handsome young man completely awed by her. "Are you glad you came?" she asked and there was a seductive quality in her voice.

"I'm not quite able to believe I'm not dreaming. You are

so beautiful. You seemed beautiful last night—but today—you're magnificent."

She laid her hand on his—a long, tapering hand with slender fingers that could caress or coil. Paul swiftly raised it to his lips and kissed it hungrily. She watched him and her eyes changed. The mocking look went from them and instead there was a smoldering quality that seared through him as he looked at her. He lowered his head until his lips met hers and the room reeled about him. In his small world he had not known that caressing a woman could be so electrifying. A kiss had been a simple thing—but this was different. Her hand was around the back of his neck, pressing his lips against hers—and those vivid red lips were soft and yielding. They seemed to drain all the strength from him, and releasing her lips for a moment, he laid his head against her breast. It was smooth and warm and as she gently ran her fingers through his hair he was divinely happy.

"You're so wonderful," he murmured. "I had no idea any woman could be like this."

"Would you like to love me?" she asked in a low voice.

In his inexperience he had to wonder how deep was the meaning of her question. He was so afraid of his callowness—afraid this lovely moment would be spoiled and she would send him away in disgust.

"Yes," he answered. He put his arm about her and it was a shock to feel her flesh immediately beneath her flimsy gown. He lifted his head and looked into her face again. How perfectly formed her features were—the delicately chiselled nose, the curved full lips and her dark eyes.

"I will teach you to love—the way I like it," she said. He wondered why she would be so patient and tender with him when so many other men wanted her. He kissed her again and then felt the touch of her flesh against his hand. He saw that her gown had fallen away, exposing her breast. It was the first time he had ever looked upon woman's flesh and it embarrassed yet fascinated him. She held his hand against her firm, round breast and it made him dizzy. Then she drew his head to her breast and he felt her body stir. With moments flying he took his first lesson in love from her.

When, hours later, Paul walked back to the farm, he had learned a new lesson and learned it well from an experienced teacher. His first visit to the land of Eros had been a beautiful one and all that night he tossed restlessly because of the memory of a white body and eyes in which there was a smoldering blackness. His nostrils were filled with the fragrance of the exotic perfume she used. Paul Boissart was deeply, madly in love.

CHAPTER IX

ONE MORNING some weeks later, Paul came to breakfast with an unusually glum expression on his face. During the meal he said little. Then as Jacques got ready to go into the fields he said abruptly: "I'm leaving for the woods very shortly, father."

Jacques looked at him sharply, evidently not quite sure he had understood him. "You're doing what?" he asked quietly.

"I'm going into the woods . . . with Charles Péchard."

"Am I to understand you intend becoming a coureur de bois?" Jacques asked in a tone that could not be mistaken.

"Yes, father, I am," Paul said deliberately.

"Oh no. No son of mine can do a thing like that," Jacques replied.

"I'm sorry, father—my mind is made up. We can't all continue living off the farm . . ."

"I think I am the best judge of that. You have been acting strangely of late, Paul. I have said nothing because I did not want to interfere with your life. But—if you become a coureur de bois you will not return here."

They looked at each other, both determined to have their own way. "I'm sorry, father," Paul said again, "but I feel your attitude is unfair. Why must you consider all coureurs de bois as bad men? There are the le Moynes, the Sieur de Lhut . . ."

"Then why associate yourself with a man like Péchard?"

"He's changed since the Major's death."

"Men like him do not change . . ."

"At least he should be given a chance . . ."

"If Father Dollier has not been able to change him, you certainly will not succeed. I repeat, Paul—if you go into the woods with Charles Péchard you cannot return here."

With these words Jacques turned and walked outside, leaving Paul glaring angrily after him. Then he went into his bed-room, gathered up his things and left the house.

A few days later they saw him paddling down the river with Péchard and his crew. Marguerite and Old Pierre stood on the bank and waved to them. Neither of them had seen Paul after he left the farm. Later on the day of his departure for the woods, an Indian brought Marguerite a note. He merely wrote:

I am sorry, Marguerite, to leave this way but it has to be. I cannot explain now. Perhaps when I return I shall be able to tell you. Believe in me. Your devoted brother—PAUL.

Paul could not explain the reason for his sudden departure to anyone. He was too deeply hurt and scarcely spoke during the first days of the voyage. Since the night of the ball he had been living in a new· world which had suddenly collapsed. Several nights each week he had gone to see Hélène de Matier. They had quarreled and made up again, loved and argued, for there was too much difference between them to be able to agree all the time. The more Paul saw of her, the more confidence he gained in himself until he became master of the situation. This was a new experience for Hélène and she rebelled against it. At first she had insisted Paul come in the afternoons but he could not leave the farm during the day. With new-found assurance he told her if she wanted to see him she would have to see him in the evenings. This had angered her and she had sent him away. But the next day he received a contrite note from her and that evening ʰe found her very docile. He never came bearing gifts as other lovers had done. He brought her nothing but his magnificently virile body. She found this young lover exacting yet could not refuse him. He gave her an exhilaration and excitement that made her feel young again. But she realized her aging body could not continue to yield to his untiring demands. Long into the night he insisted upon making love to her. Sometimes he fell asleep with his red-gold head on her breast while she lay awake dreading the moment when he would awaken, ready to sap her waning passion.

That last night they had quareled because he was so insistent. She had been very angry with him and then he had become penitent, kneeling beside her and stroking her dark hair. Looking beseechingly at her he had pleaded: "Forgive me, darling. I am sorry I was brutal but it is your own fault. You are so beautiful. You taught me all this." Her anger subsided but her desperate tiredness remained. She had not meant to make up this quarrel. She had purposely become angry, thinking he would go away as he had done sometimes before and then she could leave in the morning, letting him believe it was his fault. She could not bring herself to tell him she had made up with de Favien and was going to Quebec with him the following day. She had planned to stay away for a while and then when she was rested, return to him. But it had not worked out that way. She forgave him and because they had quarreled it was all the sweeter. When he left she clung to him and almost gave up the idea of the Quebec trip.

The next night when he came to the house at the appointed time he could not believe it when the lackey told him Madame de Matier had left that morning for Quebec.

"But . . . that . . . can't be!" he stuttered. He could not tell the servant he had been with her until two that morning. "There must be some mistake . . ."

"I'm sorry, monsieur, but madame left this morning," the lackey repeated.

"Didn't she leave me a note?"

"No, monsieur."

Paul had walked away completely nonplused. Then disappointment had given way to anger and he had lain awake all night trying to understand. He hardly knew what he had said to his father the next morning. He only knew he had to get away from everyone until he could get over this disappointment. His arrangements to go into the woods with Charles had been made for some weeks but he had not been able to bring himself to leave Hélène. He had about decided to tell Charles he had changed his mind. For one thing he was now glad this had happened before the coureurs de bois had left. To be deserted in this way and have to remain on the farm would have been unbearable.

It was the Chevalier de Favien who had made it possible for Paul to obtain his license and equipment. Before Hélène had come to mean so much to him, Paul had gone to see de Favien. When a servant informed the Chevalier that Paul was calling, he wondered if it could be because of Marguerite. "The little fool has probably told her brother about the mill and now I suppose he has come to demand that her honor be saved," he thought. He had not bothered to see her again and feared she might be angry. De Favien's expression therefore had been guarded as he came into the room. He was relieved when he found Paul had come with a proposition and not to demand retribution.

Paul disliked de Favien but he put his personal feelings aside to serve his own ends. He accepted the glass of brandy and then came straight to the point.

"I gather you don't care for Montreal, monsieur," he said.

"Would you expect me to?" de Favien's thin lips curled.

"No, I wouldn't. There is, however, another side of life here with which you are not familiar—the fur trade."

"I have heard about it."

"It occurred to me you might be interested in it."

"I!" de Favien exclaimed with contempt. "People here have the strangest ideas. The Sieur suggests I become a farmer and now you suggest I become a fur trader!" He opened a silver box and took a pinch of snuff. He offered the box to Paul but he declined.

"No monsieur," Paul explained. "You misunderstand. If you will allow me, I would like to tell you my plan."

"Certainly."

"The future of this place is going to rest upon fur trading . . ."

"If such a place can have a future!" de Favien interrupted.

"I am sure it has, monsieur. Its growth has certainly been very slow—chiefly because people have been so much against the fur trade and have devoted all their time to farming. But I have friends who are coureurs and they are willing to take me on their next trip if I can provide my license and equipment." Paul paused a moment to see what impression he was making. De Favien's face was noncommittal, but he listened carefully. "I am going to make a bold suggestion, monsieur— if you will provide my license and equipment—we could become partners on an equal-share basis. It would be to your advantage."

Unintentionally Paul said the last sentence slowly and it gave the impression of having a hidden meaning. De Favien misunderstood it and because he was uneasy over Marguerite interpreted everything through the thoughts in his mind. He wanted Paul out of the way before he found out. There was the risk of losing the money he invested if Paul should get killed, but that was a minor matter. Normally de Favien would not have worried over an affair with a young girl, but lately things had been going badly with him. He had heard the father of the girl in Paris was coming to New France, and if this happened, there was the chance he could still have de Favien arrested. Madame de Matier had imparted this unpleasant news to him only the day previously. Another scandal added to the Paris one—and the Chevalier de Favien would be in difficulties.

Also there was another reason why he wanted Paul out of the way. Quite frequently of late Hélène had refused to see him and he had begun to suspect she had found another interest. This was confirmed when he saw Paul going into the house one evening. He had mentioned it to Hélène, taunting her with getting old and becoming infatuated with young boys. This had caused a serious quarrel. De Favien was tired of her but she was the only one who could make him forget his boredom, and, what was of more importance to him, her influence at Versailles was what he relied upon to return there. He had never been able to fathom her reason for following him from France. She had been his mistress but that was not sufficient to make Hélène de Matier forsake the brilliance of Court life. She had merely answered his question by saying: "I am bored too," and beyond that had never confided in him. He did not know the details of her political intrigues—Hélène de Matier was too clever a woman to confide those to anyone.

"What expense would it involve?" he inquired of Paul.

"A thousand francs for a license and then there is my equipment. I do not know exactly how much that would amount to." He did know but hoped in this way to get de Favien to make a larger investment.

To his surprise, de Favien had consented to the proposal. Later that day they had gone into Montreal to have an agreement drawn up.

CHAPTER X

THE TOWN OF LACHINE lay about nine miles up the river from Montreal—a small village founded twenty years previously by the Sieur de La Salle. Driven by a restless urge to explore, he had subsequently abandoned the settlement to rove farther west in quest of China—hence the name La Chine given somewhat derisively to the settlement. It was the first main stopping place for the coureurs de bois after they left Montreal, as they rested from their heavy portage over the treacherous rapids just below the town. It took them a night and two days to drag their canoes and supplies over the raging waters of the rapids, trudging back and forth with heavy loads over a path well beaten down by the feet of natives and voyageurs.

Their rollicking songs acquainted the villagers with their arrival, and men immediately dropped their farming tools to join the women who hastened to the water's edge to welcome the coureurs. Jeanne Benet, large with the coming of her third child, hastily wiped her hands on her apron and came out of the house. A little girl, not quite two, clung to her skirt, impeding her progress. A few paces from the house she paused to watch the canoes being banked. She had always liked these rugged, carefree men who livened the monotony of life with their short visits. Jeanne was only nineteen but early marriage and the cares of a growing family had matured her beyond her years. With one hand she shielded her eyes from the hot August sun and smiled benevolently as her husband, Louis, came and stood beside her. Then suddenly she leaned forward looking more intently at the men clambering out of the canoes, for she had seen a curly, tawny head that was familiar.

"Surely—that's—but it can't be!" she exclaimed.

"What is it, my dear?" Louis asked in his soft voice. He was a dark-haired little man, with a subdued air which gave him the appearance of being rather tired of the struggle for life. He was ten years older than Jeanne.

"That man there—he looks like Paul . . ."

Louis looked intently and then smiled. "It surely is," he said and both hurried forward, Jeanne picking up the smaller Jeanne so she could make better progress. The next moment they were welcoming Paul, who was grinning like an overgrown boy.

"Why, Paul!" Jeanne exclaimed. "I can't believe my eyes. How does it happen you are with the coureurs?" Her pleasure at seeing her brother was obvious and when he gave her a large, smacking kiss, she clung to him.

"Surprised you, didn't I?" Paul said and laughed again. "Hello, Louis. You look well." They exchanged greetings.

"Are you really a coureur de bois, Paul?" Jeanne asked.

"Don't I look like one?" Paul asked proudly.

Jeanne nodded her head, for Paul was wearing the conventional garb that distinguished the coureurs. It was a half-civilized, half-savage dress designed for comfort and practicability. The heavy blanket coat that characterized them lay in a bundle at his feet, for the day was warm. He looked rugged and strong in his striped cotton shirt, leather leggings fringed at the seams and strong deerskin moccasins. As he drew his sister's attention to himself he straightened up proudly, his hand thrust into the belt of varigated worsted from which hung a large knife, tobacco pouch, powder horn and other implements. He had thrown his coonskin cap carelessly on top of his coat—a cap which Charles had given him as they started on their journey.

"Yes . . . yes, of course, Paul," Jeanne said, "but it is so surprising. I have always thought father was against it . . ."

Paul's bravado faded. "He is," he said in a crisp, defiant tone. "I'll tell you about it later."

"Yes, later," Louis echoed and took Paul by the arm. "Come along to the house and have a drink. We must celebrate."

The serious moment was gone and they became merry again. Louis' dark beady eyes were mischievous as he looked at Paul and said: "I presume now you have become a coureur de bois you take something stronger than milk?" Paul's smile broadened to a grin as he replied in the affirmative. He had a feeling of being approved and it was soothing after the recent unhappy days.

As he walked away between Jeanne and Louis he turned to the other men who were being welcomed by the villagers. He could not see Charles but knew he must be with one of the groups.

"Come on up, Péchard, as soon as you are free," he shouted.

"Péchard!" Jeanne said sharply.

Paul felt awkward as she looked at him. "You remember Charles?" he said a little defiantly.

"Yes," Jeanne said flatly.

At that moment Paul observed a small face peeping at him from behind Jeanne's skirts. He breached the awkward moment by saying:

"Whom have we here?" He bent down to speak to his niece but she ran to the other side of her mother and then peeped back.

"Shy, eh?" Paul said. "Well, we'll get acquainted later. She's grown," he remarked to Jeanne.

"Nearly two now," she replied. "You haven't seen her for over a year."

"No, of course not. Haven't I a nephew whom I've never seen?"

"Yes, he's asleep. You'll see him later."

Sitting in the Benet parlor, fraternizing with Louis over a glass of brandy, Paul realized their hard struggle for existence. After the large acreage around his father's farm, the small holding that belonged to Louis appeared very unproductive. By the same comparison the parlor with its sparse homemade furniture looked bare. There were only four straight chairs placed around a plain wooden table and one armchair near the fireplace. In the corner was a wooden bench used as an extra bed if travelers stopped overnight. The floor was devoid of any covering, though it was scrubbed to meticulous cleanliness.

While the men chatted, Jeanne was busy at the stove preparing a meal. Marie's plain, heavy features were duplicated in Jeanne, who was already beginning to grow fat. She was only two years older than Paul, yet to him she had always seemed much the older sister, for she had devoted herself to her older brothers before she had married.

Today Paul felt more drawn to Jeanne and Louis than ever before, perhaps because it was the first time he had been with them away from the rest of the family and more likely because of their approval of his becoming a coureur de bois. He felt they were entitled to an explanation.

"About father . . ." he begun and Jeanne paused to listen. "I may have done wrong but I don't feel I have." He leaned across the table intent upon presenting his side of the case. "I cannot see how we are all going to remain on the land. There are too many of us."

"I agree with you, Paul," Louis said and sighed heavily. "Anyone who says the land will continue to support us is talking stupidly. It's good land—no one can deny that, but we haven't the money or materials to develop it so that the yield is abundant enough."

"That is exactly my contention, Louis," Paul said and his voice was eager. "Also, well, perhaps I shouldn't feel this way, but frankly the monotony of farm life irks me. I have so much energy and ambition. And maybe I should have put this first, but I want to make money so that when I eventually settle down on my own farm, I will have some means to develop it."

Louis leaned towards his brother-in-law and for a moment the tired disappointed look left his face. "Believe me, Paul, I would have become a coureur de bois had I had the opportunity. The farmer's struggle is a hard one. Sometimes we seem to be getting ahead and then enemies come and all our labor is lost. Take the opportunity you have and make the most of it."

Louis slumped back into his chair. He seldom talked at length and it appeared to have exhausted him. He drained his glass, holding it empty in his hand as though debating whether he should fill it again or preserve what little was left in the bottle.

"Thanks, Louis," Paul said. "It is encouraging to hear that you approve. I hated to cross father." He looked at Jeanne. "I'm afraid I have angered him by going against his wishes. He . . . he says I am not to return to the house."

Jeanne paused in her cooking and turned to him. "That's bad, Paul. He's very stubborn. Perhaps by the time you return he will have thought better of it. Why did you have to make things more difficult for yourself by joining Péchard? You know how father has always felt about that family—and with good cause."

"Charles is better than he used to be. He is trying to improve his way of living . . ."

"About time."

"I know. He told me—and I believe he is sincere—that he wants to give up fur trading and settle down—with a wife."

"No woman would marry him—least not a woman who was any good."

"We can all change, Jeanne," Paul said but Jeanne did not reply. Paul continued: "Péchard is the best coureur in Montreal. I thought I might as well learn from the best." But Jeanne was not to be talked into altering her opinion.

Later that evening when Charles stopped in, his attitude did not improve the situation. He had evidently consumed plenty of brandy and was in one of his morose moods, making no effort to be friendly. As long as he remained there was restraint.

The next morning at daybreak they were off, cheered by the villagers who stood on the shores and waved to them, until at the bend of the river they were lost to sight. Jeanne and Louis watched with the others and Jeanne's eyes were misty as the canoes disappeared.

"He's a fine boy, Louis," she said.

"Aye, indeed," Louis agreed and walked away to attend to his work. There was envy in his heart that he had not had the courage of his young brother-in-law.

As the journey proceeded Paul's anger over Hélène began to fade and in its place came a feeling of gratitude. She had been the first woman he had ever made love to and from her deep experience she had taught him well. One evening, Charles became confidential and told Paul the difficulties of his own life. He had been only thirteen years old when one of his father's mistresses had taken him into her bed, and since then it had been Indian women with whom he had consorted on his trips. It explained Charles' attitude towards women. Paul made up his mind he would have nothing to do with the squaws who he understood frequented the forts where they would stop—but it was a young and inexperienced mind that made that decision.

Their next stop was St. Anne's where the waters of the stately Ottawa greeted but refused to mingle with those of the St. Lawrence. It was as though the smaller river agreed to tolerate its larger rival but would not admit the supremacy and so brown and green waters flowed side by side but never mixed. Here the coureurs pulled their canoes ashore for their last touch of civilization for many months. Through custom and superstition all the coureurs went to the little church that long ago had been dedicated to them. There they offered up earnest prayers for the success of their venture and the preservation of their lives. Though these men were wild and led irregular lives they never entirely forgot the Catholic faith in which they had been reared.

After they left St. Anne's, however, if prayers were said at all, they must have been strictly in private for Paul never saw them engage in any devotions. Having been reared in a home where prayers were said faithfully every night and morning he found the habit hard to break, but, like many other things, he learned to keep it to himself.

He soon discovered these devotions at St. Anne's were largely a matter of habit, for the moment the service was over the men threw themselves into an orgy of feasting and drinking. Around a table laden with simple but plentiful fare they ate, sang and drank heavily. It was a merry feast and Paul thoroughly enjoyed himself.

Then, when the excitement was at its height—the women came. With screams and yells they descended upon the men, picking out the one they wanted and going with him to the woods. All the men, including Paul, were very drunk by this time, but if the men stumbled as they got up from the table, the sturdy squaws helped them along, unperturbed by their condition. The sudden appearance of the women startled Paul and for a moment he held to his determination to ignore them. But his flaming hair and his youth made him conspicuous. Excepting Charles, he was the only young man among them —and Charles had already disappeared. Paul was left no time for decisions for two husky squaws pounced on him and fought to possess him. He tried to thrust them off and his struggles called forth ribald jests and laughter from the men who were still at the table.

"Don't let him go—it's his first trip. He's got to be initiated. Give him a good lesson," they shouted and the women increased their struggles. When Paul stood up he realized he was intoxicated and his knees buckled under him. Immediately they fell upon him and the three of them tussled on the ground, a struggling confusion of arms and legs.

What the outcome of the fight would have been no one could have predicted, for a voice of authority, speaking in the native tongue, shouted to them. Instantly the two women ceased their struggles and, getting to their feet, walked away. Paul looked up from where he lay and saw a woman in a deerskin dress looking down at him. Two long, thick black braids hung over her shoulders and she was not unattractive. Somewhat sheepishly he got to his feet, holding on to the table to support himself as he swayed uncertainly. The Indian girl was taller than he, her face set and expressionless.

"Come with me," she said. "I am Nadeea." She was evidently accustomed to having her own way, for when he did not move, she grasped his arm firmly and led him to a hut. He was much too befuddled to resist. The moment they were inside the hut, a quick change came over the girl. She laughed— and the sound so surprised him that he stared at her in amazement. She had seemed so fierce outside, but now, as she stood close to him, she was gentle. Maybe it was the brandy, but he found her not unpleasant. Even when she deftly slipped out of her deerskin dress, exposing a dark, swarthy body that gave off a pungent odor, she did not seem repulsive.

It was getting light when he wakened. He was lying on a bed of straw and the hut was empty. As she sat up he groaned, for his head felt as though it had been split with an axe. For a moment he wondered whether he had been injured, but when he felt his scalp it was all right. He lay back, dozing off again, and when next he opened his eyes, Nadeea was standing over him offering strong coffee. It tasted bitter and he pushed it away, but she was insistent.

"It will clear your head," she said, speaking in the native tongue, much of which he was able to understand. She held the cup to his lips and he drank without further protest. "The men are starting," she said. "You had better hurry."

He threw off the blanket and reached for his clothes. Someone had evidently undressed him the night before, for he did
not remember doing it himself. The Indian girl helped him
dress, quite unconcerned.

"I shall wait for your return on the next trip. You will not
be bothered again by the others. I am in charge here," she
told him and evidently he was expected to feel flattered. He
did not answer her. He was annoyed with himself for having
drunk so much that he felt sick. Also he wished he could remember something of the previous night.

He found the other men were also in bad moods from their
night's debauchery and all that day it was a tired, sullen crew
that manned the canoes.

They left the St. Lawrence and were proceeding up the
Ottawa, taking a course that had been mapped out long ago
by those who sought the beaver. They paddled up the winding
river between banks clothed in the majestic beauty of fir
and hemlock, where numberless rapids made pictures of un-
surpassed beauty. On they roamed until they turned to sweep
down the French River to the Georgian Bay and Lake Huron.
Between Lake Huron and Lake Michigan stood a fort and
Jesuit mission well known to every trader—Michilimackinac.
Here some of the traders ended their journey while others
branched off in one of two directions—a southwesterly course
through Lake Michigan or a northwesterly course in the direction of Lake Superior.

Paul felt the rugged beauty of his surroundings take hold
of him and though all nature around him was savage, it had
a soothing effect. Many times he found himself stopping to
gaze in wonder at his surroundings, so that often the men
called to him, sometimes petulantly because he was not taking
his share of the heavy portage. To them a leaping, spraying
rapid, swirling in all directions, was a tiresome freak of nature
which necessitated much hard work and made them strain

and curse. Perhaps, Paul thought, when he had made the journey many times he might lose the beauty of it all, and because he was afraid he would never recapture this first impression, he remained spellbound. He had not the power to express what he saw—he could only feel it deep within him.

CHAPTER XI

MARGUERITE had come to dread the nights. As they grew longer, with the waning of summer, it meant more hours in which to toss restlessly, unable to sleep because of the worry on her mind. One night towards the end of September, she had lain awake so long that in desperation she threw off the bedclothes and got out of bed. It was weeks since she had had a full night's sleep and the strain was beginning to take its toll.

The night was chilly and she took down her beaver coat and wrapped it around her. She threw open the wooden shutter and looked out into the darkness. There was no glass in the windows, for that was a luxury they could not afford. Cool air rushed into the room and in the blackness outside there was little comfort to be gained. She leaned on the sill and as her eyes became accustomed to the dark, she could see the waters of the river rippling along in their contentment. The thought came to her that if she plunged into the river her worries would be drowned in the silence of the waters. But even as this thought crossed her mind, youth asserted itself and she knew that, despite her troubles, she wanted to live. Her life had always been happy and carefree but now she faced a serious problem. All during the month of July she had feared it; by August she was frightened and now that the end of September was near, she was frantic. There could be no doubting her condition and soon she would be unable to conceal the truth from her family. The thought made her tremble, and overwhelmed by her despair, she rested her head on her arms and sobbed.

"Holy Mother, help me," she prayed but no soothing answer

came. She had committed this sin and now must face the consequences. She felt so desperately alone. To whom could she
turn for help? Her mother? No, Marie would merely be horrified and tell Jacques. Her sister Jeanne? No, Jeanne would not
understand. Although they had always been fond of each other
in a sisterly way, they had never shared their secrets and Jeanne
would merely be aghast that a sister of hers should bring such
shame upon the family. Old Pierre? This thought shed a slight
ray of hope but she dreaded to have to disappoint him. He had
always been so proud of her—had loved her much more than
the others, and though he had always helped her through her
difficulties, this was something beyond ordinary problems. She
was bitter in her loathing of de Favien, now enjoying himself
in Quebec, probably with some other woman. Yet she knew
she could not blame him entirely. She had allowed herself to
be too easily tempted—had gone to the mill knowing that she
should not have done so. But remorse now would not help and
she must somehow decide what to do.

Again she cried out to the night, "What am I to do?" and
out of the stillness came a thought, a rather strange thought
considering the circumstances. Her mind turned to one whom
she had always loved—the Mother Superior of the Congregation of Notre Dame. In all Montreal there was no one so beloved as Sister Marguerite Bourgeoys. She had come to Montreal on the same ship as Old Pierre and his wife and son. For
thirty-five of her sixty-five years she had devoted her life to
helping and inspiring others. During that time she had been a
constant friend to the Boissarts. When Old Pierre had returned
broken in body, it was Sister Marguerite who had come every
day to the farm to help little Jacques. She had founded the
first school in Montreal and to this all the Boissart children had
gone—the boys until they were ten years old and the girls
for all the education they could expect. Marguerite had been
one of her pupils and though Sister Marguerite could never
outwardly show favoritism, she had grown especially fond of

this vivacious girl. Since Marguerite had left school, scarcely a week had passed that she did not pay her a visit.

Marguerite Bourgeoys had been the daughter of a tradesman of Troyes and had felt the call to come and help colonize New France. Unlike some of the other splendid women who answered this same call, she had neither known miracles nor received visions. She was less austere than many of the others and her religious zeal was tempered with an abundance of understanding and human affection. Her face was a mirror of frankness, loyalty and womanly tenderness and whenever her small black-clad figure was seen coming along the streets of Montreal, or whenever she entered a home, faces immediately showed reverence and love. The hardest, toughest farmer, the wild rough coureur de bois—all knew her and when she passed pulled off their caps.

Dawn came—and Marguerite was still sitting by the window. A bird gave an early morning greeting but because she was miserable the happiness of her winged friend found no response in her heart. Though she dreaded the idea, she decided to go that day to see Sister Marguerite. It was going to be terrible to have to tell her what had happened. She would have to watch a pained expression come into those beautiful, kind features. She tormented herself with her thoughts and they brought another flood of tears. If only there were some way in which she could pluck out this new life which was stirring within her. She felt faint with nausea and crept back to bed to fall asleep from exhaustion.

As they all assembled in the morning for prayers, Old Pierre was shocked when he looked at Marguerite. There were dark lines under her eyes contrasting with the whiteness of her face. He had known for some time that something was troubling her but had not been able to get her to confide in him. He watched her furtively. There was something in her appearance that brought a suspicion to his mind, yet almost immediately he dismissed it, because such an idea seemed absurd. As they rose from prayers he caught her eyes and there was a terrified look in them. It seemed to him that as she met his eyes, hers filled with tears.

The shock of his thought so upset Old Pierre he could not eat his breakfast. Suppose his suspicion were right, whatever would the child do? He must find an opportunity of talking to her that day. But though he hung around all the morning, she seemed to avoid him and when afternoon came—it was too late.

Since Paul's departure, Jacques had been more silent than ever before. Not once had he mentioned Paul's name and the others did not dare. If he spoke at all, it was about matters pertaining to the farm. In the evenings he and Old Pierre would sit outside smoking their pipes and often exchanged only a sentence or two.

It was after dinner that the storm broke. To the surprise of the others, and the consternation of Marguerite, Jacques did not leave for the fields, but sat inside smoking his pipe. During dinner he had noticed Marguerite toying with her food, as she had done at breakfast.

"Why aren't you eating your food?" he had asked in a gruff but kindly way.

"I'm not feeling very well today, father," she had answered.

"What is the matter with you?"

"Nothing," she answered, but as he looked keenly at her he saw her color rise. He said no more but his face was stern. As she helped her mother clear the table, he watched her.

Marguerite noticed it and knew that the dreaded moment had come. She was deciding whether she should leave the house when her father said sharply:

"Marguerite, come here."

As she turned, the contour of her figure stood out and Old Pierre knew then that his suspicion had been correct.

"What is it, father?" she asked and remained where she was.

"Come here," he repeated. As she came slowly towards him every drop of blood drained from her face, accentuating the dark circles beneath her eyes. Jacques grasped her arm and turned her sideways, confirming his own suspicions. His hand on her arm was like a vise, making her wince, but she did not cry out. The cup she had been drying broke in her hand from the tenseness of her grip.

"Marie, come here," Jacques said tersely. Marie in her dull way had missed what was happening and in her flat voice said:

"What do you want?" and went on swilling water in the pan.

"Come here," Jacques repeated and, taking her time, Marie came over wiping her hands on her apron.

"What is it?" she said again.

"Look at your daughter. Am I mistaken in what I think I see?"

"I don't know what you're talking about," Marie said but her remark went unheeded. Marguerite could stand the strain no longer. The pieces of the broken cup which she held in her hands fell to the floor, as she threw herself down beside her father and buried her face against his knee.

"No, father, you're not!" she cried.

Jacques jumped up as though he had been struck, pushing her from him and looking down at her as though she were something unclean.

"What did you say?" he asked in a low voice. Marguerite did not answer. Her face was buried in the chair beside which she crouched. Jacques took her by the shoulder and wrenched her around so that she faced him. "What did you say?" he repeated and she tried to pull herself away from his firm grasp. "I demand an answer!" he cried.

Old Pierre sat there, digging his mangled hands deeper into his pockets, not knowing what to do but wanting desperately to help her.

"You are right, father," Marguerite said between sobs.

"How am I right?"

"I am . . ." She could not go on but buried her face again, her body shaking with sobs. Jacques was relentless. He grasped her shoulder again and forced her to face him.

"You are—what?" he said.

The tears were streaming down her face and she could not answer him.

"I am waiting for your answer," he said slowly.

"I am—going—to have a baby." The last words came rapidly in a voice scarcely above a whisper.

"Merciful God!" Jacques exclaimed and covered his face with his hands for a moment. Around the edges of his weather-beaten face, his skin was greenish white. There was not a sound in the room but the ticking of the clock and this seemed twice as loud as usual. "Whose baby?" he asked. There was no answer. His anger increased and when Jacques' temper was out of control it was something to be feared. "I'll make you answer me!" he cried and strode over to the door where his horsewhip hung. He took it down and uncurled it as he strode back to where Marguerite still crouched. "I'll give you one more chance—who is responsible for this?" His voice was slow and deliberate. The leather thong of the whip hissed through the air and came down upon her shoulder. She screamed but it came down again, wrapping its stinging tongue around her arm. "It's that fellow your worthless brother has gone off with! I might have known you were two of a kind. You always have been. I should have thrown you out with him!"

"It wasn't Charles," Marguerite managed to say.

"Now you lie to defend him!"

"I'm not defending him. It has nothing to do with him."

"Then who is it?"

Why should she defend de Favien? Yet what was the good of naming him? He was in Quebec and it would only involve the Sieur de Courville.

"Will you answer me!" Jacques shouted and when she remained silent, he wielded the whip so unmercifully that it cut through her flesh. Her cries went unheeded as, blind with rage, Jacques forgot what he was doing.

Marie was too aghast to make a move beyond saying several times, "Don't, Jacques." She had not fully comprehended what had happened. Marguerite could not be going to have a baby —she was not married.

It had all happened so quickly it left Old Pierre stunned. Each time the whip struck, he flinched, until, unable to stand it any longer, he jumped from his chair and rushed at Jacques.

"Stop it, you fool!" he shouted. "Do you want to kill her?" With his mutilated hands he grasped the thong of the whip as it waved through the air and he and Jacques struggled for its possession.

"I'd rather see her dead!" Jacques shouted. Both men were powerful but Old Pierre was the calmer and after a short tussle he secured the whip and threw it across the room.

"It's not for you to take life," he said to Jacques. "God alone has the right to do that."

"Then may God strike her dead," Jacques said, and exhausted from the force of his anger, he sank into the nearest chair and buried his face in his hands.

Old Pierre helped Marguerite to her feet. She looked for one terrified moment at her father and then fled from the room.

CHAPTER XII

PAUL'S FIRST TRIP into the woods lasted eight months. As the winter snows thawed and the ice in the river disappeared, he and his teammates made their way towards Montreal. It had been a successful trip and both canoes were loaded to capacity with beaver pelts. Soon Paul would know the thrill of receiving the first profits he had ever earned. These months in the wilds, filled as they had been with many hardships, had yet been the happiest Paul had known. Even the thought of his father's displeasure did not spoil his longing to get home and show the family he had made a success of the venture. It seemed to him every day had brought new experiences and now he could consider himself a fairly good trader. It had amazed him to see how often beautiful beaver pelts changed hands for a mere gimcrack. Once while trading with the Indians he had taken out a comb to tidy his hair, only to have it seized from his hand and admired as though it had been a thing of great value. He had learned to humor the Indians, so he had waited while they jabbered to each other about it and then had been astonished to have them hand him a large beaver skin. He had laughed and pushed it away, shaking his head to mean the comb was not worth such a price. The Indian had misunderstood the gesture and at once added a second pelt, urging him by signs and entreaties to accept it. There had been many such instances as this, so that the ultimate profit on the trading was usually very satisfactory to the coureur de bois.

All day bevies of canoes swirled down the St. Lawrence, the men chanting their familiar songs and waving to the farmers who were standing on the banks watching them. Charles had told Paul they could only stop for a short visit in Lachine in order to reach Montreal in time for the annual fair. As they dragged their heavy canoes ashore, Paul saw Jeanne and Louis waiting to welcome him. He hurried over and threw his arms around them, happy to tell them of his success.

"You look fine, Paul," Jeanne said admiringly.

"Even with all this growth!" he said, running his hand over his rough red beard. "Didn't know whether you'd even recognize me."

"You certainly do look different," Louis said. "But you look as though the trip had agreed with you."

"It has! I've never enjoyed anything so much."

"Have any trouble with the Indians?"

"A scrap here and there. How about you people?"

"Nothing to speak of. It's been a good year all down the River. There have been rumors of a raid here and there up above Montreal, but nothing bad."

"That's good news. Surprising too. When I left Montreal everyone was expecting some retaliation for the trouble last year."

"Aye—but it hasn't come—yet."

They walked up to the house as they talked. At the door Jeanne stopped and looked at Paul with a rather strange expression on her face.

"We have a surprise for you, Paul," she said.

"Surprise?" he said and looked at her questioningly. Then remembering the outward journey, he exclaimed: "Ah! Another nephew or is it another niece?"

"Oh, yes—that too. Another nephew. But I was not referring to that . . ."

"Some other surprise?"

"Yes. Come inside."

Paul followed Jeanne inside, his face expectant. Louis left them and went back to his farming. The next moment Paul had leapt half across the room and was hugging Marguerite to him. As she disentangled herself from her brother's embrace, her face was anxious.

"To think I should find you here, Marguerite, instead of having to wait until I get to Montreal! This is wonderful. Had you thought I would be back about this time?" The words poured from his mouth in his eagerness. Marguerite's reply was not so eager.

"No—I'm staying with Jeanne now," she said quietly.

"Stay . . . staying with Jeanne?" he asked, puzzled. "You don't mean father was angry with you, too, because of me?"

"Oh, no—not because of you." She dreaded having to make these explanations to Paul. "It's a long story. You'll have to give me time to tell you."

"Yes, of course, take your time, dear." He saw then that there was an extra bed in the parlor and beside it a wooden cradle.

"Is this my nephew?" He turned to Jeanne but she had slipped from the room.

Marguerite's face flushed deep crimson. "Yes, he's your nephew," she said, "only—he's not Jeanne's son."

Paul wrinkled his forehead, completely confused. "You mean you are married and living in Lachine?"

There was an awkward pause and then Marguerite said: "No, I'm not married—but this is my son." Paul's eyes met hers. "Sit down," she said. "I'll get you something to drink and then I'll try to tell you."

Paul drew up a chair near the wooden cradle and looked down at the tiny little person in it. There was a convulsive movement and a wee hand pushed jerkily against a rosy cheek. Paul rather gingerly put a finger into the clenched fist and smiled as it was gripped.

"How old is he?" he asked.

"Five months," Marguerite said, her face softening with motherly tenderness as she saw her little one hanging on firmly to his uncle.

"Then he was born about Christmas?"

"Just after. He was born prematurely."

"I see."

Marguerite handed him a glass of brandy and sat down at the table wondering how she should start her story.

"I'm afraid you won't love your favorite sister any more, Paul. I'm a disgraced woman."

"He is illegitimate?" She nodded. "Was this after I left?"

"No—it began before . . ."

"Then—you knew about it when I left?" he exclaimed.

"Yes."

"I'm so sorry. I had no idea. Why didn't you tell me?"

"You were very busy."

Paul looked at her a little sheepishly. "Yes, I was. But still I would not have left had I known. After all—we have always shared our troubles with each other."

"Almost always," she answered.

"Well, up to the time I left. We both seem to have kept the most important trouble to ourselves. I'll tell you later or would you rather I told mine first?"

"No, I'll tell you about this. It was—the Chevalier de Favien . . ."

"De Favien! I didn't know you loved him!"

"I didn't." Marguerite pressed her lips together tightly and could not meet his eyes.

"You mean he seduced you!" Paul said angrily.

"No—not exactly. Oh Paul! It's so hard to explain. I didn't mean to do wrong . . . I don't know what made me do it."

Paul leaned across the table and took her hand. "Let me tell you my story. Perhaps you will feel better. It seems we were both having a similar experience, only being a man I did not have to suffer any consequences. I was Hélène de Matier's lover."

As they faced each other their twin likeness was apparent: the shape of their faces, the color of their hair and eyes and at this moment even the expression on their faces.

Marguerite smiled rather ironically. "They seem to have involved us both."

"Did you know she was his mistress?" Paul asked.

"No, though I have heard it since. Did you?"

"Yes, and I was rather proud of having taken her away from him. But he won in the end. She went off to Quebec with him without leaving me even a note. That was why I was angry, and left so abruptly. I shouldn't have let it get the better of me. But I was very upset."

"Of course."

"I suspect now that this was why he helped me get my license. He wanted me out of the way not only on account of Hélène but because of you. Tell me what happened after I left."

"It was the day after the ball that he asked me to meet him . . ."

"The same day I went to Hélène de Matier for the first time!"

"That was the only time I saw him . . ."

"The only time! You mean he went away and left you to bear the consequences! Of course, he would. He was that type of man . . ."

"He probably did not know he was the father of a child."

"Then he soon shall know—even if I have to go to Quebec."

"That wouldn't help now. He's not in Quebec any more."

"Then wherever he is . . ."

"You'd have to go to France."

"You mean he has gone back?"

"He's in the Bastille . . ."

"Bastille!"

She nodded. "The Sieur de Courville had him sent back to France. It seems he had done something wrong there and the moment he landed he was arrested and put in the Bastille."

"Good! I never did like him and should not have accepted his help. Go on, dear."

"I'll be as brief as I can. The months went on and I became terrified."

"You poor child!"

"Then it was no longer possible to conceal it. Father noticed my condition. I hardly remember the details. I ran from the house after grandfather had stopped father whipping me. I ran practically all the way to Montreal and don't remember anything until I found myself lying on a bed with Sister Marguerite sitting beside me."

"Sister Marguerite!"

"She was so good to me, Paul. If ever there was a saint on earth it is she. Father Dollier was wonderful too. It was he who told the Sieur de Courville."

"That it was de Favien?"

"Yes."

"It must have upset the Sieur."

"It did. He came to see me and was very kind. He insisted upon being present at the baptism. They kept me at the Congregation all the time. I don't know whether the story is known in Montreal—I suppose it must be. Grandfather is the only one of the family I have seen since. He came nearly every day and he never once reproved me. Sister Marguerite sent for father but he would not forgive me. I did not know of this until grandfather told me. He told me also that the Sieur left at once for Quebec. He went to the Governor himself and asked him to send de Favien back to France. When Paul was born . . ."

"Paul?"

"Yes. Do you mind? I named him after you," she said a little anxiously.

"Of course I don't mind. I'm glad you did."

"When he was born there was the question of what should be done with us. I prayed he might never be born alive and that was wrong. But I could not bear the thought of his having to face life with this awful stigma hanging over him. It is still awful for me to think of—yet I do love him. The first suggestion was that we should be sent to Quebec. Then one day Jeanne came to see me. I don't believe we have ever really understood or appreciated Jeanne. Before the baby came I had thought of telling her but was sure she would be shocked. She probably was, but she came to see me and asked me to come and live with her and Louis. At first I refused, thinking my disgrace would reflect upon them. But people have been surprisingly kind here. There are some who ignore me—but most of them don't."

"Bless Jeanne."

"I don't know what I should have done had she and Louis not come home on a visit just then. I could not bear to have Paul taken from me and that is probably what would have happened."

There was silence and before they spoke again Jeanne came in. She glanced quickly at each of them.

"Your friends said to tell you they are leaving, Paul," she said. Paul got up from the table and put his arms round Jeanne.

"Thanks, Jeanne, for helping Marguerite," he said and kissed her.

"Somebody had to help," she said briefly. "Have another glass of brandy before you leave. Here's Louis."

Louis came in and they drank together. "Stop on your way back, Paul," he said. "I presume you're going out again."

"Yes indeed," Paul said eagerly and then as a thought crossed his mind, he said: "I'll probably have no choice. Father won't let me stay home."

Charles was standing a few yards from the house and when Marguerite saw him she drew back into the shadows. "Don't tell Charles," she said hurriedly.

"Wouldn't it be better if I told him the true story rather than have him hear a garbled account in Montreal?"

Marguerite hesitated and then said, "I suppose it would."

"He has always thought a great deal of you, Marguerite."

"He'll be able to change his mind now," she said bitterly.

"Charles is hardly in a position to judge anyone," Paul reminded her.

"No. He'll probably place me in the same class as the women he's used to," she replied and hurried indoors.

CHAPTER XIII

SILENTLY AND SWIFTLY the canoes sped on their way towards Montreal, skimming over the dangerous Lachine rapids and accomplishing in a few hours what had taken two days and a night on the outward journey. Before they had stopped at Lachine, Paul would have welcomed this speed, but now he dreaded it and sat silently paddling in unison with the other men, having no heart to join with them in their songs. Strengthened by the success of his trip, he had felt he would be able to overcome his father's objections but now all such hopes had faded. It was impossible to regard Marguerite's trouble lightly. He kept turning over in his mind what he should say to his father. Ought he to give up this new life he had chosen and accede to his father's wishes? It was a difficult decision for he knew he could never be happy on the farm again after the broader life which had now opened to him. On one point he had made up his mind even before they had reached Lachine—he would not join in the wild revelries of the men. Perhaps if he could show his father he had not become reckless, Jacques might be persuaded to change his views about coureurs de bois.

Presently Charles asked: "Wasn't that Marguerite I saw?" There was resentment in his tone.

"Yes, it was," Paul said.

"Why didn't she come and speak to me?"

Paul was silent. Then said: "Marguerite's in trouble."

Charles looked at him sharply. "What kind of trouble?"

"Serious," Paul said and then after a moment added: "She didn't want me to tell you. But I told her it would be better for you to hear it from me rather than get some garbled account in Montreal."

"Go on," Charles said abruptly.

"Marguerite has a baby."

There was another silence and then Charles asked: "Who'd she marry?"

"No one."

"You mean . . ."

"Yes. It was the Chevalier de Favien."

"De Favien! Was that why he helped you?"

"That's what I'm wondering."

"This explains much that has puzzled me," Charles said bitterly.

"In what· way?"

"Oh—it doesn't matter now. But you know I've always been fond of Marguerite . . . too fond for my peace of mind. I understand now why she would not see me before I left Montreal."

"She was in trouble then—only I didn't know it."

"And having got her into trouble, the gentleman of the French Court refused to marry her, I suppose," Charles said with a sneer.

"I don't believe there was any question of marriage. From what Marguerite said, it is doubtful whether he knows he has a child. He left for Quebec soon after."

"Then, by God, I'll go to Quebec and see he does know he has a child!" Charles exclaimed angrily.

"That's just what I said. But he's in the Bastille." Paul explained to Charles what Marguerite had told him. He sat sullenly for a while and then said:

"We coureurs may be wild—but at least we don't seduce innocent girls. What I can't make out is how she could have loved a man like de Favien." Jealousy welled up in him.

"It was more infatuation than love. She certainly has no love for him now!"

"I don't imagine she has."

As they passed the Boissart farm, Paul glanced eagerly towards it, but there was no one in sight. He made the excuse to himself that they probably were at their midday meal. The fields looked in good condition, as they had all along the river —and this sign of freedom from devastating raids was comforting.

Montreal was the usual scene of pandemonium which always attended the annual fair. They had to wait in a long line to deliver their beaver skins to the magazines, have them appraised and receive their money. There was little cash in circulation in New France, the medium of trading being convertible bills of exchange, except in many instances when the pelts themselves were used for barter. Paul's share of the profits was considerable, and for the first time since leaving Lachine, he brightened up, unable to resist the thrill of receiving his first earnings.

"Come over to Dillon's," he said to Charles and his companions. "We have to celebrate. This is too important to let pass."

At the tavern they ran into many old friends and before Paul realized it he had consumed far too much brandy and was singing raucously with the rest. There were several brawls that evening but these were expected during the fair. Paul forgot his troubles until jerked back to remembrance by a drunken farmer who made a besmirching reference to Marguerite. Her name was not actually mentioned but no one could be in doubt as to whom the man meant. Immediately Paul was on his feet and fists were flying. The two men fell and rolled over and over on the floor, pummeling fiercely at each other and landing blows that took their toll. Paul came out the victor but was far from unscathed. Blood poured from a deep cut over one eye and there was a long gash across his cheek.

When he awoke the next morning in Charles' home and looked in the mirror, he was disgusted with himself. How could he appear before his father looking like this? The obvious conclusion would be that he had been drunk and brawling the night before and this was exactly what he had hoped to avoid.

All his good intentions were now refuted. Yet he must go that day to see them. He washed his face carefully, trying to patch up the injuries. He then discarded his coureur outfit and put on the homespuns he had always worn.

As he walked towards his home, a feeling of nostalgia came over him. He loved these people who were his flesh and blood and did not want to be considered an outcast.

He could see his father and his two elder brothers working on the far side of the farm. His mother would undoubtedly be at the bake oven. He decided he had better go to see his father first. As he made his way across the fields, his two younger brothers saw him. With the impetuosity of youth, they raced over, and the enthusiasm of their welcome was comforting. Standing with an arm around each, he answered their many questions and found it difficult to get away from them. There was no doubting their admiration, which amounted almost to worship.

His two older brothers, however, were reserved and there was disapproval in their manner, though this may have been because their father was working with them. Jacques looked up as he heard the greeting but immediately resumed work without speaking. Paul hesitated a moment, glanced at his brothers, who gave him no help.

"Hello, father," he said awkwardly.

Jacques stopped work and looked up, his eyes hard and stern and his face set. Paul was shocked to see how he had aged. Immediately pity and regret for the trouble he and Marguerite had caused surged over him and he was penitent. As Paul had feared, Jacques' eyes went at once to the injuries on his face.

"Am I welcome, father?" he asked doubtfully.

"If you are ready to come back and take your place on the farm," Jacques answered coldly.

This was what Paul had expected and dreaded. He hesitated before answering. "I have done well on this trip. I have made a good profit and want to give it to you to help with the farm . . ."

"If we were starving I wouldn't touch it! You should know that," Jacques said contemptuously.

"I have done nothing wrong," Paul said, defending himself.

"Your appearance shows me exactly what kind of a life you now lead."

"That was an accident. I slipped . . ."

"I am not interested in what you did. Nor do I intend to waste time discussing it with you. You know my opinion of the trade you have chosen. I have no more to say."

With that Jacques turned his back and went on with his work. Paul stood looking at that stern back, uncertain what to do. He glanced at his brothers, both of whom had heard the conversation, but they were working industriously. Despondently he walked away. He hesitated whether he should go to see his mother, but he could not leave without doing so. Her broad back was bent as she kneaded the dough and she did not see him until he was standing beside her. At the sight of him, her face changed—mother love vying with fear.

"I have returned, mother," he said.

"Yes, Paul. You look well," she said, and her mouth trembled into a smile.

"I am. I had a very good trip."

"I'm glad."

The conversation was stilted and Marie continued with her work.

"I saw Marguerite in Lachine," Paul said. He saw his mother's arms stiffen and then resume their work. "I'm sorry we have both caused so much trouble." Marie did not answer. "Father won't let me come back home," Paul said and his voice wavered. Marie stopped for a moment and turned to her son.

"Give it up, Paul. Your father is a broken man. Marguerite's disgrace has nearly killed him. Don't add to his grief."

"I've no wish to, mother. But I can't see that I am doing

wrong. I have made a very good profit on this trip and I offered it to father to help with the farm. I have behaved myself and I don't see why I should be treated as an outcast." His voice rose in his own defense. "It is narrowness that makes father act like this."

"Perhaps—but you can't blame him."

There was another long silence. Paul broke it by asking:

"Where's grandfather?"

"He went into town."

"I think I'll go and see if I can find him."

"Very well," Marie said. Paul hesitated and then put his arm round her. She looked up at him and her eyes were sad. "Don't be too hard on me, mother. I'll make good and some day you'll be proud of me."

For just a minute she relaxed against him and he tightened his arm round her. Her movement was hardly perceptible but it was enough so he knew she was not really against him. He kissed her gently on the forehead before she turned and went on with her work. As he started to walk away she asked in a low voice:

"How was Marguerite?"

Paul's face softened, for this question told him his mother's real feelings. "She was very well, mother, and quite happy with Jeanne. Shall I give her your love when I return? I shall stop there."

"Yes," she said quickly and, turning back to her dough, began kneading it as though she were angry with it.

Depressed and unhappy, Paul walked across the farm. He changed his mind about going to Montreal and instead turned in the direction of the Manor House. Perhaps the Sieur would advise him what he should do.

"Come in, my boy, come in!" the Sieur exclaimed when he saw him standing in the doorway. He did not get up from his chair but held out his hand eagerly. "I am so glad to see you, Paul."

To his confusion, Paul felt his eyes fill with tears. This

warmth after the reception at home quite unnerved him. With long strides he crossed the room and clasped the Sieur's outstretched hand. He was shocked by the change in him, as he had been by the appearance of his father. He, too, had aged considerably and seemed quite feeble.

"Thank you so much for your welcome, monsieur."

"You are very welcome, my boy. Old Pierre left only a little while ago for Montreal. He saw Charles this morning and learned you were back. We have been anxious about you. You do look well. The life has evidently agreed with you. Draw up a chair and tell me all about it."

Paul pulled up a chair and sat opposite him.

"Now," the Sieur said with keen interest, "tell me all you've been doing."

"I shall be glad to, monsieur, but first of all permit me to ask after you."

"Me—oh, I'm just an old fool as I always have been."

"You have been ill, monsieur?"

"Yes, yes. The old heart's giving out. I'm not the man I used to be. But, come, pour yourself a glass of brandy. I'm impatient to hear your news."

Paul poured the brandy and handed it to the Seigneur. He took the glass and made a face. "Not supposed to drink it—so they tell me. But I'll be content to live a few years less and enjoy myself rather than linger along without a glass of brandy with my friends. A *votre santé*, my boy."

Paul held his glass up to the Seigneur and drained half of it.

"Now—you've had a successful trip?"

"Very good, monsieur, and profitable."

"Splendid. I knew you would like it. When do you leave again?"

"I don't know, monsieur. I wanted to talk to you about it."

"Not had enough of the woods already, have you?"

"Indeed no—but—father . . ."

"Oh, yes, Jacques. Poor Jacques . . . his load is a heavy one."

"Yes, monsieur. And I don't want to add to it."

"No—of course not. Have you seen him?"

"I've just come from there. That was why your warm welcome meant so much to me, monsieur. Father forbids me to come home unless I give up being a coureur de bois."

"Hm," the Sieur said thoughtfully. "That is bad. I had hoped he might feel differently now Marguerite has gone away."

"On the contrary, I think it has made him more bitter with me. I saw Marguerite in Lachine."

"I expected you might." All the eagerness had gone out of the Sieur's face now and it was ashen grey. He sipped his brandy in heavy silence. "It was a terrible shock to us all, Paul. To think that any kin of mine should bring such disgrace upon a fine family. And such a lovely girl—I had hoped much for her future. I never should have risked bringing him here." He paused for a moment and then looked at Paul with anguish in his tired eyes. "I don't know what to do to put things right. I feel entirely responsible."

"I don't see how you can be responsible, monsieur. He was your nephew, but . . ."

"He wasn't my nephew . . ." Paul looked at him and the agonized expression on the Seigneur's face wrung his heart. "He was—my *son*."

Paul opened his mouth, but his astonishment was too great for him to speak for a while. Then he said in a tone hardly above a whisper: "Your—*son*."

"Yes, Paul—a natural son."

"I had no idea, monsieur," Paul said.

"No one knows this, Paul—except Old Pierre. I wanted to tell Jacques, but Old Pierre would not let me."

"I don't see what good that would have done."

"That is what Old Pierre said. I would gladly have told it

to everyone in Montreal if it would have cleared your family from this stigma."

"Even though he is your son, that still does not make you responsible, monsieur."

"I feel it does. I'll tell you why. Give me another glass of brandy first." Paul filled the Sieur's glass and waited for him to continue. The old man sat with his hand over his eyes for a moment and then looked at Paul. "His mother was my mistress. We had many happy years together. As you may know—or perhaps you don't—my wife and I were not congenial. She gave me three sons but none of them has ever cared for me. She is dead now, so we won't discuss that. I turned elsewhere for comfort and Madeleine de Favien gave it to me. She was a very wonderful woman, Paul, the finest woman I have ever known. When Nicholas was born I was very happy for I hoped to find in him what I had lost in my other sons. But it was not to be. When I was sent out here many years ago, Madeleine wanted to come with me. But she was very frail and I felt could never have withstood the hardships of the life here. To the day she died we were devoted. I had always hoped I could have seen her again. That also was not to be. When I received word of her death, I wrote to Nicholas and asked him to come out here to me. The answer I received shocked me, for he had become associated with the worst elements of Court life. Then, last year, I received a letter from him saying he had changed his mind. On the same ship came another letter from an old friend from whom I learned the reason for this change. The letter informed me Nicholas had involved himself in an intrigue with the daughter of a prominent minister and had had to flee Paris to avoid arrest." The Sieur paused and drained his glass. "I was happy at the prospect of having a son of mine out here and overlooked the indiscretion, hoping it might have been just such an escapade as many young men get into. When I saw Nicholas getting off the ship in Quebec, I knew it was no such thing. I disliked him the moment I saw him."

"I am sorry, monsieur, sincerely sorry. It must have been a great disappointment."

"It was. I blame myself because I feel that what has happened is largely due to his irregular birth. He had learned his mother was my mistress and he took every advantage of it to prevent my speaking plainly to him. How could I reproach him for having mistresses when his mother had been my mistress? I had no idea how vile he was until he threatened one day to spread the story all over Montreal unless I financed his return to Quebec. I gave him practically all I possess—except this seigneury. This, Paul, is what comes of letting irregularities get into our lives."

"Yes, monsieur," Paul said and his thoughts went to Hélène de Matier.

"Get yourself a wife—a good wife."

"I would like to, monsieur. I must say I have not given it a great deal of thought. I wanted to make some money first and then settle down perhaps on land of my own that I could build into a fine seigneury."

"It is a good plan. Did I understand you to say you were going back to the woods?"

"What would you advise me to do, monsieur? I don't want to add to father's sufferings, yet I do want to continue being a coureur de bois."

"That's not an easy question to answer. I must think it over. My feeling now is to advise you to lead your own life. Perhaps we should talk it over with Old Pierre."

"I'm anxious to see him."

"He'll probably come here when he doesn't find you in Montreal."

"Perhaps he will. Meantime, monsieur, there is another question I should like to ask you. What shall I do about de Favien's share?"

"Share of what?"

"The profits, monsieur. We were partners—he is entitled to half."

"He's entitled to nothing! What motive did he have in doing it anyway?"

"I don't know, monsieur—perhaps on account of Marguerite. Or—it might have been to get me out of the way."

"Why?"

Paul hesitated a moment and then said: "Hélène de Matier had become my mistress . . ." The Sieur looked at Paul with surprise. "It was probably wrong, monsieur," Paul said apologetically.

Then the Sieur threw back his head and gave a hearty laugh. After the seriousness that had hung in the air, it was surprising. Paul did not quite understand the meaning of it.

"Forgive me, Paul. But this really is the only good piece of news I have heard. I can just imagine Nicholas' fury when he found you had taken his mistress away from him—he who thought he was so much grander than any of the men here." Then the Sieur said with some concern, "But I hope it's over."

"Yes, monsieur, it was over before I left for the woods."

"I'm glad to hear that. She was a very dangerous woman."

"And what about de Favien's share of my profits?" Paul asked, diverting the conversation from Hélène de Matier. He did not want to discuss her even with the Sieur.

The Sieur thought for a while, his chin in his hand and his lined face serious. "I have an idea. His share of the profits shall go to Marguerite. I have been concerned over what I could do for her. As I just told you, Nicholas took practically all I have. It has worried me because I have been able to do nothing for Marguerite. Would you be willing to give her Nicholas' share?"

"Most willing, monsieur. It would be a very good way—if she will take it."

"She must take it. It will be necessary, however, for us to have this handled carefully. I shall send for a notary and he shall draw up legal papers. You can hand me de Favien's share which I shall place, technically at least, against the debts I paid for him here. He is in the Bastille now but I don't know for how long and he might some day come and demand the money from you."

Paul felt in his pocket for some papers. "There is the bill of exchange for the amount," he said, handing the paper to the Sieur.

"Keep it now. I will let you know when I can get a notary and arrange it." He glanced at the paper before handing it back. "A nice profit. I wish I had spent more years fur trading. It's a good healthy life. I know if I were a young man I'd spend some years in trading."

"That is encouraging to me, monsieur," Paul said.

The Sieur thought deeply for a while. He did not want to add to Jacques' troubles by advising his son to go against his wishes, yet he could not truthfully advise Paul to remain on the farm. It was the ambitious spirit in Paul that had made him a favorite with the Seigneur. During these past years of disappointment over his own family, he had been forming a plan in his mind—but he did not want to tell Paul about it yet. While they were talking over the future, Old Pierre came in. Paul jumped up to greet him.

"You young rogue, where have you been? I've looked all over Montreal for you. If I've had too much brandy—it's your fault. I went into every tavern looking for you!"

"Sorry, grandfather. But I haven't been near town today."

"You weren't so good yesterday, I'll wager. Or did you just slip and cut your eye?" Old Pierre gave him a roguish grin. The Sieur thought how much of his grandfather's spirit Paul had inherited.

"I did celebrate a little yesterday and I'm afraid I got into a fight."

"Well—I hope you won. Saw your partner in town—he's still celebrating."

"Was he drunk?" Paul asked a little anxiously.

"I should say he was—very drunk!" Old Pierre said and

grinned again. Then he turned to the Sieur: "Where's the brandy, Jean-Baptiste? I need some . . ."

"Thought you said you had already had too much," the Sieur chided.

"You don't think I'm going to celebrate my grandson's return by drinking water, do you! You've a bad heart and aren't supposed to drink but my heart's all right . . ."

"You haven't a heart," the Sieur snapped back.

"So much the better—give me the brandy."

Paul poured the brandy and they toasted each other.

"Now, tell me about the trip," Old Pierre said as he settled himself in a chair. "I heard from Charles that it was a profitable one."

"Very profitable."

"It seems to have agreed with you. I hope you learned your lessons well?"

Paul shrugged his shoulders. "I learned a lot if that is what you mean."

"And you like the life?"

"Yes, it's a fine life."

"Go on—tell us all that happened," Old Pierre urged.

Paul enjoyed the part of narrator, though he was frequently interrupted by the older men who had anecdotes of their own to add.

"How soon are you leaving again?" Old Pierre asked.

"I don't know, grandfather," Paul said thoughtfully. "I saw father before I came here—he won't let me come home unless I give up the fur trade. What should I do?"

Old Pierre kicked back his chair and got up abruptly. He walked to the window and stood looking out over the farms. "You know about Marguerite, of course?" he said without turning.

"Yes—I saw her in Lachine," Paul replied.

"You must make your own life, Paul," Old Pierre said. "Jacques is a fine man and this trouble with Marguerite has been a terrible blow to him. But your giving up your ambition will not help. He hardly speaks to any of us and though it would please him if you stayed, it would not make him forget his unhappiness. There are others who can look after the farm—too many others actually. You're the only one who has ambition and some day you will be in a position to help this country—perhaps even to help it grow into something more than the desolate colony it is at present."

"Then you would advise me to continue as a coureur de bois?"

"Yes." The word came out with a snap as though Old Pierre were afraid of hearing himself say it.

Immediately Paul felt a sense of relief. He knew then how bitterly disappointed he would have been had he had to give up the fur trade.

"Stay here with me, Paul, until you leave again," the Sieur said.

"That is very good of you, monsieur."

"Not in the least. I'm lonely," the Sieur said and smiled sadly.

CHAPTER XIV

PAUL STAYED IN MONTREAL less than a week and then set out again with Charles and the men. The St. Lawrence was covered with fleets of canoes, as Indians and coureurs left at the close of the fair. Their songs filled the air and from the banks of the river many of the habitants joined in as they waved their men good-bye. One lone figure stood on the bank by the Boissart farm—a tall, rugged figure with white hair, and Paul's face quivered as' he saw his beloved grandfather. He called to him and Old Pierre shouted back his encouragement. Paul had not seen his father or any of the family during his stay and had been into Montreal only once to get supplies. He had enjoyed his days with the Sieur, though it had worried him to see how feeble he had grown. As they talked through the long evening hours, Paul learned of his many disappointments.

"When I die, the seigneury will revert to the Seminary again as I have no heirs. Unless . . ." He paused and looked at Paul. "Unless I can sell it to one of the habitants who has always lived here. I have the right to sell . . ."

A pair of young and a pair of old eyes met and the Sieur smiled. "I believe you have caught my thoughts, Paul. It is something I have been brooding upon for a long while. My own sons have failed me—I should like to adopt one—*you.*"

"Why, monsieur!" Paul exclaimed. "I was thinking that I could make enough money in the fur trade so that some day I could help you carry out your plans for the Seigneury."

"You know that you and Marguerite have always been my favorites. Perhaps in this way I could make recompense for the trouble my family caused yours. I cannot make you my direct heir—but a little legal arranging making the transfer appear a sale—and I would acquire a son while you would acquire a seigneury."

These arrangements were made but no one was to be told about them for the present. It gave Paul something to work for and made him less unhappy over his father's attitude. Marguerite alone was to share the secret.

When they reached Lachine, Marguerite came to welcome them. As Paul hugged her to him, Charles Péchard watched— jealous of the brother who had the right to do this while he could only stand by. He had asked Paul to try to get Marguerite to see him and Paul had promised he would speak to her. He had reminded Charles of the sodden condition in which he had been during the week they were in Montreal and Charles had defended himself by saying:

"When you told me about de Favien all my hopes died. I drank to forget my disappointment. And then it occurred to me I might be able to help her. I'll behave better if she will give me a chance."

Paul had so much to tell Marguerite that he did not get to the subject of Charles until late that evening. First he was eager to tell her the news of his ultimate inheritance of the seigneury and she was delighted. But when he mentioned the Sieur's idea that she should receive de Favien's share of the profits, she was stubborn.

"I don't want anything that has to do with him," she said.

"But it doesn't come from him," Paul insisted. "Don't you see? The way the Sieur has arranged it, he took de Favien's share in payment of debts and now he gives you this money instead of keeping it himself."

"It's a legal twist, of course, but the fact remains the money was de Favien's and I don't want to touch it."

"Don't be obstinate. You must have something to live on and shouldn't you forget these qualms and think of Jeanne and Louis?"

Marguerite's face brightened. "That would be a solution. Give the money to Jeanne for my keep. I would rather feel that the Sieur was repaying her for helping me, than that I was getting de Favien's share."

"Whichever way you like, as long as the money does some good. I'll talk to Jeanne presently. Meanwhile, there's something else I want to talk to you about—Charles."

"What about Charles?" she asked guardedly.

"He wants to marry you."

"Why?"

"He's been in love with you for a long time. He told me he had looked forward to his return from the last trip because of you. He was deeply hurt that you would not even come and speak to him."

"You told him about little Paul?"

"Yes." Marguerite was silent. "Won't you see him and let him speak for himself?"

"I don't know. I'll think it over. Maybe tomorrow . . ."

"Our time's very short. We have to leave tomorrow morning. Why not see him tonight?"

"I'm so unsettled, Paul. I wouldn't know what to say to him . . ."

"It would do no harm to have a talk with him." She still hesitated. "You didn't even greet him last time we were here."

"All right, then," she said reluctantly.

"You'll find him in the canoe."

She walked down to the water's edge. It was a beautiful night for a rendezvous, with the moon high in the heavens and casting a silvery streak across the rippling waves. The thought crossed her mind how beautiful this moment could have been had she been going to meet someone whom she loved.

Charles saw her coming and stood up in the canoe. As they met, their faces were in the shadow and neither could see the expression of the other.

"It is good of you to come," Charles said and his voice was unusually gentle.

"Paul told me you wanted to see me," she replied.

"Yes. Will you come into the canoe?"

He held out his hand and helped her. As they sat down, the moon reflected upon his face. The impression upon her was not favorable, for his sleek black hair and high cheek bones accentuated his Indian blood.

There was an awkward silence and then Charles said:

"Paul told you how I feel?" She nodded. "I have always loved you, Marguerite . . ."

"I was unaware of it."

"Not entirely unaware of it, surely. Before I left on the last voyage . . ."

"So much has happened since then. Things are not the same."

"I know you have been through great difficulties. That is why I want to help."

"Out of pity, perhaps. No man wants a woman who has an illegitimate child." As she lowered her head, the moonlight touched her burnished hair. With the easy movement of a man accustomed to canoes, Charles moved quietly over beside her and put his arm around her. The movement startled her.

"Do you remember the sleigh ride we took together, Marguerite?" he asked.

"Yes."

"I kissed you then. At the time I thought little of it. You were just the girl next door. But afterwards I found myself thinking about it more and more. I believe it was then I first fell in love with you."

It was difficult for Marguerite to realize that this man talking to her in soft, pleading tones was the wild, dissolute Charles Péchard. Except for a few occasions, when she had talked with him before she had always found him cynical and bitter, bearing a grudge against a world that had never given him a chance.

"I have not led a very exemplary life," he went on, "but I could change if I had something to live for. I have made a fairly good fortune in trading, and if you will marry me, I will give up the woods. I promise I will make my seigneury as fine as any in Montreal. Won't you give me a chance?"

"I can't help feeling, Charles, you are doing this out of pity . . ."

"Why should I be pitying you! For the love of God, Marguerite, can't you see I am the one who is unworthy, not you? Because some scoundrel takes advantage of you . . ." His tone was angry and he stopped. Then in a calmer tone he said: "Marguerite, couldn't we both make a fresh start? We are young and in time the past will be forgotten. We could help each other and little Paul would have a name—even if it's not one that is thought much of at the present."

For the first time Marguerite brightened, for in mentioning little Paul, Charles had touched a vulnerable spot. She turned to him and gave him a weak but kindly smile. His arm tightened around her.

"Don't analyze the situation too keenly, Marguerite. There are too many obstacles if you do. Please say you will marry me."

"Let me think it over while you are away, Charles. I will give you my answer when you return."

"That will mean long months of uncertainty for me."

"I promise you this—I will not marry anyone else."

He thought for a while and then reluctantly agreed. "Very well—only I wish you'd let me hear you say it now."

"I can't, Charles. It's something I have not thought of and I must have time."

"Very well. Will you at least let me kiss you?"

She hesitated and then turned her face to his and their lips met. Charles was gentle—and surprised himself that he could be so, for his love-making had always been brusque. But as he held her in his arms for that brief moment, it was as though he held a bird with a broken wing which must be handled gently lest it suffer further injury. The kiss did not satisfy him for there was no warmth in it.

He walked back to the house with her and when they reached the door kissed her again. Then he returned to the canoe feeling confused and dissatisfied.

CHAPTER XV

MARGUERITE THOUGHT OVER Charles' wish to marry her, and despite the difficulties which it would involve, she decided she had better accept his offer. She could not go on living indefinitely with Jeanne and Louis, and Charles' proposal offered a solution. She did not love him and could not but doubt his promise to reform. Men as hardened as he did not change easily and she felt sure it would be only spasmodic. It would mean living in Montreal in close proximity to a family who would not accept her. Some people would say scornfully: "What else could you expect of her?" She would have to rear her son in an atmosphere where he would soon begin to question why he could not have friends and enjoy himself with the other boys. The prospect was not encouraging.

August came and the weather was freakish, being unusually stormy and sultry. On the night of the fourth, Marguerite went to bed as soon as it was dark and for a few hours slept fitfully. Then she awakened suddenly. She sat up in bed with every nerve in her body tingling. As she listened another crashing peal of thunder shook the house. Beneath the door and through the cracks in the shutters lightning flashed, zigzagging around the room. Storms always upset her, and when little Paul began to whimper, she jumped out of bed and lifted him from his cradle. Her body was hot and clammy and her legs shook. Dropping into the nearest chair she held him to her, crooning until he was quieter. Outside the noise and confusion was terrific. As the downpour of rain turned to hail, battering against the door and making the shutters rattle, Marguerite's nerves reached a tension where she felt she must scream. Trying to control herself, she laid little Paul in his cradle and then lit the tallow candle in the bowl.

Jeanne and Louis came in and their presence helped to calm her, for she was ashamed to have them see her so frightened.

"Bad storm," Louis said and went to see that the shutters were all secure.

"Very bad," Marguerite agreed. "I've never known one to make me feel so nervous."

"It'll be over soon, dear," Jeanne said. "It's beginning to abate now. I'll . . ." She never finished the sentence. Above the waning storm they heard a bloodcurdling yell. The sound petrified them.

"Indians!" Louis said hoarsely. While the two women clutched each other, he rushed to the peephole near the door and peered out. "Mon Dieu!" he exclaimed. As he turned back to them his face was blanched. Outside the yelling increased, mingled with the terrified cries of the villagers. There was no doubting what was happening and no time to be lost. "Quick, the muskets," Louis shouted but the women had already fled to the bedroom. They snatched the children from their beds and rushed back with them.

"Hold him—I must help Louis," Jeanne said and thrust her baby into Marguerite's arms. The two older children clung to their mother's skirts and she had difficulty in disentangling them, until Marguerite collected her wits and, putting the baby into the cradle with Paul, pulled the other children to her.

Louis was frantically loading the two muskets. The rain had ceased and a red glow showed outside as the Indians set fire to the houses. Under cover of the storm the savages had descended upon the sleeping village and were burning and plundering everything in their path. The yells and screams outside increased. Watching through the peepholes, Jeanne and Louis could see dark figures leaping about, dragging people from their houses and murdering them. Their naked bodies streaked with war paint, the savages swarmed everywhere, hacking with their tomahawks and throwing lighted brands into the houses.

There was no hope of escape, for soon the house would be surrounded. What was the use of two muskets against such odds? The three grownups and the children huddled together, Jeanne and Marguerite clutching their babies to them, too terrified even to comfort the crying children who clung to them. Louis looked again through the peephole and saw their neighbors dragged out, their scalps torn off and their child impaled on a spear. He knew then that there was no hope.

He turned back into the room and looked at them. "No—no—I can't let them do it. I'll kill you myself. It is better than having you butchered."

Gripping the musket, he looked appealingly at Jeanne and she understood. He looked at the two crying children who were burying their faces in their mother's skirts. Slowly and with hands which trembled he raised the musket and fired. One small body fell. Then he took the second musket and fired and a second child lay dead. He leaned back against the wall and covered his eyes. Jeanne dropped to her knees, touching the little bodies and crying out in prayer.

As Louis pulled himself together and hurried to reload the muskets, the savages battered on the door. He managed only to reload one before tomahawks smashed through the door and three screeching savages rushed in. The women screamed and hugged their babies to them, while Louis made a last valiant effort to protect them. Placing himself in front of them he raised his gun but the shot went wild. A tomahawk cleaved his head in two. A yelling savage tore the baby from Jeanne's arms and threw it outside, where another savage stuck a spear through it and left it impaled against the side of the house. Jeanne fell forward across the body of her husband. A savage seized her by the hair and dragged her outside, adding her scalp to the others dangling from his belt. On her knees Marguerite tried to plead with them to spare her baby but it was useless. The savage grabbed little Paul and smashed his head against the portals of the door. Marguerite stared horrified and then all was darkness. As she dropped to the ground a savage leapt upon her.

In Montreal they heard it; at Longueil and La Prairie across the river from Lachine they heard it; at every seigneury between Lachine and Montreal they heard it, and within a few hours the news was carried by fast horses to every place east and south of Montreal. Men listened with set faces and hurried their families to safety, for all feared this was but a prelude to a concerted onslaught by hostile hordes all over the country. Those whose property—like that of the le Moynes at Longueil—lay on the south side of the river, hurried their families to the armed forts built on their seigneuries and stood guard in case the havoc should spread across the river.

This was the Iroquois' answer to Denonville for his treachery and it shook the colony. For long months they had feared reprisals and now, before the ripening harvest could be gathered in, the blow had been struck.

That stormy night of August 4, 1689, was the worst massacre the colony had known. Few slept, for the storm kept them restless and they were soon aroused when they heard the firing of the warning cannons from the outlying forts. They rushed to the doors of their farms and saw the red glow in the west. A horseman galloped wildly along the road to Montreal, firing his gun and shouting the news to all of them. He had miraculously escaped the massacre and raced to get help from Montreal.

The shots awakened the Boissart household and Old Pierre and Jacques reached the door together. The horseman reined up for a moment and shouted, "Massacre at Lachine!" and galloped on again.

"Lachine!" they all cried together, for the rest of the family were now aroused. Immediately their thoughts went to Jeanne,

Louis and their children, and Old Pierre thought at once of his beloved Marguerite. He sank weakly on to the seat that flanked the doorway and buried his face in his hands.

Jacques roused the family to action. "We must get to Montreal without delay. Get dressed. I'll harness the horses." When he returned Old Pierre was still sitting there, his limbs trembling as he recalled the horrors he had once endured at the hands of the savages. Jacques looked at him kindly, understanding, and then gently helped him up from the seat. "I will help you dress, father," he said and led the old man into the house.

The boys had collected the muskets and were piling them into the cart by the time Jacques and Old Pierre were ready. They stopped on the way to see whether Pierre and Raoul needed any help and then whipped up the horses, eager to get within the sanctuary of the palisades that surrounded Montreal. On the way they met neighbors hurrying in the same direction and when they reached the western gate there was confusion everywhere. Carts jammed into carts and those on foot were in danger of being trampled, as every anxious family tried to get within the barricades before savages could overtake them.

At every gate leading into the town, the scene was the same and inside the people were wild with terror. Vehicles of all kinds blocked the roadways, standing at all angles and in all directions, for the few police which the town possessed were unable to keep order. Soon the forts were filled and those who were fortunate enough to have friends in town left their carts and continued on foot. The tavern keepers opened their doors and plied their trade while giving refuge to the frantic populace.

Outside the Governor-General's house was the principal place where people gathered, waiting for him to make an appearance. But the Marquis de Denonville remained inside. It was learned that the leading men of the town and the heads of the regiments were with him and all night the people waited for some decision to be reached.

Then the crowd began to murmur and a young man jumped up calling for volunteers to march to Lachine.

"For all we know it is too late to help them but it is not too late to pursue the red devils who have murdered our people. Most of us have relatives there—are we going to stand here while in there"—he pointed angrily to the Governor's house—"they waste precious time debating?"

"No!" the crowd roared angrily and the next moment Jacques Boissart jumped up beside the young man, offering to join him. Raoul and Pierre followed their father and soon all the men had volunteered. Jacques' behavior would have surprised even himself had he had time to think. The shock had now stirred him to action and had brought back his fighting spirit.

As they neared the gate a black-clad figure strode towards them and placed himself beside Jacques. When the crowd saw him they cheered, for the sight of Father Dollier girding himself for action was encouraging to all. The priest, who had once been a captain in a French regiment and had seen action on many of the battlefields of Europe, carried no gun but he had more powerful weapons—his great physical strength and his spiritual courage.

They were a silent group as they marched, the only sound being the crunch, crunch of their feet upon the rough ground. Every face was set and determined—men bent upon revenge and the saving of their families. At the end of three miles they reached the first fort, where two hundred regular soldiers stood ready for the order to march. But their commander was in Montreal, in the conclave with Denonville and they could not move without him. They waited until dawn and then a figure on a horse came galloping towards them. It was Captain Subercase, who, disgusted with the delay in Montreal, had left them to their haggling and had come to join his men.

The early morning sky had cleared as the two hundred soldiers, followed by the hundred armed Montrealers, moved towards Lachine. The sight that met them when they reached their destination made every man draw in his breath. The savages had done their work thoroughly and an indescribable scene of horror lay before them. Some of the houses were still burning and amongst the charred ruins were the mutilated bodies of those who had once been their friends or relatives.

Father Dollier's face was grim as he surveyed the scene and his powerful jaw set. He dropped to his knees and everyone did likewise. His deep voice shook as he prayed to God for help and guidance and for those who had been made prisoners. Then he rose and walked with the others among the ruins, hoping that perhaps there might be some who could yet be saved. Captain Subercase, his face white and drawn, directed his men to remove the human sacrifices that stood impaled on stakes, pierced through with arrows and fastened to the walls, hanging from trees with heads down and scalps severed or lying strewn over the fields, evidence of the horrors of the previous night.

Jacques, followed by his sons, went to where Jeanne and Louis' house had stood. It was a heap of ruins which still smoldered and they knew they were only adding to their agony by looking at it. Yet something compelled them to do so, perhaps a hope they might learn the fate of their loved ones. The first sight that met their eyes was the body of little Paul, crushed as though it had been an eggshell. Then they came across Jeanne's mutilated body and the sight completely unnerved Jacques. He sat down on the ground beside her and wept.

Pierre and Raoul stood beside their father and shared his sorrow. Presently he looked at them. "Have you found any trace of Marguerite?" he asked and they shook their heads. Father Dollier came over and laid his hand on Jacques' shoulder.

"Come away, Jacques," he said kindly. "There is nothing that can be done." He took Jacques by the arm, helping him up, and they walked over to where Captain Subercase was talking to a stranger. The man was without a coat and his face was streaked with dirt. Bloodstains marred his clothes. As they approached Captain Subercase looked towards them.

"Messieurs," he said. "Permit me to present Doctor Menoir. He miraculously escaped the slaughter last night and has been giving me a detailed account of what happened."

Father Dollier, Jacques and his sons exchanged greetings and then listened to the narrative. The doctor told them how he had escaped the massacre by hiding beneath a pile of bodies and as soon as the savages had departed had gone all over the village hoping to be able to save some of those left behind.

"But they had all been too well tortured," he said. "The fiends did their work well. The storm covered their approach and they were on us before we had any idea of what was happening."

"Did they take many prisoners?" Jacques asked.

"Yes—I'm afraid so, though I have no way of knowing. I did not dare move in case they discovered me."

"Doctor Menoir tells me the savages are encamped about a mile and a half distant behind that tract of forest," Subercase told them, pointing to the west. "By this time they will all be stupefied with drink and we should be able to take them by surprise."

"Then don't let us waste any more time," Father Dollier said. As Captain Subercase drew his sword and shouted to all to follow him, Father Dollier walked beside him. Quickly the regulars fell in behind their leader and the armed civilians followed their example.

They approached the forest and were about to enter when there came a command from the rear to halt. Subercase heard it and repeating the order to his men went to the rear to investigate. An officer of high rank was approaching followed by a company of regular soldiers. As Captain Subercase recognized the Chevalier de Vaudreuil, commander of the French forces, his face lit up with delight.

"You come at a vital moment, monsieur. We have learned the savages are encamped just beyond this forest and are stupefied with brandy. We should be able to wipe them out and avenge the massacre of last evening." There was an eagerness in Captain Subercase's voice.

"Thank you, Captain Subercase," de Vaudreuil said. "I carry orders from the Marquis de Denonville." There was something in his tone that made Subercase suspect that de Vaudreuil's mission was an unpleasant one. "The Governor-General's orders are that we are to run no risks and stand solely on the defensive."

"On the defensive! Allow them to recover from their stupor and repeat these horrors?" Subercase exclaimed.

"Those are my orders, Captain. You will please relay them to your men."

"I will not!" Captain Subercase exclaimed, his anger overruling military training. "Do you think these men will stand by and permit this devastation to go unavenged? If we strike now, we can probably surprise them and prevent their undertaking further massacres. More than that, we can free the prisoners which I understand they have taken in quantity."

General de Vaudreuil permitted the Captain to finish his indignant protest, for he was much in sympathy with him.

"You heard the orders, Captain," he said kindly.

"I heard—but I do not have to obey! I have these people to think of—men here who have found their loved one brutally massacred . . ."

"You heard the orders, Captain," de Vaudreuil repeated. "We are soldiers—it is our duty to obey."

"Obey the orders of a man who was too frightened to come out of his house! I would rather be punished afterwards," he shouted. "I will lead these people as a man and not as a soldier."

General de Vaudreuil ignored the statement. "Take Captain Subercase into custody," he said. "The sights he has seen are enough to unnerve any brave man." Then he stepped forward and ordered the soldiers and civilians to return to the village. There were loud murmurings but they had to obey. They marched in silence. Faces that a short time ago had been eager and determined were now sullen and angry. The position of General de Vaudreuil was an unhappy one for he shared Captain Subercase's feelings and was bitter that he had had to carry out such an order. How grave was Denonville's mistake was proven the next day when the savages, having slept off their orgy, sallied forth to perpetrate further massacres.

CHAPTER XVI

THE FIRST THING Marguerite saw when she recovered consciousness was a muscular pair of brown legs against which her face kept hitting. She was being carried unceremoniously by an arm which gripped her around the waist, her head and feet hanging down. The next moment she was flung roughly into a canoe, landing on top of other bodies, and as her head struck the side of the boat she again lost consciousness. Later when she opened her eyes she was lying on the ground surrounded by yelling, whooping savages who danced gleefully around the group of prisoners. At first she thought she had been taken to an Indian village, but when her mind became clearer she recognized the St. Lawrence and knew they had crossed the river and were somewhere along the south bank. From where she lay on the ground, she could see a red glow in the sky and with horror realized its meaning. Raising herself on one elbow she saw naked men and women tied to stakes; some were already writhing in agony as flames licked at their bodies; others waited in terror for the faggots at their feet to be lighted.

Men and women were huddled in groups all around her. Some had recovered sufficiently to pray—pray that soon they might be released by death. Marguerite got to her knees and prayed with them. Was this tragedy which had befallen her punishment for the sin she had committed? She bowed her head trying to reconcile herself to the fact that she deserved her fate. For a few moments her mind cleared and she remembered the last moments at Lachine—remembered her little son being smashed against the door and Jeanne and Louis being slashed to death. A piercing shriek cut into her thoughts and she opened her eyes to see a live body being hacked to pieces, not with quick strokes that brought instant death, but a limb at a time so that the unfortunate victim writhed in the agony of slow torture.

Those across the river heard the terrible screams of the tortured and burning prisoners. For miles the flaming fires could be seen and agonized relatives on the opposite bank fell on their knees and prayed. Night after night this horror went on, as for weeks the savage tribes roamed the neighborhood, swooping down on unprotected settlements, slaughtering and taking as many prisoners as possible. It was by the number of prisoners that the magnitude of the victory was reckoned. Each warrior secured as many as he could so that those in the villages at home could later enjoy the victory. When at last they were satisfied, the savages moved off, brazenly bringing their canoes within sight of Montreal and as a final salute giving ninety yells to indicate the number of prisoners in their possession.

They sent a defiant message to the Marquis de Denonville: "Onontio, you deceived us and now we have deceived you."

Thus they avenged themselves for Denonville's fatal mistake two years before.

The days which followed became increasingly terrible for Marguerite until her mind was so filled with horrible sights that it became numb. It was a mercy it did, for a clear mind could not have endured the suffering. The prisoners were divided into groups and with nine others Marguerite was taken far inland until she lost all sense of direction and time. After what seemed interminable days of traveling, with nights so cold some of them—the more fortunate ones—died from it, they came to an Indian village. Birchbark wigwams were ranged in a circle round a central spot of clearage where stood a raised wooden platform in preparation for the orgy to come. Several huge fires had been lighted and around these the children were dancing. A loud whoop greeted the warriors when they appeared with their prisoners, and men, women, children and numberless curs raced towards them. The dogs nipped at the legs of the unfortunate captives and the children ran around them, pinching them. Then they all formed into two lines—old warriors with faces scarred from battle, grisly old squaws, younger women decorated with ochre and wampum, and the children. All were armed with sharp pointed sticks, clubs and tomahawks and as the terrified prisoners were made to run the gantlet, each one was jabbed and clubbed. The men were pushed forward first and by the time each reached the end of the line he was dripping with blood from his injuries. Some fell before they reached the end and when this happened one of those in line stepped out and dragged the victim by the hair and threw him to one side.

Marguerite was the last in line and had to witness the torture of the others. She was so terrified that when it came to her turn she could not move. She stared before her and trembled, until a savage pounced upon her and tore off her coat. She had only a nightdress underneath for there had been no time to dress on the fatal night. She crouched with her arms folded around her. The savage pushed her forward and as she stumbled and fell, others yelled and rushed upon her, dragging her to her feet and jabbing their sharp sticks into her, propelling her along to the end of the line. By the time she reached there her nightdress was torn to ribbons and blood oozed from a dozen or more gashes. Yet she was not as badly cut as many of them, for the savages had now become bored. Many of them had already turned to the next piece of entertainment.

Those who had fallen had been revived by buckets of water thrown over them. Then all the men were dragged up on to the scaffold and tied to stakes. Indian torture was administered by slow degrees so as to give the greatest amount of pain before the captive was allowed to die. It was not until the third or fourth day that the tribe would be ready to feast upon them. Marguerite now learned how Old Pierre's hands had become such a hideous sight. The savages, young and old, having first consumed plenty of brandy, rushed with blood-curdling yells onto the platform. Each man grabbed a prisoner's hand and began chewing on the fingers. Some took an arrow and, thrusting it through the palm of the man's hand, held it up as though it were a piece of meat on a skewer and then chewed on the fingers. Some first tore off the nails with their teeth, while the older men, whose teeth were not so good, drew on their pipes until the inside of the bowl glowed red and then thrust the men's thumbs into this. If they did not cry out for mercy, then the torture was increased, for it was considered ill luck not to have a captive scream.

Nor were the children merely onlookers. They jumped about excitedly running from one captive to another and when the men called to them to come and "caress" the prisoners they grabbed clamshells and proceeded to tear off what thumbs had not already been mangled.

Two of the women among the prisoners were wives of the men and their agonies as their husbands screamed were terrible. Nor were they permitted to close their eyes to shut out the horror. If they persisted in doing so, their heads were firmly tied against the stake where they were bound. One woman, who could not keep her eyes open to witness such horrors, had splinters run through her eyelids and into her forehead so that she could not close her eyes.

Marguerite watched it all with eyes that were dilated and fixed. It seemed to her such things could not possibly be happening—that these people before her could not be human but some kind of demons let loose from hell. She was so numb with terror that she could not notice she was being watched by a boy about fourteen or fifteen years old. He stood among the savages but took no part in the orgies. He kept moving nearer to her and, taking advantage of a moment when the savages were all intent upon their torturing, tried to say a word of comfort to her. Unfortunately he could not speak French and she was too terrified to realize he had spoken. She was tied to a stake, the remnants of her torn nightdress hanging about her waist. She sagged against the ropes and became unconscious. The boy saw it and, pretending to be callous, said in native language: "I'll take care of her." Jerking her head roughly, he held a cup of brandy to her lips but his hands were gentle. She opened her eyes and for an instant her mind registered surprise at seeing a face with features definitely not Indian. "Have courage," he whispered but she had become unconscious again and did not hear.

The men were now taken down from the stakes and stretched upon the platform, their arms and legs splayed and fastened to pegs in the ground. The children then put red-hot coals or live ashes upon their tortured bodies.

Then came the turn of the women captives, all of whom had fainted. Water was thrown over them and as soon as they had revived they were given brandy. The young braves retired into the largest wigwam, where they sat smoking their pipes around a huge fire in the center. The old squaws dragged the white women to the entrance of the wigwam and thrust them forward between the fire and the circle of men. The first woman was so weak she fell forward into the fire. The braves scarcely took any notice as a squaw stepped in and dragged the woman out of the fire, extinguishing her burning hair. The men took up sharp pointed sticks and prodded each woman as she passed, trying to make her dance. Marguerite longed for death. Again and again the women in front fell down into the scorching fire, only to be dragged out and pushed forward. Soon the braves, tired of pulling them out of the fire and picking them up, tossed them outside where hungry curs pounced upon them.

The atmosphere inside the wigwam was nauseating for there was no opening except at the entrance. The place filled with smoke from the fire and the odor of perspiring and burning flesh was sickening. Around and around Marguerite went, trying to dance rather than have to endure the torture of the sticks that were prodded into her flesh. Her red hair fascinated them and presently a young brave jumped to his feet with a shout. He was a tremendous man with a lithe brown body in which the muscles stood out. He was the Chief's son and in his way was a handsome man. With one hand he grasped her small body and held it above his head, laughing as the heat of the flames scorched her. The other men yelled and whooped as he tucked her under his arm and carried her off to his own hut.

CHAPTER XVII

ERIC WALKER lay on his blanket, his face buried in his arms. He had crept away when the women had been driven into the big wigwam. To have to watch human beings subjected to such brutal tortures and be unable to help them was unendurable. He had had to witness such orgies before, but this time it had been worse because the moment he had seen the youth and beauty of the red-haired girl he had longed to get her away before they disfigured that beauty. Yet it was more than his life was worth to interfere. Only by pretending to sympathize with these Indian rituals, had he been able to remain alive.

Two winters had passed since his capture by the Indians and thus he knew he had been a prisoner for about two years. He had lived with his parents and two brothers in a comfortable home in Schenectady. With his father and brothers he had gone on a hunting trip and, curious to see what was beyond the forest, had wandered away and had been captured. It was his own fault, for his father had repeatedly warned him not to stray away, but he had disobeyed. He had always been a dreamer—yet with this quality had combined a love of adventure—two things which frequently clashed with each other. Had he not been dreaming that day, the Indians probably would not have surprised him. When the savages had pounced upon him, he had been too frightened to make a sound and this probably had saved his father and brothers. Had he screamed they would have rushed to his aid and in all probability would have been captured or slain.

The Iroquois had taken him to the village but to his surprise had not tortured him. It had been a peaceful hunting party and this apparently did not call for the same ritual with prisoners taken in a raid. Moreover when the Chief discovered he was English, he ordered his adoption into the tribe. From the moment of his capture, Eric had but one thought—escape. This he knew he could not accomplish until he had learned where the village was situated. He set himself to appear friendly towards his captors and willing to learn their ways. He had carefully studied their language, and whenever they took him on hunting trips, he observed the paths and surrounding scenery.

From where he lay he could see the entrance to the big wigwam, where the unfortunate women were being made to dance. He heard their screams and dreaded that these might be coming from the red-headed girl. He saw first one lifeless body and then another tossed out. Then the massive frame of Onego, the Chief's son, appeared carrying an apparently lifeless form under his arm. As Eric saw who the woman was he clenched his hands and waited to see the form tossed on top of the others. Instead Onego carried it across to his own hut. Hatred welled up in Eric's heart. Onego had always been good to him but now he wanted to rush in and kill him. In the two years he had been a prisoner, he had seen white women distributed among the men and made to suffer all kinds of indignities until disfigured and tormented beyond endurance.

When the village became quiet, Eric crept out of his hut and, taking great care no one saw him, drew step by step nearer to Onego's hut. The moon shone in through the entrance and he could see the girl where Onego had dropped her. She was huddled up, one arm thrown over her head, hiding her face. She had no covering over her and the whiteness of her body made Eric nostalgic for his own people. For so long he had seen nothing but dark husky bodies and stringy black hair. Even his own skin was now burnished by the sun. Onego lay a few feet away—a gigantic brute reduced to helplessness by too much "fire-water." Eric's hand went to the knife he carried in his belt but he drew it away.

Creeping back to his own tent, he thought long into the night until exhaustion made him sleep. With the coming of dawn he was awake and immediately began thinking of the previous night. The village still slept and Eric knew from experience that after these orgies it would be late before anyone stirred, except the old squaws. To evade suspicion he went first to the hut where the prisoners had been placed the night before. In case anyone should be watching, he had a hard expression on his face as he went in, but the moment he was inside his expression changed to one of deep concern. In one corner the bodies of a man and two women were thrown in a heap and these he knew were dead. The other four men lay stretched on their backs with limbs extended and fastened to stakes in the ground. Eric was not hardened enough to look at these torn naked bodies without shuddering. They were lacerated beyond description and above each wrist tied to a stake was a hand from which every finger had been chewed off. The last "caressings" of the children had left the soles of their feet covered with blisters.

He was violently sick. He had come in to avoid suspicion before going to see what had happened in Onego's tent. Also in the hope that perhaps he might be able to help the captives in some way. The unfortunate men were still alive and groaning. Defying detection, he went for water and gave each one a drink. Beyond that he could do nothing though he would gladly have sunk his knife into each heart rather than leave them to suffer further tortures which would be begun as the sun went down.

Sick at heart, he walked along so that he would pass Onego's hut. At the entrance, Marguerite crouched with a blanket wrapped about her. As he approached her a look of fear came into her face. He smiled at her and her expression changed to surprise and bewilderment. He was a tall lad with fair hair and this alone made him appear incongruous among this horde of black-haired people. He made a sign to her not to move, and having made sure no one was around, he sidled up to the entrance. Deep snores from inside told him that Onego still slept.

"Have courage," he whispered. "I will try to help you."

Marguerite knew from his tone that he was being kind even though she could not understand what he said. Eric's heart sank—they were two white people, yet each spoke a different language. He tried the native tongue but this was equally incomprehensible. He searched frantically in his mind for any French words that he could remember.

"Courage," he said. He tried pronouncing it in several different ways until she finally understood him. Then she smiled —and to Eric it was the sun coming out. Marguerite was as surprised as he to find she could still smile. After the horrors of the previous night she had never expected to smile again.

Eric returned her smile. Then he tried to make her understand he was planning to get her away. It was not easy and he tried all kinds of words. *Escape* she could not understand; *free* was equally difficult; but *assist* and *aid* conveyed his meaning and she nodded to him that she understood. The rest of the conversation was carried on in sign language. Then he saw squaws coming out of their huts and hurriedly moved away.

The conversation heartened Marguerite but as the day wore on she began to lose heart again. When Onego wakened he took little notice of her. Still huddled in the blanket which she had found in the hut, she crouched in a corner. Presently she saw the captives brought out and given food and drink, while incongruously, their wounds were tended. If this gave them hope it was soon gone. The attention was merely to revive them as much as possible so that they would make better sport that night.

"Tie her up also," Onego said. "She might try to escape." He spoke in his native tongue so that Marguerite did not understand, and when they bound her hands and feet and left her for the rest of the day in the hut, she feared what the night might bring.

Night came—and the savages were hilarious with drink.
They first dragged out the bodies of the three who had died
and tore out their hearts. One was given to the Chief, the second to Onego, and the third to the head man. They were devoured with weird and awful sounds that made Marguerite
vomit. Then the bodies were hacked to pieces, placed, head
and all, in a large stew pot and the evening meal was ready.
Marguerite and the other captives were forced to witness these
sights. All of them were now tied, naked, to stakes, ready for the
"exercises" which would begin as soon as the feast was over.
The awful sight was too much for Marguerite and she fainted,
sagging in the ropes that bound her. She remained unconscious until a terrible scream wrenched her back to life. The
men had now been placed on the platform again and lighted
brands were held to different parts of their bodies. One man,
who had refused to give them the satisfaction of screaming,
was cut down from the stake, dragged along the ground and
suspended by the ankles from a tree. Then they cut him up
piece by piece until his heart was torn out of him while there
was still life in his body.

Again the mercy of unconsciousness saved Marguerite from
witnessing all the horrors. She remained unconscious so long
Eric feared she had died. By pretending to be ill, Eric avoided
witnessing as much as possible. Once he had been forced to
eat of these human sacrifices and it had made him dreadfully
sick. Fortunately, his companions were all too busy to bother
about him and he lay unmolested in his hut. It was to his advantage that lately they had become so accustomed to his being
with them that they had relaxed their attention. He had made
his own small hut himself, purposely making is so small that
only one person could get into it, and no objections had been
raised. Now he was glad he had made this subtle move, for it
would have added to his difficulties had he still been in the
large wigwam with the other men.

Marguerite again lay in Onego's hut, bound hand and foot

and hoping death might come to her. Now all the others had been killed, her turn must come and she feared her lot was going to be even worse. She had been made to understand by one of the old squaws, who had brazenly inspected her body, that she would be the concubine of the Chief's son. The meaning had been conveyed by sign language which left no doubt in her mind.

When Onego stumbled drunkenly into his wigwam and stood towering over her, she closed her eyes and waited. Her bound limbs trembled and she uttered a prayer that the end might come soon. Onego grunted and through her half-closed eyes she saw him draw his knife and drop on his knees beside her. She expected him to gouge out her heart and eat it but with two quick strokes he slashed her ropes and dragged her over to his blanket. Then her fear was worse than if he had driven the knife into her flesh. She tried to cry out but no sound came from her throat. It was useless to push her weak hands against his strength. She felt the weight of his great body on her. Then all was darkness as she sank into unconsciousness.

CHAPTER XVIII

When Marguerite next opened her eyes, all around her was pitch black and a dark face was peering into hers. She opened her mouth to scream but a hand was roughly clapped over it and a voice hissed at her. She closed her eyes in terror. Then as her mind began to clear she realized a voice was talking gently to her. Again she opened her eyes and saw she was no longer in Onego's hut but lay beneath a large tree with a blanket covering her. The face that now looked at her she recognized as that of the fair-haired boy who had spoken kindly to her a few days before. What had happened to her in that blank period? She asked the question but he put his finger to his lips and shook his head.

"We must hurry," he said anxiously. "Vite." In these past few hours he had suffered tortures of anxiety, first because he could not bring Marguerite back to consciousness and secondly because, having to carry her, he had not been able to make much progress. Overburdened as he was he had been able to carry her only a short distance. The delay meant precious hours lost, increasing the possibility of capture. Unless they could travel a good way during the night, it would be fatal. In the morning Onego's lifeless body would be discovered. Then the whole village would be aroused from its stupor and take to the warpath to capture the murderer.

Eric had tried to lay his plans carefully but there were, he knew, many flaws, and if they were captured he would be shown no mercy. The uttermost that the Indian mind could devise in the way of torture would be his punishment for having killed the Chief's son. During those frantic moments while he tried to bring Marguerite back to consciousness, he began to regret having let sentiment influence him. There was no reason for him to rescue this woman who was completely unknown to him. He told himself several times that he should have taken care of himself. Then he would not have had to kill Onego and would by now have been miles through the forest. For a brief moment he was even tempted to cover Marguerite carefully and leave her there—but as though to provoke him, it was at that moment she opened her eyes and he knew he could not desert her. He held some brandy to her lips and she swallowed a little, choking as the burning liquid went down her throat.

Desperately he tried to make her understand they must hurry as much as possible. He went through all kinds of pantomime before her numbed mind grasped his meaning. She scrambled to her feet, the blanket falling away as she did so, revealing her nakedness. Quickly she grabbed at the blanket and held it to her as Eric handed her a bundle of clothes. He had stolen a deerskin dress several sizes too large for her and which reached to her ankles. At least it covered her and the moccasins fitted quite well. She swayed a little as she put on the dress, for she was dreadfully weak.

On through the night they tramped, resting at intervals, and when the dawn began to show through the trees, they made their first halt. Marguerite dropped to the ground exhausted and Eric unrolled a blanket and laid it over her. His greatest worry was food, for he had scarcely enough for two days and must rely upon the forest to feed them. He prepared a little now and ate it, putting aside a share for Marguerite when she should awaken. He prayed that the sun would come up for by that he must guide them, and if fortune favored them, in two days they should reach the river where he hoped to be able to make a canoe. He was used to tramping in the woods and was capable of traveling a long time without tiring, but even had Marguerite not had to endure so many hardships since her capture, he did not expect she would have been able to make long treks. His mother had been a strong pioneer woman, capable of enduring almost as much as his father, and perhaps this woman he had with him also came from pioneer stock. That was something he would find out presently. As he looked at her he wondered who she was and what her name was.

When Marguerite was rested, they tramped on, and when the day dawned fine and clear, they made better progress. When he discovered Marguerite could handle a musket he was able to get some rest while she stood watch. They soon began to know enough of each other's language to make themselves understood. They would point to different things as they tramped along—trees, leaves, birds, stones, sky and so on and tell each other their respective names for each. Eric had difficulty in grasping Marguerite's name. The first name was simple, but Boissart as pronounced by her he found himself quite unable to remember. Words and signs made up their conversation, for sentences were still beyond them. It was a fascinating game and it made the long tedious hours pass very quickly.

For three days they made good progress but on the fourth day rain fell. Not only did this soak them but by nightfall Eric knew he had lost his course—and this was what he had most dreaded. That night when he took the first watch while Marguerite slept, he was more concerned than he let her know. As he kept his lonely vigil, no one would have taken him for a boy of fifteen years. His face was lined and the grime had seeped into his weatherbeaten skin. His fair hair was matted and straggly and his clothes as well as Marguerite's were already beginning to suffer from the branches and bushes which snagged and tore at them.

Halfway through the night he woke Marguerite and she took her turn at watching. It seemed to him he had hardly closed his eyes when he felt her shaking his shoulder. She signalled to him to listen and he sat up quickly. The wind had changed and on the breezes wafted unmistakable sounds of Indian warwhoops. Without wasting words they hastily rolled up their blankets, Eric carrying the musket and Marguerite grasping the hatchet. Fear was on their faces, for the dread of capture had never ceased to haunt them. Treading carefully, they made their way as far as possible from the direction in which Eric judged the Indians would be camped. But his knowledge was very limited and many times they had to stop to listen. Sometimes they could hear nothing and then again the sounds would become very clear. They were in the depths of a wilderness and it was impossible to break through the dense growth. Often it seemed they were getting nearer to the Indians instead of farther away. Repeatedly Eric stopped and put his ear to the ground in the hope of being able to detect the direction of the sound. In the darkness the path was scarcely discernible and the crack of a twig in that tense stillness sounded as loud as a shot.

On they tramped, silent and tense, while Marguerite's lips moved repeatedly in prayers for guidance. Suddenly Eric stopped and Marguerite waited behind him, for directly ahead the thicket cleared.

He made signs for her to wait, while he stealthily moved forward to the end of the path and then stood still. Had it not been for their danger he would have yelled with joy, for the river he had been seeking for the past two days lay before them. But—also across the river the Indians were camped and as he stood there wondering what would be best to do, a terrible agonized scream rent the air—the scream of a human being in torture. Marguerite heard it and rushed up to Eric. He put his arm round her to support her and whispered anxiously to her not to make a sound. He could feel her trembling and when a second scream followed by a deep choking sound came through the night, Marguerite broke away from him and fled. Eric hurried after her, fearful that the moon might silhouette them against the night and betray them to the savages across the river. Fortunately Marguerite had fled in the right direction and had so far uttered no sound. As Eric caught up with her, she stumbled and fell. He quickly helped her to her feet and tried to calm her, but the horrors of Indian torture which she had witnessed were too recent and her terror was beyond control. She leaned against him for a moment and then began running again. All he could do was to follow her and hope that the whooping and screaming across the river would drown the sounds of snapping twigs and branches. Again Marguerite stumbled and this time did not get to her feet. Eric lifted her in his arms and continued along the path beside the river. Every muscle in his body ached but he braced himself and strode on, his elation at having found the river buoying him up.

The sounds of Indian revelry became fainter and presently Marguerite was able to walk again. Eric's feet began to drag but still they tramped on, for each time he thought of stopping, the dread that they might not be far enough away from the Indian encampment urged him on. At last they were too exhausted to go farther and when they found a spot well hidden by the trees they stopped. In a moment he was asleep and Marguerite, who had had some sleep earlier, took the musket and sat with it across her knees. That lonely vigil was terrifying and she sat tense and frightened but determined not to give way to her fears. The sound of an animal scurrying through the forest, the drop of a leaf or the movement of a branch in the trees made her heart pound. Every time she saw a shadow she would grip the musket between icy hands and look around from side to side, expecting a dark form to pounce upon her. Her only comfort was to pray and this she did unceasingly.

The sunlight awoke Eric from a deep sleep. Marguerite lay across him, the musket still clutched in her hands. She did not remember when she had dropped off and he smiled at her reassuringly as she tried to explain. They collected their blankets and cautiously returned to the bank of the river. In the early morning light it was very beautiful—a quiet, flowing stream that moved peacefully between banks covered with fir and hemlock.

Eric stooped down, cupping some water in his hands and throwing it over his face. Marguerite did likewise and the water was cool and refreshing. They had no food for breakfast and must rely on what the forest would produce later that day. They followed the bank for several miles, afraid to turn inland lest they lose their course again. There was no pathway and the going was rough but Marguerite followed closely behind Eric, tracing his footsteps. Presently they came to a bend in the river and Eric proceeded cautiously. Before he could stop her Marguerite gave a cry, for coming towards them was a canoe of Indians. Eric grabbed her arm and pulled her behind a tree. But the Indians had seen them and before Eric could decide what to do, a shower of arrows came in their direction, one hitting the tree. To remain behind the tree with the canoe coming nearer was certain death.

"We must run," he whispered hoarsely and, grasping her hand, he turned back the way they had come. Another shower of arrows whizzed past, one grazing Eric's shoulder. He clapped his hand over the wound and they ran on, plunging into the forest at the first opening. Every twig and branch seemed to reach out and tear at them. They raced along without caring in what direction they went. When they had to pause to regain their breath, the sound of twigs breaking told them that they were being followed.

On and on they ran, plunging through thickets and tearing at branches with their hands. There was only one hope—that they might be able to hide themselves in the denseness of the forest, though Eric felt this was practically hopeless since their pursuers undoubtedly knew the forest well. Eric went first, tearing down branches and crawling under others until they came to a clearing. The open space, he felt, would be their undoing. They paused again for breath and he whispered:

"We must make a dash for it." Without waiting to see whether she had understood his words, he grasped her arm and together they raced across the clearing. In another moment they were both gasping as water came up over their shoulders. They had plunged into a hidden pond—a stream the beavers had dammed and covered carefully with weeds and tangled branches so that it had looked like solid ground. Eric's head came to the top dripping with slime and rank-smelling leaves. Quickly he wiped it off with his hand and looked around to see how they could get out. Marguerite had only plunged in up to her shoulders and her face as she looked at him was white with terror. Holding on to her arm, he waded to the edge of the pond and found a surer foothold.

"Crouch down," he hissed and she followed his movements. Raising one arm, he pulled the weeds and branches over their heads. There they waited with water up to their necks, not daring to move to brush off the insects that swarmed over their faces, biting at their eyes and getting into their nostrils.

A twig snapped and they held their breath. Voices came nearer and it seemed to them that the sound of their thumping hearts must be heard. They could hear the voices arguing in a language that Eric knew was some tribe other than the Iroquois. When the voices ceased, he wondered whether with typical Indian humor they were squatting waiting for the fugitives to reveal themselves or whether they had gone away. It grew cold and Eric became concerned over Marguerite. It looked as though they might escape Indian torture only to die of cold and fever. Yet he dared not move or climb out of the pond until he could feel sure their pursuers had left. On the other hand it was impossible to stay crouched in their present positions for very long. Presently he stealthily raised his head to look about him, and as far as he was able to make out all was quiet. He lowered his head again to whisper to Marguerite and as he did so the full force of her weight came against him. His wounded shoulder was nearest to her and as he moved it to support her, the pain was excruciating. The suddenness of her movement also made him lose his foothold and as he fought desperately to get a purchase on the slimy bottom of the pond, he lost his balance and they both went under.

CHAPTER XIX

A WEEK LATER Eric Walker sat crouched before a fire in a deserted hut. He had come to realize there was no limit to what some human beings could endure. He had seen and marveled at this often as he had watched prisoners writhing under Indian torture. He marveled now that he could have come through the experiences of the past few days and still be able to sleep and breathe. For seven days he had waged a fight with death—and now knew he had won, for that afternoon Marguerite had opened her eyes and looked at him, the first sign of recognition during all those harrowing days.

It would always be a miracle to him how he had been able to get them out of that stagnant pond. It had not been so deep but the entangling weeds had held them down and with Marguerite unable to help herself and his left arm almost useless, he had fought a desperate battle. Several times he had managed to get a grip on the bank, struggling to keep Marguerite's head above water, only to have the branches he held break in his hand and his feet slip on the slime. Once he lost his grip on Marguerite and when he regained his hold could not get her away from the weeds so that he was afraid she would be drowned. When at last he was able to clamber onto the bank and drag Marguerite after him, he had dropped across her body and lain there exhausted. How long he had remained like that he would never know. When consciousness returned he was aghast at the sight of both of them. Marguerite's legs and arms were swollen twice their size and as fast as he brushed the mosquitoes off her, further swarms settled back. It made him hysterical and his courage gave way, so that he lay across her, shielding her with his own body and crying in agony and despair. The moment passed and in its place came a desperate urge to get away from that filthy pond with its stagnation and fever. He scrambled to his feet and tried to lift Marguerite, valiantly endeavoring to ignore the burning pain of his wounded shoulder.

"I must do it! I must!" he kept saying and tried to lift his burden. For all he knew she was already dead but he could not leave her there. "Oh, God help me," he cried and, kneeling down, tried again to raise her. He managed to get her body onto his knee and then over his shoulder. It was his wounded shoulder but he had to have one good arm free to get through the forest. For a moment, as he stood up, he swayed and everything around him whirled but he recovered himself and ran rather than walked towards the forest. Desperation drove him as he tore and wrenched at the low-hanging branches—branches which insisted upon encircling him or Marguerite, holding them back, tearing at them, scratching his face, entwining themselves around his feet and making him stumble so that several times he whimpered in his despair. Terror gripped him as he thought of darkness coming before he could reach the river. "I must reach the river—I *must*," he cried. He stumbled on, blood running into his eyes where thorny branches had torn at his forehead, and several times he almost lost his burden as Marguerite's dress became entangled in the branches.

Then the forest cleared and as if by a miracle he saw a hut. He gave no thought as to whether enemies might be concealed in the hut—nor was he able to care. He pushed open the door and, lowering his burden, fell across the threshold.

What happened during the next two days he never would be able to recall clearly. All he remembered was that between bouts of fever and unconsciousness he had managed to get Marguerite onto a bench that took the place of a bed and to build a fire. Somehow he had managed to get her soaked dress off and had covered her with some old blankets which he found in the hut. When his strength returned he heated water in a kettle he found there. Into this he placed huge stones and, when they were warm, put them, wrapped in rags, near her body to drive out the fever. Her body was a terrible sight from the bites of the insects, and as his mind began to clear he searched around for something to counteract the fever and poison. His Indian training was now useful and he searched the trees around the hut for a balsam fir. Gathering leaves and bark from this he pounded them to powder and boiled them in water. The Indian squaws believed this was a cure for all diseases and he forced some of the infusion between Marguerite's lips and drank some himself. The remainder he applied to the infected parts of her limbs and also to his own wounded shoulder, which had now swollen dangerously.

During those first two days he had hardly known whether she was dead or alive, and more than once, spent with hunger and want of sleep, he had thrown himself down beside her and cried out to God. Only a miracle, it seemed to him, could save either of them for he was at the end of his endurance. And a kindly Father wrought the miracle. When he awoke on the morning of the third day, he saw that there was a change in her. Her face was less flushed and that was a hopeful sign. All day long he kept a fire going and as fast as the heated stones cooled, applied fresh ones. He made more of the balsam infusion. It seemed to him, too, the swelling was less, but this he was afraid might be only his imagination.

He was able then to give thought to food and went outside to see what he could find. All that he had had in these past days had been roots which he had dug from the ground, eating them raw and hardly stopping to scrape off the dirt. He had discovered gratefully that they were near the river and wondered whether he could risk fishing. He had learned to spear fish the Indian way with sticks sharpened to points which were then hardened over the fire. He made some sticks and, keeping as much out of sight as possible, waded along the edge of the water. It was not long before he had a pile of shimmering silver bodies lying on the bank and he devoured some raw. The rest he took back to the hut and cooked. When he had finished his first real meal for days he felt considerably stronger.

He found some waterfowl eggs and beat them up, hoping that Marguerite would eat them, but she was still in a coma. If only he had some brandy, but that was out of the question. They had lost every possession they had—blankets, musket and hatchet—and the two ragged blankets that he had found in the hut were hardly sufficient to keep Marguerite warm. He had dried her dress and had piled this on her and everything else he could find, including large strips of soft bark.

He now began to plan what they should do when she recovered. For one thing he fervently thanked God—there had been no intruders and the owner of the hut had not returned.

As he sat outside the hut, he looked with pride at the string of fish drying on a line. He had also collected a good supply of waterfowl eggs, ready for the time when Marguerite would be able to take some food. He was making himself a crude hatchet for he had seen the tracks of deer. These would not only supply food but he could make the hides into clothing. When the hatchet was ready, he waited for the deer to come down to the river to drink of an evening. He did not have to wait long and he watched for a moment or two while they drank. When the leader raised his head and began to sniff the air suspiciously, Eric lifted his arm and took careful aim. The hatchet hurtled through the air and landed in the center of a deer's head. The rest of the herd scattered and he went to his victim, now quivering in the last spasms of life. Grasping the antlers, he dragged the body back to the hut and soon had it skinned and the meat hanging. In the days that followed he killed more deer until he had plenty of food for the future and several skins stretched out to dry.

Marguerite made slow but steady progress. Her fever gradually abated and her swollen limbs returned almost to their normal size. She began to talk but to his disappointment it was in delirium. He listened carefully, but though he had learned much of her language, he still could not understand what she said. She seemed to be worried over a child and this was beyond his comprehension.

It was several days later as he sat on the bed watching her that Marguerite smiled at him. It was the sun coming out after a terrible storm. He took her hand in his and thought how small it looked lying in his large one. Then she spoke his name and he could hardly believe it.

He spoke her name in return and there was recognition in her eyes. Once more she closed them and drifted off into a coma. It seemed hours while he watched for further signs of recovery. Presently, as the room was growing dark, she opened her eyes and smiled at him again.

"You are better," he said and she seemed to understand. "I will get you some food."

He hurried to the fire and piled wood on it. He beat up some eggs and she ate them and also some of the fish.

That night she slept her first normal sleep and Eric rested more peacefully. The next day he knew the crisis had passed and though she was weak, she was able to talk to him and learn what had happened. Eric now began in earnest to prepare for the time when she would be strong enough to travel again. He had begun to make a canoe and hoped that as soon as this was finished they would be able to proceed on their journey. The dress he had made her was crude and he laughed as he handed it to her, but Marguerite took it tenderly, for she realized all that had gone into the making.

CHAPTER XX

SINCE THE NIGHT of the massacre, Montreal had remained in a state of terror as each day reports came of the Iroquois being in undisputed possession of the open country and of parties of savages scalping and pillaging for an area of more than twenty miles around. Behind the palisades surrounding the town, the people remained, crowding the fort beyond its capacity and filling every available dwelling. Still the Governor-General did nothing and the angry murmuring grew louder, until the people threatened to take matters into their own hands. The men crowded each day into Dillon's and the other taverns and tried to formulate plans. What the result would have been no one could have foretold, but at the beginning of October news came that the Comte de Frontenac was on his way back to New France. Actually his return had been arranged before the Lachine massacre but the news had only just had time to reach them. Nothing could have brought greater encouragement, for he was the one man on whom they all knew they could rely. Immediately the tension relaxed and as though he were already there to help them, the inhabitants began to talk of returning to their own farms. When shortly afterwards it was learned that the hostile tribes had taken to their canoes and were returning to their own territory, the exodus from Montreal began in earnest.

Paul had returned home at the end of September. This time there were no canoes heavily laden with beaver pelts, and manned by rugged men singing their lusty songs. Instead it was a single canoe manned by Charles and Paul and bearing two badly wounded men lying painfully in the bottom of the boat. They, too, had encountered the hostile tribes, and though they had succeeded in beating them off, they had lost six of their men and their supply of furs. Charles had sustained only minor wounds but Paul had a badly injured leg.

When they had reached Lachine they were hungry and weary. They had been sustained by the thought that here they could replenish their food supply and get help for the wounded men before making the descent of the Rapids. But they were confronted with charred ruins that told their own story all too clearly. Cries of horror came from Charles and Paul at the same time. There were no words they could utter as they viewed the scene. As the same thought came to each of them they uttered one name—"Marguerite." Hunger was forgotten as in their anxiety they quickly pushed the canoe away from shore and paddled with all the strength they could muster towards Montreal. The sight of every farm they passed added to their distress, for crops lay unharvested and houses were deserted. As Paul passed his home he looked anxiously for some sign of life, but it too was uninhabited, and without delay they went on to the town.

Charles looked after the wounded men while Paul hurried into the town as fast as his injured leg would allow him. The moment he had entered the palisades he was besieged with questions and when he mentioned the word "Lachine" he found they could tell him more than he could tell them. He inquired for his family and was directed to the Fort. Here he found them all huddled together in one room and old feuds were forgotten in the joy of finding him alive. While the younger children clung to him, his older brothers wrung his hands. When he could release himself and go to his mother, he saw that Jacques' eyes were wet and no longer looked harshly at him. Quickly they pieced their stories together as his father and his brothers told him of their journey to Lachine, of the hopelessness of it and how they had been ambushed on the return journey when Pierre had lost an arm.

"And grandfather?" Paul asked anxiously.

"He's a very sick man," Jacques told him. "He collapsed the day we came back from Lachine."

"It was while father was telling him we had been unable to find any trace of Marguerite," Pierre added.

"You mean—she may have been taken prisoner?" Paul asked and his eyes were scared. They nodded. "And only grandfather knows what that means," Paul said and sank down on to the nearest bench. He was weak from the pain of his leg and want of food. Then he crumpled in a heap. When he recovered, his mother was sitting by him.

"Are you all right, son?" she asked.

He moved and a twinge in his leg made him wince. He sat up and shook his head. "What happened? Did I faint?" She nodded. "Come to think of it, I haven't had any food for days," he said weakly and forced a feeble smile. Immediately Marie began preparing a meal for him and when he had devoured it he felt stronger.

"I must go to grandfather," he said and young Etienne volunteered to take him to the hospital.

"Is your leg badly hurt?" Etienne asked him as he limped along.

"It'll be all right after a time. I'll have them look at it while I am at the hospital."

The sight of his grandfather was a shock to Paul. He appeared to have shrivelled so that his cheek bones stood out and one side of his face was drawn down. His eyes, when he looked at Paul, were wide and staring. Paul leaned over the bed.

"It's Paul, grandfather," he said, but there was no reply. "Paul," he repeated several times, and Old Pierre's eyes searched his face. The mouth opened and quivered as he tried to speak and the maimed hands seemed to claw the air. Paul knelt by the bed and took one of the hands in his. "I've come back to take care of you, grandfather." Again the mouth moved and Paul leaned closer, trying to hear the words.

"Marguerite—come—home?" he heard and each word was a struggle with a long pause in between.

"Not yet," Paul said and the white head sank back on the pillow and the faded eyes were troubled.

Paul did not leave his grandfather's side, and though, through the long hours, Old Pierre neither moved nor spoke, the presence of his grandson seemed to help. When Paul left the bedside for a few minutes, the anxious eyes followed him and only when he returned would they close with relief. The family brought Paul his meals and at night he lay down on the floor beside the bed.

A few days after his return, Jacques told Paul they were going back to the farm and the news was a welcome relief. Old Pierre was lifted carefully into a cart and when he saw the farm he seemed to rally. It made it easier for Paul to watch over him, and again and again Old Pierre would repeat the same words: "Marguerite—come—home." At first they had taken it to be a plea for her return but Paul realized it was a question. Each time he would give the same reply, "Not yet, grandfather," and it seemed to him in the long days of watching that Old Pierre clung to life only because of this hope. He would sleep long hours. Each time Paul would be afraid he would slip away during his sleep, and his heart was heavy. The two people who had meant the most to him were gone or going from him. As he sat by the bedside through the long hours, sleeping in the same room and leaving only for short intervals, he thought of his beloved twin sister. It did not seem possible she would not be with him any more. They had always been inseparable, had done everything together and even the thing which had set them apart for a time had been from much the same cause. He wondered, too, what he should do with his life from now on. On the day of their return to the farm, while Old Pierre was sleeping, Paul had stood by his father and had surveyed the devastation. All around was desolation, and the crops which should have fed them through the winter were all ruined and would have to be ploughed under. It would have been the time to remind his father of their argument about the land not being able to support them all, but he remained silent. Jacques had suffered enough and the tragedy of Marguerite had made him an old man before his years. Instead, at the first opportunity, Paul went into Montreal and with some of the profits he had made from his furs bought food and comforts for the family. There was little food that could be bought, for the ships that came in did not bring nearly enough for all. Paul purchased what he could, and when the food appeared on the table, he saw a strange look come into his father's face, but he did not refuse to eat and Paul was satisfied.

The days seemed very long to Paul and he constantly thought of the long winter of idleness ahead of him. It was not a pleasant thought and he made up his mind that if his grandfather had passed away when spring came, he would go into the woods and perhaps stay away for a year or more. Then when he had made enough he would return and perhaps could help the Sieur with the seigneury. He was much worried over the Sieur. Marguerite's tragedy had not only aged him too, but had brought on a severe heart attack so that he was now bedridden. Paul had been able to see him only a few times and the Sieur was worrying because his own ailment prevented his seeing Old Pierre. Whenever Paul could get away, he hurried over to the Manor House and gave the Sieur the news, although there was really no news he could give him except to say that his grandfather's condition remained unchanged. During these months this became Paul's life, divided between two aged men both of whom were bedridden.

Shortly after their return to the farm he had wondered about Charles and had gone over to see him. What he saw did not please him for Charles had returned to his old habits, even to the presence of a young and slatternly Indian girl in the house. Charles had greeted him sullenly, and rather than get into an argument, Paul had left in disgust. Nevertheless it worried him during the many hours in which he had nothing to do but think. Charles had been so different on their treks together and he had grown quite fond of him. It was because of this that Paul went to see him again, hoping he would find conditions better. But they were not. The house was still filthy and untidy and empty bottles gave evidence of the amount of brandy being consumed. This time Paul remonstrated with him and as he talked Charles eyed him bitterly.

"Leave me alone. I am going to lead my own life and no one is going to interfere."

"I thought you had decided to change all that."

"It was changed for me again. Whatever shades of my father's ancestors may have tried to make a better man of me have now all departed. They lay in those charred ruins we saw at Lachine. At the very first sight of spring I am leaving these parts *forever*. What do I want with a seigneury? You can have it, my friend. I will bequeath it to you or sell it to you or whatever has to be done with a seigneury here. But I shall never return again to darken the shores of Montreal. I only wish to God this winter were over!"

And Paul had left him alone. There was so much of despair contained in Charles' words that he could not argue with him. He had not actually mentioned Marguerite's name, but Paul remembered how Charles' face had looked that day at Lachine when they had surveyed the ruins, and he knew how much he really suffered. The depression which Paul had felt lately became deeper, and he stood for a while watching the River that was already beginning to look wintry, although it had not yet frozen over. Dusk was falling but he stayed there thinking for a little longer, for there was peace in the stillness. As he looked towards the water he was surprised to see a canoe drawing into the shore. Someone was getting out, and uttering an exclamation of annoyance Paul strode towards them, sure that he had surprised his younger brothers out much later than their father would have approved.

"What are you doing out this late?" he shouted in a big-brotherly voice. There was no answer but the one on the shore bent to say something to the one in the canoe. Paul wondered what story they were concocting between them, and though he was looking stern, he knew very well he would support them in it. He shouted to them again and this time the one on the shore came slowly towards him. He opened his mouth to give the proper reprimand but the words froze in his throat.

"Paul—don't you know me?" a voice said, and unless his imagination was playing tricks with him, there was no mistaking the voice. For a moment he stood still and then with long strides covered the distance between them. "Marguerite!" he cried, and as she stretched out her arms to him, he caught her as she fell. He picked her up and ran shouting towards the farm.

Eric Walker watched with sad blue eyes—watched while people poured out of the farm and gathered around the form in Paul's arms. Then, satisfied he had fulfilled his mission, he turned the canoe and quietly paddled away into the night, hoping that in the darkness he could make his way safely from this hostile shore and reach English territory without being captured.

CHAPTER XXI

THE NEWS THAT Marguerite Boissart had escaped from the Indians quickly spread through Montreal and to the outlying settlements until finally the story reached Quebec. Furthermore when it was learned she was not frightfully mutilated, questions began to be asked and people flocked to the farm eager to get firsthand news of the escape. Also those who had lost close relatives or friends in the massacre hoped to learn exactly what had happened. All, however, had to wait for several weeks before Marguerite could be questioned and then only for a little while at a time. She suffered a complete collapse and there were days when her condition was so serious they feared she might have reached home only to die before anyone, even her own family, could know her story. For days she lay in a coma and when she came out of this a new fear haunted them—that her mind might be deranged, for she talked in incoherent sentences and many times let out fearful screams that made them all shiver. In the derangement of her mind it was evident she still thought she was in captivity and sometimes struggled to get out of bed, fighting with her fists when they tried to restrain her. Paul was able to do more to calm her than anyone, and he hardly left her bedside, except to sit for a while with his grandfather. Day and night he devoted his time to them, reluctant to leave them even to get some rest himself.

The effect upon Old Pierre was immediate. On the night of Marguerite's return, as soon as Marie had her comfortably in bed, Paul went into Old Pierre's room and waited for him to waken. Then, gently, he told him the news. He repeated it several times to make sure it had penetrated the old man's mind. Old Pierre said nothing, but a contented smile crossed his face, and with a sigh he went to sleep again.

As soon as Marguerite had recovered sufficiently for Paul to leave her for a little while he hurried to break the news to the Sieur and to Charles. He went to the Manor House first and tears rolled unrestrained down the Sieur's face when he heard the news. "Mother of God, be praised," he said. And then instantly his face became anxious again. "Is she . . . mutilated?" he asked, and Paul shook his head. "It's a miracle!" the Sieur said and from that day he, too, began to recover.

As Paul crossed the Péchard land, a feeling of revulsion swept over him. His feet caught in entangling weeds as he walked up what had once been a path. The interior of the house was nauseating. Empty bottles lay all over the place and the dirty squaw who had opened the door to him had made no effort whatsoever to clean up the mess. Charles was sitting in front of a miserable fire and looked as though he had not shaven since the day they had returned. Paul was so disgusted that he hesitated whether to tell him about Marguerite. Charles merely looked up at him as he came into the room and then continued staring sullenly into the fire. Paul leaned on the mantlepiece, the disgust he felt written on his face. Presently Charles said petulantly:

"Well, what do you want? If you've come over to preach, you might as well save your breath . . ."

"I came over to tell you some news but I'm trying to make up my mind whether you're worth telling it to," Paul answered.

"Please yourself," Charles replied and reached for the brandy bottle. Paul swung out and sent the bottle spinning out of reach, the contents splashing over the floor.

Charles swore and shouted at him. "Get out of here and let me alone, will you?"

"That's just what I'm going to do," Paul said angrily and strode towards the door. When he looked back, Charles had slumped into his chair and because he had learned to know him while they had been in the woods, Paul had a moment of pity. He hesitated and then said: "I came to tell you Marguerite has returned."

"Paul!" Charles shouted and jumped to his feet. Paul came back into the room. "What did you say?" Charles asked.

"I think you heard."

"Is this your idea of a way to make me pull myself together? You wouldn't joke over a thing like that . . ."

Paul walked over to Charles and put his arm across his shoulder. "No, I wouldn't joke over a thing like that. Marguerite has returned, Charles . . . she is very ill, but we think she will recover."

Charles dropped into the armchair again, his hands covering his face and his shoulders shaking. For some time he sat there trying to get control of himself and Paul did not disturb him.

"When can I see her, Paul?" he asked presently.

"I'll let you know as soon as it's possible. She is very weak and as yet we don't know how she escaped."

"I can hardly believe it. Marguerite . . ." He said her name softly. "Let me see her soon, Paul. It means so much." The bloodshot eyes that looked up at Paul were full of unshed tears. The blotchiness of the skin and the straggly black beard made him a pathetic object.

"I'll arrange it just as soon as I can. Meanwhile . . ." Paul put his hand on Charles' shoulder. "Try to get yourself straightened out. You wouldn't want her to see you like this."

Charles shook his head and soon afterwards Paul left him to his thoughts.

As Marguerite began to recover she was able to tell Paul a little of what had happened, but the memory distressed her so that, fearing a relapse, he did not encourage her to talk. Little by little he was able to piece the story together but there were still many gaps to be filled in.

It was the afternoon after he had seen Charles that she startled him with a question.

"Where is Eric Walker?" she asked.

"Eric Walker?" he asked with surprise for it was a name he had never heard before.

"Yes . . . he brought me here . . . he was in the canoe with me."

In a flash Paul remembered the other figure in the canoe and felt guilty for not having thought of it before.

"I owe him my life, Paul. We must find him. It was he who rescued me from the savages and when I nearly died he nursed me back to life. We must find him. He is English and it would be awful if he were captured again. The people here—they hate the English. We must find him." She clutched Paul's arm as her hysteria rose. He tried to calm her by talking gently and reassuringly.

"I will search for him, dear. Please don't worry." And then he added rather apologetically: "You see, dear, you collapsed in my arms that night and we were all so astonished and excited at finding you alive that everything else was forgotten."

"But you will find him, Paul? He must not be captured again. He has been through so much. Please, Paul . . ." Tears coursed down her cheeks. Paul took her hand in his and patted it comfortingly.

"I promise you I will do everything to find him. Can you tell me what he was like?"

"He was fair and tall, very tall for his age—he was only fifteen . . ."

"Only fifteen . . . and rescued you from the savages!"

"Yes . . . he was marvellous. He seemed so much older and he was wonderful the way he took care of me. I can't remember now—some day perhaps I can tell you all of it."

"Don't try to tell me now, dear, it will only upset you. We are not worried as to how you escaped—only thankful that you are safe."

"Yes, but, Eric . . . he may not be safe. He had scarcely any food in the canoe and was quite exhausted. Oh, Paul . . . do you think they may have captured him again? I tried to get him to let me go my own way the moment we reached French territory . . . but he would not leave me. We . . . must . . . find . . . him." Her head dropped back on the pillow and Paul watched her face anxiously.

This was a new turn in events and he wondered anxiously what could have happened to her rescuer. It was certain he was not in Montreal or the vicinity or they would have heard about it. He might possibly be hiding somewhere and Paul began thinking how he could organize search parties. He did not want to leave Marguerite alone too long—and then his face brightened as he thought of Charles. Here was something that Charles could do for Marguerite, something that would keep him busy while he waited until she was well enough to see him.

The next day he went over to Charles and was relieved to see the change in him. Though his face still showed evidences of his dissipation, he had shaved and had put on clean clothes. The squaw was not there and some attempt had been made to clean up the house. Paul told Charles about Eric Walker and readily he undertook to try to find out what had happened to him.

Inquiries in Montreal proved negative. No one had heard any mention of a young English boy being in those parts, and knowing how news spread, Paul gave the name to everyone he spoke to and asked them to be sure that if they heard of an English boy by that name being taken prisoner, to let him know and also, if they could, to see he came to no harm.

As soon as Marguerite saw Paul the next day, she inquired whether he had been able to trace her friend. Her face clouded when he told her he had been unsuccessful, but brightened again when he told her that Charles was going to take out search parties. This gave him an opportunity to talk to her about Charles. She listened quietly while he told her of the many fine qualities he had discovered in Charles on their trips together, omitting any mention of the condition he had been in since their return.

"I believe much of Charles' behavior is because he has never had anything much to live for," Paul said. Still Marguerite did not answer. "He wants to see you, Marguerite—very much."

"Some time, perhaps," she said.

Paul was quite concerned as to how he was going to arrange for Charles to see Marguerite. He knew it would be quite impossible for him to come to the house, for some of the family were always there. The best that Paul had been able to devise was for Charles to come to her window at some prearranged time and perhaps that would satisfy him until she was better.

Charles was gone a week searching for Eric Walker. He had found several men willing to go with him and Paul waited anxiously for their return.

It was on a Sunday afternoon and they had finished their midday meal, when a knock came on the door. Young Etienne opened it and then stared with his mouth open as he saw Charles Péchard standing at the door. He had shaved and was neatly dressed. Jacques looked up and when he saw who it was his face clouded angrily.

"I am not aware, Monsieur Péchard," he said in a deliberate tone, "that I have ever given you permission to come to this house."

Charles had expected this and replied in a tone of studied politeness. "That is true, monsieur, but I had hoped that recent circumstances might have changed that."

"What circumstances?" Jacques asked coldly.

"Marguerite's return," Charles said quietly.

"And what has that to do with you?" Jacques asked. Before Charles answered, the door of Marguerite's room opened and Paul came into the parlor. He had heard voices and thought he recognized Charles' though it hardly seemed possible. For a moment he was alarmed that Charles might have been.

drinking and out of bravado had come to the house, but he appeared sober.

"Charles!" he exclaimed and glanced quickly at his father.

"Paul. I . . ."

"Were you able to find out anything?" Paul asked anxiously.

Charles shook his head negatively. "No trace at all."

In the hope of making Charles' visit more welcome, Paul turned to his father to explain.

"I told you about the boy Eric Walker who brought Marguerite home. Charles and some other men made up a search party to see if they could find him."

Jacques stared hard at his son. "Why did you not ask your brothers to undertake the task? This man has nothing to do with our family. I . . ."

"But I have, monsieur," Charles interrupted. Jacques turned towards him angrily. He did not like to be interrupted. "Before she was captured, Marguerite had promised to be my wife."

There was a moment of dead silence and then Jacques said slowly, "Your . . . wife . . . !"

"Yes, monsieur, I have loved her for many years. I know that in the past you have had many reasons to disapprove of me. But I assure you that is all over and I shall lead an exemplary life from now on."

A vision of the degraded, sullen individual he had seen only recently crossed Paul's mind but he thrust it away. Jacques turned to Paul again, his eyes blazing.

"So! This is what you have been up to! Not content with leading the kind of life you know I heartily disapprove of, you involve your sister with a man who since his birth has led a life of utter degradation. I had thought better of you, Paul."

It was the first time any word had passed between Paul and his father about their former quarrel. Before he could answer, Charles spoke.

"This has nothing to do with Paul, monsieur. I have loved Marguerite for many years . . ."

"And now you would like her to become one of your squaws, I suppose?" Jacques sneered. "I am surprised you even mentioned marriage. It has not been a custom with the Péchards to bother about marrying their women!"

Jacques' words were hard, and Charles' eyes became two black darts.

"I appreciate how you feel, monsieur," he said in a controlled voice. "Our reputation has been very bad but the worst of us can reform. I do not want to add to your burdens at this time; all I can say is that our religion teaches us forgiveness . . ."

"Our religion!" Jacques replied, his voice rising angrily again. "You and your father have been outside the church as long as I can remember."

Paul felt that Charles was overdoing it a little. This humble, sanctimonious attitude did not befit him very well.

"But that does not prevent my coming into the church now, monsieur. I saw Father Dollier about a week ago and talked with him."

"Do you really expect me to place my daughter in your care after all she has already been through? You really expect me to sanction such a marriage? You think I believe you will reform? Such as you do not reform. Drink and women have been your life and unless I am mistaken were still your life up to a week or so ago." Jacques paused to let this sink in and Charles looked uncomfortable. "You are even the product of an irregular union between your own father and an Indian squaw," Jacques said contemptuously, "and I'll thank you to leave this house."

Charles' jet-black eyes did not flinch when Jacques arraigned him as a bastard, though the twitch of his mouth told Paul the accusation had hurt.

"I'll not argue with you, monsieur. I admit we have been worthless—but a man can change, particularly when he loves a woman as I love Marguerite."

"He deserves a chance to prove himself, father," Paul said quietly.

Jacques gave him a scathing look. "Using your sister as an experiment?" He turned to Charles, his face twitching angrily. "Please leave this house before I lose my patience. If you ever set foot in it again, I warn you, I shall not hesitate to use my gun."

At this threat two red spots began to glow in Charles' cheeks and Paul could see his control was beginning to break. He wished Charles had not tried to force the issue in this way.

"Please allow me to see Marguerite for just a moment," Charles asked, "and then I will go quietly and I promise I will never intrude again."

"Leave this house at once," Jacques said and his tone was ugly.

Paul had left Marguerite's door slightly ajar and now imperceptibly he put his foot behind him and touched the door, so that it appeared to swing open of its own accord. Inside, Marguerite was lying against her pillows, her red-gold hair spread out and her eyes closed. Charles' expression changed when he saw her and for a moment he stared in awe. Then before anyone could stop him, he darted past Paul and was inside the room, kneeling beside the bed and kissing her hand. As he touched her she opened her eyes and a faint smile crossed her face.

The movement had been so sudden Jacques had no time to intercept it and Paul had made no effort to do so. As soon as he could collect himself, Jacques jumped from his chair, but the sight of Charles kneeling beside Marguerite's bed, with such a profound look on his face, made Marie restrain him.

"One moment, Jacques," she said. It was so unusual for Marie to interfere that even Jacques was surprised. By the time he had recovered, it was all over. Charles rose to his feet, straightened himself and walked past his staring audience and out of the house.

CHAPTER XXII

WINTER BEGAN to fold its icy veil over Montreal and the inhabitants settled back for the long idle months. The last vessel had left for Quebec and for the next five or six months there would be no news from outside. There was much for idle tongues to chatter about. In the taverns the men talked of the Comte de Frontenac and there was satisfactory praise in most of their remarks; in the homes the women also discussed the political situation and gossiped about their neighbors, the gossip still centering with much interest around Marguerite Boissart. A few of the women who knew the Boissarts intimately had been to see Marguerite and had talked with her, but she was still too weak to relate her experiences and so throughout Montreal there spread fragments of her story, enhanced each time they were repeated by the imagination of the teller.

Not all the settlers were as charitable as their pious upbringing should have made them and more than one of them voiced the opinion that her capture at Lachine was what she deserved. To these people she was a woman who had strayed from the path of virtue and no amount of repentance could ever wipe out the stain. Some even went as far as to call her a *prostituée* and a wanton while others doubted whether she had ever been captured by the Indians. The news that she had been brought safely home by a young Englishman was twisted until some said she had run off with a man before the Lachine massacre and had lived with him in the woods, using the massacre to cover up her behavior. In support of this theory they pointed to the absence of wounds.

"We all know no one ever escapes from the Indians completely unharmed, especially when they are taken to the villages," one woman assured her listeners.

"Why, of course," they agreed. "Look at her grandfather—he escaped but was badly mutilated."

"Are there no scars at all?" a more charitable neighbor inquired.

"A few minor ones, they say. And we all know those savages always disfigure white women."

Others, who were willing to admit that she had been captured during the massacre, sneered because her rescuer was a man. "What were they doing in the woods for two months?" these asked and when someone added that it was said Marguerite had lived in a hut with Eric, pious eyebrows went up. "What would you expect?" they asked. The fact that Eric was only fifteen years old was ignored and as the tongues wagged the story grew.

Of all this Marguerite was fortunately ignorant—at least until she was able to appear in public again. Then she noticed that some of the women averted their eyes and drew their children hastily from her path as though she would contaminate them. These gestures hurt her though they were compensated to some extent by others who were more tolerant and willing to forget her past sins and give her a chance; while a third group even went to the opposite extreme and regarded her as a heroine for having endured such a terrible experience.

Her greatest happiness was the day when Sister Marguerite and Father Dollier came to visit her. The sight of these two who had befriended her when she was in trouble brought tears to her eyes. Sister Marguerite seldom traveled outside Montreal any more, for she was nearly seventy and growing frail. Father Dollier brought her out in a carriole.

When Marguerite saw the gentle little lady in black standing in her doorway she held out both arms and in a voice full of joy cried: "Mother!" For several minutes Sister Marguerite held her in her arms and then sat by the bed, one hand resting in hers.

"It is so good of you to have come all this way to see me," Marguerite said gratefully.

"I was so happy when Father Dollier offered to bring me . . ."

"Is he here too!" Marguerite exclaimed.

"Yes, my dear. He will come in and see you before we leave. We were both so overjoyed when we heard you had been returned to us."

"It is almost unbelievable. I never thought it possible I would get back alive. They tortured the others so horribly and the journey back was terrible . . ."

"We prayed for you unceasingly, my dear, and God was good to answer our prayers."

"Indeed He was. It was a young English boy named Eric Walker who rescued me. He was so good to me, and so patient. Many times it seemed as though I would succumb before we reached here. He nursed me through fever for weeks. And now, I don't know what has happened to him. It worries me so."

"Paul told us about him. The Holy Mother will protect him. We will offer up prayers for his safety every day."

"I have, and I shall never cease praying for him."

They talked for a long while and it was the first time Marguerite had given a complete account of all her adventures.

"Have I atoned for my sin now, Mother?" Marguerite asked anxiously.

"Indeed you have, my dear. And God has shown He has forgiven you by bringing you safely back to us."

"Thank you," Marguerite hesitated before asking the next question. Then she said: "Charles Péchard wants to marry me. Would that be wrong?"

"Charles Péchard?" Sister Marguerite said and there was concern in her voice.

"He wants to lead a better life and believes I can help him."

"I had heard that from Father Dollier," Sister Marguerite said and smiled faintly. "Has he spoken to your father?"

Marguerite's face looked anxious. "Father disapproves of him very much. He has forbidden him to come to the house. It would be wrong of me to go against father's wishes, wouldn't it?"

"Yes, dear, particularly after all the trouble he has already been through. I would consider the matter very carefully before making my decision. Do you love Charles?"

"No . . . but . . ."

"Do nothing hastily. Think it over very carefully, my dear."

Marguerite did think it over very carefully, long after Sister Marguerite and Father Dollier had gone. She had not seen Charles since that day he had thrust his way in. Paul had brought her a note from him every day. It was a decision she found very difficult to make. She had told Charles at Lachine she would marry him, yet knew she was not in love with him. Having returned to the good graces of her family, she did not want to displease them again, but there was an urgency in Charles' notes that could not be ignored. She procrastinated as much as she could and a series of events helped her to delay the matter.

The first day Marguerite was strong enough to get out of bed, Paul helped her to her grandfather's room. She walked unsteadily to his bed and fell into the arm which he held out. His left arm he could not move but his right held her in a strong embrace, while the tears coursed down his wrinkled cheeks. As she sat down by the bed he clutched at her hands and looked at them anxiously, and his expression was one of great relief when he saw they had not been mutilated.

"They did not injure me, dear," she said.

"Thank God for that. I was so afraid," he said. To Marguerite this complete sentence gave no surprise for she had not known her grandfather had not spoken since he had received the news of Lachine. The words came out unfalteringly and Paul went to tell the rest of the family about it.

Those were the last words he spoke. As Paul had surmised, the old man lived only to see Marguerite return safely and then was content to slip quietly away. All the rest of the day Marguerite sat with him, ignoring her own weakness. He lay there, his white head sunk into the pillow and a smile of contentment on his face. Somehow, Marguerite knew when his spirit had left, although outwardly there was no change. There was something so peaceful about him that she did not hurry to call the family, but sat there quietly holding the hand which gradually grew colder.

"Good-bye darling," she whispered. "Maybe it was you who brought me back. I shall always think that in those silent weeks while you have lain here you have been communing with God and guiding me back. I shall always love you and always remember you. Good-bye."

She bent and kissed the hand she held and her tears warmed it. Then she got up slowly and opened the door. The family looked up and her face told them even before she spoke.

"Grandfather has gone away," she said quietly and Paul hurried to help her to a chair.

As soon as Marguerite was well enough to go out, Charles' notes begged her to arrange to meet him somewhere. During these winter months that would keep him in Montreal, Paul devoted much of his time to the Sieur de Courville and the remainder to Marguerite. When he handed her the note from Charles asking her to meet him, she turned to him for advice.

"What shall I do, Paul? Do you think I should marry Charles?"

"How can I answer that? I wouldn't want to influence you."

"I know, it isn't fair to ask you. But I am so confused. I know him so little; only what other people have told me and what you have added."

"Then why not see him? Perhaps that will help you decide."

"But—father?"

"Yes, that is the difficulty." Paul shook his head anxiously.

"What is Charles' home like, Paul?" she asked curiously.

"Why not go and see for yourself?" he parried.

"That would certainly make father angry! Has he said anything to you about Charles since that time he came here?"

"Nothing. He scarcely speaks to me at all. He blames me for it."

"Why do you and I always seem to be doing things the family don't like?" She laughed nervously. "Perhaps I had better write Charles a note and tell him it is impossible because of father. I've already caused so much trouble."

"I think you should see him instead of writing. It's only fair to him. He has been trying very hard to behave himself and it's all because of you."

"How am I going to arrange to see him?"

"Leave it to me."

The following Sunday Paul had it all arranged. Sunday afternoons had always been their one chance to get away from the family, and on the pretext of taking Marguerite for a sleigh ride, Paul had been able to arrange the rendezvous. He did take her for a short ride, but on the return journey took her to Charles' home.

"To his house!" Marguerite had exclaimed when Paul had told her his plan.

"Yes. You said you wanted to see it."

They entered on the side away from the Boissart homestead and hoped they had not been seen. Charles' appearance certainly bespoke the effort he had been making and Marguerite was agreeably surprised.

"Welcome to Péchard Manor!" he said as he took her hand, his black eyes burning as he looked at her. "I was afraid you would not come. Come and warm yourself by the fire. Your hands are cold."

Paul found the room almost unrecognizable. In the idle months Charles had repaired the broken furniture, and instead of the miserable fire that he had usually seen, a bright one blazed in the hearth. The entire house had an elegant appearance that it had never shown before and Marguerite did not fail to admire it.

"Your home is charming," she remarked to Charles as he removed her fur coat.

"I had hoped you might find it so," he said and the significance of the words did not escape her.

Paul left the room, knowing they wanted to be alone. The moment he had gone, Charles sat down beside Marguerite and, taking her hands in his, began covering them with kisses. She did not withdraw them, although it made her feel uncomfortable. It was going to be impossible to tell him what she had intended, if he were going to continue kissing her hands.

"Oh, Marguerite," he murmured, "it has been so long. Don't keep me waiting forever."

He looked up at her appealingly.

"But, Charles, I . . ."

"No. . . ." He put his hand up and covered her mouth. "No, don't say you have changed your mind. I couldn't bear it. You must marry me, Marguerite. It's the one thing I have to live for. Don't you understand? You must." Again he was smothering her hands with his kisses and she did not know how to answer. She stared into the fire and watched the flickering flames, thinking how much they reminded her of the jumpiness of her own heart.

"Won't you answer me, Marguerite?" he pleaded.

"How can I, Charles? I can't hurt father again. And living next door . . . it would be impossible."

"Then let us leave Montreal and go to Quebec. I will do anything you want, just so I can have you."

"Go to Quebec!"

"Wouldn't you like that? It is a much gayer life there and I would give you beautiful clothes to wear . . ."

"Are you trying to bribe me?" she said with a smile.

"I am trying to do anything, say anything, so you will marry me . . ."

"But we couldn't go to Quebec until the winter is over," she hedged.

"Then marry me secretly and we will go as soon as the ice melts."

"You're being foolish. You know it would be impossible to be married secretly in Montreal. Everyone knows us and besides there is no priest who would do such a thing."

"I know," Charles said helplessly. The suggestion had, however, given Marguerite an idea.

"Wait until the winter is over and then perhaps Quebec might be the solution," she said.

Charles' face brightened and then clouded. "All those long months . . . ?"

"I know you so little, Charles. In those months I would try to see you as often as possible and we could get to know each other better."

"And you won't let me ask Father Dollier to marry us before then?"

"You know he wouldn't without father's consent!"

"Not if we told him our side of the story?"

"No, it's quite out of the question."

Charles stood up and, leaning on the mantelpiece, looked down at her. His eyes were flaming as he watched her and he swallowed with difficulty.

"Always so many difficulties. I'm so afraid I shall lose you." He sat down on the arm of the chair, his black eyes searching the depths of her greenish-blue ones. He did not speak but his nearness seemed to vibrate through her. Then he drew her to him and pressed his lips against hers. He held her mouth a long while and for a moment his hand touched her breast but he drew it away quickly. Then he released her abruptly and walked over to the window, his back turned to her. Marguerite watched him, wondering what quality this plain little

man with the hard features had, which always stirred her so
much. She was trembling and afraid to move. Charles turned
back into the room.

"I'll call Paul," he said, but as he passed her to go to the
door, he stopped. He gave her a half smile. "Not angry with
me?" he asked.

She shook her head and smiled back.

"Don't keep me waiting too long," he said. "I want so much
more than that kiss."

CHAPTER XXIII

DURING MARGUERITE'S CONVALESCENCE the Comte de Frontenac had reached Montreal. News of the Lachine disaster had been given him as soon as he arrived in Quebec, and despite the lateness of the season, he continued up the River. The quay at Montreal had been crowded with people awaiting his arrival and the moment he appeared, every throat gave a cheer that came right from the heart. He was the personification of what they most needed—a man who was fearless, an indomitable leader and above all one who possessed the faculty of knowing how to handle the red men. He had about him an air of distinction, his manners were those of a grand seigneur and he was elegantly dressed, for no one knew better than he how to impress. He was a man of contradictions and at times his arrogance, boastfulness and quick temper outweighed his finer characteristics, but these were details that could be forgotten at this critical time. He had grown stout in the seven years of idleness in France but beneath his bushy white eyebrows his eyes burned fiercely. This return was not only a personal triumph but a triumph over his ecclesiastical enemies who had forced his recall to France. It was also a triumph over the French King, who for seven years had ignored the Comte and had left him to idle away his time at Court without the slightest recognition. Then had come the day when Louis XIV had sent for him and the stern old soldier, now nearly seventy years old, had faced his monarch with a proud and steady countenance.

"I am sending you back to New France," the King had told him. "I know you will serve me as well as you did before and I ask nothing more of you."

There was a hidden depth in these words that did not escape the Comte and when later the King told him he now believed the charges made against him were unfounded, de Frontenac was satisfied.

The Marquis de Denonville was waiting on the quay to welcome his successor and there was a tense moment as they formally greeted each other. A carriage waited for them, but the Comte ignored it.

"I will walk," he said and in this gesture his admirers saw a desire to greet the people who had come to pay him homage and his enemies sneered that it was the old desire for display. It was only a short distance to the Governor-General's house and it was a triumphal journey, with frequent stops as the Comte paused to greet an old friend or acquaintance. Everywhere flags were flying and those who did not have anything else had hung colored material and ribbons from their windows. All day the people celebrated, while behind closed doors sharp words passed between the returning and the retiring Governor-General.

The Comte de Frontenac lived up to his reputation as a man of action but the task before him was almost hopeless. So much harm had been done by the former administration that it was difficult for him to re-establish the reputation of the French. He reviewed the troops in Montreal and found about seven or eight hundred there and the remainder in garrison at various forts. At Lachine he surveyed the desolation and began to plan reprisals.

To his extreme disgust he learned from the Marquis de Denonville, before he sailed, that he had ordered the abandonment of Fort Frontenac—the Fort which had been the Comte's greatest pride. At once he dispatched troops to the Fort in the hope of countermanding the order, but it was too late and scarcely had his men left than Valrenne, the commander of the garrison at the Fort, arrived in Montreal with his men. Valrenne stated that he had set fire to everything before leaving the Fort but this afterwards proved to be untrue. Instead the Fort became a stronghold for the Iroquois.

The Iroquois tribes took advantage of this and on a snowy day late in November—a time of the year when the settlers were usually safe from Indian raids—news came that they had descended upon the village of La Chesnaye, a settlement a few miles above Montreal, and had laid waste to it, setting fire to the houses and carrying off many prisoners. Nothing but mangled corpses lying in the snow were left to tell the story and panic struck again at the hearts of the people. They had been basking in a false sense of security, putting all their faith in de Frontenac, yet knowing that one man alone could not bring them peace. The Comte was faced with a grave problem, for he knew that unless he could achieve a decisive victory over these marauding tribes, the morale of the people would break.

So desperate was the situation that it seemed to him nothing but a miracle could save the day. Half of the families in and around Montreal were reduced to a daily diet of peas and eels, and hungry stomachs made voices angry. De Frontenac decided to make one more attempt to bring the Iroquois tribes to reason. On his return voyage he had brought with him thirteen of the captives sent to the galleys by Denonville. With the leader of these—a famous Cayuga chief called Ourehaoué, he had established a firm friendship and he now sent him, with three of the other captives all gorgeously attired, to negotiate with the Iroquois. The deputation went to Onondaga, the Iroquois capital, and carried with them this message from the Comte de Frontenac:

"The great Onontio, whom you all know, has come back. He does not blame you for what you have done, for he looks upon you as foolish children and blames only the English, who are the cause of your folly and have made you forget your obedience to a father who has always loved and never deceived you. He will permit me, Ourehaoué, to return to you as soon as you will come to ask for me, not as you have spoken of late but like children speaking to a father."

Laying quantities of wampum—the recognized medium of

communication without which no pact or speech had any weight—at the feet of the Iroquois chiefs, Ourehaoué delivered his message with dignity and pride. The chiefs listened in silence but would give no reply until they had communicated with their English friends at Albany. No amount of urging or bribing would make them change this decision, and the delegates from the French were forced to wait until the English sent a reply urging the Iroquois to make no peace with the French. The English had a scheme by which they were trying to unite all the tribes of the Great Lakes with the Iroquois, and this alliance, aided by the English, would have meant the greatest disaster for the French. The tribes of the Great Lakes had always been allies of the French, but they had become so disgusted with Denonville's treachery that they no longer looked upon the French as their friends.

Ourehaoué's mission was a failure. He brought as his answer from the Iroquois the words: "Tell Onontio that his council fire is out." At the same time the distracted Governor received word, brought by a messenger who had traveled over the deep snows, that the tribes at Michilimackinac were on the point of revolt. Though the lateness of the season made it almost impossible to plan a successful attack, the Comte de Frontenac knew that some action would have to be taken at once. Despite the odds against them, the French must attack the trouble at the source—the English—and this de Frontenac boldly determined to do without waiting for the spring.

He drew up a bold plan of attack. From the three focal points, Quebec, Three Rivers and Montreal, three armies would leave simultaneously and march upon the English. He chose his men chiefly from the coureurs de bois because these men were used to winter hardships and would be able to withstand the fierce climatic conditions under which they must march. For the leadership of the Montreal party he made his choice from the indomitable le Moynes and selected Jacques, Sieur de Sainte-Hélène to share the command with D'Ailleboust de Mantet, an intrepid fighter who had fought many wars against the Indians.

The men of Montreal were roused from their winter lethargy and responded to the call. In every farmhouse and throughout all Montreal there was activity. The Boissarts were in the depth of a second sorrow within a few months, for Jacques now lay buried beside his father. He had slipped on the ice, breaking a leg and fracturing his skull. Ironically enough it was Charles Péchard who had found him and helped to get him to the farm. Pierre, the eldest son, now had to take his father's place and because of the loss of his arm after Lachine, he could not answer the Comte de Frontenac's call. The others, with the exception of Philip, who was only eleven, all offered their services without hesitation.

Charles Péchard also went. A week before he left, he and Marguerite were quietly married by Father Dollier, and if the members of the Boissart family had any objections, they kept them to themselves. That one week was their honeymoon, and perhaps because they knew they would soon be separated, they lived it ardently. It was not as Marguerite had wanted it, but when she would raise any objections, Charles would plead that he soon must leave her. During the entire week she never left Péchard Manor, and though many of her hours were undeniably happy, yet there was much to worry her. She found Charles an exacting lover. He had never known refinement in women, and as his passion welled up, he would sweep her off her feet and carry her to their room, ignoring her protests. The first night she had not minded for they were both emotionally keyed up. But on the third day they quarreled, when she protested at his uncontrolled passion and, losing her temper, had stormed at him. He, too, had lost his temper and had flung out of the house, staying away for hours. When he returned he was a different person. He came in quietly, and rather too dramatically threw himself at her feet, his arms clasped round her knees and begging for forgiveness. She was to have many

scenes like this as she tried to understand his changeable
moods. But for the rest of the days together he was more gentle,
and as she stood and watched him marching away with her
brothers, there were tears in her eyes.

The snow was falling heavily as two hundred and ten men
marched out of Montreal. Ninety-six of them were Indians
from the two nearby villages and the remainder were Frenchmen. Each man wore a heavy blanket coat with the hood
drawn well down over his head. In a mittened hand he grasped
his gun, and from his belt hung a knife, hatchet, tobacco-
pouch and powder horn. On his back was slung a pack and in
a leather case around his neck hung the inseparable pipe.

Across the vast white field of the frozen St. Lawrence the
men trudged on their snowshoes, turning to wave frequently,
and when they were mere dark specks upon the horizon, Marguerite walked back alone to her house. Her mother and sisters urged her to return with them, but she wanted to be alone
for a little while.

For five days the men strode along, crossing the forest to
Chambly, gliding over the frozen stretches of the River Richelieu and Lake Champlain and then halting to hold a council.
The Comte de Frontenac had left the precise point of attack
to the discretion of the leaders. The men had been told nothing
of their proposed destination and the Frenchmen were content to leave it to the leaders. But the Indians did not like
being left in ignorance and began to grumble and then demanded to know whither they were being taken. When Albany
was mentioned, the Indians demurred and a definite decision
was postponed until they had journeyed farther.

For eight more days they trudged through insect-infested
swamps and over snow that had begun to melt, necessitating
their wading knee-deep in slush and mud. Then the weather
changed and faces were whipped by icy blasts that froze them.
The leafless trees afforded them no shelter as they stood gaunt
and bare like white spectres with arms outstretched against

the windswept ridges. The coureurs withstood the hardships well, but as days lengthened into weeks, even they suffered as lips cracked with the bitter cold and limbs froze. They toiled through drifts of whirling snow banked higher than their shoulders and the raquettes on their feet became heavier and more difficult to manœuvre.

Paul and Charles withstood it as well as any. Paul was concerned over his brothers, particularly the two younger ones who were making their first trip. When at last the small army reached the point where the paths to Albany and Schenectady diverged, a halt was called. The men were half dead with cold, fatigue and hunger—yet to have lighted a fire would have been to risk detection.

Sainte-Hélène, who had endured many harder journeys than this, went among the men cheering and helping them. The sight of him and his brothers ruggedly withstanding the strain, brought new courage to failing spirits. He came up as Paul was showing Charles and Etienne how to rub their feet and hands to keep the circulation going. Paul was so busy speaking words of encouragement to the young boys that he did not at once notice Sainte-Hélène.

"Good work, Paul," Sainte-Hélène said and Paul looked round gratefully at this praise from the indomitable leader he had always admired.

"My two young brothers," he explained. "It is their first trip."

"A tough one for a start—but it's better to begin the hard way."

The two young boys smiled their thanks, their eyes wide with pleasure at this interest from their leader.

"Keep moving, men," Sainte-Hélène kept saying. "You'll freeze to death if you stand still."

About four in the afternoon the Indian scouts sent out to survey the territory returned to say they had found a hut with four Iroquois squaws in it. They had captured the squaws without any resistance and had brought them back with them. Sainte-Hélène ordered the scouts to direct them to the hut. The possibility of shelter from these expanses of frozen land encouraged the men and when they reached the hut all crowded into it and warmed themselves at the fire. The squaws were left outside in the cold and muttered sullenly as they watched the men.

It had been decided not to attempt to attack Albany, as it was learned a strong garrison of English soldiers was stationed there, but to push on to Schenectady. For several more days they made a forced march and then again the leaders halted them and took council. The original intention had been to wait until daylight and then attack, but the condition of the men was getting desperate, and a night of waiting in the intense cold with no means of keeping warm would probably have meant the loss of a large majority of the stalwart little army.

Through the blinding snow they could see the palisades that surrounded Schenectady—the farthest outpost of the New York colony. Scouts who were sent to reconnoitre reported that the village was oblong in shape, with a gate at either end of the palisades. The leaders divided the men into two groups —Sainte-Hélène leading one group and Mantet the other. In dead silence the two groups closed in on the village, one going to the right and the other to the left. Not a sound came from the sleeping village and to their surprise they found the gates unguarded. Stealthily they crept through, filing around the village close to the palisades until the two leaders met.

There was a pause for a few moments and then the signal was given. The Indians let out their ghastly war whoop and then Indian and Frenchman rushed to do his work as he had been instructed. With hatchets they broke down the doors of the houses, dragging out the scared villagers aroused from their sleep and slaying many of them in their beds. What Paul now witnessed made him sick, for he suddenly realized he was par-

ticipating in a massacre that was identical with that of Lachine. Only it was worse, for Lachine had been attacked by
Indian savages whereas this was white men attacking white
men and being as merciless as those they called savages. The
sight paralyzed him and he stood behind a house watching
while women were dragged out by their hair and scalped and
defenseless children were crucified against the sides of the
houses. In his hand, Paul had his musket ready but he could
not use it. He thought of what Marguerite had told him of
that terrible night in Lachine and he wanted to yell to the men
to stop. Why were they killing these people who were white
like themselves, except that their inheritance was either Dutch
or English instead of French? In horror he watched while
white men hacked at white men and did not even stop there
but slashed at women as well. The white snow was now stained
red—red with the blood of innocent people and the glow of
raging fires which destroyed the houses.

For two hours the horror went on, the leaders urging on
their men, and those who a short time ago had seemed heroes
and idols to him now were maniacs, crazy with the lust for
blood. And still Paul stood behind the house to which he had
first rushed—stood there paralyzed and horrified.

"Come along, Boissart," a voice shouted to him—the voice
of le Moyne d'Iberville to whom this kind of thing was not
new. He rushed past Paul, sword in hand, and as he spoke
cleaved the head of a man in two. It made Paul vomit and
when he looked again he saw an Indian with hatchet raised
stealing up behind d'Iberville. Paul lifted his gun and fired and
the Indian fell, knocking d'Iberville over. Before Paul could
reload, another savage rushed at him and he had to use the
butt of his gun and his hatchet to defend himself. D'Iberville
scrambled to his feet again and came to Paul's defense.

"Well done, Paul," D'Iberville said when they had killed
those who were attacking them. "You saved my life. I shall
remember it," and then he was off again like a madman.

Paul lost all sense of what he was doing. The noise and screaming were terrible and it drove him temporarily insane. He ran from one place to another, fighting anyone who attacked him, unable to distinguish friend from foe. He had one desire—to get away from it—and even though he would be called a coward, he ran as fast as his legs would carry him towards the gate. Then his foot slipped in a pool of blood and he fell flat on his face. Before he could get up, feet trampled over him and something hit him in the back. For several minutes he lay there gasping for breath, his mouth filling with the blood in which he lay. When he recovered he struggled from under the load on his back and got to his feet unsteadily. He looked down to see what had hit him—and his blood froze. It was the body of his brother Raoul—Raoul with his head scalped and his face almost unrecognizable.

"Raoul!" Paul screamed, though he did not know that the sound he made was a scream. He knelt down and lifted the gruesome head onto his knee and thought of the wife and children at home waiting for Raoul to return. Paul began to blubber like a child.

He recovered himself and stood up unsteadily, wiping away the tears with the back of his hand—and the back of it was red. Half dazed, he noticed it and, as a drop of blood trickled down his cheek, realized that he had a large gash on his forehead. Only then did he realize that the din of battle had ceased, though there were still screams from the wounded. Nearby some of his fellow men were herding prisoners into a group in the center of the devastated village. The leaders were placing sentinels at important points and calling to the rest of the men to rest and refresh themselves.

Le Moyne d'Iberville patted Paul on the shoulder as he passed. "Well done, Paul," he said again. Well done, Paul thought. What had he done but stand paralyzed behind a house and vomit? Well done to massacre women and children. It made him feel terribly sick and as he looked around at the gruesome picture before him, he vomited again.

As his mind cleared he remembered his other brothers and Charles Péchard and went to look for them. The houses had yielded plenty of food and wine, and the tired, hungry men were now devouring these ravenously. Someone held up a bottle to Paul and, still in a daze, he took it and drank some of it. Then the bottle was snatched from him and he stumbled on. He found Charles sitting among the wounded, his left arm hanging helplessly by his side. It had been slashed with a hatchet and he was waiting his turn to have it dressed. The sight jerked Paul's mind away from the horror surrounding him and into action. His experience in the woods had taught him what to do, and without a word he took his knife and slit Charles' sleeve up to the shoulder and examined the wound. It was a deep gash and was bleeding profusely. He snatched some material from a pile beside the doctor and, cleaning the wound as best he could, bound it up tightly. In a moment the bandage was red and Paul wound more around it, but they were running short of material and nothing more could be done.

"Ghastly wasn't it?" Paul said as he worked on Charles' arm. Charles shrugged his good shoulder. It had not affected him as it had Paul—but then in his wandering life he had seen many more ghastly sights than Paul.

"What's the difference between this and Lachine?" Paul said bitterly. "And they call the Indians savages!"

"They did most of it," Charles said.

"Urged on by us and our brandy! Where were you during the fight?"

"Standing behind a house and taking care of my own skin," Charles said with a grin.

"You didn't do such a good job," Paul said and laughed hysterically.

"You've got a messy gash on your forehead," Charles told him.

"I know. I'll get it dressed later," Paul said and put his hand to his head. It had stopped bleeding as blood and dirt had congealed. He pulled his hand away quickly for the wound was painful.

"Raoul's dead," he told Charles.

"Too bad," Charles said feelingly.

"Where are the boys? Have you seen them?"

"Not lately."

"I'll go and look for them."

Paul's feet dragged for he was desperately tired. He found his brother, Charles, lying among the pile of dead with five shots in his body and Etienne was lying on the ground nearby with a doctor bending over him. As Paul came up the surgeon handed his assistant the right arm which he had just hacked off Etienne's body. Paul's face went a greenish shade and he fell on to his knees beside Etienne.

"Who are you?" the surgeon said irritably, pushing Paul aside. The doctor's face was hard, and smeared with blood and dirt—but his was a hard job and he could not afford to have feelings.

"His brother," Paul answered.

"Oh," the surgeon replied and went on with his work.

"Will he live?" Paul asked.

The doctor did not reply and as soon as he had done what he could for Etienne, he turned to the next casualty. Paul knelt beside his brother and spoke to him, but he had lost consciousness. It had been a bitter fight—two brothers killed and another wounded, perhaps mortally.

A bugle sounded and the men were told to get into line. Paul heard the command but it only half penetrated his mind. Charles saw him and came over to him.

"I'll look after him, Paul," he said kindly. "You'd better get into line."

Paul looked up at him, anguish on his face and then struggled to his feet and fell into line. A hasty retreat had been ordered, owing, it was learned, to the fact that a Dutchman had escaped and had gone to raise the alarm in Albany.

The battle had yielded much booty and nearly ninety prisoners who were to be taken back to Montreal. Some old men,
women and children who had not been slaughtered were to be
left behind. Among the booty were forty horses and these were
harnessed to the sledges so that a hasty retreat could be made.
As fast as possible they crossed the ice and when they reached
the far side of Lake Champlain, a halt was called. The food
supply had run so low that some of the horses had to be eaten
and from then on the journey was slow. The wounded rode in
the sledges and the rest of the men trudged along on snowshoes.

Paul was weary and disheartened. He had started on the
journey proud and thrilled with the thought of adventure. Soldiering had never appealed to him, but he had thought, from
what the Comte de Frontenac had said, that this was to defend
his own home and the homes of the settlers and to secure
peace. Perhaps the Comte was right, yet Paul could not help
feeling that those innocent settlers in Schenectady were no
more responsible for all the unrest than were the peaceful settlers in French villages. It was governments that made wars
and not those who had sought these new countries in the hope
of making a new life. He thought bitterly of the task before
him—the task of telling his family that Raoul and Charles
were dead. That made four deaths in the family in a few
months and two of the men, if Etienne lived, crippled for life
with only one arm.

On and on they trudged and though Paul was accustomed
to raquettes, they now dragged on his feet and his soles were
blistered and sore. At last, after what seemed to be days without end, they came within a day's march of Montreal and
bivouacked for the night. Paul rolled himself in his blanket
and, huddling close to his fellow men for warmth, fell asleep.
Hardly had they closed their eyes, however, than the alarm
was sounded and every man jumped to his feet and gripped
his gun with an ice-cold hand. Over the snows a dark mass
was moving towards them and soon a flight of arrows whistled

through the air. The leaders hastily organized their men and a volley of fire was returned. Word came that a band of Mohawks which had persistently pursued them from Schenectady were the attackers. The fight was short and violent and when at daybreak the Indians were driven off, fifteen more of Sainte-Hélène's army were dead.

They dared not now wait to rest for there might be more following that band of Mohawks. So on to Montreal they plodded with the remnants of the army and the prisoners they had brought with them. Cheer after cheer greeted them as they crossed the last lap of the frozen St. Lawrence, but there were no answering smiles from the weary men. As they entered the town, though people still cheered, anxiety and pity were upon every face. Anxious eyes searched the faces of the returning men—eyes that looked for brothers, husbands, fathers and loved ones. So many of those eyes searched in vain—and some turned away to weep alone.

BOOK II

Paul

CHAPTER XXIV

SOME EIGHT MONTHS LATER, Paul wound his way up the steep, serpentine road which led to the top of the mountain on which the Upper Town of Quebec was situated. Each few steps he took he looked around, fascinated by the sight of a place which all his life he had longed to visit. It was quiet now but there were many evidences both in the people and in the damage wrought, of the siege from which only recently the city had emerged victorious. The Comte de Frontenac had just achieved one of his greatest successes in routing the English fleet under the leadership of Sir William Phips.

As Paul climbed the hill he was in a thoughtful mood, for much had happened upon which his mind could dwell. After he had recovered from the attack on Schenectady, he had spent much of his time with the Sieur de Courville. The Sieur had reminded Paul that it was time he found a wife and had also suggested a visit to Quebec. "The right woman can do much for you, Paul," the Sieur had told him. "In Quebec you would have a larger choice." The idea had been in line with Paul's own thoughts. These last years had been so full of changes, that he had given no thought to his own matrimonial future. Hélène de Matier had shown him the charm of a cultured woman, and though he was reluctant to admit it, even to himself, had made him look beyond the farmers' daughters in Montreal. He did not want to be thought overly ambitious, particularly now the Sieur de Courville had announced to the habitants of the Seigneury that Paul would ultimately take his place. The announcement had been made at the May Day festival and the news had been well received. Paul hoped it was because they liked him and not because at that time he was basking in what he felt was false glory. The Sieur d'Iberville had spread throughout Montreal the story that Paul had saved his life and all Paul's protests had been regarded as modesty. Even when he insisted that during the attack he had hidden behind a house, they would not listen.

However, before he could make arrangements to go to Quebec, news arrived that the English were planning a concerted attack by land and sea in revenge for Schenectady. The Comte de Frontenac had immediately hurried to Quebec and, finding the rumors true, had ordered Governor de Callières to muster every able-bodied man and follow him. Not only de Callières, but the Chevalier de Vaudreuil and four of the le Moyne brothers had begun recruiting and Paul and Charles had joined Sainte-Hélène's company. Thus, instead of going on a visit, Paul had sailed for Quebec at the expense of the government of New France.

Now the siege was over. He paused to look down at the lower part of the town which spread around the base of Cape Diamond. He had been stationed below during the siege, and from where he stood, looking out across the St. Lawrence, he was impressed by the precipitous appearance of the place. Towards the St. Lawrence it presented a bold front and he could understand now why Sir William Phips had attempted the ruse which had succeeded in Acadia—that of first trying to intimidate the Comte de Frontenac into surrendering without a fight. From his position along the shore, Paul had thought how formidable the English ships in the Quebec Basin had looked. But from this height he now realized why the aim of the English gunners had been so poor, for from this vantage point the French guns at the Fort could sweep the decks of the English ships.

During the siege Paul had performed another feat which had brought him praise. The French cannon had struck the flagstaff on the Admiral's ship and the Cross of St. George had

crashed into the water. The incoming tide had caused the flag
to drift towards the shore and when Paul saw this, he had
plunged into the water and had secured it. He was a strong
swimmer but the opposing current was treacherous and he had
a hard fight with shots falling all around him. His life seemed
to be charmed and he reached the shore unharmed, his com-
rades cheering him as they pulled him from the water. When
all was over, he had been called before the commanding
officers, highly praised and given the honor of bearing the
captured flag to the Cathedral and of placing it in position
while the Te Deums were sung.

The north side of the town was bounded by the St. Charles
River where the ascent from the shore was more gradual. It
was here that Phips' troops had successfully landed under his
second-in-command, Major John Walley. Again it had seemed
to Paul a stroke of good fortune that he had been one of the
men selected by Sainte-Hélène for the counterattack against
Walley's troops. Paul had found the fighting this time very
different from Schenectady. Here they had fought as soldier to
soldier and not against trapped men, women and children.
The excitement of it had appealed to him and he had fought
as fearlessly as any man.

There could be no denying that it had taken much strategy
and courage on the part of the leaders and their men to stem
that tide of thirteen hundred trained men who had landed
from the English ships. The skirmishes had been fierce and in
many instances the fighting had been hand to hand. Dodging
behind trees, hiding behind rocks and bushes, the Frenchmen
fought Indian fashion. Then Sainte-Hélène had fallen mortally wounded and Paul had rushed out in the thick of the
mêlée and had dragged his leader behind a rock out of range
of the fierce English fire. Leaving the fighting to the other
men, he had worked to save the life of Saint-Hélène but to
no avail. Sainte-Hélène had looked up and smiled:

"No good, Boissart. This is my last fight." Blood gushed

from his mouth and his head fell to one side, and Paul knew
there was nothing more to be done.

Paul turned from his reveries and went on his journey up the
steep mountainside. He was on his way to present a letter of
introduction which the Sieur de Courville had given him to
the Chevalier de Luc.

"He's a minister of some kind," the Sieur de Courville had
told Paul. "Just exactly what kind I don't know. He has one
of those ambiguous titles to cover up the fact he has been sent
over here by the King to watch what is going on. He has influence and should be able to see that you meet interesting
people."

Paul had delayed nearly two weeks before presenting the
letter, partly to get some clothes made and partly because he
felt it would be better to let things settle after the siege.

He looked well in his newly tailored clothes though he felt
conspicuous. Having worn moccasins all his life, the high
leather boots hurt his legs and feet and he had walked about his
room for hours, trying to get accustomed to them. Many times
during that uphill climb he wished he had on his moccasins, for
the boots kept making him slip, and when finally he reached
the top, his shin bones were aching.

Quebec had made a favorable impression upon him and
there were moments when he found his loyalty to his own town
a little strained. The Sieur de Courville had so often said that
one day Montreal would be a great city, and though Paul
respected the Sieur's opinion, he could not help being rather
sceptical. Here in Quebec there was a charm and polish of
manner absent in Montreal. The people dressed more fashionably, particularly in this upper part of the town where the
quality lived. The thought came to him that perhaps he had
been a little hasty in accepting a seigneury in Montreal and
should have sought his future in Quebec.

He made inquiries as to where the Ministry was housed
and then asked for the Chevalier de Luc. For more than an

hour he waited in the anteroom, while well-dressed men passed to and fro. They all looked very important to him. At last a lackey came forward, bowed formally and told him the Minister would receive him. He was ushered into a large room, at the far end of which he could see a man seated behind a desk. The lackey announced his name, but the man did not look up from studying the papers he held in his hand. Paul waited, feeling very self-conscious and not knowing what he was expected to do. When at last the Minister looked in his direction he had a heavy frown upon his face and appeared annoyed.

"Yes, what is it?" he said in a sharp, irritable voice.

Paul's mouth was dry and he moistened his lips as he made a polite bow.

"Paul Boissart—at your service, Monsieur le Chevalier," he said and walked towards the desk. He held out the letter which the Sieur had given him. With the same irritable expression the Chevalier took it. Then he looked up sharply at Paul and his expression changed. He broke the seal but before looking at the letter kept repeating:

"Boissart? Boissart?" as though trying to remember the name.

The Sieur de Courville had told Paul: "You will find him rather a testy little man, but it's only a pretense. He's very kind and his snappishness is only a pose."

"Boissart?" the Minister repeated, and just as Paul was about to explain that he was a stranger, the Minister's face broke into a smile. "Ah yes, I remember now. You are the man who captured the flag?" And then he began rummaging furiously among the papers heaped on top of his desk. "I have a note somewhere to communicate with you. Strange you should have come this morning. Now what is it de Courville wants?" He stopped rummaging to read the letter. "Hm," he said and as he looked at Paul his face showed interest. "Seems to think a lot of you. How is the old rogue?"

"Only fairly well, monsieur," Paul answered politely.

"Feeling his age, eh?" he said with a chuckle. "Well, we all do when we get as old as he. Fine man, though . . ."

"Indeed yes, monsieur," Paul agreed.

"He says you'll inherit his seigneury. Don't know how you can do that unless you're his flesh and blood but I'll wager the old devil has thought of a way."

Paul was about to explain when the Minister said sharply: "Sit down—sit down."

The Chevalier was fussing again among the papers on his desk and Paul wondered whether he ever found anything in that muddle.

"Devil take these secretaries! Why don't they leave things where I put them!" He picked up a handbell and rang it violently. Immediately a young man with a very obsequious manner appeared and de Luc shouted: "Where's that memorandum about Boissart?"

"Boissart, monsieur?" the puzzled secretary asked and looked completely bewildered.

"Yes, yes. The man who captured the Admiral's flag . . ."

"Oh, yes, monsieur. It's right here . . ." the secretary replied and he too began rummaging frantically. "I placed it here but . . . it seems to have disappeared." De Luc and the secretary kept moving piles of papers and stacking them on top of other piles. Fortunately the paper was found and the secretary grasped it with relief.

"Here it is, monsieur," he said and hastily retreated.

"Yes," the Minister said and proceeded to ignore the paper that had caused so much trouble. Instead he sat back, putting his fingertips together, and scrutinized Paul. "Longueil was talking to me about you—le Moyne de Longueil. He says you are a neighbor of his."

"Yes, monsieur, his seigneury is almost directly opposite the de Courville seigneury. My father's farm is on the de Courville seigneury," Paul explained. "We've all grown up together."

"Yes—sad about Sainte-Hélène being killed. Longueil mentioned your name in connection with that. You tried to save Sainte-Hélène, I hear."

"No, monsieur, I . . ."

"Well, that's what de Longueil said," de Luc interrupted, a little of his testiness returning. "And you were at Schenectady with Sainte-Hélène, weren't you?"

"Unfortunately, yes, monsieur."

"Unfortunately?" the Minister snapped. "What do you mean by that?"

"It was massacre, monsieur," Paul replied and faced the Minister unflinchingly.

"They massacre us—we have to do the same. Anyway, that's beside the point. From the looks of you, what the le Moynes say appears to be true. We need young men like you and we want to encourage you. Where'd you get that rusty hair?" the Minister asked suddenly.

Paul's face colored to match his hair. He took the remark as a reproof because most gentlemen in Quebec followed the fashion and wore wigs.

"I'm not used to wearing a wig yet, monsieur," he apologized.

"Wigs! Who cares about wigs! They're all right for old men like me who have no hair! If I had hair like yours I wouldn't wear a wig either. Infernally hot things!"

Paul was relieved. He had spent unhappy moments that morning trying on those that were being made for him but he could not bring himself to wear one.

"Well—what were we talking about? Now what do you want me to do for you? What is it de Courville says in this letter?" He began reading it aloud. "Introduce you to some interesting people. Hm . . . he doesn't say what sex." He looked at Paul and smiled mischievously. "Are you married?"

"No, monsieur."

"Looking for a wife, I suppose?"

Before Paul could answer, the Minister went on. It was obvious he liked to do the talking. "You shouldn't have much trouble with your looks. Take care you choose the right one. Don't be hasty—take your time. Once you're married—well, there you are. You want a woman who'll help you build up a fine heritage. The trouble with the women here is they won't leave Quebec. So be careful who you choose."

While the Minister talked, Paul wondered whether he was married. The Sieur had not mentioned this.

"Montreal is far away, of course," Paul said, "and a dangerous spot."

"Not thinking of remaining in Quebec? We need strong men back in Montreal."

"No, monsieur, I was not thinking of doing so."

"Montreal's all right. I've spent some time there. If it weren't for those marauding, murdering savages, the place might develop into something. We've got to find some way of settling those Indians."

"The Comte de Frontenac may be able to find a way," Paul ventured to say.

"If he can't—no one can. Have you met him?"

"No, monsieur."

"You should. Come to the ball tomorrow evening at the Chateau. I'll have an invitation sent over to you. Where're you staying?"

"At the St. Louis, monsieur."

"Down below, hm," the Minister said, rubbing his nose. "Well—it's all right for now. Got some clothes?"

"Yes, monsieur. I've had some made at a tailor that the Sieur de Courville recommended."

"Good. Very well, I'll send over the invitation. I'm very busy now. See you tomorrow night. Good-bye."

And abruptly the interview ended.

CHAPTER XXV

As Paul dressed for the ball the next night, there were moments that bordered upon despair and he began to wonder whether he should not have stayed on the farm where he belonged. In the midst of dressing, he slumped into a chair and ran his hand through his hair in a disgruntled way. Across his mind flashed thoughts of the le Moynes and this encouraged him. They had come from the same kind of stock as he and it was they upon whom he had always modelled his ambitions. He thought it over for a while and then started again to don his elegant clothes. He had no servant to help him—in fact, this would only have added to his confusion, for by himself he could struggle and fume without anyone watching. He had to admit it felt fine to be wearing silks and embroidered satins instead of the rough homespuns—only it made him feel foppish and reminded him of the Chevalier de Favien. Nevertheless when he stood before the long pier glass and surveyed himself, the difference in his appearance was pleasing. He found comfort in the fact that his legs, always until now hidden by heavy leather leggings, looked shapely in their silk stockings. From moccasins to buckled shoes was a wide jump and he wished the shoes had not looked so new and were less stiff on his feet.

As he was adjusting his lace cravat, there was a knock on the door and the man from the wig maker's came in with his perruque. This was the one part of the whole business that Paul would have gladly omitted. It was difficult enough to accustom himself to wearing a sword, but to have his head encased in this long, full, curly perruque with absurd curls over each shoulder was exceedingly uncomfortable. He only half listened to the flatteries as the man adjusted it, realizing that it was part of his trade to flatter all his gentlemen. When he had finished, he handed Paul a mirror and suggested he admire himself. Accustomed all his life to seeing himself with a reddish crown of wavy hair, this dark auburn affair was quite startling and it changed his entire appearance. He peered at himself closely, looking from one side to the other, but it was not meticulousness that made him do it, although the man probably thought so. With much deference he handed Paul his coat and helped him into it. With the coat on, the perruque looked a little less absurd.

"Handsome, monsieur, handsome," the man kept saying as he bobbed around adjusting this and that. When the man had gone, Paul gazed at himself for a time in the pier glass, a heavy frown on his face. The tailor had suggested a coat of a soft shade of green with heavy gold braid down the front, and Paul had to admit that the choice was good. It flared out from the waist, showing the embroidered undercoat or vest and the jewelled hilt of the sword which the Sieur de Courville had given him before he left Montreal. He dangled his wrists and made a wry face at the lace cuffs which draped themselves over his heavy masculine hands. This sort of thing was all right, he told himself, for simpering fools like de Favien with delicate white hands that had never been used to work. He sighed and turned away from the mirror, walking about in an effort to feel more at ease. It was fortunate for his ego that he could not appreciate how handsome he looked.

This was immediately evident an hour later when he arrived at the Chateau and was ushered into the ballroom.

"Monsieur Paul Boissart," a stentorian voice called out and the eyes of those nearest the door widened with interest. Paul glanced quickly around for The Chevalier de Luc but could not see him. Immediately a young man came toward him and bowed stiffly.

"The Chevalier de Luc's secretary at your service, monsieur," he said. "Philippe de Fouberg."

As Paul returned the bow, he recognized the young man who had helped search for the paper on The Chevalier de Luc's desk the day before.

"The Chevalier de Luc is in attendance upon his Excellency. They will be here presently. In the meantime, monsieur, permit me to introduce you."

"Thank you, monsieur," Paul replied and followed de Fouberg towards a group of people.

"Mademoiselle de Luc, permit me to present Monsieur Paul Boissart," de Fouberg said. Paul made his first leg without a fault. Before him was a young girl curtseying low to the floor, and as he took her hand and raised it to his lips, his eyes met hers. They were as black as velvet and equally as soft and appealing.

"You are most welcome, monsieur," she said. "My father told me you would be here."

So the old rascal has a daughter, was Paul's immediate thought.

"Thank you, mademoiselle," he said, and as she smiled, the velvety eyes danced so that Paul could not take his away.

"Allow me to present you," she said and to her other qualities Paul added a soft, gentle voice. He hardly heard the names of the other people to whom he was introduced.

"My father tells me this is your first visit to Quebec, monsieur," Mademoiselle de Luc said.

"Yes, mademoiselle," Paul replied politely.

"I do hope you will find it enjoyable."

"I am sure I shall," he answered and their eyes met again. For a fraction of a second he held hers, and when she dropped them, he knew she felt his admiration. He tried desperately not to act like a fool the first time he was introduced to a charming girl and concentrated upon the conversation of the others.

"We have all been looking forward very much to meeting you, monsieur," a stout dowager said to him. He could not remember her name and wondered how she knew anything about him.

"Thank you, madame," he said and then became tongue-tied.

"Monsieur Boissart is to be honored tonight," Mademoiselle de Luc said, coming to his rescue.

"I, mademoiselle!" he exclaimed.

"For having captured the Admiral's flag."

Paul colored with embarrassment. "That was only in the line of duty, mademoiselle, and nothing compared to the valiant deeds performed by others," he said.

"Hark at the modest boy," the dowager said and tapped his arm approvingly with her fan.

"No, really, madame, it is not modesty. Too much is being made of it and it embarrasses me."

Paul glanced quickly at Mademoiselle de Luc.

"My father does not think so. He is very proud to be introducing you tonight," she said.

"I wish I could feel I deserved it," he answered.

"I'm sure you do," she said and smiled again. There was an ease of manner and a poise about her that gave him confidence. At first glance he had thought her beautiful but as they talked he realized this was not really so. It was her large black eyes that dominated her face and put other features in the shadow. Her nose was sharp and pointed like her father's and her mouth too large for beauty. Paul watched it and a disturbing sensation ran through him. He wanted to feel those lips on his and the suddenness of the thought after so short an acquaintance rather shocked him. How stupid of him to be wanting to kiss the first woman to whom he had been introduced!

As they stood there in a group, conversing and listening to the soft music which wafted to them from the far end of the room, Paul had time to observe his surroundings. He had thought the balls at the de Courville Manor magnificent but

they faded before this splendor. The room was furnished in
elegant taste and lighted by thousands of candles which reflected in the crystal chandeliers and in the windows changed
into mirrors by the blackness of the night outside. Never had
Paul seen such beautiful clothes on the women and on the
men too and such jewels. There were many officers present
and their brilliant uniforms added to the splendor.

Mademoiselle de Luc turned to him again. "Are you staying
long in Quebec, monsieur?" she asked.

"For the winter, I expect," he replied.

"I am so glad. We must try to make your stay as pleasant
as possible."

"You are very gracious, mademoiselle," he said. There was
a happy smile on his face but a moment later it disappeared
so suddenly that Mademoiselle de Luc was startled. Across the
room floated a low provocative laugh and the sound of it made
Paul's heart stop beating. He was almost afraid to turn his
head in the direction whence it had come—and when he did
he looked into the face of Hélène de Matier. She recognized
him immediately and he saw her coming towards him. He was
so confused he wanted to run for the nearest door. It had
never occurred to him she would be in Quebec; he had
thought her back in France.

"Why, mon petit sauvage!" he heard her deep fascinating
voice saying and when he turned to look at her his face flushed
with anger. How dare she address him in such a way before
all these people! It had been an expression she had always
liked to use and they had many times argued about it. She was
curtseying to him and he had no recourse but to take the hand
she held out and kiss it. As his eyes met hers, he saw that
mocking look he hated so much. Inside he was trembling, for
again her beauty stirred him in a way he did not wish. Beside
her every other woman's looks faded—a fact which she knew
only too well. As always she was perfectly gowned, and as on
the former occasion when he had seen her at a ball, she was

conspicuous by the difference in her headdress. Practically all the ladies wore their hair dressed high while she wore her long tresses au naturel, and partly covered by a de Maintenon hood. Paul did not know until later that she was responsible for introducing this new hood into the colony.

"How magnificent you look, my friend!" she said in a patronizing way. "We have progressed, have we not?"

Each sentence she uttered had a barb in it and Paul fought to keep his anger under control. What right had she to come and spoil his evening, particularly when it had started so well? He began bitterly to regret the past. He had come here in search of a wife—and a mistress had turned up.

"You are looking as beautiful as ever, madame," he said formally.

"Thank you, monsieur," she said and curtseyed to him again, still with that mocking look that infuriated him. Then she slipped her hand through his arm and, turning to Mademoiselle de Luc said in the same patronizing way: "Paul and I are old friends. We came to know each other *very well* during my stay in Montreal a few years ago." The tone of intimacy which she used could not have been missed by anyone. Paul was furious that Mademoiselle de Luc should hear it.

"Monsieur Boissart is very well known to all of us," Mademoiselle de Luc said, and when Paul looked at her, her black eyes, which so short a time ago had been soft and velvety, were hard and piercing.

"Indeed, my dear Ann?" Hélène replied, and then, turning to Paul, "So you have forsaken the plough for the sword! You used not to wear one."

"A farmer has little use for a sword, madame," Paul replied cryptically.

"And you look so strange in a wig!" she laughed and Paul colored with embarrassment. "He has the loveliest red hair!" She directed her remark to Mademoiselle de Luc, a possessive triumph in her manner.

Fortunately at that moment the doors at the far end were flung open and all conversation ended.

"Here they come," Ann de Luc whispered and when Paul looked at her some of his discomfiture disappeared.

The guests separated into two long lines, Paul standing between Mademoiselle de Luc and Hélène de Matier. The Governor and his suite came down the room, stopping to greet each one in turn so that their progress was slow. With the Comte de Frontenac were several men whom Paul knew—the Chevalier de Callières, the Chevalier de Vaudreuil, the Chevalier de Ramezay, le Moyne de Longueil with his arm still in a sling, le Moyne de Bienville, and le Moyne de Maricourt. Paul felt proud of this fine representation from Montreal. The Chevalier de Luc walked behind the Comte de Frontenac and when they reached Paul, the Chevalier gave him a friendly smile.

"Your Excellency—would you permit me the privilege of presenting a young friend of mine from Montreal?" The Comte nodded and the Chevalier de Luc continued: "Monsieur Paul Boissart."

Paul bowed to the Comte de Frontenac. "Ah, yes," he said. "I am glad to have this opportunity of thanking you for the fine work you did during the siege. We are all grateful to you. I have asked the Chevalier de Luc to bring you to the levee tomorrow, in order that you may be suitably rewarded."

Paul was so surprised that for a moment he did not know what to reply. "Thank you, your Excellency," he said simply.

This was the first time he had seen the famed Comte de Frontenac face to face and the fine qualities of that face impressed him. The eyes were fierce and gray, deep set beneath shaggy eyebrows, and the nose was rather beak-like. Despite his age, the Comte carried his tall figure erect and moved with an easy grace. His weather-beaten face was heavily lined and looked very red against his white wig—probably because he had just dined exceedingly well.

When he had passed, Paul was further flattered by greetings from the le Moyne brothers and the other Montrealers who all treated him as an old friend. Le Moyne de Longueil dominated the conversation. "This is the first opportunity I have had of thanking you for trying to save Jacques' life." For a moment Paul was not sure of whom he was speaking until he remembered Sainte-Hélène's name was Jacques. "This is the second time, gentlemen, that this young man has helped my family. He saved my brother d'Iberville's life at Schenectady."

"It was nothing, monsieur," Paul said quickly. Then, in the hope of changing the subject, he inquired after de Longueil's wound.

"It's mending. They told me I should not be here tonight but I did not want to miss the occasion."

As they talked, Paul was conscious of the eyes of both Mademoiselle de Luc and Hélène—the latter's still mocking. She was, however, soon too busy making quick repartee to the compliments paid to her to bother about Paul.

The dancing began, and before Hélène could claim him, Paul bowed to Mademoiselle de Luc and asked: "Would you permit me the honor, mademoiselle?"

"With pleasure, monsieur," she replied and sounded as though she meant it. The touch of her cool hand in his was soothing. As they danced the minuet he watched her. Her nearness to him did not arouse the violence of feelings he always experienced with Hélène but he was stirred with a deep emotion near to reverence.

All too soon the dance ended. The moment he relinquished her she was surrounded and then Hélène came to claim him. It was impossible to refuse her without being openly rude, so he submitted with as good a grace as possible.

"Come, Paul," she said, "I will introduce you to some of my friends." From the tone of her voice he evidently was expected to consider this a privilege. She claimed him for the next dance and Paul was angry with himself for finding her so attractive. He wanted to hate her, yet could hardly refrain from crushing her to him.

"I must see you, Paul," she whispered as they danced. He did not reply and hiding the urgency of her tone with a smile she asked: "Did you hear what I said?"

"Yes," he replied coldly.

"Meet me after supper on the balcony outside this room," she said imperatively.

"Is it necessary?"

"Yes, Paul, it is. Please don't be difficult."

They danced on in silence and Paul wondered how anyone so beautiful could be so vicious. The Creator had incased a serpent within a body that was irresistibly fascinating, coupled with a beauty and quality of voice that stirred pagan emotions in every man present—be he young or old.

Paul was privileged to take Mademoiselle de Luc into supper but all through it he kept remembering Hélène's insistence that he meet her afterwards. He kept wishing something might happen so he would not have to go. The lighting of the huge bonfire was to follow and people began to drift out to gain a good vantage point. Paul saw Hélène leave the room and caught the significant glance she gave him, but he remained talking with Ann and her friends. Presently, when the ladies excused themselves, he stood for a while chatting with the men and then went into the gambling room. While he stood there a lackey came up and handed him a note and' without reading it he knew what it would say. He strolled apart and opened it, trying to appear nonchalant.

I am waiting for you at the far end of the balcony. Come. —Hélène.

It was just what he had expected.

The balcony ran the length of the Chateau and looked on the water. Paul strolled slowly along admiring the view, for the night was dark and clear and the sky filled with myriads of stars. How much he wished the figure at the end might be Ann de Luc and he prayed she might be too occupied with her guests to see him talking to Hélène. Hélène was gazing out over the water as he came up and then turned swiftly so the light caught her face. She had a cloak thrown over her shoulders, and against its dark background, her loveliness was silhouetted. Against his will memories of that figure as he had often seen it, lying white and appealing in his arms, flooded his mind and he struggled to control his emotions.

"Paul," she said in that liquid tone which had once so thrilled him and still did. "Thank you for coming. I had to see you—there is so much I must tell you."

"Is it necessary?" he said and tried to make his voice sound hard and cold.

"You said that before—and I told you it was," she said. There was the faintest note of annoyance in her voice. "First of all I want to say I am sorry I had to be so horrid to you in there before others—but I had to do it, Paul." She came closer to him as she spoke and looked up into his face. "I was so astonished at seeing you here, I could have fainted—and I have never fainted in my life except for convenience. I had to make myself hard to cover up my real feelings for my heart was beating so fast. Were you surprised to see me or did you know I would be here?"

"Certainly not. I had no idea you were in New France. Frankly I had given it no thought." He was pleased with himself that he could sound disinterested.

"I don't blame you for being hard, Paul. But you don't know why I went away so abruptly and left you . . ."

"Presumably, madame, because your lover, Monsieur de Favien, objected to me . . ." he said cruelly. He saw her face change for a fleeting moment at the mention of de Favien's name. That affair had involved her in more difficult situations than she would have cared to mention but when she spoke her voice was well under control.

"I went away because I loved you so much—so desperately. I—"

"That is all finished," he said quickly.

"It need not be, Paul." Her voice was soft and seductive and she leaned closer to him, making his blood race. "You want me just as much as I want you."

"I do not!" he said furiously but there was no conviction in his voice. "You finished it yourself in Montreal and—"

"And I can start it again in Quebec."

"Oh, no. I have forgotten all about you and I don't want anything more to do with you."

"Your actions belie your words, my dear Paul. You know you can't resist me and—I always get what I want." She leaned up against him but he thrust her aside.

"I have other interests here and shall thank you to stay out of my life."

"*You* have other interests!" she said and gave a low laugh. "Do you realize the compliment I am paying you? There is hardly a man here who would not give everything he has to be in your shoes at this very moment . . ."

"Then go and find someone else if you think yourself so desirable," he said angrily, for he felt his resistance weakening.

"Why try to fight it, Paul?"

"Because I hate you!" he said desperately and, turning, walked quickly away. Her low, tantalizing laugh followed him, and as he turned into the ballroom he saw her standing where he had left her, watching him and very sure of herself. The ballroom was empty and he hurried across it to join those watching the bonfire—hurried in case she should follow him, though he knew he was running away from himself as much as from her.

He looked around quickly until he found Mademoiselle de Luc and then went over to join her.

"Ah, here you are Monsieur Boissart. I was wondering what had happened to you," she said sweetly. He smiled at her and was ashamed of his own weakness, for he wanted to beg her to stay near him and give him strength.

CHAPTER XXVI

PAUL MADE HIS WAY up the hill towards the Chevalier de Luc's house. Mademoiselle de Luc had intimated to him the previous evening she would be "at home" that afternoon and he was taking advantage of the suggestion. Had it not been for Hélène de Matier his happiness would have been complete. All night long thoughts of Ann and Hélène had vied with each other and for the hundredth time he wished there had not been this interference with his plans. He felt sure Mademoiselle de Luc returned his interest and he wanted to be free to pursue his advantage. In his inexperience he did not know how to deal with a woman like Hélène de Matier.

That morning he had been conducted to the levee by the Chevalier de Luc and the wily old Minister had given him more than one hint that he had made a good impression at the ball. At the levee he had been decorated for his services and had also been informed by the Comte de Frontenac that a recommendation had been sent to Louis XIV that he be vested with the title of Sieur de Courville-Boissart. Afterwards the Chevalier de Luc had told Paul this had been done at the recommendation of the Sieur de Courville and that Paul's behavior during the siege had furnished the opportunity. The Lettre de Noblesse could not now arrive until communications were again established after the departure of winter, though the recommendation would leave by the last ship from Quebec. The Comte de Frontenac, as representative of the French King, had the power to bestow the title, though Paul felt he would not be officially in possession of it until the Lettre de Noblesse came from France.

When he entered the drawing room and gave his name to the servant, he was announced for the first time as:

"The Sieur de Courville-Boissart."

The sound of it thrilled Paul. He felt a momentary disappointment at finding the room so full of people for he had hoped for a more intimate gathering and an opportunity of talking with Mademoiselle de Luc. She was seated at a table dispensing that most expensive luxury—tea—and Paul went toward her to pay his respects. She greeted him with her lovely smile and its warmth enveloped him like a soft cloak.

"Congratulations," she said as he bent over her hand.

"Thank you, mademoiselle," he replied and looked into her eyes. He was not sure whether his imagination was playing tricks but he thought her fingers pressed his before he relinquished her hand. It was only a fleeting moment but one he cherished.

Then she introduced him to her other guests. There were so many people and so much idle chatter that Paul could not get another opportunity to speak to her until just before he was leaving. She was standing near the door receiving the parting compliments of her guests, and when Paul saw she was alone, he made the most of the opportunity.

"I must leave, mademoiselle," he said, although he had nothing to do for the rest of the evening.

"I am sorry there were so many people and I did not get a chance to talk with you more," she said.

"I'm sorry too, mademoiselle. Perhaps I shall be more fortunate next time."

"I hope so. Father told you, I hope, that we are giving a small dinner next Saturday and would be honored if you would be our guest?"

"Thank you, mademoiselle. It is most kind of you."

"Father is so absent-minded I was afraid he would forget to tell you."

"He mentioned it just before we parted this morning. He is such a busy man."

"Too busy. It tires him and he is no longer young."

"He is fortunate in having you to help him."

"There is so little I can do. Since mother died I have tried to look after him but it is difficult."

This was the first mention that had been made of family matters. Paul had been wondering where Madame de Luc was.

"You do it very charmingly, mademoiselle. In fact—if I may be personal, it has amazed me that anyone as young as you could be so accomplished."

"A very pretty speech, monsieur," she said and again her candid smile made him happy.

Several people were waiting to say their farewells, and after kissing her hand, Paul took his departure.

All the way down the hill he thought of her and wished Saturday were not three days away. This afternoon had confirmed his impressions of the evening before and he knew he was in love. He was impatient for the moment when he might tell her and hated all the conventions that must be observed, delaying that longed-for moment.

He opened the door of his room and then stopped abruptly on the threshold. Into his beautiful thoughts the unpleasantness of the outside world thrust itself—for seated in a chair opposite the door was Hélène de Matier. A frown immediately replaced the happy expression on his face.

"Such a countenance with which to greet an old friend," Hélène remarked and laughed.

There was no retreat so Paul came in, leaving the door ajar.

"May I ask, madame, what you are doing in my room?" he asked coldly.

"What else would I be doing but waiting for you and believe me it is the first time that Hélène de Matier has ever waited for a man!"

"Then why break a precedent?" he said roughly.

"Because I had to see you. And, by the way, would you

please close the door. I thought I had broken you of the habit of leaving doors ajar." The reference annoyed him and because of its implication he kicked the door violently so that it slammed. "You *are* in a bad temper," she said.

He stood by the door, glowering at her, yet all too well aware of her charms. As always she was excellently groomed and the picture of enchantment as she sat watching him with mocking eyes.

"We might as well understand each other, Hélène. I don't want anything to do with you," he said emphatically.

"Oh, yes you do!" she replied and held out her graceful hand. "Come here."

With his mouth set firmly, Paul ignored her outstretched hand and walked past her into his bedroom, where he took time to compose himself. When he turned, she was standing in the doorway, a seductive and beautiful figure exuding temptation.

"Don't be foolish, Paul," she said in a low voice. He tried to glare at her but in a moment her arms were around his neck. He grasped both wrists firmly and tried to wrench them apart. "Paul! You're hurting me!" she cried and then used her own way to make him release his grip on her. She planted her mouth directly on his and the feel of those luscious lips against his sapped all his strength. He let go of her arms and tried to get his face away from hers but she clung to him more tightly.

"I love you," she murmured and pressed her body hard against his. She pulled off his perruque and threw it across the room, running her hand through his thick hair. "Why try to resist me, Paul, when you love me with every fibre of your body?" How true her remark was! He did love her with his body but he hated her with his mind. "You have grown so much more charming than you were in Montreal. I always knew you would. You were such a good pupil and I am very proud of my work. I have never forgotten you, Paul, and those glorious hours we spent together. And now I know it was all so worth while. I love you," she repeated. He did not dare look into the eyes raised appealingly to his.

"Can't I make you understand I want nothing to do with you?" he cried, averting his head. "I hate you!"

"No, you don't—you love me."

"I do *not* love you—I love someone else. Have you no vestige of pride that you force yourself upon me in this way?"

"Pride? Not where you are concerned, my darling." She released her arms from his neck but remained leaning against him. "Listen to me, Paul. I—Hélène de Matier—who have been annoyed all the morning by men who fell in love with me at the ball last night—I who could snap my fingers and have all I want—I have ignored them all because I love you. *Love you*—can't you understand that? Marry me, Paul, and I will give you everything I have—my fortune, my influence, myself, soul and body. Marry me and I will make you the most powerful man in this colony."

"I don't want power—and I don't want to marry you."

"No—?" she said and taunted him with a smile.

"No! You seem to have forgotten you are old enough to be my mother!" he said brutally. The shaft went home but she had another weapon ready for use. She buried her face in his coat and began to cry. A woman's tears—an old trick but Paul was duped by it. He stood rigid for a moment and let her cling to him.

"Don't, Hélène—please don't," he said and his voice was softer. She noted the change in tone and took advantage of it.

"You're so cruel to me, Paul—and when anyone loves as I do it hurts so dreadfully."

Paul was young enough to be flattered. "But, Hélène, I have told you I love someone else," he said lamely and thought how awful it would be if Ann could see him in his present position.

"I'll never let you marry anyone else," she said fiercely. "I can't let you—I love you," and she raised her eyes to his

—black, smoldering eyes bright with her tears. He looked on forbidden ground and his legs began to tremble. Hélène felt him trembling and knew that she was breaking down his resistance. With a desperate effort he tried to pull himself together and, pushing her away, walked back into the other room. He went to the window and stood with his back to her trying to calm himself. She did not follow but watched him from the doorway.

"Why try to fight me, Paul?" the soft, alluring voice went on. "You know when I make up my mind, I always get what I want. And I have made up my mind that I want you."

"Leave me alone," he cried desperately and hated himself for his weakness.

"No, I shall not," she said and he started when he heard her voice so close to his ear. She insinuated herself between him and the window, bringing her face close to his. He thrust her aside.

"Go to the other men who want you! Why do you cheapen yourself with a man who keeps telling you he has no use for you?"

"Because that man is not telling the truth. You have forgotten how well I know you and I can tell from the way you are acting that you want me." She came over to him again and clung to him and his mouth quivered as he looked at her. "Don't you remember how I taught you to love? How you adored me? I shall make you adore me again." Her mouth was on his, pressing his lips apart and sapping his strength.

"Remember?" she whispered and, taking his hand, pressed it inside the bosom of her dress.

"Oh, God, help me in my weakness," he cried within himself.

"You do remember," she said as she felt his fingers at her breast.

With an inarticulate cry he lifted her in his arms and carried her into the next room.

CHAPTER XXVII

PAUL WAS UNHAPPY. He stayed in his room most of the next day brooding over the development of things and growing increasingly angry with himself. He realized remorse was foolish and that he should have thought of the consequences before he involved himself. His mind kept reverting to Ann, longing to see her, yet afraid to face her. He walked about his room tormented by the vision of Hélène's loveliness, until he could stand it no longer. Quickly he packed his clothes and left the Inn, moving to a room in the Upper Town. It was nearer to where Hélène was staying but it was also nearer to Ann. He hoped, too, that Hélène would be unable to find him, though he knew that hope would not last long, for it was inevitable they should meet. Strangely enough, he kept wishing he could talk the situation over with Ann. Somehow he felt she would know what to do and then he wondered why he should feel this confidence in one whom he knew so slightly.

On the following Saturday, when he went to the dinner party at the Chevalier de Luc's, his hopes sank lower. All through dinner he tried to catch Ann's eye, and when he did, it brought him little comfort for the warmth he had seen there before was absent. She was coldly formal throughout the evening although Paul tried to think this was because of the other guests. After dinner he had to sit over the port with the men, trying to take an interest in their conversation. When they joined the ladies, he covertly watched Ann for a glance or a smile but the black eyes never once looked in his direction.

When the guests rose to depart, there was no intimation from Ann that he should remain a little longer. He expressed his thanks for the evening in the conventional manner.

"It was a pleasure, monsieur," she said coldly.

He pressed his lips to the back of her hand but the fingers remained still and icy.

"I hope I may have the pleasure of seeing you again very soon," he said.

"I am sure we shall meet," was her reply.

He walked past the Chateau St. Louis and thought of the ball there. For some time he watched the water playing in the moonlight while the evening passed in review. The more he thought of it, the more he was convinced there was a change in Ann's manner and wondered what poison Hélène had been distributing. He was too restless to sleep and walked for hours trying to decide what he should do. By the time he returned to his room he had made up his mind—he would woo Ann in every way possible and the very first time they were alone would tell her of his love.

With this determination he sent her a note the next day. All day long he waited for a reply but it did not come. He was determined not to give in easily and each day sent her a note, but all his requests to see her remained unanswered. When he did see her it was in the presence of throngs of people, for Paul was now besieged with invitations from those he had met at the ball. The evenings were gay with dancing and entertainments, petits soupers and theatrical parties, but he received little enjoyment from them.

It was at a ball at the home of the Intendant that he saw Ann again. She was not there when he arrived, but feeling certain she would be among the guests, he lingered near the door. She came in on the arm of her father, looking lovely in a gown of soft rose that set off the color of her hair and eyes. The Chevalier de Luc greeted him warmly and Ann gave him a smile.

"Thank you for your notes," she said as he bent over her hand.

His eyes pleaded with her as he looked into hers and replied: "You did not answer them . . ."

Her eyes returned his gaze steadily but there was still no warmth. "I have been terribly busy," she said. "The winter season leaves me very little time."

"Not even for the things you *want* to do?"

"Oh, yes, I usually find time to do the things I want to do," she replied and his heart sank.

"I see," he replied, and as she was drawn into conversation by those who had gathered around her, he walked away disconsolately. He entered a long gallery where cozy chairs nestled among the palms. It was as yet empty and Paul stood looking out over the River and watched the first snow falling.

"Ah, mon cher, how fortunate to find you alone." At the sound of the voice, he swung round, and glowered for a moment at the speaker. As he strode from the room, Hélène's soft laugh followed him. Without pausing he walked out of the house and did not return.

Paul's days were further complicated by the many ambitious mothers who had eligible daughters. In order not to get the reputation of being thoroughly unsociable, he accepted their invitations. Young girls, many of them quite beautiful and with handsome dowries, tried to make themselves attractive to him because he was young and handsome, but their wiles and schemes bored him. It was not long before his disinterestedness began to be talked about in Quebec and the reason sought. This suited Hélène de Matier's scheme perfectly, and as she heard the chatter she took every opportunity of subtly suggesting that she was the reason.

When a rumor reached Paul that Mademoiselle de Luc was about to become engaged to a Major attached to the garrison, he was in despair. It was impossible to try to storm her citadel and call at her house uninvited, for there were strict hours for social calling. He could have gone during these hours but it would have been to no purpose since there would have been so many others present.

Finally he called on the Chevalier de Luc. This time he was

not kept waiting but ushered in the moment he gave his name.

"Well, young man, having a gay time?" the Chevalier greeted him cordially.

"Oh, yes," Paul replied flatly.

"Oh! Have we neglected you in some way?"

"On the contrary you have been most kind, monsieur."

"Then what is troubling you? You look unhappy."

"I am, monsieur."

The Chevalier's face folded into a smile. "A woman, I'll warrant!"

"Yes. I . . . er . . ." Paul felt foolish as he began to stutter. "The truth is, monsieur, I . . . er . . . fell in love with Mademoiselle de Luc the first time I saw her. Have I your permission to pay court to her?"

"Why, yes, you have my permission," the Chevalier said, rather surprised. Then he added: "But the rest is up to Ann. I don't interfere with that part of her life."

"Would you mind if I asked a question?"

"Not at all."

"I have heard she is to become engaged to a Major at the Fort. Is that true?"

"Oh, Major Soubrué—yes, he has been at the house quite often," the Chevalier said drily and Paul was consumed with jealousy. He had been denied and his notes had been ignored, yet this other man had been "at the house quite often."

"I have not been having much success, monsieur," Paul went on. "The fact is I don't quite know what to do. Would you mind my asking your advice? Being a stranger here, there is no one to whom I can turn, and I am very worried."

The Chevalier studied Paul before answering. He knew that things were not running smoothly between him and Ann. After the ball she had talked admiringly about Paul, but since then, whenever he referred to him, Ann avoided the subject.

"Tell me anything you want to, Paul. I will try to help you if I can."

"Thank you. Er . . . at the Governor's ball there was unfortunately a lady whom I had known in Montreal. She . . . er . . . became my mistress for a little while and then left abruptly for France. I had not seen her again until that night."

The Chevalier's eyes widened with interest and then narrowed. He had not thought this young man matured enough to have had a mistress already.

"And she has been giving you trouble?" he asked.

"Plenty of it. She insists I marry her."

"O-oh," the Chevalier said seriously.

"But, monsieur, she is years older than I and I don't love her," Paul went on hurriedly.

"Mistresses can sometimes be very tiresome," the Chevalier agreed. "Do I know the lady?"

"I expect so—everyone in Quebec knows her." Paul hesitated and then said: "It is Hélène de Matier."

The Chevalier nodded his head. He had already heard the rumors. There was a half smile on his face as he said: "So you were one of the many fascinated by that lady."

"Yes, monsieur," Paul said a little sheepishly.

The Chevalier was thoughtful for a few moments and then looked at Paul. "I'm glad you came to me. To be frank with you I have already heard rumors. This town, you know, thrives on gossip."

"I was afraid she had been saying things. And no doubt Mademoiselle de Luc has heard them too?"

"No doubt. If Madame de Matier has any idea you are interested in someone else, she would make a point of seeing that that person heard about it. Strange that Hélène should insist that you marry her." He paused long enough to take a pinch of snuff. "I have never known her to talk of marrying again. I wonder what her reason is."

"I wish I knew, monsieur. I deeply regret now that I was ever foolish enough to be caught by her wiles . . ."

"But I presume it seemed very much worth while at the time," said the Chevalier drily.

Paul's face went very red but when he saw the mischievous look on the Chevalier's face, he smiled.

"Most men have mistresses some time or other, Paul. You were unfortunate in having chosen a very dangerous one."

"I don't know what to do about it. I am not experienced in handling women like her."

"Very few men are. But we can possibly find some way out of it."

"I would like to tell Mademoiselle de Luc about it myself. I wanted to speak to her before this but she would not give me an opportunity. I believe she would understand."

"I believe she would. She has wisdom beyond her years. You see—she and I have lived very close to each other. I have had to be father and mother too. I am anxious for her to marry. But I want it to be someone with whom she can be happy. I saw she was interested in you and I have also noticed that things were not progressing well. When I heard these rumors about Hélène de Matier, I guessed the reason."

"Isn't there some way in which you could arrange for me to see Mademoiselle and explain it all to her?"

"As I said earlier, I do not interfere in these matters with Ann. But"—he scratched his chin thoughtfully—"in this instance perhaps I could do something to help you. How would it be if I had a talk with her tonight?"

"I should be very grateful, monsieur."

"Let me make this suggestion. I will speak to her tonight. Tomorrow send her another note and if she answers it, then you will know I have been successful. If she does not reply, then . . ." He threw up his hands. "Women can be very difficult, you know."

"I am very grateful to you, monsieur. And thank you for letting me tell you my troubles."

"I'm glad you came to me, Paul. I will think over the matter of your former mistress and see what suggestions I can make to you. We'll talk about it again some time later."

When Paul left he felt more lighthearted than he had since the night of the ball.

CHAPTER XXVIII

Paul spent hours composing a note and destroying it, until small balls of paper littered the room. Then he gave up in despair and wrote simply:

Please see me.—Paul.

He sent it by messenger the next day. All the morning he paced the floor, and when her reply came, his fingers trembled so much he could hardly open it. It read:

Come at three this afternoon, if you are free—Ann.

She received him in a small room off the large drawing room. As she came forward to greet him, she was smiling, and her eyes were soft and velvety again.

"Thank you so much for seeing me," he said as he kissed her hand.

"I'm glad to see you," she replied.

"Do you mean that?"

"Why not?"

"You have been angry with me . . ."

"No, not angry. Perhaps, not understanding. Shall we sit down?"

She led the way to a small settee and he sat at the opposite end.

"There's so much I want to say but I don't know how to begin," he told her.

Her smile was kind as she answered, "Father told me you have been finding things rather difficult in Quebec."

"Did he tell you why?"

"He mentioned one or two things, I believe."

"Did he mention Madame de Matier?"

"He did not need to." Her voice was low and full of meaning.

"Oh," he replied and became more crestfallen. He put his head in his hands and rumpled his hair. Ann looked at him tenderly and wanted to comfort him but she had to hear his story first. When Paul looked up she was staring into the fire. "What has Hélène been saying?" he asked.

She turned and looked at him. "That you and she have been engaged for a long time and will be married as soon as convenient."

Paul jumped up as though he had been struck. "She said *that*," he cried angrily.

"Then it isn't true?" Ann said and her eyes were mischievous.

"No wonder you didn't answer my notes, if that's what you have been thinking!"

"She came to see me and talked of nothing but you." Ann knew she was torturing him but she felt he deserved a little punishment.

Paul leaned against the mantel staring down into the fire. "I don't know what to do, Ann." Her name slipped out before he realized it. "I feel as though a net had been drawn round me."

"Why not tell me the whole story, Paul?" He looked at her quickly. It was the first time she had used his name.

"I want to, but it isn't easy, particularly to you."

"I know."

"Two years ago, Hélène de Matier came to Montreal. I . . . I was fascinated by her beauty. It was the first time I had met a woman like her and—well, I was swept off my feet. Then suddenly she left Montreal and I heard she had returned to France." He paused, wondering how much more he should tell. "I had no idea she had returned to Quebec."

"She arrived two days before the Governor's ball. She was on one of the ships that was nearly captured."

"I wish the English had captured it," he said fiercely.

Ann smiled faintly. "Isn't that rather unkind?"

"I don't feel kind where she is concerned."

"But surely when you have been in love, there should be some feelings of kindness left."

Paul sat down beside her. "I was never in love with her. It was infatuation. She has a fascination that draws men to her."

"Oh, yes, no one could deny that."

"It is something more than that. You saw the way she behaved at the ball."

"Yes, I did." Under her breath she added, "And I could have killed her."

"I told her after we had danced that it was all over but she merely laughed. Then the afternoon of your reception, I found her in my room when I returned. She made a scene and insisted I marry her."

Ann's eyes watched his face as she said, "Then there was something to the rumor that you were to be married?"

"Believe me, Ann, it was her invention. I told her I was in love with someone else. I love you, Ann, as I have never loved any woman, but I am not worthy to be telling you." He buried his head again in his hands. Ann placed her hand lightly on his arm.

"Don't condemn yourself unnecessarily. I want to hear the story from you. You are not the first man who has had difficulties with her. She is a very dangerous woman. Did you tell her you were in love with me?"

"I did not mention your name but it would not have been hard for her to guess since at that time I had met so few people here."

"She hates me, Paul, and has probably done this out of spite."

"Why should she hate you?"

"That is a story I will tell you. About three years ago in Paris, a man tried to involve me. He was anxious to get into favor at Court and was using me as a channel to my father's position. I was young and though he was older than I, I found him attractive, or thought I did. One night he climbed through my bedroom window and into my bed. I screamed and fortunately father heard me. There was a very unpleasant scandal. Father obtained an order for the man's arrest but he had already fled France. It was Hélène de Matier who helped him escape. He was her lover."

Paul gripped her arm. "What was his name?"

"Does it matter? It's an old story and there's nothing you can do about it now."

"That's not why I asked you, though I would kill any man who harms you. I have another reason for asking his name. Would you mind telling me?"

She hesitated a moment. "It was Nicholas de Favien."

"Mon Dieu! I thought so!"

"You know him?"

"Indeed I do! You have heard your father mention the Sieur de Courville whose name I now bear?"

"Yes."

"He was the Sieur's son."

"His son!"

"He came to Montreal as the Sieur's nephew. Actually he was a natural son. No one else knows it and you must respect the confidence I have imparted."

"Of course I will."

"The Sieur told me himself. It was when . . . after de Favien had seduced my sister."

"Oh, Paul, no!"

He nodded. "Now we can link the two stories together. The Sieur told me de Favien had to leave France because of a scandal. And to think that it should have been you!" Paul clenched his hands. "Some day I will make him pay for this. The two women I love the most have suffered at his hands."

"You know he is in the Bastille?"

"Yes, the Sieur went to Quebec and asked the Governor to have him arrested and returned to France."

"And father had him put in the Bastille as soon as he returned. Father is powerful in France and will keep him there as long as he can, even if the crime does not warrant so drastic a punishment."

"It warrants it all right. Because of him my sister was disgraced. She had a child by him and because of that was living in Lachine at the time of the massacre. She was captured by the Indians . . ."

"Oh, Paul!"

"Fortunately she escaped."

"Escaped?"

He nodded. "It was a miracle. She went through an awful ordeal though."

"And is she all right now?"

"Yes, she has since married. She is my twin sister and we are very devoted. If your father wants further evidence to keep de Favien in the Bastille, her story should be enough."

"I shall certainly tell him. This brings us very close, Paul."

"I wish we could have become close without all these complications. Without Hélène de Matier I might have been worthy of you."

"She is our common enemy. We'll fight her together."

"You mean that?"

"Yes, I do."

"And you're not angry with me over her?"

She shook her head. He looked into her eyes and there was a depth he had never seen there before. "Oh, Ann, I do love you so much." He leaned closer to her and she turned her face up to meet his lips. It was the moment he had longed for but despaired of ever having. He released her to look again into her eyes. "Can this be real, Ann? I have thought of it so many times. I can't believe it is real."

"Don't I seem real?" she teased.

"So very real." He drew her to him again and there was no coquettish resistance. "Let me hear it in your own words, Ann."

She put her arms around his neck. "I love you, Paul. I've loved you since the night of the ball."

"I loved you the moment I looked at you. From that moment I have wanted to kiss you."

The day had faded and the room was soft in the flickering firelight as they talked of their lives.

"When will you marry me, Ann?" Paul asked.

"As soon as you want me to."

"Then it will be very soon. We have wasted so much time. Oh, Ann, I have been in agony because I thought I had lost you."

"And I have been consumed with jealousy. It was the day after the tea that Hélène told me about you."

"She didn't waste much time! I knew the night of your dinner party you were angry with me. I watched for your eyes to give me a kinder look but they were cold."

"I was very unhappy. I nearly sent you a note not to come."

"I would have died of despair."

"I nearly asked you as you were leaving whether you were going then to see Hélène."

"You wouldn't have been so cruel."

"I wasn't, was I?"

"No. But I walked about all night in agony. Your eyes were so black and angry."

"They shall never be that way again, darling."

"I'll never do anything to make them that way. Let me look at them now. They're so beautiful. Deep velvety pools."

"In which is mirrored my love for you."

"Let me kiss them to seal that love there." He kissed each eye softly. "And now your lips?" Her eyes had spoken and now her lips spoke more than words.

CHAPTER XXIX

IT WAS NEARING the end of April and the snows had melted, the frozen expanse of the St. Lawrence giving way to slowly moving waters already dotted with canoes. Everywhere nature and people had sprung to life, eagerly preparing for a new season after the prolonged idleness. That winter had been restful and pleasant for most of them in Montreal, with hopes sustained by Frontenac's victory over the English. All were now eager to get grain sown before the men might be called away again to fight against an English revenge from the east or an Indian attack from the west.

Marguerite stood at the door of her house watching the evening fade in a myriad of colors from the sinking sun. Her face as she looked out over the river was sad. She had finished her supper and had put her six-month-old son, Pierre, to bed. In her hand she held a letter which had come that day from Paul. There had been much in it to make her happy, particularly the news that he was on his way back to Montreal. That winter without him had seemed interminably long, haunted by the fear that he might decide to remain in Quebec. It told her of his marriage to Mademoiselle de Luc. With the pleasure of learning he was married, came a twinge of jealousy, not a vicious jealousy but a fear that now she and Paul would never again be as close to each other.

After a while she went back into the house and its loneliness made her shudder. She lit the candle on the table and when she had barred the doors and windows, sat down to read the letter again:

I am bringing home the loveliest wife, the Ann de Luc I mentioned to you in my former letters. As I think I told you, she is the daughter of the Chevalier de Luc, to whom the Sieur de

Courville gave me an introduction. You will love her, Marguerite. She is about your own age—a year younger to be exact—and you will have much in common. You and she have a secret you can share and this, I believe, will make you very good friends. I have not time now to go into details as I want to get this letter on the first boat so you will know we shall be on our way shortly. We shall leave on the second boat, providing the weather is sufficiently clear by then. I do not want Ann to have a rough trip in her present condition—you will know what I mean . . .

She wondered, as she had done so many times that day, what "the secret" could be that they would share.

"I do hope I shall like her," she said half aloud and sat thinking about it. Would Paul be angry when he knew Charles had gone off into the woods again, despite his many statements that he was giving up fur trading now he was married? Marguerite thought of the fifteen months of her marriage. Many of the days had been happy though she had found Charles' changing moods hard to understand. He could be sweet and gentle or crude and brutal; he could be sullen and bitter when he had been drinking or gay and entertaining when he was sober; he would be violent in his bad moods and contrite and full of repentance afterwards. She had not always known how to handle him and they had often quarreled. After his return from Schenectady he had kept his word and for the first time the Péchard seigneury had looked well kept. But after his return from Quebec he had been very restless and the long winter following immediately had not made things easy. He had nothing to do with his time and inevitably formed the habit of spending hours in the taverns, often returning far from sober. Had it not been for these months of idleness perhaps he would not have fallen back into his old ways. When Marguerite saw him collecting his equipment for the woods, she had reminded him of his promise.

"I can't help it," he had said sharply. "This idling is driving me mad."

"The idle months are over now. What about the farm?" she had asked.

"I'm not meant to be a farmer. I tried it last year and hated it. I must go my own way." His tone had been brittle yet at the same time he seemed to be trying to justify himself.

"And you are the man who was going to change if I married you!" she had reproached him.

At her words he had looked at her sullenly and then his brows knit together as though he could not make up his mind whether to be cross or apologetic. He had simply shrugged his shoulders and turned away. "I'm sorry, Marguerite," he had said after a while. "I thought I had had enough of the woods but when I heard the men talking about it at the tavern and they asked me to go—well, I couldn't resist it. I'll go this once and then I'll try to settle down."

Marguerite had not answered him for her own thoughts were too confused. She wondered, as she had often before, how she could sometimes feel love for this man and at others feel she hated him. They had not spoken of the matter again and though he had tried to be considerate before he left, there had been bitterness in her heart as she watched him paddling away.

Her brothers and other members of her family had said nothing in the way of reproach. They had offered to help her with the farm but she had shaken her head. "You have enough to do with your own land," she had told them. "If the boys will keep the place tidy, that will be all right." She had tried to keep bitterness out of her tone but had not succeeded. She saw her family every day and on Sundays they all gathered at Pierre's house, where her mother was now living.

She took up the letter from Paul again and read it through. She knew it almost by heart. Perhaps, with Paul home, things would be better.

She took the candle and went into her bedroom where little Pierre slept peacefully in his cradle. She sighed as she looked at him.

Paul stood beside Ann, one arm around her to support her against the motion of the ship, as they watched eagerly while the ship slowly approached the shore. Ann had enjoyed every minute of the trip, for the elements had been kind and it had not been rough. She had never been beyond Quebec and had been fascinated by the rows of white houses dotted all along the River's edge, giving the appearance of a long straggling village all the way to Montreal. Paul had been much concerned over the change in the mode of living which Ann must now face and had talked long and earnestly to her both before and since their marriage.

"I shall prefer that kind of life, Paul," she had assured him but he had shaken his head.

"You say that, darling, because we are in love, but there will be hardships to face. Even though I am now a seigneur— in my part of the country, seigneurs work in the fields with the other men. There may be times when we have little to eat— there may even be Indian attacks. It will be so different from your life in France or even in Quebec. We are not nearly so fashionable in Montreal."

"What makes you think I want to be fashionable?" she had asked giving him one of her lovely smiles.

"It's what you have always been used to, dear. You were reared at the French Court and now . . ."

"And now I am going to learn the realities of life instead of the superficialities. I hated Court life . . ."

"Yes, dear," Paul had continued to argue, "but the contrast is going to be so great and I'm afraid . . ."

"Afraid of what?"

"Afraid that when some of the fire of our love has died down, you will be bored with the life."

"Couldn't we let that rest until I have proven myself?"

"Proven yourself? You've done that already, proven to me that you are the most wonderful girl in the world. I do love you."

"Then love me enough to know I am looking forward to this new life—really I am, Paul. I want to get to know your people—these people who are pioneers. There is a lot of the pioneer spirit in me—and, darling, you needn't be afraid that I shall—well, how should I put it?—not be able to make myself one of them. They may not take to me at first—sometimes farm people are apt to resent townspeople."

Whenever she talked this way, Paul was full of admiration. "How did you learn so much in so few years?" he had asked her one day.

She had merely smiled. "Instinct perhaps."

More than once during their talks he had repeated: "I know they will love you."

Ann would then remind him that they were not in love with her as he was but his only reply would be: "They cannot help but love you."

That morning as they made the last lap of the journey, she had said to him: "Paul, I want to work beside you and help you build up your seigneury in the way you have told me. We can do it together—it is something to work for, something to make life worth while." It was probably looking at the partially developed farms that had prompted the remark.

Before leaving Quebec they had discussed this angle several times. It was not until Paul had had a serious talk with the Chevalier before the wedding that he had discovered he was marrying a rich woman. He was so much in love that he had given this side of the matter little thought. When he had learned the amount of her dowry, he was perturbed. He had protested and the Chevalier had thrown up his hands and exclaimed:

"Sacré nom! That's the first time I ever heard a man protest that his wife's dowry was too *large*!"

"It probably sounds like an affectation to you, monsieur, but I do wish it were less . . ."

"Why?"

"Because I have so little . . ."

"You have plenty that isn't counted in money. I would
rather see Ann marry a young man with your prospects than
the richest man there is. As it is you are well balanced—you
have the ideas and she has the dowry to help you carry out
those ideas."

"But I couldn't use her money for that!"

"Bah! Stop being a fool! Colonizing this territory is a difficult job. It is going to be worse unless we have some strong
men who can pull us through. Listen to this." The Chevalier
picked up a paper from his desk. "I received this report yesterday. Quebec—a town that is eighty years old and its population is only thirteen hundred people and that includes outlying settlements. Your town—Montreal—fifty years old nearly
and only eight hundred people—less than a thousand in all
those years. We need young men like you to help this colony
grow. And its growth must come from here—we can expect
nothing or next to nothing from France. Those blockheads
across the water won't listen. They insist upon retaining these
colonies as a matter of pride but they won't help. That's why
I'm going back—to try to convince them something must be
done. How far I shall succeed—I don't know. Better men than
I have attempted it and failed."

"You are returning soon?" Paul had asked.

"By the first ship that sails for France. I'm going back to
have my say—and then I'm going to retire. I'm an old man,
Paul." Paul had protested politely but the Chevalier had
stopped him. "I know my limitations. I was forty-six years old
when Ann was born. She's had an old man for a father most
of her life and it is time she was with younger people. I'm leaving her with you and I'm happy to do it."

The Chevalier had sailed for France on the first ship. It was
hard for Ann to part from her father. They had always been
together and she cried for several days after he left.

Hélène de Matier had also left on the same ship. From the

moment Paul's engagement had been announced, Hélène had left him alone. Paul never knew what passed between her and the Chevalier, though he knew there had been some conversation. To the surprise of all, Hélène had suddenly married in January—married a man twenty years older than herself. What had caused this sudden decision no one had been able to find out. Her husband was the old Duc de Chamois and most people presumed it was his great wealth that had attracted her or perhaps the security of his position.

As Paul and Ann discussed the matter, she had remarked: "It seems they suspect her of being an English agent . . ."

"A spy!"

"Well, not altogether. That was the reason father was sent here. There has been a leakage of information to the English and they have not been able to find out the source. He thinks Hélène has something to do with it, but she is so clever, they have never been able to prove it. But father knows enough to be able to keep her quiet—and he also told me she had been ordered back to France. It's all very complicated and confusing. I have never understood these intrigues and politics."

"Nor I," Paul had agreed.

"Perhaps that will make you understand why I am glad not to be going back to France. One's whole life is a confusion of scandal and intrigue. You never know who is your friend and who is courting you because of your influence."

As the ship came closer Paul ran his eyes eagerly over the crowd waiting on the shore.

"There she is!" he suddenly exclaimed and drew Ann over to him so she could see where he indicated. "See there—standing with the baby in her arms. The one with the red hair—see now, the sun has caught it." His voice was eager and excited.

"I see her," Ann said, keenly interested. "Why, Paul, she's beautiful!" He smiled with grateful pride. He was so anxious for these two to like each other.

"Yes, she is, isn't she?" he replied.

"You never told me. I don't wonder . . ."

Paul looked at her curiously as she stopped. "What were you going to say?"

"Oh, it wasn't very nice to mention it. But—I was thinking of it as a compliment. I was thinking that I didn't wonder de Favien found her so attractive." Paul scowled for a moment. "I shouldn't have mentioned it. I'm sorry."

"It's all right, dear. It's only that the mention of his name makes me angry."

A little while later they were rowed ashore. Everyone was trying to reach friends and it was difficult with such a crowd and so much cargo blocking the way on the wharf.

When Marguerite saw them, she handed Pierre to her mother and ran to greet them. Ann stood by trying to be unobtrusive while these two who looked so much alike clasped each other in their arms and kissed almost as though they were lovers. Then Paul turned to Ann.

"Ann—this is Marguerite," he said and two pairs of eyes quickly appraised each other.

"I'm so glad to meet you," Marguerite said and held out her hand.

"I have been looking forward very much to meeting you," Ann told her with a friendly smile. Then she looked from Paul to Marguerite. "There would be no doubting she is your sister —you are identically alike."

"Almost," Paul said and laughed.

"He told you we were twins, of course?" Marguerite remarked.

"Oh, yes. He has told me all about you."

Marguerite gave Paul a quick look and there was alarm in her expression.

"It's all right, Marguerite. Wait until you hear Ann's side of the story. But—here's the rest of the family."

Paul introduced his mother. Marie held out a hard, gnarled

hand and Ann took it in her soft, white one. Marie was not a woman of words and Ann felt the keen eyes looking her over.

"I'm so glad to come here and be with you," Ann said.

"We're simple folk," was Marie's reply and there was doubt in her voice. She never had understood this son of hers. All her other sons had married peasant women.

"That's why I am glad to be here," Ann told her and tried to be reassuring. She was not offended by the abrupt words of Paul's mother, for she had expected them.

"This is my eldest brother, Pierre," Paul went on, "and this is the next one, Etienne." The two one-armed brothers extended their hands. They did not bend over her hand and kiss it, but she was prepared for this.

"We own a pair of arms between us," Pierre said and laughed. "We make quite a good team!" There was a warm friendliness in their manner.

"Paul has told me about you too. The men here have to give up much in defending their families."

"The women too. It's a hard life you have chosen."

"Yes, I'll have a lot to learn."

Little Marie and Philip were waiting impatiently to be presented and eyed their new sister-in-law with awe. When the sisters-in-law and their families had been introduced, Marguerite presented her little son whom Paul had not yet seen.

"Well—so this is my new nephew!" he said and bent over him. Little Pierre yawned as though he were bored with it all and the action broke the awkwardness of the family introductions.

"Isn't he sweet," Ann said. "How old is he?"

"Six months . . ."

"What's his name?"

"Pierre."

"Why didn't Charles come down?" Paul asked.

"He's gone to the woods," Marguerite said without looking up.

"What!" Paul exclaimed.

"Yes, they left early this year," Marguerite said, trying to sound nonchalant. She was being very occupied with the baby and Paul knew she did not wish to discuss the matter further at that time. Marguerite saw the Sieur de Courville coming towards them and grasped the opportunity to change the subject. "There's the Sieur, Paul," she said.

"Where?" he exclaimed and then saw the stalwart figure coming towards them, his white hair waving in the wind. "Ah! Come with me and meet him, Ann," he said and hurried her towards the Seigneur.

"Paul, my boy," the Sieur said and his face was wreathed in smiles. "I am glad to see you. I was becoming anxious for your return." Then he turned to Ann. "And this is your wife." He gallantly bent over the hand she extended to him. "Welcome, my dear, welcome. And how is that old rogue of a father of yours?"

"He sent his respects to you, monsieur, and many messages."

"Thank you. I had hoped he might come with you. But you can never get him farther than Quebec."

"He has left for France, monsieur."

"Oh, I'm sorry. I had hoped to see him again." He looked at Ann with admiration as he said: "I don't know how he could have such a beautiful daughter."

Ann curtseyed to him and thanked him.

"You're to be congratulated, Paul."

"I am indeed, monsieur."

"Are you glad to be back or was Quebec too attractive?"

"No, monsieur, I am very glad to be back. I wanted to get here before the spring planting began."

"Still a farmer, eh? Was afraid Quebec would spoil you."

"No, monsieur. I am more anxious than ever to get back to work."

"Good. I've arranged a little celebration tomorrow night. You remembered that tomorrow was May Day?"

"Yes, that is why we came on this ship. I want Ann to see the celebration. She is as anxious to get started here as I am."

"Different life than you've been used to, my dear."

"I know—but I shall like it."

"I hope so. It's a hard one but you look as though you'll be all right. Your father said in his letter that you were very sensible. Father's prejudice probably." He laughed and they joined in with him. Then the Sieur looked serious. "Paul, I've a favor to ask you. I came down here to meet you especially to do so. I don't go out much any more—in fact, this is the first time I have been into Montreal for months."

"You know, monsieur, I am happy to do anything you ask."

"Will you bring your wife back to the Manor and make it your home?"

"Why, thank you, monsieur," Paul said and there was relief in his voice. On the voyage he had thought frequently of what he was going to do and hoped the Seigneur would make this offer. It would make things so much more simplified, than having to follow the usual routine and build a house.

"Your family won't mind?"

Paul hesitated a moment. "I don't believe so. I'll go and speak to my brothers."

Paul left Ann with the Seigneur while he went to explain matters to his family.

"You have a fine man there, my dear. You two should be very happy and do much for this colony," the Sieur said.

"I am anxious to, monsieur. I want to help Paul build a fine heritage."

"You will," the Seigneur said confidently.

Paul returned to them. "It is all right, monsieur."

"That is good of them. I must go and speak to them."

Shortly afterwards they drove off with the Sieur and along the way Ann's eyes took in every detail.

"This is the beginning of the seigneury," Paul explained.

"It stretches as far as you can see." He pointed out his father's farm and then said: "The farthest house—you can just see the top—is where Marguerite lives. That is the Péchard seigneury."

A few minutes later they drove up before the de Courville Manor.

"And here, my dear, is your future home," the Sieur said. Paul watched Ann's face eagerly. She knew it but did not turn his way. When he had helped her out of the carriage, she stood looking up at the old house, built of half stone and half timber. She looked at it for several minutes.

"It's lived a long while, Paul—and we'll make it live longer and always be a memory to you, monsieur." She held out both her hands—one to Paul and one to the Sieur.

CHAPTER XXX

For the first time in all the years that he had received the May Day homage, the Sieur de Courville was really happy, for beside him was the family he had always longed for, and though not his own flesh and blood, they meant as much to him. As he stood at the door of the Manor House, Ann on one side and Paul on the other, his bearing was proud, and when the cheers had died down, he spoke of Paul and his new wife.

"My friends—I have reached the age when many changes must come. This may be the last time I shall stand here to receive your homage . . ." Protests greeted this remark, but the Sieur waved them aside, smiling patiently. "Last year we had to celebrate this day with two of our oldest friends missing— Old Pierre and Jacques Boissart. This year we are not going to look back, but forward, for the man who will step into my shoes is young and he has returned from the expedition to Quebec, loaded with honors for his bravery during the siege and showing that the faith we had in him was not misplaced. To me he is like a son. While in Quebec, he was fortunate enough to find a very lovely wife. Her father is one of my oldest friends and the fine characteristics which I always admired in the Chevalier de Luc are reflected in his only daughter. In the short time I have known her, I have grown to love her and I know you will do the same as you get to know her. I shall leave it to Paul to introduce her to you later. His Gracious Majesty, King Louis XIV, was pleased to recognize Paul's valiant services during the siege of Quebec and has bestowed upon him a title he well deserves. My friends—the Sieur de Courville-Boissart."

He turned to Paul and they exchanged smiles, while the

crowd gathered at the foot of the Manor steps cheered their new Siegneur. Paul spoke to them briefly and then, taking Ann by the hand, proudly introduced her. She made a deep curtsey as the habitants cheered. She spoke a few brief words, choosing them carefully and expressing her happiness at being among them. But during breakfast Paul could detect a little reticence, particularly in the older people. Ann was of the noblesse and unused to the rigors of farm life, and for all her simplicity and friendliness Paul knew that they were asking themselves—and later would ask each other—whether this girl bred in Court society could ever fit into this rugged pioneer world.

The breakfast was happy and gay. Afterwards, as Paul went from table to table and chatted with friends, he received many congratulations from the men—but the women, these dour, hard pioneer women, merely smiled and reserved their judgment.

During the next few days, as they went from farm to farm while Paul talked to the men in the fields, Ann sat in the kitchen and pleased the women by asking them to teach her the things she must know. She dug her white hands, which had never done any hard work, into flour and learned how to bake bread. She was awkward at first and laughed at herself but the women soon learned that her desire to become one of them was sincere and then they began to vie with each other in helping her to learn their ways.

At the first opportunity Paul went over to Marguerite's house and talked to her about Charles. He felt largely responsible for her marriage and was anxious because things did not seem to be right. Marguerite did not want to spoil Paul's own happiness and made light of Charles' departure.

"There's nothing to worry about, Paul," she tried to assure him. "Fur trading has been his life; we can't expect him to give it up all at once."

Paul looked at her quickly, trying to read her face, but she was prepared for this. "Do you really mean that you don't mind?" he asked.

"Not now you are back," she replied evasively. "I have missed you dreadfully."

"And you are going to like Ann?"

"I'm sure of it. She is lovely."

"I hope she is not going to find the life too hard here . . ."

"It will take some adjustment. But she seems very sensible."

"She is indeed." His voice was proud. "She has told you about de Favien?"

"We talked of it yesterday. It has already made a bond between us. You have not yet told me how you came to meet her?"

Paul told her the story but as soon as he had finished he returned to the subject of Charles.

"Are you sure you are happy with Charles?"

"We have had some very happy times together, Paul. You know he is moody and I have found his changeability hard to understand at times."

"I can believe that . . ."

"But don't worry. I am all right and I have little Pierre. And now I have you and Ann. We can all be happy together."

Beyond that she refused to be drawn out. It was not that she would not confide in Paul but she was not sure of her own feelings about her husband and until she was able to clarify her own thoughts she would keep them to herself. She had been lonely these past weeks, particularly during the long evenings and nights, yet with it there was a certain relief, for Charles was an exacting husband.

The friendship between Marguerite and Ann grew. For the first time in her life Marguerite had someone her own age to whom she could talk. Ann naturally was eager to know about her brother-in-law whom she had never met and at first Marguerite spoke only of Charles' more attractive side. But as their friendship grew deeper, Marguerite let down the barriers and confided her doubts and heartaches, telling Ann details she could not mention to Paul.

A day never passed that they did not spend some part of it together, sometimes at Marguerite's house and sometimes at the Manor. Marguerite delighted in Ann's stories of life in France and at the Court and Ann was equally interested in what Marguerite told her of colony life. Now that it had receded into the past, Marguerite was able to tell her about the attack on Lachine and her capture by the Indians. If Ann felt any misgivings or fears that there might be Indian attacks again, she did not voice them. Paul was delighted that the two women had become such friends, for his days were very full with the work on the seigneury and he did not have to worry about Ann being lonely.

The harmony of the summer was broken by the death of the Sieur de Courville. Now that everything was settled for the care of the seigneury, there was no need for him to struggle to hold on to life, and three weeks after the May Day festival he died. When he did not appear in the morning, Paul went to his room and found him peacefully sleeping the last long sleep, a smile of contentment on his parchment-like face. They buried him in Montreal with all the honors due his long service to the colony—and Paul and Ann took up the reins, prepared to carry on in his memory.

Shortly after the Sieur's death, Paul suggested to Marguerite that she come and live with them until Charles' return but she would not do it. She spent many evenings with them and often they went over to her and she cooked the supper. She enjoyed being with them, yet their idyllic happiness with each other sometimes hurt, not because she would have had it otherwise but because she was desperately lonely for someone to love her the way she desired. She had never yet found love and there was at times despair in her heart.

That summer was a hard one, for the English ships blocked the mouth of the St. Lawrence. When Phips had left Quebec he had said: "We shall make you another visit in the spring," but lack of supplies and ships precluded another attack. So he did the next best thing and sent what ships he had to prevent the much-needed supplies from France reaching the colonists. At the same time, the English sent their Iroquois allies to block the western supply line by encamping at the mouth of the Ottawa so that the coureurs de bois could not return and the settlements were kept in constant alarm as marauding parties of savages ravaged the farms. Blocked at both ends, food became alarmingly scarce and famine faced the settlers. There was a variety of fish to be caught in the region and ducks and partridges were plentiful, but men were fearful of going far from their homes to fish and hunt. Many of the people had to live on a daily diet of eels.

Valiantly the men continued to farm the land, forming a communal system whereby they worked together first on one farm and then on another, taking turns to stand guard while the rest worked. Seigneur and servant, habitant and hired man worked side by side, laboring to produce food that they might all survive. Paul had not until now realized what Jacques' death had meant on the farm, particularly with Pierre and Etienne having only one arm with which to work. He felt a twinge of conscience when he realized that he had left them with only twelve-year-old Philip to help them. He plunged more deeply into the work and at times he could not help feeling angry with Charles for having gone away. They tried to keep the land around the Péchard farm cleared, for their own protection as well as for Marguerite's sake, but beyond this nothing could be done as it required too much labor to farm it.

Not for a moment could the tension be relaxed, for every few days news came of villages being attacked, and towards the middle of July the tension increased as news was received that Point aux Trembles, below Montreal, had been burned and many people killed. Many of the families living outside Montreal moved into the forts and Paul discussed with the men of the seigneury the advisability of doing the same. The majority were reluctant to leave, for many times they had moved their families into the forts, neglecting their farms so that the crops were ruined, and then they would find the alarm had not been necessary. Some took their womenfolk to friends in Montreal but these were in the minority.

Paul tried to urge Ann to go with Marguerite and stay in town but she refused to leave.

"If there is danger, Paul, I would rather be with you," she persisted and all his persuasions were unavailing.

It was at this time that Paul was able to test the reaction of the habitants to some of the changes he ultimately hoped to make on the seigneury. He called them together and made his proposal. If they would help him build it, he would erect a strong stockade around the seigneury, with lookout towers to the west. He would bear the expense, he told them, and hoped it would not look too obvious that it was because of his wife's handsome dowry he was able to do this. If they thought of it, they gave no indication; on the contrary they received the suggestion with enthusiasm and for days afterwards the air echoed with the sounds of their labor. There was the question of the Péchard seigneury, which, being the farthest west, was the logical place where the lookout tower should be erected. Paul talked it over with Marguerite and they agreed to continue the stockade to include the Péchard land as well. "If Charles does not like it when he comes back, he can pull it down," Paul said.

Marguerite merely smiled. "He'll *have* to like it, Paul. I am entitled to some protection and there is little enough with him away."

Paul agreed and was tempted to say much more, but he let it pass.

Paul in farm clothes, with roughened hands and dusty sweat on his brow, looked very different from the casual gentleman Ann had known in Quebec. At first he was apologetic about it but soon ceased to be as Ann was able to convince him she would rather have a husband who was doing real work. While the men labored building the stockade and tending the fields, she joined the women in preparing food to be taken to them and for this the women loved her. Aristocrat though she obviously was, there was no snobbery in her and had she not been pregnant she would have joined them in the harder work.

It worried Paul that Ann should have had to begin her life in Montreal during a time of threatened famine and possible attack. He talked of it many times as he lay in her arms at night.

"If only you could have had this summer in peace," he told her anxiously, but she would not agree.

"This has given me an opportunity of showing your people that I want to be one of them," she said.

"But it may get worse, Ann. The food shortage is very serious, and unless the blockade is lifted before winter comes, it will make our lives very hard."

"By that time I shall have learned how to live like a seasoned pioneer."

"But you are not used to it, dear," he argued. "And then there is the child . . ."

"He might as well start life the way he is going to live it . . ."

"He?"

"You want a boy, don't you?"

"I don't mind which it is, as long as it looks like you," he said and nestled his head against her and was almost immediately asleep, exhausted from his labors of the day.

CHAPTER XXXI

In July the news came that the English were advancing from Albany with a strong force under the command of Major Peter Schuyler, with Montreal as their objective. Once more every able-bodied man was called upon to leave his farm and join Governor Callières, who led seven or eight hundred men to meet the English.

The stockade around the de Courville seigneury was quickly finished and a temporary structure erected as a look-out tower. With this protection those who remained behind felt safer. The physically unfit, the old and the women would continue to look after the farms until the men returned. Paul was now able to persuade Marguerite to come to the Manor House and be with Ann while he was away. For the first time he commanded a company of his own, and much against his will, took his young brother Philip with him. Like most boys in the colony Philip had matured early and Paul did not have the heart to refuse him.

"I'm the only man left in the family, Paul, besides you—I mean the only one who hasn't lost a limb," Philip pleaded.

"And now you want to go and lose one too," Paul said, trying to dissuade him. "Don't you think you should stay home and help with the farm?"

Philip's face fell and there was a little defiance in his attitude as he looked up at Paul. "I don't want to be a farmer," he said and watched his brother's face anxiously.

"Oh . . . and what do you want to be?"

"You ought to know that answer, Paul. I used to hear you arguing with father about it."

Paul smiled. "What is it—the fur trade?" he asked.

"Of course," Philip replied and set his mouth firmly.

"Then why not wait for that instead of soldiering?"

"Because I want to go with you," Philip replied stubbornly and Paul had to give in.

They met the English at La Prairie de la Madeleine on the opposite bank of the River across from Montreal. The fight that followed was the fiercest in Canadian history, for Major Schuyler was one of the ablest leaders and though he was outnumbered, his strategy was so skilful he outwitted them. The French were handicapped by the fact that the Chevalier de Callières was stricken with fever and was forced to remain in his tent.

As the English retreated, they burned the land and inflicted heavy losses upon the French. The honors of the day went to Valrenne, an officer of great ability who had been sent to Chambly to prevent the English reaching the canoes they had left on the banks of the Richelieu. The fighting was so intense that often men's shirts were scorched by the flash of the enemy's guns and several times the combatants became so intermingled that it was difficult to know whether they were killing friend or foe.

The French counted it a victory because they had driven off the English, but it was a costly one in lives and homes. As they had done many times before, the women gathered to welcome the returning army, every face anxious and drawn as they searched for the men of their families. Again many a home that had started so hopefully was now left without its main prop and a woman had to bring up a large family as best she could.

Ann and Marguerite, accompanied by Pierre and Etienne, stood among the crowd. Anxiously they watched for Paul and Philip. Ann was the first to see her husband, carried on a litter, and breaking through the crowd she rushed to his side.

"Paul—my darling, you are hurt?" she cried and her large black eyes were fearful as they looked into his. He patted her hand and smiled.

"Only a leg wound, dear. Don't be alarmed."

"Is it serious?" she asked anxiously.

"Bad enough. It's the same one that was injured before—but it will be all right," he reassured her and turned to greet Marguerite and his brothers. "Philip's back there somewhere —came through without a scratch."

"Thank God," Pierre said and went to find him.

Paul was a long while convalescing. Fortunately the harvesting was over and the fields ready for the winter. Paul was thankful the idle months were coming and that he would be able to rest his leg and be ready for work when spring came again.

On a day early in October when the first snow began to fall, Ann gave birth to a son. Marie had come to take care of her and assisted by Marguerite they helped Ann through this difficult period of giving birth to her first child. Paul had wanted to help but his mother had pushed him angrily from the room and had told him to keep out of the way. She was not really angry but she knew how prospective fathers acted and would have none of them. It was a day of agony for him, but when later that evening he was allowed to go in and see Ann, he found her radiant. In her arm she cradled a tiny little form, red-faced and wrinkled, with eyes shut tight against a strange world.

"Here's your son, Paul," she said and smiled proudly.

"You're wonderful," he said. "How could you go through all that pain and now, a few hours later, look so beautiful?"

Ann smiled—the enigmatic smile of a mother who knows how quickly pain and suffering are forgotten. She looked down at her small son with pride.

"What shall we call him, Paul? Our future seigneur . . ."

Her remark gave Paul an idea. "Would you want to call him after the Seigneur—could we call him Jean-Baptiste?"

"It would be lovely. Jean-Baptiste de Courville-Boissart—I like it. I hope he looks like you."

Paul smiled at her indulgently. "Maybe by the time he grows up the land will be more peaceful. I so often think of my own family—six boys and now all that's left intact are Philip and myself. It worried me so much at La Prairie—the fighting was so fierce . . ."

"That's probably how you got wounded—thinking about Philip instead of looking after yourself."

"Probably. When we're his age we are so reckless and it all seems an adventure. I was never meant to be a soldier, Ann . . ."

"But you've made a splendid one . . ."

He shook his head. "Not really. I hate it. I don't want to fight and kill people. I want to live in peace. I want to be able to rear a family and have them live so we can enjoy them . . ."

"There won't always be fighting . . ."

Paul shook his head again. "I wonder," he said.

The winter was long and because of the scarcity of food there was little entertaining in Montreal. Deep snows muffled them within its boundaries and men went with armed guards to hunt bear and elk that their families might not starve. Despite the hardships, Ann loved that winter, with Paul always beside her. It also gave her a better opportunity to know his family, now they were not busy in the fields. Among their own small circle on the seigneury they had their fun, visiting each other's houses and amusing themselves in the simple way that these folk enjoyed.

When again the river ice broke and spring came, it brought with it alarm after alarm. Frantically the Comte de Frontenac had written to France:

What with fighting and hardship, our troops and militia are being depleted. The enemy is upon us by land and sea. Send us a thousand men next spring, if you want the country to be saved. We are perishing by degrees; the people are in the depth of poverty; the war has doubled prices so that nobody can live;

many families are without bread. The inhabitants desert the country and crowd into the towns.

Months passed before an answer came to this plea but eventually a squadron arrived strong enough to beat off the English ships that blocked the St. Lawrence and then supplies reached Quebec. The people fell on their knees at the wharf and gave thanks. The ships did not bring nearly sufficient for the needs of the colony but they were grateful for even a little help. Some of the newly arrived troops were immediately dispatched to break up the Iroquois camp at the Ottawa and the inhabitants began to breathe more easily.

But the relief was short-lived. Instead of a horde of savages to ruin the crops, another destructive force descended upon them—an army of caterpillars that laid waste to the crops and devoured the food that was so badly needed. The farmers were unable to cope with them and many fell on their knees in their fields and prayed for help. Help came, but not in a manner they had expected. Multitudes of squirrels came after the caterpillars and the farmers scrambled from their knees to trap and shoot these little animals that would provide food and also clothing for their families.

Pleas to the mother country brought only conflicting orders that drove the Comte de Frontenac nearly frantic. When an order came to abandon such strongholds as Fort Frontenac and Fort Michilimackinac, he refused to obey and braved the anger of his Royal master by ignoring it.

Ann wrote desperate letters to her father imploring him to intercede for them and get help. Returning ships brought his reply but it gave them little hope, for there was not much that he could do. As they had expected, he urged them to come to France and when Paul read it he turned anxiously to Ann.

"Shall we go, dear?" he asked.

Ann looked at him in astonishment. "And leave all these people to battle alone? You know you could never do that. What about your family?"

"But I have you to think of—and little Jean-Baptiste. What kind of an inheritance is this for him?"

"He was born here and we will teach him how to live this life . . ."

"But you were not born here . . ."

"Haven't I convinced you after all this time that I am part of this life now?"

Paul shook his head and smiled. "No, darling. You do it for me . . ."

"I do *not*, Paul. Though this first year was hard it has meant more to me than all those other years leading a selfish, empty life."

"All right, dear, but . . ."

"No buts . . ." she said and put her hand over his mouth. He pressed it against his lips but still was not convinced.

There was one paragraph in the Chevalier de Luc's letter that interested them particularly.

"You will be interested to know," the Chevalier wrote, "that Madame Hélène de Matier died last August. She died in childbirth leaving behind her a son—a son whose fatherhood is doubtful since the old Duc de Chamois can hardly be credited with the parentage at his age. There are many here who think this impending pregnancy was the reason for her hasty marriage to the Duc. But who shall know? She has gone and taken her secret with her, and the boy, if he grows to manhood, will never know the truth—at least it is doubtful if he will."

"A son?" Paul exclaimed and became very thoughtful. For the rest of the day it was on his mind as he recalled that day in Quebec when Hélène had come to his room. Could he possibly be the father of her child? It was a question that haunted him—but he said nothing of his fears to Ann. Difficult though Hélène de Matier had been, her death left Paul sad. He did, after all, owe her a great debt of gratitude for many happy hours he had spent with her and she had taught him how to love. Perhaps inadvertently she was responsible for the great happiness of his marriage. Since Ann had given him a son, he knew now how women suffered in childbirth and it hurt him to think of Hélène's beauty being distorted by pain, evidently pain far greater than Ann had suffered, since it had taken her life.

"Poor Hélène," Paul murmured and, forgetting any hatred he had had for her, he burned candles for the salvation of her soul.

It was not until the following summer that relief came to Montreal. When at last the Iroquois blockade of the St. Lawrence was broken, the coureurs de bois were able to come down the river with their furs. The people crowded to the shores to watch the hundreds of canoes laden with beaver skins. For over two years now they had waited, and the songs of the men were music in their ears. Montreal became gay again.

Marguerite waited at the water's edge with Paul and Ann. They scanned each canoe for Charles and, when dusk fell, returned silently to the house. For several days she watched but he was not among the returning coureurs. Marguerite remained silent and Paul did not bother her by talking about it. She had not worried about his prolonged absence, knowing that none of the coureurs could get through the blockade, but she had not thought of the possibility of his not returning.

Paul brought her the news. He had been into Montreal and at Dillon's Tavern had met several of the men of Charles' crew. They told of the hardships they had suffered and of being ambushed by the Indians. Charles Péchard had been killed during the fight.

Marguerite sat quietly while Paul repeated the story to her. He came over to her and put his arm around her, their coppery heads against each other. But Marguerite could not cry.

CHAPTER XXXII

MARGUERITE'S WHOLE LIFE now centered around little Pierre. He had inherited Charles' dark hair and eyes but to these were added some of his mother's characteristics. His black hair had Marguerite's luxurious waves and his eyes were large and dark, giving promise of his growing into a handsome man. This, combined with the reckless, roving spirit of his father, were danger points to be carefully schooled. It was almost with horror that Marguerite saw him one day unconsciously imitate one of Charles' habits. He had been very naughty, running off alone into the woods as he loved to do. After a frantic search they found him and brought him back to his mother, and when she faced him sternly, he rushed over to her, clutching her around the legs and burying his face in her lap as he pleaded for forgiveness. It was what Charles had often done when he had hurt her and the same action in her son paralyzed her. Then when he looked up at her, his large black eyes misty with tears, it was all she could do to refrain from hugging him to her. It needed all her self-control to withstand his pleading and to punish him.

Desperately Marguerite realized how much Pierre needed strong masculine control, and though Paul helped her, he was not his father. Besides, Paul soon had a family of his own to occupy his time. A year after the birth of Jean-Baptiste, Ann gave birth to twins—twins as red-headed as Paul and Marguerite. They named them André and Elise after Ann's parents. There was some argument over the names because when Ann saw their little red heads, she had wanted to name them Paul and Marguerite.

"Let them have their own identities," Paul argued and he carried the day.

These were the last children Ann was to have. She had almost died in bearing them and it had frightened Paul. Over-ruling his mother's objections he had called in a doctor from Montreal and, when the crisis was over, learned that the bearing of further children would be fatal to Ann. His disappointment at not being able to have the large family they had hoped for was counterbalanced by relief that Ann would not again have to pass through such an ordeal.

Despite everything that Marguerite could say or do, she could not break Pierre of the habit of going off alone into the woods. She tried to scare him by telling him of her experiences when the Indians captured her, telling him how Eric Walker had been taken prisoner because he had strayed off into the woods. Instead of curing him it seemed to make him worse and for days he would rush around the house, letting out warwhoops and pouncing upon everyone from hidden corners as he pretended to be an Indian. He feared nothing and darkness, which was the terror of every other child in the colony, possessed no fears for him.

"What am I going to do with him, Paul?" Marguerite would repeatedly ask, but he could only shake his head.

"Frankly I don't know, Marguerite. Unfortunately he has inherited many of Charles' qualities with an added fascination that Charles never possessed. You can't help loving the little imp and sometimes I think he is sweetest when he is being naughty. After all, though these qualities are very trying, as he grows older they will probably develop into qualities which will be invaluable in this wild country. I'd rather see him that way than dull and unambitious or weak and afraid, like many we see here."

"Yes, I agree with you, Paul. The fear I have is that this courage of his will carry him into danger. I don't mind his wildness as much as I am terrified of his running away by himself."

"That is bad. We'll all have to help you keep watch over him."

But all the watching did not prevent his getting into trouble. For a little while, Marguerite thought she had found the solution. She talked seriously to him about protecting her since his father was not there to do it. This impressed him and for a time he took his new rôle of protector very seriously. Paul had fashioned him a wooden musket and he carried this everywhere, following his mother about and often getting in the way, but this she did not mind since she could keep an eye on him. At night he would shoulder his musket and go round the house seeing that the door and windows were barred. Sometimes Marguerite could not refrain from smiling as she watched him, his handsome face serious as a soldier on duty.

Fortunately he and his little cousin, Jean-Baptiste, developed a liking for each other and when he was over at the Manor House his mother was relieved of worry. She would stand at the door and watch him cross the fields and wait for him to turn at the Manor House steps to wave back at her.

One evening as she was preparing supper, Paul kicked open the door and came in carrying Pierre in his arms. Marguerite dropped what she was doing and ran to them, holding out her arms to take her child, but Paul shook his head and carried him to the couch.

"What has happened, Paul?" she cried.

"I don't know. I found him lying by the lookout tower."

"By the tower! But he was with you—he went to play with Jean-Baptiste . . ."

She knelt down by the couch and called his name but he did not answer. "Get a doctor," she cried desperately. "He is badly hurt." She smoothed back the dark hair from his forehead and felt a large bump on his head. "He must have struck his head. Oh, Pierre, my darling, speak to me . . . it is mother." He did not answer. "What happened, Paul?" Paul shook his head and something in his expression brought one of alarm to Marguerite's face. "He's not . . . not dead?" she cried. "Pierre! Oh no . . . no . . ."

Paul knelt down beside her and put his arm round her, tears coursing down his cheeks too.

"Oh, my baby . . . my baby! Don't you leave me too," she moaned and buried her face in his thick hair.

Paul stood up and went to the door trying to regain his composure. He could hear Marguerite sobbing but there was nothing he could do to comfort her. When the spasm passed he heard her ask:

"How did he get to the tower?"

"I don't know, dear," he said helplessly. Later he learned from Ann that Pierre had told her he could only stay and play for half an hour. At the end of that time she had watched until he reached the farm. Evidently then he had slipped round the other side of the house and gone to the tower.

"He must have climbed to the top and fallen from there," Paul told her. "One of the men went to look—there were scratches on the outside of the wall where his feet had scraped as he fell."

Marguerite looked at the little feet and the badly scuffed toes of his moccasins bore out this statement. She broke down again, pressing her face against Pierre's.

"Oh, Paul, why did he have to be taken? Two children. . . . I wish the Indians had killed me instead! Oh, my darling, my beautiful darling—and you so loved life!"

The news spread over the seigneury and people came from all directions and stopped in hushed silence when they saw Marguerite crouched beside the still form of her son. Marie was in Montreal with Pierre and nobody seemed to know what to do. The crowd increased and gathered outside the farmhouse. Then Ann came and the crowd parted to let her through. Never was Paul so relieved as when he saw the calm gentleness of her face. They did not speak, for no words were needed. Immediately she went to Marguerite.

"Come with me, dear," she said softly and put her arms about Marguerite to help her up.

"No . . . no . . . leave me alone with him," Marguerite cried.

"Paul will look after him, dear. Come with me. There is nothing we can do now—he is in God's hands."

"God's hands that have taken away everything I loved," Marguerite sobbed. "If only He would take me too . . . so that I can't bring unhappiness to more people. Oh, Ann . . . he was so beautiful. Look at him now—he looks just as he did when he was sleeping. Oh, Pierre . . . my darling . . . open your eyes and tell me you are still living." She threw her arms around him and hugged him to her.

Ann could do nothing for a moment for her own tears blinded her. Then she regained control of herself and was able to persuade Marguerite to go with her. The crowd parted respectfully as Ann led her away, leaving Paul to take care of little Pierre.

All night long Ann sat with her until eventually she fell into a troubled sleep.

After the funeral, Marguerite collapsed and Paul and Ann took her home with them. For days she lay in bed, not ill but staring at the ceiling as though her mind were blank. When later she was strong enough to get up, the change in her wrung their hearts. Her beautiful face was lined and drawn and instead of twenty-five she looked forty. They kept their children away from her but it was not possible to still the sound of their voices.

Winter closed in and she remained silent and brooding. Then one day she came to the door of the parlor dressed to go out.

"Paul, would you take me into Montreal?" she asked. "I would like to go and see Sister Marguerite."

"Why, certainly," Paul said and hurried away to get the sleigh ready.

"Shall I come with you, dear?" Ann asked.

"Thank you, no. I would rather go alone," Marguerite said.

Ann did not question her. With both arms around her she kissed her tenderly and went with her to the sleigh. All the way into Montreal Marguerite sat muffled in her fur coat and did not tell Paul why she had decided to see Sister Marguerite and he did not ask.

Sister Marguerite at seventy-eight was very feeble and administered all the affairs of the Congregation from her room, moving from there only to attend services. Her mind, however, was still alert and she was cognizant of all that went on in Montreal. She had heard of Marguerite's tragedy but was hardly prepared for the change in her appearance as she walked into the room. She made no comment but held out both her hands.

"I am so glad to see you, dear," she said gently. "Come and sit here by me."

"Thank you, Mother." A deep sigh escaped her as she slipped off her heavy coat.

"What can I do for you, child?"

Marguerite looked into the wrinkled, gentle face. "I want to enter the Congregation, Mother."

"You do, my dear?" If Sister Marguerite felt any surprise she did not show it. "I don't need to ask why. You have had many troubles to bear." She laid her hand over Marguerite's. "I would have come to you had I had the strength."

"Thank you."

"Are you sure you want to do this?"

"Yes. I have given it very careful thought. The ordinary life does not seem to be for me. My husband and both my children have been killed . . ."

"Life in a pioneer country like this is very hard and unfortunately accompanied too often by violent deaths . . ."

"Nothing seems to have gone right with me . . . since . . . my mistake several years ago."

"You have atoned for that, my dear. I had hoped you had been able to forget it."

"I had—until this happened. Now I feel I want to renounce everything and come and live here. I want to be cloistered . . . the same as Jeanne le Ber . . ."

At the mention of the name of Jeanne le Ber, Sister Marguerite's faced showed concern and her brows contracted in a slight frown. The story of Jeanne le Ber was known throughout the colony. She was the daughter of Jacques le Ber, one of the most prosperous merchants in Montreal and brother-in-law of Charles le Moyne. Jeanne had been an ardent and affectionate girl with a very sensitive nature, extremely susceptible to religious impressions. Against the wishes of her family and friends, she had insisted upon renouncing all her suitors and had wanted to renounce her inheritance also, to devote the rest of her life to solitary confinement in a cell behind the altar of the Church of the Congregation. Here she lived a life of rigid discipline, dressed in a garment of coarse serge, worn, tattered and unwashed and sleeping on a pile of straw that was never moved lest it should become too soft. Every day she scourged her body as a penance, occupied her days in spinning and making exquisite embroidery for the churches, never permitted herself to see anyone but the girl who brought her food. All the persuasion of her family would not make her emerge, not even when her father lay dying. Many regarded her as a saint —many considered it a selfish life of unnecessary sacrifice. Even those of the church were not all agreed upon the wisdom of such a life and among those who disagreed with it were Sister Marguerite and Father Dollier.

"No, my dear," Sister Marguerite said decisively. "I would not wish you to do as Jeanne has done. I wish I could have persuaded her to live a less austere life but she was determined and we must leave her guidance to God. All the years I have lived here—and it is nearly forty-four years—I have never led a cloistered life nor have those who worked with me. There is

too much work to be done and we must go among the people
to help them."

"I should only bring them misfortune . . ."

"I don't think so, dear. How old are you now?"

"Twenty-six . . ."

"That is still very young." Sister Marguerite smiled kindly.
"You have had much to suffer in a short space of time. But
you still have many years ahead of you. Let us not make hasty
decisions . . ."

"I assure you I am not, Mother. I have been thinking of this
for many weeks. I have lost all interest in living . . . I am
afraid to go on . . ."

"I can understand that, child." The gentleness of Sister
Marguerite's voice was soothing. She had never been known to
raise it, though there were many times when she had cause to,
as she fought for the rights of the people associated with her.
No one could understand Marguerite's problems better than
Sister Marguerite, for few days passed that someone did not
come to her seeking help and advice. "Come and stay with
me for a little while. Maybe I can help you find peace."

"I would like to remain here away from everyone."

"You can do that. I shall be glad to have you. Did you
come alone?"

"Paul brought me. I didn't tell him why I wanted to come.
If you will let me remain here . . . now . . . they can send
on anything I need."

"As you wish, dear."

Marguerite rose. "I'll go and tell Paul."

"Why not have him come in here? I would like to see him.
It is a long time since I have."

"If you wish it."

Sister Marguerite tinkled a little handbell and a sister appeared. "Sister Nicholas—Marguerite is going to stay with us
a little while. Will you have a place made ready for her? And
also, the Sieur de Courville-Boissart is outside.' Will you ask
him to come in here?"

As Paul entered the anxiety he felt showed on his face. Sister Marguerite greeted him cordially.

"I am going to stay with Sister Marguerite, Paul," Marguerite told him. "You have probably already guessed what I have in mind. I shall stay here to prepare myself."

Paul's face was distressed. "Whatever you want to do, Marguerite," he said kindly and glanced at Sister Marguerite. She smiled at him reassuringly.

"Come and sit by me, Paul. I am a little hard of hearing now and I want to hear all about your family. Marguerite, go with Sister Nicholas. She will show you your room."

Marguerite gave them a quick glance. "Don't try to get Paul to persuade me to change my mind," she said at the door. "It is made up."

"Paul wouldn't want to do that I am sure," Sister Marguerite said.

"Certainly not," Paul said, but the moment the door had closed he turned to Sister Marguerite with concern. "Is she going to become a religieuse?" he asked.

Sister Marguerite shook her head. "I don't believe so, Paul. Many come to us when their hearts are in anguish and the world seems too hard a place to live in. God has given us peace within these walls and here they are often able to find themselves again. Marguerite has had much misfortune . . ."

"Do you think it is all because of what happened some years ago? You know to what I refer."

"That is something I cannot answer, Paul. We have to have our share of unhappiness—at least most of us . . ."

"I seem to have been one of the fortunate ones. It seems so unfair sometimes—Marguerite and I are twins, yet she has all the unhappiness and I have had none."

"Your lives have only just begun. I am only too glad, Paul, that things have gone so well with you."

"I have been most fortunate . . ."

"And your wife and children are well?"

"Splendid. Ann is a wonderful wife and mother. Everyone loves her."

"I am so glad. You must bring her to see me again."

"She would be so happy."

"So would I, Paul. Bring her soon."

"I will . . . If only Marguerite could have half the happiness I have . . ."

"Perhaps she will. Let us not be impatient. She is stunned by sorrow now. It will pass."

"Thank you for looking after her."

"That is my work, Paul."

He terminated the interview there for he could see that Sister Marguerite was tired. On his way home his heart felt lighter, as many did after they had left her presence.

CHAPTER XXXIII

IT WAS NOT UNTIL the year 1697 that there came a ray of hope that at last peace might be established with the English and the Iroquois. Each year French troops had sallied forth to ravage the English frontiers, while the Comte de Frontenac, aged though he now was, had himself led picked men to revenge the colonists against the hostile tribes who continued to burn and plunder around Montreal. There was no doubt that each time the Comte made these attacks, he built up the prestige of the French, and he began to receive peace overtures from the Five Nations.

When the spring of 1698 came, the hopes of the settlers rose to new heights as the news was received that the long-drawn-out war in Europe—subsequently to be known as the War of the Grand Alliance—had at last come to an end with the signing of the Treaty of Ryswick. The winter snows prevented the news reaching New France until spring and then it was brought to Montreal by a deputation of English under Major Peter Schuyler, who came to propose an exchange of prisoners and discuss peace terms.

The white men were weary of the slaughter—the red men were said to be resigning themselves to the disagreeable fact that these white man had come to their territory to stay and the best thing was to bargain with them, accept what advantages were offered—to most of them the advantages of firearms and firewater—and try to live with them. It was not a peace, for even when outwardly friendly, the red man hated the white man and the feelings were heartily reciprocated. The white man considered his civilization made him superior to those he called savages—and these savages despised the pale-faces' ideas of civilization.

On a May evening in this year of 1698, Marguerite was visiting Paul and Ann and they discussed these things. Paul had gone to Montreal that day and had brought Marguerite back with him for a few days. He had brought them news of the arrival of Peter Schuyler's deputation and they built their hopes upon the result. Marguerite, in a plain grey dress of coarse serge, looked peaceful and resigned, but there was no trace of the vivacity that had always made her seem so beautiful. The green eyes had a dull look and it seemed to reflect into her coppery hair which had lost much of its lustre. It might have been the drab dress—it was more probably the loss of that inner fire. All the winter she had stayed with Sister Marguerite at the Congregation, visiting her family at infrequent intervals, and now they had become reconciled to the fact that she would ultimately become a member of the sisterhood at the Congregation.

Sister Marguerite had been quite ill during the winter and Marguerite had enjoyed nursing her. The close contact had evidently brought her the inner peace she needed, but when Paul had called that day, he had had no difficulty in persuading her to come and stay with them for a while. He had noticed a little more spark in her when they drove up to the Manor House that afternoon. She had paused to look over the land and had remarked:

"It does look beautiful, doesn't it, Paul?"

"I'm glad you think so," he answered. "I have always thought it did."

"You've made a lot of improvements!"

He was glad she had noticed it. That spring they had taken down the rough stockade that had been so hastily erected in anticipation of an Indian attack and had built strong palisades of selected wood that could withstand attack. The defenses stretched from the Péchard property to the opposite boundary of the de Courville seigneury with gates at intervals. At Marguerite's request Paul had taken over her property, pulling down the old house and in its place erecting a new mill. The old mill had begun to crumble, and because of the unpleasant memories, Marguerite was glad to see it had disappeared.

It grew chilly as the evening faded and Paul had a fire lighted. They sat around it, talking of the affairs of the colony, and then Paul read aloud while Ann and Marguerite worked on their embroidery. Presently the hired man came in to say a messenger had arrived with a letter for Marguerite Boissart.

"Marguerite *Boissart?*" Marguerite said, puzzled. "He probably wants my sister-in-law, *Madeleine* Boissart . . ."

"No, madame," the servant answered. "The messenger says he has been to the farm and they sent him here."

"Better have him come in, Marguerite, and we can see," Paul said.

"All right—only I'm sure it can't be for me."

The messenger was an Indian convert who worked at the Congregation and other places in town and he nodded quickly to them as he stood hat in hand. Marguerite took the letter he had brought and puzzled over the handwriting.

"Should I open it, Paul?" she asked. "I don't recognize the writing."

He thought how few times they saw the writing of any of their friends. "As it appears to be addressed to you—I would open it."

Marguerite broke the seal and, after she had read a few lines, let out an exclamation. Paul and Ann watched her expectantly.

"It *is* for me—it's from Eric Walker—you remember, the English boy who rescued me from the Indians. He's here with the English commission." Her voice revealed her excitement. "Of course, he wouldn't know I had married and changed my name. That's why he addressed it to Marguerite Boissart. I'll read you the letter . . ."

"Just a minute, dear," Paul interrupted and with a movement of his eyes reminded her that the Indian messenger was still in the room.

"Oh . . ." she turned to him.

"I am to take an answer back, madame, if there is one," the man said politely.

"Oh . . ." she said again. "Er . . . well . . . it will take a little while."

"Go into the kitchen and have some refreshment while madame writes the answer," Paul said.

When he turned to Marguerite again, she was eagerly reading the rest of the letter and for the first time in many months there was animation in her face. Paul and Ann exchanged a quick glance and waited.

Marguerite looked up and became conscious of the silence. "Oh . . . let me read it to you," she said quickly. "He says . . ." and then interrupted herself. "It's written in beautiful French—I wonder if he wrote it himself. He used not to be able to speak a word of French—I tried to teach him—he did learn a good many words, enough so we could make ourselves understood. He taught me many English words too—but I'm afraid I have forgotten most of them." She broke off abruptly and said: "Well—the letter says:

"Mademoiselle,

I hesitate to send you this letter not knowing whether it will reach you and also, if it does, whether it will be welcome. I hope you have not forgotten me because I have never ceased to remember you.

I am here with Major Schuyler's commission and as their mission is one of peace, I hope you will not think me too presumptuous in asking permission to call upon you, if only to assure myself that you suffered no ill effects from our hazardous journey several years ago.

I do not know whether we remain here hours or days and as I am subject to the orders of my superior officers, may I request

—at the risk of appearing impatient—that if you will see me, it may be as soon as possible lest the opportunity be lost.

I am staying at the house of Governor de Callières and I have instructed the messenger to bring your reply to me here. I pray it may be the answer I hope for.

Your obedient servant,

ERIC WALKER."

When Marguerite looked up from reading the letter, there was a faraway look in her eyes as she recalled incidents of her journey with Eric. "I have always been afraid he might have been captured again. He was such a kind, sweet boy . . ."

"The boy will be nine years older now," Paul reminded her with a smile.

She looked at him thoughtfully. "Why, of course, yes. Let me see, he was fifteen then—he would be twenty-four now . . ."

"You're going to see him, aren't you?" Ann said quietly and there was a little anxiety in her voice.

"Oh, yes, I must," Marguerite answered quickly. "I have never thanked him for all he did for me."

"Why not send him a note to come over this evening if he is free? It is still early—and I think he said something about his stay being limited," Paul said.

"This evening! Oh . . ." She broke off and looked at the letter again. "He's staying at the Governor's house."

"Yes, the entire deputation is staying there," Paul remarked.

She read the letter again. Then, looking up quickly, said to Paul: "You think it would be all right to ask him this evening?"

"I don't know why not. By tomorrow the commission may be leaving."

"Yes. I'll send him a note." She went to the desk and sat for a while sucking the end of the quill pen. "I'm so relieved he wasn't captured again. It has always haunted me," she said and then they heard the scratching of the pen. When she had finished she brought it over to Paul. "Will this do?" she asked. "Read it aloud so Ann can hear."

She went to the window and looked out thoughtfully while Paul read her reply:

"My Dear Friend,
It was such a pleasure to get your letter and at last be able to assuage my conscience. I have always been concerned because we never knew what happened to you.

As your time is limited, my brother has suggested that you call this evening, if convenient. The Chevalier de Callières house is not very far from the de Courville Manor, where I am at present staying with my brother. We shall welcome you if you are able to come.

There was some delay in finding me as since we last met I have been married (and widowed) and my name is now

MARGUERITE PÉCHARD."

When Paul went out to give the letter to the messenger, Ann said quietly: "Would you want to change your dress, dear? I would be glad to lend you one of mine—we are about the same size . . ."

Marguerite looked down at her drab grey dress and it reminded her of the resolutions she had made.

"Oh, I don't know . . ." she said.

"It would be nice to have on something brighter . . ." Ann said tactfully.

When Paul came back into the room, having delayed long enough to select a bottle of his best wine and give instructions for it to be brought in when the guest arrived, he found a complete metamorphosis had taken place in his sister. Instead of the straight-cut grey dress, she was wearing a simple frock of pale green with a wide flowing skirt. He stood in the doorway and gazed at her, and the expression on his face was very gentle.

"Now you look like my twin sister!" he said and gallantly took her hand and kissed it. Her fingers contracted over his and she smiled up at him.

The minutes dragged. Though Marguerite held her embroidery in her hands, she put in very few stitches. At last the sound of horses' hoofs came over the night air—in the distance at first and then growing louder as they neared the house.

A moment or two later the door opened and a servant announced:

"Captain Eric Walker."

A tall, lean man with fair hair and very blue eyes, filled the doorway. His appearance was so different from the gangling boy she had known that, for a moment, Marguerite just stared at him, and then, collecting herself, came forward to greet him. Eric Walker had not noticed that moment of hesitation for he too was experiencing surprise. The charming lady curtseying to him was hardly recognizable as the tortured girl whom he had rescued.

"Madame . . ." he said and his voice shook as he bent over her hand.

"Monsieur . . ." she answered and her voice was also unsteady.

"It is very good of you to let me come," he said.

"But I am delighted. I have worried so much all these years because I could not find out whether you continued your journey safely."

"My presence here speaks for itself."

"Yes, it does." Then remembering there were others in the room, she presented him. "My sister-in-law, Madame de Courville-Boissart, and my brother, the Sieur de Courville-Boissart."

"Your servant, madame," he said as he bent over Ann's hand. "And yours, monsieur. I hope I am not an intruder?"

"On the contrary, you are most welcome, monsieur," Paul assured him and offered him a chair. There was a momentary lull in the conversation and Paul filled in the gap. "I feel that I am responsible for my sister's concern over you. It was I who saw her get out of the canoe and was so amazed I never noticed you were also there."

"I did not expect you to, monsieur. I realized you must have given her up."

"We certainly had."

"Please tell me; I have been so anxious," Marguerite asked. "Did you have many difficulties after you left me here?"

Eric turned to her and smiled—a quick smile as though he did not smile often and did it quickly in case the moment should pass. Marguerite noticed the deep, strong lines in his face, yet also there was an aesthetic quality—a firm chin that vied with a sensitive mouth.

"Yes, I had some difficulties," he replied, "but I reached home safely."

"I have never been able to thank you properly."

He held up his hand in protest. "Please, no. The joy of being able to save you was enough."

"But still I want you to know how deeply I appreciate what you did. You saved my life."

"For which I thank God. You were so ill when I left you here. I hope you soon recovered." He searched her face and the strained lines did not escape his notice.

"Yes, thank you. I was ill for a few months."

"You must have been." Then he turned to Paul. "Your sister was remarkably brave, monsieur. It's astonishing how she could have lived through all the exposure and fever, particularly after the dreadful horrors she had to witness."

"Without your help, monsieur, she never would have lived through it. We shall always owe you a great debt of gratitude. How about yourself? I trust you recovered in due course."

"I collapsed when I reached Schenectady . . ."

"Schenectady!" Paul's voice was horrified.

"Yes, monsieur, that used to be my home," Eric said and

smiled faintly because he thought he knew what was in Paul's mind.

"I am sorry," Paul said and looked distressed.

"Meaning, monsieur?"

"Meaning that I was unfortunate enough to be there when it was burned and have never ceased to regret it," Paul said and his tone was fierce.

"Wars are regrettable, monsieur . . ." Eric said gallantly.

"Wars are one thing—massacres another. What happened at Schenectady is something I shall never forget and never cease to regret that I had a part in it . . ."

"Yes . . . it was a terrible massacre. I lost my family then . . ."

"Oh, Eric!" Marguerite exclaimed, forgetting that up to now they had been formal in addressing each other. He turned and smiled at her.

"How did you escape?" she asked.

"I was in Albany at the time . . ."

"Oh, I am glad . . ."

"I wish I had known your family were there . . ." Paul said. "But what good would it have done? I was helpless . . . in fact, I spent the entire time standing behind a house and vomiting."

They all laughed and it broke the tension.

"Now we are doubly indebted to you, monsieur," Paul said.

"We live in difficult times, monsieur," Eric replied.

"Indeed we do and let us hope that your mission will bring peace."

"I sincerely hope so."

"Would you join us in a glass of wine that we may all drink to peace?"

"I shall be glad to, monsieur," Eric answered.

"And the ladies?" Paul said to Ann and Marguerite.

"Oh, yes," Ann answered, "we must drink to that too."

Paul poured the wine. It was a burgundy of a reddish amber

color and Eric held his up to the light for a moment and then looked at Marguerite's hair. He did not make any comment but she smiled at him as she read his thoughts.

"To peace—long, lasting peace," Paul said and they all repeated the toast. "How do things look, monsieur?" he asked.

Eric considered the matter for a moment. "It is difficult to say—there is much wrangling over the exchange of prisoners."

"Has the war really ceased in Europe?" Marguerite asked.

"Yes—with the Treaty of Ryswick . . ." .

"It's been a long war," Ann remarked.

"Longer than most of us remember—by that I mean it started so many years ago."

"Unfortunately wars are made by kings and governments and we here in the colonies have to go on fighting them when often they are little concern of ours," Ann said.

"A very true statement, madame," Eric said and looked at Ann with admiration. With the firelight playing on her dark hair and gentle face, she was charming. It was strange that anyone wearing the hated red coat of the British could sit in a room with three French people and yet feel so warmly drawn to them. Eric Walker, whose life had been one of so many difficulties and hardships, separated most of the time from those he loved, felt very much akin to these people.

"Major Schuyler is a fine man, I believe," Paul said and then added with a smile: "I had occasion to admire his skill at La Prairie de Madeleine . . ." He tapped his leg. "It gave me a wound from which I have never properly recovered."

There was a peculiar expression on Eric's face. "We seem to have met quite often, monsieur, without knowing it."

"You were at La Prairie also?" Paul asked.

Eric nodded his head.

"How you must hate us," Marguerite said in an undertone. Eric turned to her and his eyes were flashing.

"That I could never do, madame!" he said. "As I have

been sitting here talking with you in the privacy of your home, enjoying the warmth of your hospitality, I have been realizing how foolish all this warring is. I am English—yet I don't have any cause to hate you . . ."

"Nor we you . . ." Paul interpolated.

"Isn't it foolish? This continent is so vast—greater than we have any idea, so the explorers tell us—then why can't all we colonists enjoy part of it and live in peace?"

"If only others would feel that way . . ." It was Ann who spoke. "My father was very close to the throne in France—he tried to make them understand just what you have said—but it was no use."

"No, I'm sure it wasn't—and I am sure it is the same with those close to the English throne. But it is not they who suffer —it is the simple people who have come all this way to make a new life—and want to be left alone to live it in peace," Eric said and his voice was deeply earnest.

For a while they discussed the political situation, trying, as people have done all down the ages, to settle questions over which they had not the slightest jurisdiction. They were the people who bore the brunt of all the friction—yet they did not have a word in the ordering of it.

When Eric rose to go, the feelings between them were cordial and the handclasp of a Frenchman and an Englishman was firm.

"I hope we may have the pleasure of seeing you again before you leave," Paul said warmly.

"Thank you, monsieur—I should like nothing better—if circumstances permit."

Marguerite walked into the hall with him. He hesitated a moment and then said: "There's so much I want to say to you, Marguerite." She looked at him questioningly. "May I ask you one question?"

"Yes."

"Have you been happy?"

She hesitated a moment. "Not altogether. I have had some great sorrows. But then most of us have."

"Yes, but I had hoped you might have been spared. You had your full share of hardship when the Indians captured you. That should have been sufficient."

"Sometimes I think that was the least of it."

His eyes were very kind as he said: "Maybe the future will be all happiness."

"That is doubtful too."

"I sincerely hope not. Could I see you again before I leave? I don't know when it will ever be possible for me to come to Montreal again, and as I said just now, there are several things I want to speak to you about."

"I would enjoy seeing you again."

"Would tomorrow afternoon be convenient? Or would it embarrass you to have an enemy calling in the daytime?"

"You could never be an enemy, Eric."

"Bless you for saying that," he said softly. "What time shall I call tomorrow?"

"Could you come about three o'clock?"

"I believe so."

He kissed her hand and took up his hat. "It is so wonderful seeing you again, Marguerite, after all these years. I never believed that I would, though I have always hoped. And, may I add, you were lovely then . . ."

She laughed and interrupted him. "I don't know how I could possibly have looked anything but ghastly at that time."

"In spite of it all, you were lovely. Now—you are beautiful."

"Thank you, Eric," she said.

He gave her a searching look and strode out of the door. She watched him leap on his horse and gallop away, turning to wave to her at the bend in the road.

CHAPTER XXXIV

Marguerite wakened late the following morning and with returning consciousness was aware of a light-heartedness she had not felt for some time. Then she remembered Eric's visit and lay thinking about him. She had thought about him for a long while before going to sleep, aware of the difference in him. She had not missed the many glances he had given her, nor the way he had hung upon her words. She had been excited when she had received his letter because of knowing he was alive and the anticipation of seeing an old friend again. But the moment he had entered the room, different feelings had enveloped her. It had been a magnetic moment when they had looked at each other. The night before she had gone over every moment of his visit and now she reviewed it again. She tried to analyze her own feelings. She had always thought of him as a boy, younger than she, but the boy was now gone. Her thoughts disturbed her and then came 'a warning not to be foolish. She reminded herself that he was an Englishman and a Protestant. She also reminded herself of her decision to give up worldly matters and enter the Congregation. Desperately she clung to this resolution during her morning devotions, praying for strength to resist temptation.

When Eric arrived she had herself under control. She had, however, made one concession in not wearing the drab grey dress. She had already given away her possessions to her younger sister—all except a few small things. Among them remained the last dress she had made, and this she wore to receive Eric.

He was standing by the window when she came into the room and the first thing she noticed was that he was not in uniform. She commented upon the fact.

"I thought it would be less conspicuous in daylight. I did not want to embarrass you—redcoats are not very popular in these parts."

"That was very thoughtful of you. And how are the negotiations going?"

His face clouded and he shook his head. "Not as well as I had hoped. They have been wrangling all the morning and words have run high . . ."

"What is the main difficulty . . . or are there several?"

"The return of prisoners . . ."

"Iroquois prisoners?"

Eric's face was puzzled. "Say that word again, would you please? My French is not very good."

"Indeed it is! I noticed last night how well you now speak it. Do you remember the difficulties we had in trying to make each other understand? I'm afraid I have been very bad and have forgotten most of the English you taught me . . ."

"Perhaps I'll have an opportunity of teaching you again."

She looked at him quickly and then smiled. "Perhaps."

"I remember those days very well—in fact, every detail seems to be imprinted upon my mind."

"Horrors such as we went through are hard to dismiss from the mind . . ."

"Yes—though I was not thinking only of the sufferings. There were so many other things . . . But we were talking of the language. What was the word you said—the word I did not understand?"

"Iroquois Indians—I-ro-kwa . . . the combined tribes of the Mohawks, Oneidas, Onondagas, Cayugas and Senecas . . ."

"Ah!" he exclaimed. "What we call the Five Nations . . ."

"Yes . . ."

"And now I have forgotten what we were discussing about them," he said and laughed.

"You were saying the peace negotiations hinged upon an exchange of prisoners."

"Oh yes." He was thoughtful for a moment. He leaned towards her a little. "I want this peace so very much, Marguerite . . . much more than I ever did . . . now I have found you again."

She looked up at him and then dropped her eyes for she did not know what reply to make.

"If we had indefinite time at our disposal, I would not be as bold as I now must be—because for all I know we may have to leave tonight . . ."

"Oh . . . so quickly!" Marguerite exclaimed.

"It may be. I don't know yet. That is why, Marguerite, I ask permission to say what I have been longing to say."

"Yes?"

"Don't be angry with me, and don't think me too presumptuous. I have loved you, Marguerite, since the days I first saw you under such dreadful circumstances in the Indian village. I did not know then that it was love—I was very young —I had not thought of love—not until those days when I nursed you through the fever."

"But you were only a boy then, Eric. And I was such a miserable sight . . ."

"Even so, I fell in love with you and it has remained. In this interval of nine years I have met no one who has been able to erase you from my memory. Always I have felt that one day I would be able to get to Montreal and see you again. When I heard Major Schuyler was coming here, I used all the influence I could so that I could come with him. It was only because of the hope of seeing you. I thought perhaps I should find you married or that perhaps you would have left Montreal. But I am fortunate. I have found neither of these."

"Thank you for telling me this, Eric. I had no idea."

"Not even last night?"

Marguerite hesitated. "Yes, but not until then."

"When I entered this room last night, Marguerite, I was so overcome at seeing you, just as I had imagined you all these years, that I don't know what I said or did."

Marguerite was afraid to trust herself to speak, so remained silent.

"I haven't offended you, have I?"

"Why should I be offended? On the contrary, it is flattering."

"I know it is precipitous, but if I don't ask you now, I may lose the opportunity forever. Marguerite, will you marry me?"

His sudden proposal startled her and he saw a frightened look in her eyes.

"You did tell me you were now a widow, didn't you?" he asked hesitantly.

"Yes, but so many things have happened that you do not know. I don't believe I could marry again."

The corners of his sensitive mouth drooped. "Would it be too much if I asked you the reason?" he asked.

Marguerite looked away from him. She tried to find the right words to say but her thoughts were so confused. "My life has been so complicated, Eric," she said without looking up. "You are young and should not be handicapped with a woman who . . . who is not very well thought of here."

"We wouldn't be living here so what would that matter? Or perhaps I am asking too much in taking you away from your home and those you love . . ."

"No, it is not that, Eric. Oh, it's all so horrible."

"Then why not forget it all? You don't have to tell me . . ."

"It would be better, Eric, if you went away and forgot me. Now you have seen me again, the longing will probably go away."

"On the contrary, Marguerite, it has become all the greater. Before I was in love with a memory; now I am in love with a real person."

"I wish this had not happened." She shielded her eyes with one hand, torn by indecision.

"You have told me you have had many sorrows; I would not want to add to them. Would you rather I went away?"

She laid her hand quickly on his arm as she said: "No." The gesture made his heart leap.

"Let me tell you the story—and then you can leave. You will probably feel differently when you know it," she said sadly. "It goes back to the time before the Lachine massacre. I was staying there with my sister because I had disgraced my family." With an effort she looked into his face as she said: "I had had an illegitimate child."

A startled expression crossed his face and Marguerite looked down quickly, afraid of the change that this might make in his attitude towards her. But a strong hand was placed over hers and a gentle voice said, "You poor child." To her annoyance, tears welled up in her eyes and she dared not look up. She gazed at the hand covering hers. It was a large hand with long fingers, well formed and masculine. She was tempted to place her other hand over it and hold it there, as a longing for protection welled up in her. She had to keep a firm hold on herself so as not to give way to the desire to lean towards him and let him envelope her in his strong arms.

"You talked about a child several times during the fever," he said.

"I did?" Then she looked up at him quickly and turned away again. "He was killed by the Indians."

"Good God! That too!" He tightened his grip on her hand. "Let me take care of you and protect you, Marguerite."

"There are so many obstacles, Eric."

"You mean because I am an Englishman?"

"That doesn't matter."

"Most French people would think so."

"I never seem to do the conventional thing. But there is my religion . . ."

"I will embrace your faith."

She looked at him steadily for a minute. "That is generous

of you, Eric. But it goes deeper than that. Last year another child of mine was killed—a child by my husband who had already been killed by the Indians. I realized then that this world would not bring me happiness. So I have made up my mind to enter the Church."

"No!" It was a spontaneous cry as he saw an impregnable barrier raised between them. "Oh, Marguerite, does this have to be?"

"It is best, Eric. I would only bring you unhappiness."

"I am prepared to take the risk. Are you already pledged?"

"No."

"Then please think it over. I don't have much to offer you, but I will do everything I can to make you happy. I will give up my commission and embrace your faith. We can surely find some place to live where there isn't discord between the French and English. I will do anything, Marguerite, but I can't lose you now I have found you again." He lifted the hand he held and pressed it to his lips. "Is there no hope, Marguerite?"

Her resistance began to weaken. "I must have time to think it over, Eric."

"Of course. I have been hasty, but you understand why."

"Yes."

He stood up abruptly. "Forgive me if I have made myself a nuisance. Would you let me see you again tomorrow?"

"I doubt whether I shall be able to give you an answer by then."

"Let me see you anyway. Please."

He was head and shoulders taller than she and as she looked up she saw his eyes were the deepest blue. Would she dare defy everyone again and marry a man who was an Englishman and a heretic? So much did she need the comfort he offered, that when he put his hands on her shoulders and held her eyes with his, she let go of herself and leaned against him. His arms around her were strong and comforting and she wanted to say: "Take me with you now."

He put his hand under her chin and turned her face up to his. "You do care just a little?" he asked. She did not dare speak but merely nodded. "Thank you," he said, and with a last lingering look, left her.

CHAPTER XXXV

PAUL AND ANN realized that something untoward was going on between Marguerite and Eric and when his visit that afternoon was curtailed so quickly they were a little concerned. This increased when Marguerite did not come down for supper. They discussed the matter but decided it would be better to leave her alone. When she appeared the next morning wearing her coarse grey dress again they were disappointed.

Paul went into Montreal to find out the latest news and when he returned told them that the peace negotiations were not progressing well. He noticed the color drain from Marguerite's face.

"Won't there be peace?" she asked.

"It looks rather doubtful. The English are insistent that the Iroquois are subjects of the British crown and the Comte de Frontenac scorns that idea. He refuses to give up the Iroquois prisoners, maintaining that by so doing he is acknowledging the British sovereignty over them. Each side is threatening the other."

Marguerite left the room and Paul looked anxiously after her. "Has she said anything?" he asked.

"Not a word about Walker. She made a remark this afternoon about it being time she returned to the Congregation . . ."

Paul sat biting his lips. "Do you think Walker wants to marry her?"

"Probably. He is obviously in love with her . . ."

"That was apparent last night."

"It's easy to see her difficulties. The English are supposed to be our bitter enemies."

"I saw her face blanch when I intimated the peace negotiations might fail."

"It does mean a lot to her if he has asked her to marry him."

"Everything. Poor Marguerite. She always seems to be faced with difficulties. Even if we are at peace with the English, a marriage to one would not be very well thought of."

"English or not—he seemed very attractive."

"Very . . ."

"Why don't you go up and talk to her? You and she have always shared your problems and she must be very worried."

Paul sat thinking. "Maybe I will later."

Up in her room, Marguerite was very worried. She sat by the window watching the sun sink over the River. She had thought until her head ached. She had analyzed every point and everywhere there were obstacles. Now, with the news that Paul had brought, the outlook was quite hopeless. Even if she overrode all the other difficulties, there would always be that difference in nationalities, and however much they might grow to love each other, there would inevitably be times when they would think on opposite sides.

She lay down on the bed and fell asleep. Suddenly she wakened to a knocking on the door and her heart raced.

"Yes, what is it?" she called out.

"It is I, dear," Paul's voice said.

"Oh, come in."

He opened the door and stood a moment trying to see through the darkness. "A note has just come for you, Marguerite."

There was silence from inside the room. Then she said: "A note . . . for me?"

"Yes, dear. Shall I come in and light your candle?"

"Yes . . . please."

Paul lit the candle and handed her the note. She gazed at the seal. Quietly he went out and closed the door. She still continued to stare at the seal and then broke it with hands that shook. Going nearer to the light, she sat down and opened the letter. It read:

My Dear,

We leave tonight. There was no time to come and see you before I was ordered aboard. Perhaps it is as well because I could not have left without you. On that other occasion I went away alone with despair in my heart. Must I do it again, Marguerite?

I love you with every fibre of my being and I would protect your name with my life. Dearest—come with me and let us make a new life together.

We sail at midnight and I shall watch until the last minute and not until the last light ashore is dimmed shall I give up hope.

What is your answer?

Your devoted—ERIC.

Marguerite buried her face in her hands. "Oh, Mother of God—what shall I do?" She got up and walked about the room, stopping at the window to look out over the River. From where she stood she could not see the wharf but she knew where the ship would be anchored.

Down below a horse shuffled impatiently. She realized it was the messenger waiting to take back her answer. She thought of going down and asking Paul and Ann what she should do. "No—I must decide myself," she said but could come to no decision.

Presently Paul came to her door and asked if she wished the messenger to take back an answer.

"Tell him there is no answer, Paul," she said and buried her face again in the pillow. If she could just stop thinking until midnight, then he would have gone. How long she lay there she did not know but gradually all sounds outside died. She got up from the bed and began to undress. She slipped off the grey dress and hung it up and then went to the window again. The night was warm and a gentle breeze stirred her hair.

"You're young and vivacious—you don't want to spend the rest of your life in a religious order. Your nature is warm and passionate—you need love—remember how it was yesterday when he held you in his arms. He is tall and fine and gentle—he's not like Charles or de Favien. He has loved you all these years—why don't you go to him?" These thoughts tempted her.

And then the other side of her put up an argument. "He's an Englishman. He's an unbeliever. You have already made so many mistakes. How do you know he would marry you? Remember how you were misled by de Favien. What about the vows you made to yourself that you would devote the rest of your life to God? You are weak. You already have many sins to atone for. Think what effect this would have upon your family."

"Go to him . . ."

"Resist temptation . . ."

"Go to him . . ."

"Resist temptation . . ."

Like a pendulum it swung back and forth in her mind until she felt she would go mad.

"I must see Paul," she cried and rushed to the door. But it was too late for they had already gone to bed. Should she waken them? Somewhere a clock struck eleven—one hour to go.

"On that other occasion I went away alone with despair in my heart. Must I do it again, Marguerite?" She heard Eric's voice in her ears. "Dearest, come with me and let us make a new life together." Everywhere she looked she could see his deep-blue eyes trying to hold hers. "Oh, Eric, Eric . . ." she cried and she heard his gentle voice answering: "Come."

"No, I mustn't Eric," she said half aloud. "I brought disgrace to my family before. I mustn't do it again."

"But I need you. I love you. I have waited nine long years . . ."

"No, no, Eric. Go away. Forget me."

"I don't want to forget you."

"You must."

"Think of yourself. You have never known love. You never loved Charles. He made you very unhappy. Go away and forget all that unhappiness," an inner voice tempted her again.

"Oh, Mother of God, what shall I do?" she cried.

"Come," Eric's voice urged her. "I love you. I love you."

She stood in the middle of the room, her hands pressed over her ears. "Come," she heard his voice again. Then she could stand it no longer. She ran to the desk and scribbled a note to Paul:

Paul dear—

I have gone to Eric Walker. I couldn't be strong any longer. They will say I am bad—but they have always said that. I hope I am not, but he offered me what I need so much. We shall work out our problems some way. I will let you know where I am at the first opportunity. Eric will look after me, I know. Try to forgive me, Paul—and you, Ann, who have always been so kind and understanding. Perhaps this may be my chance for real happiness. Forgive me—

MARGUERITE.

She did not read it over but left it unsealed on the desk. She ran to the cupboard and took down a dark dress and long cloak. For a moment she hesitated and the pendulum of her thoughts began to swing again. She shook her head as though to shake them off. Hastily she put on the dress and threw the cloak over it. Then she blew out her candle and opened her door. All was darkness outside and she crept slowly down the stairs. Once outside the house a feverish haste urged her and she ran as fast as she could to the River's edge. She untied a canoe and, without thinking of the danger of Indians, jumped into it and paddled away. She thought only that the ship might have left and paddled more quickly. The night was black and she kept close to the shore until, rounding the bend, she saw the great hull of the ship. Then she paused for a moment to rest her aching arms. A terrifying thought came to her. She had sent no reply and he would not be expecting her. But he had said he would watch until the last light on the shore had faded. But maybe he had grown tired of waiting. Feverishly she paddled again and the distance seemed interminably long. When finally she neared the ship, it loomed black and forbidding. Should she call out? If only it had not been so dark, she might have been able to see if anyone were on deck. Then she stopped, her paddle lifted high, for she heard a sound. She was not sure whether her imagination was playing her tricks, but she thought she heard her name called. She listened, holding her breath.

"Marguerite, is that you?" She heard it this time clearly and her voice rose hysterically as she called back:

"Eric!"

Then suddenly she was frightened, down there alone in the dark, a mere speck against the tall ship. Eric seemed so far away.

"Wait. I am coming," she heard him say. She sat huddled in the canoe, near to fainting from the exertion and fright. She felt herself being lifted and carried along. Strong arms held her. Then she was laid down and opened her eyes to find herself in a cabin with Eric kneeling beside her.

"Oh, Marguerite, dearest, you came! A hundred times this evening I have gone over this moment. Can it really be true? You have come to me. Oh, my darling!" He crushed her to him, covering her face with his kisses. "When you sent the messenger back without an answer I was in despair. Yet I still clung to a hope."

"I had a dreadful struggle with myself. I fought against it but I kept hearing your voice saying, 'Come.'"

"I did say it, dearest. I stood watching for hours and kept repeating the word over and over again, trying to draw you here."

"It reached me, Eric, and I gave in. I am in your hands now."

"Oh, dearest, you'll never regret it! I will make you love me."

"Why do you think I have come?"

"What do you mean?"

"Doesn't it prove that I already love you?"

"Oh, darling, do you?"

As they held each other everything in the cabin began to sway. Eric drew back his head and looked at her, lying there with her tawny hair spread out against the cushion and her green eyes cloudy. "You can't leave me now, dearest. The ship's moving."

She nestled her face against his coat. "Hold me very tight, Eric. I am a little afraid. I am entering a new world—and that new world is you."

CPSIA information can be obtained at www.ICGtesting.com
Printed in the USA
LVOW08s2255101213

364799LV00001B/312/A

9 781417 991433